THIS TOO SHALL PASS...

Mirador Publishing
10 Greenbrook Terrace
Taunton
Somerset
UK
TA1 1UT

THIS TOO SHALL PASS...

MARISA BILLIONS

Dedication

I DEDICATE THIS BOOK FIRST and foremost to the love of my life, Stephanie Billions and my son Alexander. My love for the both of you has been the inspiration for this new labor of love.

I also dedicate this to my father, Allen Smith – his telling of ghost stories on our weekend visits as I was growing up gave me my love for the macabre. Also, to my mother Marie Misko, who raised me with the love of psychics, mediums and all things New Age. Between both my parents, I was naturally drawn to the darker side of life and what goes on beyond the veil of the living, and I have long believed that we are constantly interacting with those on the other side.

And finally, to my chosen family. My ohana. Jenn and Hank Zemla, and Marc Roark. Without your never-ending love and support, my life would totally suck. Thank you for all that you have done for me throughout my life.

Oh, and to my Nana – Wanda Misko, too, though she's long passed, I miss her always. She was right. This too shall pass.

Part 1

Histrionics and History

Chapter 1

Twenty-Six

WHAT WILL IT TAKE TO be happy? Eva thought as she looked across the bland office – tan walls, a pine desk, pastel watercolors in gold frames matted with cream, and a beige couch in which Eva sat. Her thickly lashed light brown eyes blankly looked at Hillary, her therapist of the past 6 months. She was sad, but why, Hillary had asked.

"I'm lonely. I'm always lonely," Eva stated. "All of my friends are getting married and getting on with life and I'm just here. I remember my dad did a tarot reading on me when I was like 14, and it said that I would never find love. I don't want that to be the case."

"Do you honestly believe that could be true?" Hillary asked.

Eva pushed her long curly auburn dyed hair off her face and looked hard at Hillary. "I'm 26. When my mom was my age she already had me, had a house, was married twice. I have a bachelor's degree, an apartment with a bitch of a roommate, a bunch of credit card and student loan debt and a job I hate."

"You didn't answer my question."

"Yes. I do believe it. I don't know why I believe it. But I do. I know I'm not the prettiest girl, or the smartest or funniest girl. I don't have conventional anything. I am an acquired taste. I don't think anyone has ever, nor will anyone really acquire a taste for someone like me."

Hillary crossed her legs and folded her arms in front of her. Like her office, she is bland with not a lot of excess. Her outfit is simple and neutral colors. Her graying hair still holds some tones of mouse brown, cut in a bob. She wears little if any makeup, she is average height and build. Maybe that she is bland and utterly not distracting is what makes her a good therapist. She takes a deep breath and exhales. "Eva… What I'm seeing is that you really are feeling really low about yourself without looking at all that you have accomplished."

Like nails on a chalkboard, Eva hated to hear that. She always had a way of walking into a room like she owned it. She could command attention and make most people like her. At least in the beginning. Then, without explanations she had this beautiful talent to shut down and push them out of her life, usually with very little reason. She narrowed her eyes and glared at Hillary for calling her out.

Hillary looked at the clock. "We are out of time today. I want you to really think about what aspects of you that you like and your accomplishments. Journal about them. Bring them with you to your next appointment."

"Got it." Eva stood up and exited the office.

Eva left the building without stopping to make a new appointment and sat behind the steering wheel of her gray Hyundai Sonata with the door open. It was January in Metro Detroit. It was sunny, blustery and cold. She didn't care though. Having nothing to do with the weather outside and everything to do with the storm inside, she felt numb, and as she stated in the office, alone. She wanted to call her mom, but knew she was busy. She wanted to call her Nana but didn't want to hear the 'This too shall pass' cliche again. All her friends were busy planning weddings and having babies or sleeping off hangovers from the club last night leaving her with no one to call.

She looked at the clock on her cell phone. It was just after eleven in the morning. She was supposed to be at work at one. She had cut the night out with Drew and Dan early last night so she could get to this appointment on time. "What a waste." She exhaled watching her breath steam the windshield. She finally closed the door to her car and started the engine. She picked up her phone and called her boss, Julius.

When Eva had interviewed with him, she had been impressed. He was a retired detective from the Detroit Police. His office had a wall of honor covered in plaques and commendations. He was built like a linebacker, with close cropped salt and pepper hair, perfectly edged, and a commanding professional presence. His dark brown eyes were kind looking and deep set, but they could read anyone like a book. He seemed like he would be not just a boss but a mentor and that they would work well together. In the end, Eva felt like she did nothing but disappoint him. Whenever Eva called him or met with him, his deep resonating bass voice always preceded anything he had to say to her with an exasperated sigh.

When she had interviewed for the job – Executive Team Lead, Asset Protection, she felt she was perfect for it. Sitting in front of Julius in a crisp gray form-fitting suit, black heels, hair slicked and full of confidence, she nailed the interview. The position blended her education in Criminology and her experience in retail. She exuded confidence and Julius ate it up.

Now, as she steered her car onto the freeway, listening to the phone ring, she was a shattered illusion of that confidence. She was terrible at the job, and she had never been terrible at anything in her life. Avoiding the fact she was terrible was her only option right now.

He answered the phone, "Hello, Eva…"

"Hey, Julius. I am not feeling well. I think I ate something bad last night. I can't come in."

On the other end he was silent for a moment. The dreaded sigh came out over the phone and Eva winced. "Eva, we were supposed to meet today to discuss your performance." His voice was ominous.

"I know. But, Julius, like I can't go more than a few minutes without running to the bathroom."

"It sounds like you're in your car." He didn't miss a thing.

"I am. I am going to the store to buy medicine," she said quickly.

"Right. Right. Okay." He totally did not believe her. "Do you think you will be in on Monday?"

"I should be. I made the schedule for the week, and we are more than staffed in my department without me today. I was just an extra to make my hours."

"You usually are." There was no sarcasm or lightness in the comment. It was heavy and true.

"Yeah. I get it. I will see you Monday." Eva hung up and fought back the tears. She drove on autopilot until she got to her apartment complex.

The layer of snow on the ground was just enough to blanket the modest town home style buildings and their small front lawns in a few inches of glittering white. Icicles hung from the tree branches and a few black birds and cardinals who were tough enough to endure the cold adorned the branches. It would be so pretty if it were not so frigid.

Eva ran up the steps and unlocked her door. "Starling!" she called. Her tan and white Chihuahua came running from the couch. She grabbed the small dog's leash and went to fasten her.

"Oh... I thought you had to work today." Beth, her bitch roommate stumbled out of her room. She was wearing a pink terry cloth robe, and her hair in a greasy brownish colored ponytail. Her blue gray eyes were puffy and caked with about 2 days' worth of eyeliner and mascara.

"I called in. Starling and I are going for a walk."

Beth began fumbling with the coffee maker. "Can you at least try to dispose of your grinds when you are done in the morning? This is gross. I have to clean up after you so I can make coffee every day."

"Whatever, Beth. I will see you later."

Eva and Starling went out of the door into the cold, and down four doors to Drew's. She knocked loud on the door.

"Oh, hey darling!" Drew exclaimed as he opened the door. Drew was her best friend. Her brother from another mother. Swarthy, with impeccable hair (always), lean and muscular, with a dazzling smile that always came from the heart, most women would consider him sexy. They had met while out clubbing one night at a gay bar in Ann Arbor. Both of them drunk and striking out they decided to make out with each other. It was the furthest they had gone, but they were kindred souls and inseparable since.

Eva could smell fresh baked quiche and bacon frying on the stove top. "I am almost done making breakfast for Jose and I. Come in."

"Jose is coming over?"

"Honey, he never left. He's moving in! Didn't I tell you last night?" Drew smiled, his dark brown eyes genuinely happy.

"Of course. You, too."

"Me too, what?"

"You are turning into a couple. A pod person. Next thing you know I'm going to have to go to Macy's for your registry as well," Eva said as she rolled her eyes and sat at the reclaimed wood kitchen table he purchased from an artisan market. "Where is your dashing Puerto Rican prince?"

"He's in the shower. Be nice. I thought you had to work today?"

"I'm taking a mental health day. I don't want to deal with Julius. I think I am getting written up today. Drew, my life is a mess." Eva laid her head down on the table.

"Baby Girl... We need to talk." Drew turned the stove off and transported the bacon to a plate.

"About?" Eva pulled her hair out of her face and up into a messy bun on top of her head.

"You. And why you are so depressed all of the time." Drew pulled a piece of bacon into small bits and fed them to Starling.

"Don't give that to my dog. She's going to have diarrhea and she will shit all over your apartment."

"That's okay. You will clean it up." Drew grabbed a bottle of champagne and orange juice out of the fridge and set them on the table.

A freshly showered Jose came in and sat across from Eva at the table. "Good morning! What a nice surprise. I thought you were working today?"

Eva forced a smile. "I'm crashing your Saturday morning brunch. I skipped work. I needed your man today."

"Don't we all!" Jose grinned devilishly. He really was a handsome man, always perfectly put together, never a hair out of place. He moved to Detroit from Puerto Rico when he got hired to be a flight attendant for a major airline.

He was smaller and more compact than Drew, but every bit as handsome. His accent made him more alluring, though.

Drew began serving plates with quiche, bacon, and fresh fruit. "I was telling Eva that we need to talk to her," he stated. "I think we need an intervention."

"Yes, girl. We do. You are a downer. It sucks the life out of everything," Jose said as he poured the champagne into glasses followed by the orange juice.

"Well. Okay." Eva sucked in her breath bristling.

"Well, Baby Girl," Drew began. "I wouldn't say it quite like that."

"*I* would." Jose smiled.

"Well, *I* wouldn't." Drew continued, "I don't think you are being honest with yourself, or what you want. I think it's wearing you down and beating you down."

"What do you mean?" Eva asked sitting up. She was feeling slightly attacked.

"What do you feel is bringing you down?" Drew asked bluntly.

"I'm lonely. Everyone around me is coupling up. No one is ever free to hang out. When we do, I'm a third wheel."

"Amen," Jose retorted, lifting his glass.

Eva glared at Jose.

Drew set a plate in front of her and one in front of Jose. "Listen... What are you looking for?" He sat down.

"A good guy. Someone who will love me and take care of me. Not financially, but emotionally. Someone who will make me laugh. Go on vacation with me..."

"A guy?" Drew challenged. "Do you think that's being honest with yourself?"

"Why wouldn't that be honest?" Eva asked. "Not everyone is fighting the closet like you did with Mona." Eva was referring to Drew's ex-wife. He was married to Mona for a painstaking 7 years. Being raised devout Pentecostal, he married a Pentecostal woman, and thought he could 'pray the gay away'. This marriage not only brought forth misery, it brought forth two very cool kids that got to spend every other weekend and Wednesday nights with Drew and sometimes their 'Auntie' Eva.

"Fair enough. But you are," Drew challenged. "Who were you making out with at The Aut Bar last weekend? Who was the last person you really enjoyed going out with?"

"Let's be fair. I make out with a lot of people at the bar. Don't forget, you were on the other end of that once yourself." Eva avoided the question.

"You were making out with the little blonde girl from Estonia that was attending some art program at U of M," Jose corrected. "And the last person you enjoyed going out with was Camille."

"Drew, I don't think I like him." Eva glared at Jose.

"Honey, I don't care if you like me," Jose stated.

"He's right, though. Maybe you are trying to fit square pegs in round holes looking for a man to settle down with. I am telling you because I see my struggle reflected in you. It cost me years of happiness, and it ultimately affected Mona and my kids. I don't want to see you do what I did."

"Drew, I tried to come out to my Nana and just tell her I dated girls occasionally and it cost me dearly. I am bisexual. I can be happy with either. You are just gay."

"If you say so," Jose retorted.

Drew sat his fork down on his plate. "Honey, I used to say the same thing."

"What do you mean?" Eva challenged Jose.

"Girl… Look at you. You just look like a lesbo. Sensible shoes and all."

Eva looked down at her Lucky Brand jeans, fitted flannel shirt and Doc Martens. "Can you send him away? I'm not even dressed like a 'lesbo'. Stuck in the nineties eternally, maybe. And it's Michigan in the winter," Eva stated defensively.

Jose smiled and batted his eyes.

Eva rolled her eyes. "Drew, I see your concern. I honor your concern. But I cannot settle down with a woman. It would kill my grandmother. And I just don't see myself being able to be happy in a relationship long term with a girl.

It's intense and there's all these feelings and expectations to settle like really fast."

"But you want to settle down," Drew interrupted.

"Yes. But not in like 3 weeks. I want the long-term courtship and stuff. And I want a wedding. I want a marriage. That's not even legal."

"It is in Hawaii. And Canada," Drew corrected.

"We live in Michigan," Eva came back.

"Just think about it. Remember that story you told me about that lesbian from New Orleans? The one from that New Year's Eve party?"

"The cute butchy girl in the tux? My friend Riley? Yeah."

"Tell me the story again."

"Her girlfriend had to work on New Year's Eve, and she had non-refundable tickets to a party at the girl bar. She asked me to go, and I went. It was black tie, so I wore a cocktail dress, and she wore a tux. And yeah, she was fucking hot as Hell. Tall. Cute. Dimples. Blonde. My type."

"You told me you were so hot for her in that tux that you went back and broke up with your boyfriend the next day because you knew he would never be her. That says something. That guy, you told me, was sweet, and smart and everything a girl would want in a boy."

"Yeah. But that's different."

"How?"

"I don't know. It is. It was. This conversation is over. I've already spent an hour in therapy ruminating on why I'm depressed and lonely."

"Good. It's ruining my appetite," Jose stated as he began to eat.

DAYS LATER, AFTER BEING WRITTEN up at work and countless arguments with Beth, Eva was sitting in her darkened office in the back room of the The Big Box Retailer security space. She often referred to her office as 'The Cave'. It was always dark, and one wall was stacked with twelve monitors each focusing on different areas of the box store. Four monitors were dedicated to the check-out lines and could be focused in on specific cashiers, and with a flip of a switch she could also tap into the register to see what was being scanned or discounted by the cashier she chose to zero in on. All very high-tech for a discount big box store. In a haze of the soft blue glow of the monitors, Eva sat in The Cave, watching a cashier on camera with the register link glowing in the corner of the screen and checking her email.

'Remember Me?' is the subject of an email from a guy named Doug. "I probably don't," Eva muttered under her breath as she clicked it open.

'Hey! I found your email on Classmates. We went to Hospital Corps School in Great Lakes. I always thought you were cute. I see on Classmates you still are. I hope this isn't creepy. Anyhoo. Write back.'

"Who the fuck are you?" Eva asked as she read it again and again trying to get some memory of this person. She hit respond, 'I don't mean to be rude, but I don't remember you. Can you drop some hints as to who you were to me?' She clicked 'send' and went back to watching the cashier hoping to catch her passing merchandise to a friend without truly scanning it. She had to bust someone soon or she would be losing her job.

An hour into watching the cashier not pass a single piece of merchandise without someone paying properly, her email pinged. It was another message from Doug.

'You were one week ahead of me in Corps School. We used to hang out in the smoking pit. We are both from Michigan. You started talking to me on accident because you thought I was someone else initially. Now, do you remember?'

"Oh yeah..." Eva said under her breath. She hit reply. 'Yep. I remember you. What's up?' She hit 'send'.

She looked at the clock and watched as the cashier checked out of her register and left for the day. *No reason to stay here any longer*, she thought to herself and slipped her shoes back on under her desk and grabbed her cell phone and purse.

She contacted the two floor walkers and front security greeters on a walkie-talkie that was on its charger on the desk and let them know she was leaving and slid out without anyone else noticing she had left.

By the time she got home, there was another response from Doug in her inbox. 'Not much. I'm out of the Navy now. Living downriver and going to Wayne State. Are you still in?'

Cool, Eva thought, without absolutely any enthusiasm. She hit reply. 'Yeah. I got out 5 years ago. I'm living in Ypsi. Working in Westland. Finishing my MA. What are you doing now? Better yet. Call me.' She left her cell phone number at the bottom of the email.

Beth was not home. Eva took Starling for a walk and contemplated going to Drew's. She kept going past his apartment and turned around and went back home, neglecting to pick up Starling's mess from the grass.

She went back into the apartment, took a hot shower, put a fire on in the living room fireplace, made a bowl of Special K Vanilla Almond and sat down on a very beat up couch she had bought when she got her first apartment in the Navy. It was old, but comfortable, very cozy and cushy cream colored chenille. Eva turned the TV on. Starling curled up on the couch next to her. She was about halfway through the bowl of cereal and a rerun of Sex and the City when her phone rang.

She didn't recognize the number, but flipped it open and answered, "Hello?"

"Hi." It was a male voice.

"Who is this?"

"Doug Franz. From the Navy."

"Oh. Hey, Doug Franz from the Navy."

"What's up?"

"What do you mean? You called me."

"What are you doing?"

"Um. Eating cereal and watching TV."

"What cereal are you eating?" he asked.

"Special K. Vanilla Almond."

"What are you watching?"

"You ask a lot of questions. What are you doing?"

"Nothing. You left your number and said to call. So I called."

"Cool. You are obedient."

"Yeah." He kind of laughed. It was silent.

"So… What are you doing being out of the Navy?"

"I'm going to school at Wayne State. Nursing."

"Fun. Are you working?"

"No. I'm staying with my parents while I finish school."

Could this conversation be any more awkward? She sat there trying to figure out what else to talk about.

"So, like, are you married or kids or anything?" she asked.

"No. I never got married. No kids. You?"

"I got married for the benefits. Like contractual thing. But not like real married. I'm legally divorced now, though. No kids. Thank God! Oh my god. I would suck at the parenting thing." She kind of laughed at herself.

He laughed a little, too. "What does a contractual marriage mean?" he asked.

"We both needed money. The Navy pays extra to be married to civilians. So, as I was getting out, we got married. Split the benefits for a few years."

"I see. So you are single now?" he asked.

"Yeah. I'm single. You?" she asked.

"Yeah. I was engaged, but she cheated on me, so that's over."

"That sucks. Was it a long time ago?"

"Few months."

Silence again.

"Hey, what are you doing on Friday?" Eva asked.

"Nothing."

"My friend is in a band. She's performing at The Speakeasy, in Ann Arbor. Wanna go?"

"Are you asking me on a date?" he asked.

"I mean… No, maybe. I don't know. I don't even remember what you look like. I'm just asking if you want to go see a band on Friday. You do or you don't."

"Sure. I'll go."

"Cool. I will email you my address. Be here by like 7 Friday night. We can get something to eat first."

They said awkward goodbyes and hung up.

She finished her cereal, let her dog out for a moment on the patio and grabbed the little animal and went to bed.

THE NEXT DAY EVA CALLED a few of her friends and made sure at least a handful would be at The Speakeasy in case this was a disaster. *There is no way in Hell any good is going to come of this*, she thought, *the man can't even carry a conversation and he still lives with his folks.*

Yet another day passed by and still zero theft busts. Hours droned on as she sat in The Cave watching cashiers on monitors all day.

As she was driving home, her phone rang. She looked at the caller ID on the screen. It was Benjie, a doctor that her ex-girlfriend Camille worked with and hooked Eva up with as she broke up with her to get engaged to her (stuck up, elitist male) dentist. Eva wondered if Camille considered Benjie a consolation prize. He was tall, and in awesome shape, vain enough to spend five mornings a week at the gym no matter what, no excuses. His dark brown hair was in a preppy southern boy Republican haircut, with narrow sharp brown eyes and chiseled features. Benjie was a typical fox that only panned out to be nothing more than an occasional booty call. But he always bought dinner, and the sex was good, so she answered the phone.

On their first date, a double with Camille and Kyle the dentist, Camille slipped discreetly written notes from her placemat to Eva telling her how sexy she looked, and they slipped off to the bathroom discreetly to make out before returning to their dates. Camille's purpose, Eva figured, was that they could both marry well and keep a low-key affair going for as long as possible. It didn't work out that way. Camille married and became a virtual stranger and Eva was still Eva.

"Hey, stranger." Her voice dropped to a low purr as she answered Benjie's call.

"Hey... I'm in town. Where are you?" he asked. He had moved back to Oklahoma, where he was from, after his internship and residency at University of Michigan had ended. But it didn't stop him from coming back to Ann Arbor periodically for visits with friends, weddings, or other social events.

"I'm just getting off work. Where are you?"

"I'm staying at the University Inn, downtown. You want to meet up for some Indian food at Shalimar?"

"Let me go home and change. Meet you there in an hour?"

Eva got home, took Starling for a walk and invited Drew to come over while she got ready.

Drew sat and kicked back on her bed while she changed into something cuter for Benjie.

"I can't believe you are going to go out and hook up with Benjie," Drew said as he watched Eva select one top after another, ripping them off and putting on another, leaving the rejects in a pile on the floor.

"Don't be so judgmental. I haven't seen him in months. I'm also horny and hungry and broke and single."

Eva selected a form fitting black sweater with a low V neckline that emphasized her bust line showing just enough cleavage to be sexy, but not enough to be trashy, and low-rise jeans. "What do you think?"

"You look like you are going for a hook up. I forget sometimes, you have a cute little body! Look at those curves! You look hot!" Drew said.

Eva rolled her eyes. She piled her curls on top of her head and put a clip to hold them in place, a look that recalled her very distant Grecian heritage.

"Why do you think Benjie is in town?" Drew asked.

"I don't really care," Eva said as she put her eyeliner on.

"Remember when he broke up with you because you said you would never move to Oklahoma?"

"Yeah?"

"He was a hell of a catch. He's hot. He's a doctor. He adored you. You said it was great sex. You let him go."

"And he comes to town to hang out with his friends quarterly. He always calls me. We have a lot of fun. And then he goes back to Oklahoma, and I don't have to worry about a thing."

"You let him go. You could have been in a long-term committed relationship. Hell. Married. You let him go."

Eva threw her eyeliner back in the drawer. "What's your point, Drew?"

"You keep complaining about being lonely and single. I watch you throw away good catch after good catch. You are looking for something you will not get from these men. A man isn't what you want or need."

"Drew, I'm not going to have this conversation with you. I'm not gay. I don't think I would be any happier with a woman than I would be a man. The last woman I was with dumped me so she could marry her uptight dentist. She set me up with what is now my very consistent quarterly booty call."

Drew fluffed the pillow behind him and rolled onto his side to make room for Eva so she could sit on her bed and fasten her high-heeled boots. "Tell Jose I'm not wearing sensible shoes tonight," she remarked.

EVA BEAT BENJIE TO THE restaurant. Benjie knew this was her favorite to such an extent, half of the waitstaff knew her by name.

"Miss Eva!" Sani, her favorite waiter greeted her.

"Hi, Sani! Two please." She stepped in past the threshold of the small, darkly lit restaurant. Indian pop music played softly in the background. The dim chandeliers made the illusion of dancing lights on the wall. Small faux tea lights were lit on the tables in the booths. The tantalizing smell of spices and curry hung thick in the air.

"Let me take your coat." He stepped behind her and removed her long black velour trench coat. It was her favorite coat for looks but entirely impractical in the Michigan winter.

He hung her coat in a stand behind the host counter and led her to one of the dark booths in the back. "Who is meeting you tonight?" Sani asked.

"My guy friend, Benjie." She could see him enter as if on cue as she said it. "He's right here." She waved so that he could see her being seated in the back.

Benjie smiled and walked quickly to the booth pulling his beanie off as he sat. "For the life of me I don't know how you manage to live here. Oklahoma gets winters, but not like this." He slid his coat off and handed it to Sani.

Eva shrugged. "I hate it, too. But it's where I live. How are you?"

"Good. I haven't seen you in a while. You look amazing." He smiled wide and his eyes sparkled.

She forced a smile. He was everything her Nana would want for her. He's a doctor. He's devilishly handsome. Fit. Funny. Personable. She ran down the Nana Checklist in her head. Check, check, check. She put her head in her hand. "You look good yourself."

"I haven't seen you since Camille's wedding," he said. They had gone together, he had flown in just to accompany her. "That was a night, right?" Which it was. Eva drank a lot. She had to keep the drinks coming in to keep her feelings from falling out. Watching Camille marry Kyle, for a lack of better words, sucked, and Eva had a lot of opinions about the marriage, none were favorable or kind.

"No... I know. You haven't been back since," Eva said.

"You can always come down and visit me." Benjie cocked an eyebrow at her.

"Benjie... I don't want to go to Oklahoma. I drove through it twice. I'm good. Can we not do this? Let's keep it simple tonight. How's your practice?"

"Getting busy. What do you mean 'keep it simple'? I'm just asking you to come visit me. Change of scenery, you know? I bought a house. It's a new build. You have a good eye for art and stuff. I would love for you to come take a look and help me decorate it."

"That doesn't sound light." Eva stopped smiling and took a sip of water.

Sani came on cue to take their orders.

Benjie ordered a bottle of red wine.

They kept the conversation light and easy while Sani poured wine and brought out samosas.

"I really love it when you do your hair like that," Benjie said as he finished his samosa and set his fork down. He reached across the table and gently took Eva's hand. His hands were warm, and his eyes were soft. Eva looked down. She couldn't look at him. She didn't know why. Her heart was racing.

Sani brought the dinner order and Eva let go of Benjie's hand so Sani would have room to set the food on the table. "Thank you," she said, meaning it both for Sani and Benjie.

Benjie laughed and shook his head. "Girl. You have walls. You will never let me in, will you?"

Eva smiled at him. "You don't quit."

"Not in my nature to," he quipped.

After dinner, they walked out of the restaurant. It had begun to snow. Benjie put his arm around her as they walked down the street and drew her close. She enjoyed his size. He towered over her, and he was always so warm in his body and his personality. He was confident. He was sunshine and joy wrapped in human flesh. Easy going. *What the fuck is wrong with me?* she asked herself.

They walked in the cold snow glittering in the street lamps, the block and a half to his hotel. Laughing and chatting easily, their breath steaming in the cold, they went up to the room after walking into the warm hotel entrance. It was so easy to let go and let him undress her, caress her, let his mouth wander over her body. She let herself enjoy his warm hands and his weight on top of her.

When they had both had enough, she rolled onto her side so he could spoon her. That was her favorite part of being with him, he made the best big spoon. He nuzzled into her neck and squeezed her closer to him.

"Eva… we need to talk."

She closed her eyes and held her breath. "Just get it out," she managed to say.

"I think we are wasting time. I think we could be more. I think I could make you happy. I know you make me happy. Watching Camille get married I got to thinking. And being there with you... I really got to thinking. And I haven't stopped thinking since. Think about it. Really think about it."

She closed her eyes. She wondered if she could just pretend she fell asleep. She didn't say anything.

"Eva... I think we could really be together."

"Benjie, you have never once told me you love me. You have never once said how you feel about me. I've never told you I loved you. You are just wanting to settle because we are convenient, and the sex is good." She managed to get all of that out in one exhale. She rolled onto her back so they were now nose to nose.

"Maybe that's all there is, though? Romance and highs and lows are for Hollywood. You and I are more practical than that. Analytical. We make sense together. We fit together."

"Benjie... I can't live in Oklahoma."

"You never tried."

"You are asking me to give up my life and to go and live with you, and we are not in love."

"I believe love grows. It can come. It would come. Think about all of those arranged marriages that work out. They are not in love when they first get together, but eventually, it happens."

"Sani moved all the way to America to avoid his wife from an arranged marriage. No. I mean... Not no that love couldn't come. I agree with you. I think. But I just can't leave my life. You are asking me to leave everything for one thing. I can't do that. I agree with you, that maybe we could find the love. That it would happen. I mean... You are amazing, Benjie. You are so fucking everything I *should* want. And I'm lucky that you are here with me, and you want me, and you see something in me. But I can't give up everything for you when it's not certain. When you can wake up after a few months and realize I'm not what you thought I was. When it's not the fun little trysts and it's

~ 19 ~

every day me… The messy me. The depressed me. The bitchy me. Then what?"

This was all true. The two of them never had a serious conversation about beliefs or life. She had never once called him when she was down to talk about life. They went to bars together. They went to parties. The rented movies and had great sex. But he never really *knew* her. She doubted he could even name her political affiliation or favorite song. She certainly couldn't name his.

"You think I would get that way? That I would throw you away?" His hand was cupping the side of her face, as he looked right into her. He was mortified that she would think this of him.

"Benjie, you only know a small fraction of who I am and what I am. I've been your party girl. Your hookup. You haven't been witness to what I am like on the daily. What I can be. How I can be. I am my very best when you are around. But that's effort. It's effort I don't want to feel obligated to give every day all day. I don't think you would like who I am most of the time."

"Try me." He kissed her forehead and smiled.

She just closed her eyes and smiled back at him. She tried to picture living in a country home in the south. She knew he would be the white picket fence type. She tried to picture the golden retriever and the Mercedes Benz (he had told her on their first date when he walked her to her Hyundai Sonata, that one day he would buy her one. She should have known then they were playing two different end games. She just took it as he was buzzed, and she was particularly loose that night with her dress and her actions).

"Let me sleep on it? I'm off tomorrow. You can take me to breakfast."

He laid his head next to hers on the pillow, keeping his arm across her body.

In the morning, she woke up and he was nowhere in the generic hotel room. She started the shower. Looking around the room she saw that his suitcase and belongings were still there on the suitcase rack in the closet, so she knew he would be back.

She got under the steaming water and heard the door to the room open and shut. "Honey, I'm home," Benjie called. "I bring Starbucks. Americano, black, for the lady." She smiled.

He peeked his head behind the shower curtain. "Are you lonely in there?" His eyebrow cocked.

"Come on in. Water's fine." She smiled. She watched him slide out of his sweats and move gracefully into the water with her. The back of her brain was screaming at what an idiot she was as she assessed his tall muscular body under the water.

"So, no work for you today, you said last night."

"Mmmmhmmmm." She poured shampoo into her hand and lathered his head. He smiled and closed his eyes. "You are supposed to buy me breakfast, remember?"

"I can get used to this. Better be careful." She guided his head back under the water to rinse the shampoo.

"Maybe this is not something you get used to. This is just a special treat. Once in a while. If you get used to it, you take it for granted." She lathered her own hair and moved around him so she could rinse.

He used his hands to help the shampoo rinse off her head.

"You know, most women would be more eager for this offer," he said.

She grabbed his soap and began to lather him. "Most men would be happy with the way things are," she countered as she lathered his body.

He worked the conditioner through her hair with his fingers. He was silent. He had nothing to say.

They fell back into the bed for another round. He was trying to convince her at this point with his body and not just his words. She could feel his desperation for her in his every movement.

She knew she could have it all. She could have him and all that would come with it. Her Nana would be so pleased.

They drove separately to the restaurant. As he sat across from her, he took her hand again and smiled. "If I told you I loved you, would it change anything?" He knew.

"No... I don't think we should see each other anymore." She shook her head and refused to look him in the eye. He had to know.

"I bet I can change your mind." He smiled sadly at her. He knew.

She looked away and squeezed his hand. "If I was smart, I would make a different decision for sure. Benjie, you deserve a better woman."

"I wish you saw yourself the way I see you." He kissed her hand and let her fingers linger on his lips. Inside she was fighting a war with herself. What was right and what was wrong and why she would probably regret this decision down the road.

She left him at his rental car in the parking lot after a quiet breakfast and drove home.

The drive home was not long. The sky was the color of slate, and it was dark even though it was morning, threatening more snow. It matched her mood – cold and dark. She let herself in her apartment and saw Beth and her boyfriend on the couch with Starling. "Has she been out?" Eva asked.

"Yep," Beth replied. "And I fed her, too. Next time you plan on not coming home, let me know so I can be prepared to look after her."

"Got it," Eva said. "Starling!" she called out. The little dog jumped down from the couch and dutifully followed Eva to her bedroom.

In a random fit of wanting a change of scenery one afternoon she had pulled everything off the walls and painted them Tiffany Blue. Her purple bedspread and linens looked mismatched and juvenile against the bright cheery blue. Her television sat on the dresser across from the bed and her laundry basket overflowed in the open closet, next to the pile of rejected shirts from last night. She stood there as the muted sun tried to force itself in behind the heavy gray clouds. She tried to picture packing it all up and moving to Oklahoma and living in a real, grown-up home in a real, grown-up relationship.

She flung herself on the bed and called Drew, leaving him a voicemail.

She called her Nana. Nana wasn't home either.

Eva got undressed and crawled under the covers. She could still smell Benjie on her skin. She inhaled deeply. "You are a stupid ass bitch," she said to herself.

She fell asleep. It wasn't until Drew was sitting on the edge of her bed that she woke up.

"Hey, Baby Girl," he said. "Rough night?" He giggled and laid down next to her, letting Starling wiggle between them both.

"You have no idea. That crazy ass tried to talk me into marrying him." She stretched and yawned.

"He proposed? Did he have a ring?" Drew was grabbing at her left hand trying to find it.

"Well, it wasn't a proposal, so much as a 'let's settle down together in my country home down in good ol' Okli-homa.'" She tried to mock a country boy accent.

"So, when are you moving?"

"Bitch, please."

"Why would you turn that down? If you are so lonely and so whatever… What more could you ask for? You have known that man for 2 years. You said it yourself, he's the best straight lay you have had in forever… He's offering you all that you want, and you are sending him back like cold fish at a restaurant. You know you will not be happy with a man, Baby Girl. You need to accept who you are."

"I appreciate you, Dr. Phil, but that's not the case. I'm not going to give up my whole life and move to Oklahoma for a man. What happens when he leaves me because he has buyer's remorse? Benjie has always been impulsive. This is just one of his impulses."

"I think you are in denial. But I will support you in your stupidity because you are my best friend, and that's what friends do."

"Thanks."

"What time should I be at The Blind Pig tomorrow?" Drew asked getting up off of the bed.

"Oh. Fuck. I forgot about that." Eva put her hands over her face. "I should cancel it. I don't want to go. He was so weird on the phone."

"Girl, you gave him directions to your home. And your phone number. You have to go."

"Are you bringing Princess Jose with you?"

"No, he's on a trip."

"You don't get jealous? Him being a flight attendant in every port?"

"I trust him. I'm okay. We have parameters and rules." Drew stood near the bed. "I will see you tomorrow. What time should I be there?" He was pulling his coat back on.

"Shelley's band starts at 9. Like 8:30?"

"Okay... I will see you there." Drew leaned over and kissed the top of Eva's head. "I love you, Baby Girl."

"Love you too." Eva gripped his wrist and squeezed before laying back down against the pillows.

FRIDAY NIGHT, EVA WAS READY 20 minutes ahead of schedule. She was dressed in loose fitting jeans, a baggy torn sweater, and her hair piled in two pig tailed buns like horns on top of her head. A far cry from the sleek vixen like appearance she donned for Benjie two nights ago.

She was lacing her Doc Martens when there was a knock at the door. "Fuck," she said to Starling. "I bet it's him. I bet he's early. This is going to be weird."

The dog just looked back at her blankly.

She opened the door, and it was Doug. She remembered him the moment she saw him. He was tall and broad shouldered, lanky in the waist and long legged. He had a beakish nose and thin lips, and his eyes were a gray green, and expressionless. When they had first met all those years ago on the smoking deck at the training command, from a distance he had looked like this guy she used to flirt with. She had run up to him eagerly and thrown her arms around him and demanded he give her a cigarette. Now he was standing outside her door. He wore a backward fitted ball cap and a bulky, style-less down winter coat.

She laughed, "Hey! Long time no see."

"Hi!" He was nervous. "I'm sorry, I'm early. I expected there to be more traffic."

She opened the door wider and stepped aside. "Come in. I'm just getting my shoes on. We can go early. Finding a place to eat on Friday will be hard anyway. Ann Arbor is always busy."

"Um. Yeah… Okay." He came inside and Starling came running to him to sniff the stranger. "What is that?" he exclaimed laughing.

"That's my dog. Starling. I named her after Jodi Foster's character in *Silence of the Lambs*."

Doug followed her into the living room. "Nice apartment," he said looking around, assessing the hodgepodge of furniture and varying art types hung about on the walls. Eva liked edgier art, whereas Beth, being a Texas native appreciated a more traditional type of art, choosing art prints of famous impressionist painters and landscapes. Eva having a lot of artist friends had raw canvas art on opposing walls depicting chaotic scenes with bold colors.

"I have a roommate. It's not bad. She's just a bitch. But she's never really home and neither am I. So it works. My best friend lives a few doors down. That makes it infinitely better."

"Cool. Cool," Doug said sitting down on the couch. He slouched more than sat, rounded shoulders hovering over his knees.

Eva sat on the chair opposite and slid on one of her Docs. "What kind of food do you like?"

"Um… Hamburgers? American? Mexican… I don't know. What is there?"

Eva laughed. "Ann Arbor has it all. Mexican. Indian. Chinese. I won't eat Chinese though. I got food poisoning a few years ago, and I can't stomach it. But there's whatever. You want American, we can go to a Coney close by."

"Yeah. That sounds good." He was quiet. His energy was quiet. Everything was quiet. Inert and still.

Eva didn't know how to be around this. It was setting her nerves on edge.

"So, what are you studying at SVSU? I think you told me, but I forgot," she asked to fill the silence.

"Um… Wayne State. Nursing. I really liked being in the medical field when we were in the Navy. You said you were finishing your Master's. In nursing, too?"

"No. God no. I hated the medical field." Eva waved her hands in front of her, like the idea was physically assaulting her. "I have my Bachelor's in Criminal Justice Management. I just finished my Master's in Criminology/Sociology. I'm working at The Big Box Retailer now. I'm the Executive Team Lead of Asset Protection."

"That's intimidating," Doug said.

"It sounds more intimidating and interesting than it is. I sit and watch employees all day and wait for them to steal shit. It's actually quite miserable."

"At least you get a discount?" Doug offered.

"A whole 10%. It's so not worth it. But I don't know what else to do right now." Eva laughed and laced up her other boot.

Doug had not bothered to take off his coat. He was dressed casual, which was good. A little bland, she observed. Kind of like him. If he had a flavor, she guessed it would be vanilla. Or plain shaved ice without the syrup.

"Are you ready to go?" she asked standing up. "I can drive since I know where we are going."

"Sounds good." He gave Starling a scratch on the top of the head.

Eva grabbed her coat and her keys.

They walked out to her car, and she tried to really feel something. Excitement. Happiness. Something. There was nothing.

Neither one spoke much on the way to the Coney. They walked in and sat themselves in a brightly lit booth. Eva undid her coat and pushed it to her side. Doug followed suit. He was lanky, but muscular not having packed on the obligatory pounds most people put on when they get out of the military she noted.

The waitress came by and took drink orders. "Chocolate malt, extra malt," Eva ordered.

Doug ordered a Mountain Dew.

This was a far cry from any other date she'd been on in a long time. *Is this even a date?* she wondered.

They had a relatively quiet dinner without a lot of conversation. Eva looked at the clock on the wall. It was still way early for the show, but there was a bar at the venue, and they could get drinks. Maybe Drew will already be there, or she could see Shelley before she took the stage.

"Do you want to head over to The Speakeasy now? We can get a good spot and maybe grab a drink or two?" Eva suggested.

"Sure." Man of few words.

After a silent drive over to the venue, Eva parked on the street a few blocks away from the night club. "We are going to have to walk. There won't be parking anywhere close."

"Yeah. That's cool."

God. She couldn't read him. *This has to be punishment for how I treated Benjie*, she thought.

They walked side by side the two blocks to the club. The streets were dark, and snow was piled up on the corners. It was cold, and the sky was dark with clouds blotting out the stars. "What kind of music do you like?" she asked him.

"Kiss is my favorite, but I mostly like rock. But I listen mostly to sports radio," he answered. Eva hated Kiss and though she loved sports, she hated sports radio. She got lost in the statistics and would get frustrated.

"Oh. This is like a 90's cover band. They cover like Hole, and Rob Zombie, and Nirvana. My girl Shelley is the lead singer. She's pretty awesome. She's also my personal trainer."

"That's cool," he said without much emotion.

They walked into the bar and paid a cover to the large bald bouncer in the front. The bar was a dark dive bar. The wood on the bar was beat up and scuffed, the floors probably had never met a mop. The walls were painted a deep red and covered in posters from past performances, hand prints and bodies leaning against the walls had scuffed, smudged and dulled the paint. The stage was small and sagged in the middle. It smelled like smoke and stale beer. Eva led him over to the bar and they found two spots with a good view of the stage.

"Can you get me a vodka and Red Bull? I'm going to use the bathroom?" Eva asked.

Doug nodded. She ducked into the ladies' room and called Drew. "Where the fuck are you?" she whispered into the phone pulling her lipstick out of her pocket.

"I'm almost there. Trying to find parking," Drew said. "Why?"

"It's fucking awkward. He doesn't talk."

"You don't need him to talk," Drew giggled.

"Ugh." Eva hung up, fixed a few stray hairs, blotted her lipstick and went back to her spot at the bar.

She leaned over and got the bar tender's attention. "Is the band backstage? Do you know?"

The very rough, bleached blonde, leather skinned from too much tanning, shirt straining against very large, very round, very fake tits, bartender nodded. "Yeah… Why?" Her voice was hoarse from too many years smoking two packs a day.

"The lead is my personal trainer slash friend. Can you send someone back to get her?"

The bartender rolled her eyes and tapped the bar back on the back. Doug just sat there watching. Eva had said nothing to him since returning. She sipped her drink that he handed her. She smiled and nodded a thanks.

A few minutes later, a heavily made up, short muscular blonde woman ambled out. She could have been a knock off Pink impersonator down to the singer's edgy haircut. "Shells!" Eva jumped off her bar stool and hugged her friend.

"Doug, this incredible little bitch is my friend Shelley! She rocks."

Shelley and Doug shook hands awkwardly. Shelley side eyed Eva. "I'm glad you made it out tonight. The whole gym crew is going to be here, too!"

"I'm excited! I've been wanting to catch your show for a while now."

"I gotta go finish getting ready." Shelley hugged Eva and went back.

"She seems interesting," Doug commented.

"You don't even know the slightest. She's crazy. But she's an amazing personal trainer and I love her."

Doug just nodded and nursed his beer.

Eva scanned the bar as it was slowly filling up, looking for anyone she knew so she could talk to someone. She wondered if he was always this quiet or if it was just a new thing. *Maybe he is regretting coming out here?* she questioned.

She saw Drew and their friend Larry walk through. She waved them down. They stood out with their clean cuts and gelled hair and crisp Abercrombie outfits. The rest of the patrons were in tattered second-hand clothes, with shaggy hair and too much makeup.

She introduced Doug to them. Doug was by this point visibly uncomfortable in his surroundings.

She pretended not to notice and talked to Larry and Drew.

"Did you get to see Shelley before she takes the stage?" Drew asked.

"Yeah! She looks just like Courtney Love and Pink had a baby. It's pretty awesome," Eva said.

Doug just continued to drink his beer and fidget.

"I don't think I'm sticking around for this show," Larry said. "I'm going to head to The Aut Bar. This is so not my scene. I don't want to get jumped outside or something."

Drew looked plaintively at both Eva and Larry.

"Fine, you guys. Go. Maybe we will swing by The Aut Bar after the show."

Drew looked relieved.

Larry laughed. "Yeah. You do that."

Drew and Larry left just as the M.C. came out to introduce the band. Eva was relieved. At least there would be no more awkward silence.

Shelley and her band took the stage. Eva and Doug stood and watched and cheered the band. Eva wasn't sure, but it seemed like Doug was having a good time. It was so damn hard to tell with him.

After the show, Eva ran backstage to congratulate Shelley, and then excused herself.

She grabbed Doug from his spot at the bar and began walking back to the car. "Do you want to stop by The Aut Bar and have one more drink?"

"I would rather not," Doug said.

"Oh. Okay…" Eva trailed off.

"I just don't know any gay people. I'm a little uncomfortable with the idea."

"That makes sense. Just as an FYI… The majority of the people who are important to me are gay."

"I am sure if I got to know them, I would be better," Doug offered.

"Yeah. Of course." Eva just wanted tonight to be done. "I have to work tomorrow, so I should be getting home anyway." It was a total lie. She was off tomorrow.

"Yeah. I have a long drive back to my place," Doug said.

It was another silent drive back to her apartment. Doug silently watched the surroundings go by as she drove. When she parked, he looked at her for a moment. "I had fun tonight," he said.

"You did?" she asked. She waited a second and said, "I did too…"

He leaned in and took her by surprise and kissed her.

She pulled back. "I wasn't expecting that," she said, and she smiled.

"I'm sorry if I misread…"

"No… It's fine. I just wasn't expecting it. I can't read you. I can usually read most people. You, not so much." The weight in the car was heavy. She opened the door and got out, walking to the sidewalk in front of her parking space.

Doug got out as well. "Can we try that again?" he asked.

She nodded and leaned in and let him kiss her. It was still awkward, but better than the last.

"Goodnight," she said and turned and walked away to get out of the night, and get out of her head. It was exhausting her to be in her thoughts, trying to figure out whether or not Doug was enjoying himself, whether or not she was even enjoying herself, or why she wasn't or why she should be having a great time.

PAR FOR THE COURSE, SHE was noticing her life was in a never-ending downward spiral. Drew was infinitely busy with getting his catering business off and running and his relationship with Jose. Nana was busy with her girlfriends and enjoying her own retired life. Her mom was sidelined with her shit storm of a relationship.

She felt infinitely closed in. Work was a nightmare. Julius was breathing down her neck. He had come in and wrote her up for lack of performance. It was a hard pill to swallow - she was not good at this job. She had never been not good at something she did. She always excelled. But more and more she was learning that she was not always going to be the star and she didn't like the feeling.

And the pit of numbing loneliness was not helping this feeling.

She missed something but she didn't know what that something was.

Doug called her every day, she talked to him for a few minutes each time he called. As she engaged in conversation with him, she found it easier and easier to talk to him.

She learned he liked video game, he wasn't quite in the nursing program yet – he was waiting to get admitted. He lived with his parents and helped them out with odd jobs when he was not at school, but he was only taking one class right now which was his last prerequisite class. He helped coach the girls' tennis team with his best friend. He liked to work out and did martial arts. He was provincial. Simple. Uncomplicated. Kind of a fixer-upper in comparison to most of the guys she dated.

He drove down to see her a couple more times. She learned to enjoy the silence. And she was so busy trying to decipher if he was having fun or what he was thinking, she got out of her own head.

When he stayed the night the first time, they watched an Adam Sandler movie. He didn't really laugh out loud, he just smiled during the funny parts. She was so busy trying to comprehend him, she was able to explain away what a disaster it was. They were awkward, like two high school kids with each other. They couldn't figure out the other's timing. That he couldn't maintain an erection for her, was a first she'd ever encountered. She wrote it off as nerves.

She would never tell anyone, not even Drew about that. She made a note. She told Doug it was not a problem. She rolled to her side and turned on the television and dozed off. She didn't care.

Three weeks after that night, a few more sleepovers that got somewhat less awkward and more comfortable, they parted ways in the morning and Eva left for work.

She got to her office to find Julius sitting there waiting for her.

"Um. Hi," she greeted him and set her bag down.

"We need to talk. Let's take a walk around the store." He got up. He was imposing. His sheer size dwarfed the room. Eva felt like she was 2-foot tall next to a giant. Her perspective began to shift, and the floor seemed unsteady under her feet.

"Okay." Eva took off her jacket and put it over the back of her chair and she followed him around the sales floor. Her heart was pounding hard in her chest. She rubbed just under her collar bone as they walked. Her breathing shallow.

From the moment they hit the floor he started pointing out what she had been doing wrong in following the flow reports for each department. He started telling her what she did wrong in installing the security cameras in each department. Every word was what she was doing wrong and how she needed to do better.

She felt like he was talking to her under water. Her chest felt tight.

She smiled weakly and nodded.

She was trying to understand.

Department after department until they got back to her office, she could see his mouth moving. Heard sounds coming out of his mouth. But none of it made sense.

The only thing she heard was that she was on a final notice. If her numbers didn't get better, she was going to be fired. She had never been fired from a job. She had quit many, but never fired.

Eva nodded. She thanked Julius and walked him out.

She went back to her office and fell to her knees. She couldn't breathe. Oh my god she couldn't breathe. Something was strangling her. Crushing her ribs and pulling the breath from her body. Her heart was beating in her ears. She felt like she was dying. Tears spilled in overdrive from her eyes. She began to heave as she sobbed. She couldn't get enough breath to fill her lungs.

She called Drew and it went to voicemail.

She panicked. She called her friend Faye. She knew Faye would answer. She had met Faye when she met Camille, doing work study for extra cash in grad school. They all worked in the same office processing GI Bill requests. Faye was always the friend that would answer the phone and come and pick you up if you needed it. She was always reliable and always there. She was that friend that even if you had not spoken to her in 5 years, she would still answer the phone and pretend like no time had passed. When she answered, Eva blurted, "Help me. I'm at work. I need to get out of here. I think I'm dying. I can't breathe. Help me." She was gasping for air and the tears would not stop.

Faye was knocking on her office door minutes later. One of Eva's under cover floor walkers let her into the office. Faye didn't let the floor walker in, she blocked his view and shut the door in his face. She gathered Eva up, grabbed her purse and coat and ushered her out, coaching her as she went. "Stand up straight. Stop gasping and crying. You don't want anyone to see you like this." She shoved Eva in her car and drove her straight to the ER.

The nurse called her back after an hour's wait. During that time, Eva kept her head on Faye's shoulder and let the tears continue. It was all she could do.

The nurse asked her what was going on. "I don't know. I don't know what's wrong with me. I think I'm losing my mind."

"Do you want to hurt yourself or anyone else?"

"No. I just can't anymore."

"You can't what?"

"I don't even know. I just know I can't."

The nurse nodded and wrote something down and walked out.

A few minutes later, to Eva's horror, the doctor that came in was a friend of Benjie's that she had hung out with several times. His name was Steve. He had a beautiful wife, and they had a cute house just outside of Ann Arbor. She watched a Super Bowl there. His life, his wife and his look appeared to have been cut out from a J. Crew catalogue.

"Hey... I never knew your last name. I didn't expect to see you," he said.

"I am so embarrassed." She cried even harder.

"I can get another doctor," Steve offered gently.

"No... Just no."

"Okay... Tell me what's going on..." His voice was soft, quiet, empathetic. He sat on the stool across from Eva.

She sobbed and told him everything about the day and how she had been feeling leading up to it. "God, you can't tell Benjie you saw me like this."

"First, we have doctor patient privilege, Benjie will never know. Second, you are having a panic attack. It sounds like you have been struggling for a while though. I'm going to prescribe you an antidepressant, an anti-anxiety, and something to help you sleep. I'm going to refer you for some therapy, and to take some time off work. I'm going to write the prescriptions and the nurse will be in with some of the meds now so you can get them on board and start feeling better."

Eva nodded. "I have a therapist. But I've been avoiding her. I don't need a referral. I will just make an appointment tomorrow."

Steve smiled politely with his perfect teeth and nodded his head. "Okay... Well, hey... It will get better."

She laid back on the table and closed her eyes and tried to focus on her breathing while she waited for the nurse to come in with the happy pills.

As she was breathing and waiting, her cell phone rang. She looked at the caller ID. It was Doug. She answered.

"Hey!" he chirped at her.

"Um. Hi. Yeah. Just so you know, I'm in the ER right now. I had a panic attack. I'm losing my mind. I can't deal with anything right now."

"How long have you been there?"

"I don't know a couple of hours. My friend Faye brought me."

"Are you okay?"

"I don't know."

"Are they keeping you there?"

"No… I'm just waiting for drugs and then I'm going home."

"Are you working tomorrow?"

"No. I'm off for like 3 weeks or something. The doctor is writing a note."

"Okay. Well -" as he was talking the nurse came in.

"I got to go." Eva hung up.

The nurse handed her the medications and talked about the side effects. Tossing the pills into her mouth and downing the Dixie cup of water, Eva just pretended to listen. She grabbed the papers from the nurse, hopped off the table and found Faye reading a National Geographic in the waiting room.

Faye stood up and looked at her friend with obvious concern.

Eva just walked over to her and hugged her hard. "Thank you for being here for me."

"Of course. Do we need to make any stops? Do you want to go get your car?"

"I just want to go to the pharmacy and go home. I will get my car in a day or two."

It was dark in the night. The air was cold, but spring was definitely coming. Eva was grateful for Faye and grateful for the Xanax as she could feel her body and her mind numbing to the crumbling of her life.

After taking all the medications prescribed, she climbed into her bed and slept like the dead. It was the first time in as long as she could remember not feeling anything as she dozed off. It was the first time in a long time that she slept through the night without waking in a panic.

It was well past daylight when she woke up to Starling barking and someone knocking on her sliding door to her patio. It was Doug.

She was surprised to see him as she distinctly told him what a train wreck she was at the ER last night.

"How are you?" he asked.

"Surprised," she said as she moved out of the way to let him in and let Starling out.

"Why?" he asked.

"Because you are here. I told you where I was last night."

"That's why I'm here. I wanted to make sure you were okay."

She smiled at him. She didn't feel empty. But she didn't feel anything really. She was just calm. She walked into the kitchen and started a pot of coffee.

"You've been hanging around for the last few weeks, and last night didn't scare you away from me. I would say this is starting to be something," Eva commented.

"I guess it is, yeah," Doug said sitting on the couch.

"If it's going to be something, we need to make some changes though," Eva said. "You need to get a job. Like a real job. Not tending your parents. You also need to get accepted to nursing school. You need to branch out and apply for more than one program. You also need to not live with your mom and dad."

Doug looked at her quietly.

"I'm not saying it all has to happen like today. But by the time I get back to work, you need to have all of that handled."

Doug nodded acquiescing. "Okay. Sounds good. What are we doing today?"

"Going to get my car from work, taking my dog to the park, and somewhere in there I need to schedule with my therapist for this week."

IN THE WEEKS FOLLOWING HER breakdown, Eva began seeing Hillary twice a week instead of sporadically. Doug got over his fear of gays by hanging out with Drew and Jose for a dinner date, and that led to Drew hiring Doug to work for him at his catering business, which led to Doug moving in with Eva.

Since Eva was not working, she turned Doug into her project. Directing him to sit and apply and reapply for nursing programs. She took him shopping to spruce up his wardrobe and worked on introducing him to all the things she loved, including the Detroit Institute of Arts, Morrissey, and political talk shows on the news.

He was nonchalant about the hobbies but was an apt pupil in getting his life together for her.

He was accepted into the nursing program at Wayne State, which Eva loved the idea of. On nights he had school, he would just stay with his parents which gave her the space she craved.

She was calm. She was at peace. Everything was coming together. She was not excited nor excitable. She was just existing in a haze of calmness induced by the combination of antidepressants, anti-anxiety pills, and sedatives. With feeling like she had no needs, no concerns - she wasn't up, or down, or empty, or full. She just was.

Nearing her 3 weeks off, spring had definitely arrived. The cold dull of the Michigan winter had defrosted and all was warm and sunlight.

Eva arrived at her appointment with Hillary.

"You look well," Hillary greeted her, surrounded by her beige everything.

Eva smiled peacefully. "If I had known these meds would make me feel so good, I would have done this a long time ago."

"Meds alone are not the answer," Hillary quipped. "You have work you need to do."

"Speaking of, I'm not ready to go back. I feel like I will be triggered if I go back in there yet. I can't handle the thought of Julius."

"I will extend your absence. What will you be doing meanwhile?"

"Looking for a new job. I feel like I need to accept that I suck at Asset Protection. At least for The Big Box Retailer. I need to find a new place to work. Something I can enjoy."

"Are you already looking, then?"

"Yes. I'm avoiding my demons, I guess. But I think some can be avoided, right?"

"Sometimes. How is your relationship?"

"I feel like Benjie was right. I feel like settling is not a bad idea. This Hollywood grand romance shit is just make-believe. I think that's what Camille did, and it worked out for her. Or is working out for her, anyway. I think people can just settle and find peace with another person; it doesn't necessarily have to be love, right? You pick your person. You settle down. You make a life. Maybe love comes later. I think now that Doug is getting his life together, I can settle with him."

Hillary raised an eyebrow at Eva.

"Do you think you are rushing into anything?"

"No. I mean, he moved in. But we are not getting married any time soon, or even talking about it. We are just settling in. He starts nursing school in August. So, I will still get some alone time a few nights a week. We are talking about getting our own apartment not with Beth. Oh. And I'm introducing him to Camille to see if she can get him a tech position at the Med Center."

"Camille, your ex-girlfriend?"

"Mmmmmhmmmm. Yeah. She was a tech before she finished her nursing degree. It would be a better position for Doug while he's in school than working for Drew."

"Is he aware of how you identify?"

"Yes. I told him. I told him about my history."

"How did he deal with that?"

"Fine. He's chill. Nothing bothers him, really."

"You have done a lot to help him. What have you been doing for you?"

"Me? I've been journaling and seeing you. I'm working on letting go of expectations of perfection." Eva smiled proudly and brightly at Hillary.

Hillary only partially smiled back at Eva.

CAMILLE PULLED THROUGH WITH GETTING Doug a position on her floor as a tech. He would be working with in-patient gynecology oncology. The manager of the floor was able to honor a flexible schedule that would change with each semester to allow him to focus on school, and she guaranteed him a position as a full-time nurse once he graduated and passed the NCLEX.

Eva found a new job working as a retail manager at a gift shop in the mall. It was more pay than The Big Box Retailer, and much less stress. She maintained her prescriptions, and life went by in a drama free haze.

She filled her free time with her friends and went to bed early sleeping soundly next to Doug. She didn't even care that they didn't have much of a sex life together. He was her buddy. She would tell him what to wear and where they were going, and he was all for it.

They moved out and into an adorable loft space in a neighboring complex. Drew and Jose helped them move. Drew had approved of this move since, even though Eva was no longer his neighbor, they were still within walking distance.

It was the day after the move, and Eva had taken the day off to work on getting settled. Doug had gone to work. It was July, and it was sweltering hot and humid. Eva was in the upstairs loft undoing boxes. It was one of Doug's boxes, which she felt he wouldn't mind if she unpacked it for him since he was so busy with work.

A mix CD of her favorite New Wave and grunge music was playing loudly from the downstairs speaker and the air conditioner cranking on high as she put away his various hygiene products. She came across a pill bottle labeled with his name, and looked at it under the light. It was for Viagra. She raised her eyebrow at it and read it again. It was definitely made out to Doug Franz. She looked at the dates, it had recently been filled in June. It was for 20 pills. She thought about the last month. They had had sex two, maybe three times. She counted the pills. Seventeen. She didn't know why, but this prescription made her angry.

She set them down on the counter without putting them away. She put away everything else in the box. Then she broke the box down, took it to the dumpster, came back in, and picked up the bottle again. She counted the pills again. Seventeen.

Shouldn't he have told her he had a problem with that? They had been together for 6 months now. He knew she was crazy. She should know he struggled with his dick, right?

She called Drew, and he was over in a flash.

She tossed the bottle to him.

Drew caught it and looked at it and looked at her. "What? What is this?"

"It's Viagra. The little blue pill. Doug's dick is broken."

Drew stifled a laugh.

"It's not funny. I don't plan on being on these meds forever. I may get off them. When I am, I'm going to want sex a lot more than we've been doing it."

"Then he will take more pills," Drew reasoned.

"I've never had to deal with a guy who couldn't perform on demand."

"That you know of."

"Do you need pills?"

"Oh gaaawwwdd no."

"Yeah. Exactly."

"You can't throw him out over this."

"Who said I'm throwing him out?"

"Why am I here then?"

"Because I am having an emotion, and I'm still medicated, and I don't know how to deal with this."

"You don't, Baby Girl. You've been doing so good. Just enjoy things for once. It's all you can do."

Drew stayed and helped her unpack boxes and gossip for a few hours, leaving shortly before Doug got home from work.

Eva left the bottle of Viagra out on the counter, against Drew's judgment.

Doug came in the front door, greeted Starling and made his way up the stairs to the bedroom space. Eva was sitting there reading a book. She greeted him and didn't say much.

Doug got ready for bed. Brushed his teeth and put the pill bottle in the medicine cabinet and didn't say a word about it.

"You are not going to say anything about that?" she asked closing her book.

"About what?"

"Your pill bottle. Don't you think that is something we should discuss?"

"There's nothing to discuss. I have an issue, I take a pill, just like you."

"But, like, is it a forever issue? Or just a sometimes issue? Like I think my issue is probably temporary. I hope it will be over."

"It's not temporary. It just is."

"Why didn't you ever tell me about that?"

"It's embarrassing. And you are not exactly sympathetic."

She waited for anger to tip with the barb toward her. It didn't. God, these pills were fantastic.

And with that, she let the whole issue go. It was what it was. She considered that progress.

Chapter 2

Twenty-Seven to Thirty-One

THE MONTHS ROLLED FORWARD, AND Eva continued in her pill induced haze. Riding the wave of life, nothing bothered her, nothing ruffled her.

One night, a little over a year after they began dating, which was remarkable for Eva, who touted herself as the queen of the 3-month relationship – always insisting it was better to break it off as soon as you realized there was no real future as a couple- it was cold and February again, they had gone to the mall for a movie and dinner. They were walking around going in and out of the stores aimlessly.

Wandering into a jewelry store, Doug pulled her over to where the engagement diamonds were kept. "Do you like any of these?" he asked.

Eva pointed to a one carat princess cut solitaire in the middle. "That one is pretty."

The jeweler pulled it out and handed it to her.

She tried it on and admired her hand with the stone on it.

The jeweler declared the price.

Doug winced.

The jeweler informed him of financing.

Doug began filling out the paperwork.

"So, is this your way of asking me to marry you?" Eva asked.

"I guess it is."

"I guess it's a yes then."

And life continued in its pill induced haze from there. There was no big celebration or fuss about the engagement. It just was, as was everything else in her world.

Doug's mom was underwhelmed when they informed her that there would not be a big wedding and that it would be a small destination wedding in Key West in just over 2 years. They wanted Doug to be mostly through the nursing program first.

She pouted and threw a petty fit about not getting a large white wedding. Eva didn't care. And life went on.

Drew and Jose threw them a pre-wedding party at a local bar 3 months before the actual wedding. Friends and family came together to celebrate.

Eva had ditched the dyed auburn in lieu of her natural color with subtle highlights for the upcoming wedding and celebrations. She wore a cute white sundress that gave the vibe of a tropical bride and Drew had popped some white flowers into her hair.

The bar was decorated in tropical streamers and balloons. A large sheet cake that resembled a beach scene with graham cracker dust sprinkled across the top to look like sand and blue icing with fondant seashells sat on the bar. Reggae music spilled out over the speakers.

Eva flitted around and met Doug's family members and the very few friends he seemed to have.

She didn't care that he seemed to be spending the whole night wrapped up with his best friend and barely paying attention to her.

She didn't even notice until days later when she was sorting through the digital pictures her friends and family sent her from the night and she could only find one picture of the two of them together. She asked him, "Don't you think it's weird, this was like our pseudo wedding party shower thing, and we don't have but one picture together?"

"It's not really weird. No. My friend Rob was there, and I hadn't seen him in a long time."

Beautiful pink pill induced haze. She shrugged it off.

She finalized their plans, bought the plane tickets and a dress, and before she knew it, they were in Key West.

Her pill induced haze prevented any of the jitters or second guessing or stressing that came with the events and stressors leading up to a wedding day.

Eva thought that the wedding day would be a good day to discontinue the pills and learn to accept and cope with life. Drew kept running back and forth to the hotel bar bringing her drinks while she got ready.

Eva's dad, Jack entered her room while she was finishing her makeup. Though Jack was 22 years older than her, he hardly had any gray hair, his hair Eva's natural color, dark brown almost black, was freshly cut and nicely gelled back. He was stocky and dressed in the outfit Eva directed for all male guests, linen pants and a Tommy Bahama Hawaiian shirt.

"Are you sure you want to do this?" he asked sitting on the bed of the hotel suite.

"Jack, why would you say something like that?" Nana demanded. Her dark olive skin flushed with anger. Her silver hair was teased in a bouffant. She had insisted on wearing a white strapless jumpsuit and Eva refused to argue with her about its inappropriateness.

Eva's mom, Geri, in a black sundress with pink flowers printed on it lit a joint on the balcony. "Jack, you need to hit this and relax." The sun made her dyed blonde hair look like flames around her face.

Jack went out and stood next to her mom and hit the joint. "All I'm saying is this is forever. This is a big step, and Doug is not really... Well, Eva, he's not really dynamic for a lack of a better word."

Drew entered with another drink. Eva took a big sip and narrowed her eyes at her father. "Dad, you think you could have said something about this ... Oh... I don't know... Like months ago? Even days ago? There are 25 people who flew all the way here, got rooms and are sitting on the beach waiting for a wedding to happen."

"What did I miss?" Drew asked.

"My dad suddenly thinks I shouldn't do this." Her lack of a pill induced haze was not strong enough for this.

"Jack, you are out of your mind," Nana cut in. "This girl is finally settling down. Living a conventional life. She's not out running around like a lunatic. She's finally doing the right things."

"Mom, what do you think?" Eva asked.

She shrugged. "You gotta do what you feel is right. If you think marrying this guy is the right thing... Do it." She dragged on the joint and handed it back to Jack.

"I'm just saying, this is not what I pictured for you, but if you feel it's good, do it then. You have my blessing," Jack said, taking a long inhale and handing it back to Geri. Geri let it go out and put it back in her cosmetic case.

Eva turned to Drew, "See why I'm a fucked-up mess?"

Drew nodded and fiddled with a few of the clips in Eva's hair.

"What time is it?" Eva asked Drew.

"Time for you to get your pictures done."

Eva had a difficult time sitting through the pictures. She was suddenly second guessing everything. She was wondering if she could take a Xanax with the three rum drinks she had already downed.

She decided against it and powered through, faking smiles with Doug's mom who was making a spectacle of herself, asking for compliments for her dress and complaining that she was going to have to be barefoot on the beach.

She faked smiles with everyone leading up to the ceremony.

A golf cart drove her and her father down to the entrance of the beach. She could barely look at her dad.

"I know you're mad," he said.

"Not now," she said.

"This is your last chance," he said.

"You are so *not* funny," she said.

"Once we start walking toward him, you can't turn around."

"I can turn around at any point. But I'm not going to."

"Okay," he said.

The golf cart stopped. Jack got off first and helped Eva. She took her flip-flops off and handed them to the wedding coordinator that drove the cart.

The steel drum started playing and Eva and Jack started to walk down the beach.

The ceremony was unremarkable. The wedding dinner was unremarkable. The wedding night was unremarkable.

Doug forgot his medication, and nothing was able to happen.

Eva looked at him sadly. "I stopped my meds, today. We can all be fucked-up together," she said.

The wedding guests left 2 days after the ceremony and Eva and Doug stayed on for an additional 5 days to enjoy what was supposed to be a honeymoon. The way Eva had planned it, they would spend days wrapped up in the bed in their suite making love and doing what couples are supposed to do on their honeymoon. Eat. Fuck. Sleep. Repeat.

They never consummated the wedding. They ended up taking a historical tour of The Florida Keys, wandering the downtown area and doing a haunted tour one evening, sitting on the balcony and watching a few sunsets in silence. By the end of the trip, Eva was wondering if she should annul the whole thing when they got back.

It was 10 total days without her medication. Her emotions and feelings were coming back.

She was grateful upon returning to Michigan, that Doug's last year of nursing school was about to begin. She would have a few days without him.

She did insist on the eve of their return that he take his meds and they at least consummate the marriage first though.

Two months after the wedding, Eva stopped taking the pill. Doug mentioned he wanted to have a kid, and Eva, who had been utterly opposed to motherhood up until then, looked at him aghast.

"Why would we do that?" she asked.

"Why not? Isn't that what people do when they get married? They have kids?"

"I guess. But, like, I have Starling. She would be devastated if she wasn't the center of my world," Eva stated.

"I think we should have a baby," Doug said again.

"If we are going to do it, we need to do it soon. I don't want to be over 50 and have dependent kids in the house."

"That gives us one year to try. If we start now, and you get pregnant, you will have the baby before you turn 32, which means the baby will be 18 and not dependent by the time you are 50."

Eva shrugged. "I guess, let's do this. That means you have to take your pill at least regularly. We are going to have to have a lot more sex."

Doug rolled his eyes.

Eva began charting her cycle. By February, she was pregnant, which meant she would have the baby shortly before her 32nd birthday. Right on target.

Doug graduated from the nursing program and passed his NCLEX on the first try. He was promoted at the Med Center from tech to nurse.

They bought a modest single story ranch style house and moved out of the loft. The house was in the North East suburbs where she had grown up and close to her mom and Nana. It was a longer commute for Doug to get to and from work each day, but it was worth it, and his shifts never required rush hour driving. Eva loved the hard wood floors and muted colors painted on the walls. The home had a large basement with a lot of potential. There was also a huge back yard for tiny Starling.

Eva was so busy planning and moving and dealing with hormones that she didn't even care that she was no longer in her emotionless haze.

She was not okay with Doug's refusal to help her around the house after they moved in though.

It was another July move, and hot and humid. Eva was angry with herself for planning yet another move in the heat of summer. She was very pregnant and round and very miserable. She came home from work to find no boxes unpacked. She saw Doug, sitting on the floor in between boxes playing video games.

"What the absolute fuck?" she asked.

"What?"

"You couldn't unpack even one box?" she asked.

"I don't know where you want things."

"I would rather move things that were put away wrong than deal with boxes."

"It's my day off. I wanted to relax."

"What do you think I do on my days off?"

"But you enjoy putting things together and organizing."

"No. I enjoy resting, too. But we have exactly 4 months before this kid pops out and we don't even have his room put together yet."

"Four months is a long time."

"Not really." Eva pulled open a box full of kitchenware and started handing the contents to Doug. "Put this away."

Doug reluctantly stood up and walked across the living room into the kitchen. "Where does it go?"

"This is your house too. Figure it out," Eva said. She then overturned the whole box and stormed off to the bedroom and slammed the door.

The next day, she woke up early and undid several more boxes before going to work. Doug was still sleeping. She was loud as she slammed plates into the cupboards and put pots and pans away.

Doug groggily came out to the kitchen.

"What time do you work today?" she asked.

"Three till midnight," he stated.

"It's 8 am, and I need to leave for work in 30 minutes. There are at least 15 more boxes in the living room. I would love to see at least 3 of them unpacked when I get home. I know you don't like it, but you are an adult now. We don't get days off."

"You don't need to talk to me like that."

"I do. That's the fucking problem. I do. You show zero initiative. I have to always tell you what to do. Or it doesn't get done unless I do it or actually verbalize it to you to do it."

She didn't wait for a reply. She left the room to get ready for work.

She had a meeting with the regional and district managers today. She didn't need to be an unhinged bitch during the meeting.

She put on her cutest maternity suit that didn't look like a maternity outfit, sensible shoes, and put her wild hair in a tight controlled bun.

She got to the store and opened the gate and began to get the space ready for her guests. Her assistant, Shannon came in and began to help. "You seem a little edgy today," Shannon remarked.

"I'm pregnant. I can't drink coffee, my hormones are a mess, and my husband is lame."

"Husbands are lame," Shannon agreed. "You know you can have decaf, right?"

"That's not the same. I also don't want to meet with Joanne and Veronica today. I don't have a good feeling about this."

Two hours later, Joanne and Veronica entered the store. "It looks remarkable in here! Your set up is perfection," Joanne, the regional manager commented.

"Thank you," Eva smiled, hoping her smile didn't look too fake.

"Eva and her team have been consistent all quarter in not just making daily sales goals but exceeding them. They've also reduced asset loss by over 25%," Veronica informed Joanne.

"Excellent, however it makes today's meeting a little more difficult. Let's go to the office," Joanne remarked.

Joanne led the way and then helped herself to Eva's desk chair. Eva and Veronica opened folding chairs and sat across from Joanne.

"Let's be blunt. The internet is killing us. There are smartphones now and apps and people are not always buying in store now. As a matter of fact, our internet sales are doing better than all of our store fronts combined."

Eva sat back in her chair, her hands on her rounded belly.

Joanne continued, "We are closing all of our stores after the Christmas holiday. You will get a pay out and all your vacation. It's only July now, so you have plenty of time to prepare. However, if you seek employment elsewhere and leave before the closing day, you will not get the buy-out."

"I will be on maternity leave from November through January 15. How will this affect me?"

Joanne explained that as long as Eva was not employed elsewhere, she would still get the buy-out. Veronica and Joanne spent a few minutes engaging with small talk, and left, leaving Eva to explain to her staff that they would be closing shop after the holiday rush.

PREGNANCY WAS NOT FUN FOR Eva. She hated all food with meat, couldn't stand to handle raw meat, and was constantly tired and irritable. She hated strangers touching her belly. She hated that she felt fat. She hated that she felt that Doug was useless in helping her do anything.

She hated that her staff was slowly jumping ship and that she was hiring temps who couldn't care less about the job.

She felt like she did before she started taking her medications. She felt joyless. She couldn't feel empty because she had an entire being filling up her abdomen.

She had her baby shower. She finished decorating the baby's room. She found out she was having a son, which filled her with dread. She knew nothing of males or how to interact with them, much less children in general. She felt this was a double whammy in her life.

She and Doug agreed upon a name, Justin.

She was constantly horny, and Doug never seemed interested in doing much about that.

"Is it because I'm pregnant? I've read about men losing interest in their women while they are pregnant."

"No... I'm just not very sexual. You know that."

"You don't think you could try to be a little more for me?" Eva asked.

"This didn't bother you before."

"I wasn't pregnant, and hormonal and I was heavily medicated."

"Do you plan on going back on the meds after the baby is born?"

"I'm going to breastfeed, so no."

Doug went back to his video game without another word.

Eva went off to the bedroom alone.

She pulled out her laptop and started poking around on the internet. She kept hearing her employees at the store talk about this Facebook site. She pulled it open and created a log in.

Looking at the search bar at the top she began typing in people she could remember throughout her life that she had lost touch with. She started with her friends from high school. She was delighted to find Britt and Maddie and Holly and Chris!

She searched friends from her time in the Navy as well. Riley, Aaron, Ursula and Emily! They were all there. She sent out her frenzy of friend requests.

She put the laptop away feeling a sense of joy and curled onto her side wrapping herself around her belly and dozing off.

When she woke up the next morning, Eva was pleased to see all of the friend requests she sent out had been accepted and had received several more from others she knew throughout her past. She had even already been able to set up a reunion with Britt who was her absolute best friend throughout high school. They had lost touch when Eva joined the Navy, not because of hard feelings, but just that their lives had gone in two separate directions.

She was finally allowed to drink one cup of coffee a day. It was her day off and Doug was gone to work on day shift.

She poured a cup, added cream and called Drew.

"Have you ever heard of Facebook?" she asked him.

"As always you are so late to the party. Yes. I'm on there! Why aren't you?"

"I am now. I started an account last night."

"Welcome to the 21st Century."

"I found so many of my friends from the Navy! It was kind of exciting! I even found Riley!"

"The hot lesbian from the Navy? The one you dumped your boyfriend for?"

"Yeah," Eva grinned.

"Are you going to dump your husband for her?"

"Shut up. No. She looks like she has a girlfriend anyway. Or maybe two… It's hard to tell in her pictures."

"Is she still hot?"

"Stop it."

"So she is!"

"I mean… She always had *it*. I don't think that *it* goes away."

"So, you are dumping your husband for her?"

"She lives in California. I'm fat and pregnant. I think she has two girlfriends."

"So, if you weren't pregnant and fat?"

"Fuck off. I'm hanging up."

Drew giggled. "Come over. I'm making lunch."

"If I can get motivated to get ready I will be there."

"We can snoop on Facebook and look up your friend. I want to see her."

Eva forced herself to get ready and drive over to Drew's. He and Jose had bought a house and moved further into the suburbs. Drew's catering business was taking off and he was doing very well, and Jose had been promoted within the airline. Their house was a beautiful sprawling ranch that Drew turned into a landscape project. Their yard looked like a wedding pavilion with a gazebo, pond complete with koi and a fountain, and rose bushes and peonies. Eva compared her own home to what Drew had completed. She and Doug had done nothing to their basic home. Their yard was bare, and their landscaping was maintenance free bushes and one solitary tree in the front yard.

It was now early fall, and the changing leaves made the yard look even more beautiful.

She pulled into the driveway and waddled up the walkway to the front porch.

Drew ushered her in and sat her on the couch. He brought out two mugs of hot cider and sat next to Eva.

"How are you, really?"

"Miserable. Look at me."

"You look cute fat."

Eva rolled her eyes. She recounted her struggles with Doug not pitching in around the home and not meeting her needs in the bedroom.

"This didn't bother you as much before you got married."

"I swear being medicated was amazing."

"You know you don't want to go through life not feeling."

"I am beginning to think I do."

"Let's look up the hot lesbian." Drew reached for his laptop and handed it to Eva.

"You need to feed me first."

"You are so demanding." Drew excused himself to the kitchen while Eva logged into Facebook on his computer.

Drew came back with a loaded 3 tier tray with savories, sandwiches and sweets and set it on the coffee table, along with plates and napkin wrapped utensils.

"You so fancy," Eva said, helping herself to the bottom tier.

"It's one of my new lunch options for my business. They can order a full formal tea service."

"Bougie. But I love it."

She had pulled up Riley's profile on Facebook and handed it to Drew.

"Ooooohhhh… If I was a girl I would do her," Drew said.

Eva rolled her eyes. "Look at her pictures. I think she has a girlfriend. Maybe two. I can't figure out which one is actually her girlfriend. But the way these two girls both are in the pictures, it's more than friendly."

"You should send her a private message."

"And say what? I notice you have two girlfriends?"

"No. Just say hi."

Eva got up from the couch. "I'm going to pee. I will think about it."

She waddled into the restroom and began to think back about her time hanging out with Riley.

It was true she broke up with her boyfriend on New Year's Day after partying with Riley in New Orleans on New Year's Eve. Riley was in fact what she was looking for then. Tall, stylish, attentive, and so very sexy. The way she would look directly at someone as they were talking, the way she moved across the floor like she owned every room she entered.

Eva finished washing her hands and came back to the couch. The computer was back on the coffee table and Drew looked like the Cheshire Cat.

"I messaged her for you."

"You didn't!" Eva's face flushed red. She sat down and grabbed the laptop and pulled up the messages. "You did." She saw the sent message. 'Hi! Just wanted to say I'm happy to find you here! Miss you!'

"You wouldn't do it, I know you. So, I helped you out."

"You are going to put me in early labor. I feel stupid now."

"I also sent myself a friend request from you so we can be friends on Facebook, too."

"Anything else you did?"

"Nope."

After leaving Drew's, Eva stopped and picked up dinner for her and Doug from their favorite BBQ joint near the house. She made her way into the house and put dinner on the table.

Doug got up and grabbed plates and they sat down.

She talked about hanging out with Drew but left out the information about Riley.

She talked about finding Facebook and suggested he start a page as well.

He shrugged it off. He told her about one of his patients dying today, and how sad it was.

After dinner, he went off to play his video game and she went off to the bedroom with her laptop.

She checked her messages. Riley hadn't responded. She looked at the pictures of her friends and their lives. She was happy to see everyone doing so well, but sad for herself.

She found Benjie. She saw his house, and his new wife and their new baby. She was happy for him. She didn't bother to send him a friend request. She felt it was best to let sleeping dogs lie. She wondered if he loved his pretty wife or if he just settled. She hoped he loved her.

Regret was gnawing at her from somewhere deep inside. Unable to discern whether it was regret that she didn't settle with Benjie, or if it was regret that she indeed settled, she bit her lip and fought the tears threatening to come.

She closed the laptop and grabbed the novel she had been reading. She tried to lose herself in the trashy vampire romance novel but couldn't. She turned on the television and rolled onto her side and tried to fall asleep.

The next day she woke up late for work and was in a total panic trying to get ready and make calls to have Shannon switch with her so the store would open on time. Shannon reluctantly agreed.

This gave Eva an extra 3 hours to herself in the morning.

She opened Facebook and checked her messages. Riley still hadn't responded.

"She probably thinks I'm a creep," Eva lamented. She slammed the laptop shut and proceeded to clean up around the house and get ready for work.

She was in a funk by the time she got to the store.

She powered through her day though, closed out the registers and drove home.

She was in a bigger funk when she checked her messages that night and still no reply.

And this is how it went for the next week. Everyone around her wrote it off as hormonal. She didn't correct them.

Finally, she got the reply she had been waiting for from Riley. 'Hey! I just figured out there were private messages on here! I don't really check this very often. How are you? I see you are having a baby! That's very cool!'

Eva didn't want to talk about having babies. She didn't know what to say. So she talked about having babies anyway. 'Yeah. I'm giving motherhood a shot. We will see how this goes, right? How are you? How did you go from Gulfport to New Orleans, to San Diego?'

She hit 'send'. Whatever. She was just happy she got a reply.

She didn't feel so bad when it was nearly a week later before she got another response. Every week or so they would reply to one another with quaint messages with little substance.

Eva never figured out which girl in the pictures was her actual girlfriend who went by Jess, according to Riley.

AUTUMN FLEW BY. HALLOWEEN CAME and went and 2 weeks after Halloween, in the middle of the night, Eva was in labor.

Eva was not prepared for the pain followed by the rush of emotion.

They set her baby boy on her chest and her floodgates opened for the first time in the longest time. She cried hard as she looked at his tiny perfect face. His tiny deep dimples so like her grandfather's. His long eyelashes and big inquisitive eyes.

For the first time in her life, she knew what it felt like to love someone. Really, truly love them.

She was also afraid. She knew nothing of how to deal with a child or be a mom. While Geri was a fun mom, she was more like a sister and never really parented her. Jack only saw her sporadically as she grew up. Nana was the closest thing to a parent she ever had, and she wasn't sure that was a great dynamic either – one that vacillated wildly from being adored and revered to being chastised for her mistakes with few in betweens, all the while being stacked with high expectations to be everything that she had never been able to achieve.

This combination of love and fear shook her to the core and the tears wouldn't stop. Doug just looked at her. She wasn't sure if it was awe of the baby in her arms or fear for the raw emotion coming from her at the moment.

Geri was snapping pictures, and Nana was bustling into the room. Doug's parents were also on their way, as was Jack. The room was beginning to fill, and Eva was feeling very overwhelmed.

"Let me hold my grandson!" Geri exclaimed.

Eva nodded and Geri picked him out of her arms.

Everyone swarmed around Geri and the baby and Eva laid back against the pillows of the bed.

Every part of her just wanted to sleep.

Visitors began to come and go and from the room snapping pictures of Justin and themselves holding him.

After dinner, Eva asked Doug to make everyone leave. She had sent Drew a text message asking him to come. She had something very important to ask him.

The stream of family members made their way to their respective homes. Drew and Jose arrived after an hour of quiet peace.

Drew was holding Justin when Eva asked him to be the baby's godfather. She couldn't think of a better person. The person who has kept her grounded and been the voice of reason for her for the past 10 years.

Drew's eyes got glassy with tears. "Of course! Of course!"

Jose took the baby from Drew and sat down in the chair across from Eva. "I kind of want one now, too!"

"Oh. God. No. I have two already. Isn't that enough?" Drew laughed.

"But yours are big kids. They talk back and are sassy! I want one I can mold to be like me!" Jose teased.

After Drew and Jose left, Doug looked crossly at Eva. "Why did you ask him to be the godfather? I thought my brother was going to be the godfather?"

"No. I don't agree with your brother's religion or his relationship with a toxic God that hates gays. Drew used to be a youth pastor. He has a healthy relationship with a God that is loving and accepting. I told you no to your brother."

"You literally just make decisions without ever considering others."

"I did consider others. I considered Justin. You aren't even spiritual or religious or anything. I was raised Catholic, with a toxic and hateful God. I don't want that for him. I want him to love whoever God is and feel embraced and light when he prays."

Doug got up and left the room. Eva was not even aware of his return, as the nurse came to take the baby to nursery and Eva fell into the deepest sleep she had had since she quit taking the medications.

A night nurse came in and woke her up to feed the baby. Doug was asleep on the lounger across from her bed. She quietly whispered to Justin how much she loved him and how beautiful he was as he nursed. She went on to whisper to him memorized lines from stories and poems. She held him long after he was done nursing and had dozed off. She just stared at him and soaked in the feeling of loving someone else.

Chapter 3

Thirty-Two

THE FIRST FEW MONTHS OF motherhood were a definite adjustment. Sleep schedules and feeding schedules and housekeeping and cooking and night feedings, posts to Facebook saying how blessed she was, repeat. An emergency trip to the pediatrician because Eva was not producing enough milk to sustain nursing sent her into a temporary, emotional, downward spiral, feeling like a failure.

At 8 weeks, the pediatrician recommended putting the baby on a bedtime schedule. It was so hard at first, but within days Justin loved it. Eva loved it, too. She would feed him, sing to him (though she never bothered to learn nursery rhymes, opting instead to sing him songs she loved), and then rock him reading him books. Bedtime routine became her favorite part of the day.

He was a colicky baby which was difficult. But when he would calm, he was inquisitive. He had wise eyes that looked directly at whoever was speaking. It almost appeared to Eva, that Justin's wise little eyes could peer directly into her soul.

When he would smile, his dimples would melt Eva's heart.

She threw herself into being his mommy so she wouldn't have to think about her marriage.

When Justin was 6 months old, she was ready to work again. She found a job managing a small local spa. The spa was a passion project of a local wealthy socialite, Margaret Bronson, who wanted a spa like the ones she would visit on vacations in high end resorts. A place she could go to and escape and feel like she was on vacation for a day. She didn't, however, want the hassle of running the place.

Eva was in charge of making the schedules, the stocking of the retail shelves, and all of the day-to-day humdrum activities that Margaret didn't want to do.

Geri would come over and watch Justin, and sometimes bring Nana. Nana would fuss about her house and nitpick how messy it constantly was.

"How's the marriage? Still in the honeymoon phase?" she asked Eva one day when she and Geri got to her house early to watch Justin.

Eva pulled her curly mess of hair up out of her face and into a tight bun on the top of her head. "What are you talking about?"

"You and Doug," Nana questioned, wiping down the bathroom counter and putting the toilet lid down so she could sit on it.

"Yeah. There's nothing going on there. It hasn't in a long time. We have zero intimacy."

Geri was standing in the doorway listening. "Why don't I come out this weekend and watch the baby so you can have a date night?"

"Thanks for the offer. But a date night won't fix it. He has ED and doesn't like taking the meds. Something about them makes him congested or whatever."

"What man would have a problem with a stuffy nose if he was getting laid?" Nana asked bluntly.

"Exactly," Eva said as she touched up her makeup. "We've had sex twice since the baby was born. He goes days without kissing me. I've been going to the gym. I've been dieting. He has more interest in his stupid video games than he does me. I work. I take care of the baby. I take care of the house. Myself. I'm really, really unhappy."

"Well, you look great," Geri offered as she picked a piece of lint off Eva's turtle neck.

"Thanks, Mom." Eva forced a smile.

"Maybe you two need to see a couple's counselor?" Nana offered.

"That's an idea," Eva said. She was not above it.

She rushed off to work, kissing her mom and Nana and the baby before going out the door. She had to interview a new massage therapist. The perk of managing the spa was getting free massages by the therapists who were applying.

She came in, greeted the desk clerk and grabbed the resume of the waiting therapist.

"Lauren, come on back!" She shook the woman's hand. She was taller than Eva, with a short, tomboyish haircut. She had tattoos sleeved over her arms and was dressed comfortably in loose slacks and a t-shirt. Eva's heart began to race, and she felt flushed. She recognized that she had an instant attraction to Lauren.

Eva led Lauren through the spa giving her a tour as she would any other applicant. She discussed the pay rate and led her to a treatment room where they each sat, with the massage table between them.

"So, tell me about you, Lauren."

"My girlfriend and I just moved here from West Michigan. She's from here and wanted to be closer to her family. I had a busy client list over there, so this is going to be hard to rebuild," Lauren began.

"How long ..." Eva stopped. She wanted to ask how long she had been with her girlfriend, but she started over. "How long have you been a massage therapist?"

"Five years. I love it. I want to eventually teach it, too."

"Well, let's see what you have!" Eva said. It came out far more flirtatious than she had wanted it to.

"Oh! Yes. Certainly. Why don't I step out? You can get undressed, get on the table face up."

Eva nodded and waited for Lauren to step out of the room. She got undressed, trembling the whole time.

Lauren knocked on the door a few moments later as Eva lay on the table under the sheet and blanket.

Eva inhaled sharply when Lauren's hands touched her on her shoulders and slid up under her neck.

"Are you okay?" Lauren asked. Her voice was softer, huskier than during the interview.

"Yes. I'm fine. Just have a lot of stress." Eva tried to smile and relax. She had countless massages from applicants and the staff, but never by anyone she had been attracted to.

She managed to relax and enjoy the service and push aside her feelings once she closed her eyes and didn't look at Lauren.

She couldn't deny the woman was talented and knowledgeable. She offered Lauren the position, adding her to the schedule next week.

She called Drew on her way home.

"I made a big mistake."

"Marrying Doug?"

"Yeah. Okay. You sound like my dad."

"Well, we knew that. What else did you do?"

"I hired a new therapist. And she's hot."

"Like Riley hot?"

"Actually, yeah. She looks similar."

"It's not cheating if it's with a girl."

"That's morally ambiguous."

"It's true."

"Is this the law according to Drew?"

"Why, yes. Yes it is."

"Would it stand up in court?"

"No, it would not."

"Then I don't think I'm heeding that advice."

"Well, suit yourself. You are going to grow cobwebs if you don't start getting laid regularly. Marriage is not supposed to leave you high and dry."

"Thanks." Eva hung up and parked her car.

She had sent Geri and Nana home and ordered pizza for dinner and was waiting for Doug.

She put the baby in his swing and sat across from Doug at the table. "I want to start seeing a marriage counselor," she declared.

"Why?"

"I'm not happy."

"Then you go to a counselor. I'm fine."

"No. You are not. *We* are not."

"How are we not?"

"You haven't kissed me or held my hand in how long? It's been 2 months since we've had sex."

"Kissing and sex are not what makes a marriage. That's immature."

"Intimacy. Sex. It's all part of it, and we have none of that. I don't want to give up or just quit on this. But I also want to see if we can grow together."

Doug exhaled. "Fine. Find someone and we will try it." He took his pizza to the living room and fired up his PlayStation. Eva took her pizza to the bedroom and opened her laptop.

IT WAS 6 LONG WEEKS BEFORE they could get into a marriage and family counselor within their insurance network. In that time, Eva just threw herself into work, being a mom, avoiding Lauren at all costs, and wasting free time on Facebook.

Geri had come over to watch Justin so they could go to their therapy appointment and then go to dinner after. Eva was disappointed that she would not get her night-time routine with Justin.

They drove in silence to the therapist, filled out their intake papers in silence, and sat in silence in front of Ian, the therapist. Ian was younger than them, he smiled politely at both of them as he scanned over the intake papers. "So, why don't you tell me why you are here."

"My wife is miserable," Doug quipped. "I'm not enough for her to be happy, apparently."

"That's not it. I mean it is, but it isn't," Eva countered.

"So, then, explain it to me," Ian encouraged.

"We have no intimacy. No love. No sex. He doesn't even kiss me."

"Doug, what do you have to say about that?"

"My parents were not always touchy feely. They've been married almost 40 years. They don't hold hands. They sleep in separate bedrooms. They have since I was in high school. They are fine. Their relationship is a great example. They are solid and together."

"Your parents' relationship is my worst nightmare," Eva snapped.

"So, Doug, you recognize that for Eva to feel loved, you need to increase your physical connection with her?" Ian offered.

"I don't see why that's so important. Marriage is more than sex and physical touching. It's a partnership. An agreement on a life together," Doug offered.

"It's more than that to me," Eva pleaded. "You don't even come to bed at the same time. We don't even talk about anything."

"Because I can't talk to you. You just bark orders, shit all over anything I say, and do what you want anyway," Doug blurted out.

Eva didn't say anything in response. She folded her arms across her body and leaned back against her chair.

"Eva..." Ian was encouraging her response.

"Because all you want to do is disappear into the bathroom, basement, or play video games. I have to make all the decisions because you don't do a goddamn thing. It's like having a roommate but worse," she said through gritted teeth.

Eva felt utterly defeated in this appointment.

They eventually left with some homework. They had to take every single day the next month to write down three things they were grateful for the other partner doing and share them each night with each other.

They went to dinner, where they sat across from each other in silence. Eva picked up her new smartphone and pulled up Facebook. If he wouldn't talk to her, maybe someone else would.

"I think I want to start running," she said abruptly.

"Then run," Doug said.

"I mean like for real, training for races and stuff. I reconnected with my friend Britt, and she runs like 5k's and stuff."

"Okay. When will you have time for that?"

"I don't know. I will make time."

"Do it if you think it will make you happy."

"I wasn't looking for permission. Just your support," Eva said.

"Of course."

"Of course, what?"

"Of course, you are just seeking my rubber stamp."

"Well, this night is going great," Eva quipped.

"I just want you to treat me like a valid partner," Doug stated.

"Act like an adult and I will."

"Let's go." Doug threw his napkin on the table.

Eva got up and they left.

When they got home, Doug retreated first to the bathroom and then to the couch to have bonding time with his PlayStation.

Eva grabbed her phone and her book and retreated to the bedroom after looking in on Justin to see him sleeping soundly.

She scrolled through Facebook and messaged Riley. 'Tell me about your life in California? Are you still horseback riding? Do you still have your Mustang?'

She hit 'send' and put the phone on its charger and tried to read her book.

THE NEXT DAY SHE WAS sitting in the break room at work scrolling through running programs and picking at her lunch when Lauren sat across from her.

Eva had the incredible urge to get up and run out, but she stayed in her seat and smiled at Lauren. "How do you like working here? I see you are building quite the client list."

"I like it," Lauren commented as she sat down and unwrapped her lunch. "I can't complain. My schedule is good, the pay is good. Most of the clients are decent tippers."

"Good. I'm glad you are enjoying it." Eva went back to scrolling on her phone. She was desperately trying to think of a reason to excuse herself.

"What are you so absorbed in over there?" Lauren asked, making conversation.

"I think I want to start running. I'm looking at different training programs and thinking about training for a race."

"That sounds fun!" Lauren exclaimed. "I have two clients that are in a running group. Maybe I can have them talk to you."

"That would be great," Eva smiled at her. She went back to her phone desperately trying to not look at Lauren. She bookmarked a Hal Higdon training site.

Lauren sat quietly eating her lunch.

Eva checked her messages to see if Riley ever responded. No response. But Britt had responded about wanting to train for a race and would definitely run one with her. Eva was actually excited to get to spend more time with Britt. She and Britt had been good friends in high school. They were mischievous together and always got into something they shouldn't have. Britt had evolved into a successful co-owner of her husband's investment business and looked like she had not aged since graduation. She was petite, like Eva – they used to raid each other's closets and shoes during sleepovers. Her hair was now dyed fire red, with blonde and black high and low lights, which made her piercing blue eyes stand out more. She was stunning, and Eva envied her for her successful and happy life and how amazing she looked.

"I really do not like smart smartphones," Lauren offered. "I think they are going to be the downfall of humanity."

"Really?" Eva asked, clicking off the screen and dropping it on the table. "How so?"

"They make everything so accessible. People are getting more wrapped up in what's on the phone than what is in front of them."

Eva raised her eyebrow. "Sometimes people don't want to deal with what's in front of them or maybe they are trying to escape for a moment."

Lauren shrugged. "I've never been one to escape."

"I am," Eva stated. She looked at the clock. She finally had an excuse to escape. She had to meet with Margaret and review the new specials they were going to offer for next month. She got up and smiled at Lauren. "It was nice chatting with you. Margaret will be here soon, and I need to be ready."

"I will get some info for you about the running group from my clients. I see both of them this week."

"Great. Thanks!" She briskly exited the room and into her office. She sat back behind her desk and tried to breathe.

EVA FOUND A RACE TO sign up for the next day. The Detroit Free Press Half Marathon.

She messaged Britt about it, and Britt was game, although she questioned why Eva would want to run such a big race for her first one.

'Go big or go home,' Eva responded.

She had found a training schedule and wrote it out on her calendar she had hung on the side of her refrigerator.

Riley had not responded to her message in days. She knew she was busy and tried not to take it personally.

She was just going to keep throwing herself into challenges that kept her from feeling the loneliness and isolation she felt in her daily life. She and Doug were only half-assing the therapist's homework.

"Maybe this is all that there is?" she resigned herself.

She looked at Justin in his Pack N Play. He was standing up and babbling at Starling. "This isn't so bad, right?" she asked them as her phone rang.

It was Geri. "Hey, Mom," Eva answered.

"Nana is in the hospital," she said.

"Oh my god! What's going on?"

"They said she has COPD. All of her years of smoking."

"But it's treatable, right?"

"Yeah, if she quits smoking."

"So, it's not treatable."

"Probably not."

"What's the prognosis?"

"Who knows…"

Eva hung up with her mom and sat on the couch. She knew Nana was not healthy, but she didn't know how she was going to deal with this impending feeling that she was going to lose the one person who actually tried to raise her as a child.

She called off work and got Justin dressed and went up to the hospital to see Nana.

She sat next to Nana's bed and set Justin on Nana's lap.

Nana smiled and reached for Eva's arm. "You know you were always my favorite, right?" As she asked that, a young doctor came in and greeted Nana. Eva picked up Justin and sat in the chair next to Nana's bed.

"Ma'am, this prognosis is not good. If you don't quit smoking you are not going to make it much longer."

"Thank you, Doctor," Eva interjected. "We have been trying to get her to quit for a long time."

"I'm not quitting. It's one thing I still get joy from," Nana said stubbornly.

"Do you want to die?" Eva asked.

"No… Of course not."

"Are you going to quit smoking?"

"Are you kidding me? Back in my day they all smoked. Humphrey Bogart. Lauren Bacall! Everyone."

"And where are they now? Dead," Eva retorted. "Because of smoking."

"We all die of something."

Eva fiddled with her phone and opened Facebook to end the conversation and let the doctor handle the difficult old woman. She tuned Nana and her bickering with the doctor out.

Riley had responded. She smiled and read the message while Nana fussed over the doctor's recommendations. 'Hey you! I'm so sorry. My dad is sick in Tennessee and I'm going back and forth from San Diego to Memphis to help with him. But no, I sold the Mustang. There are a lot of ranches near me here, but I don't get to ride anymore. I miss it though! California is great. You were stationed here before we ended up in Good Ol' Mississippi together. You should remember how great it is! Maybe when life calms down you can come out and visit. Bring that husband and baby.'

"Why are you smiling over there?" Nana grilled her.

"Remember my friend Riley from the Navy? The one that was my roommate for a few months. You met her when you came to visit me. She took us horseback riding at the stables and called you Elizabeth Taylor."

"Oh! Yes! The lesbian girl. Is she still a lesbian?"

"I think that's how that works. I don't think you suddenly go to men."

"Yes. She was lovely. What a nice girl. Just a shame about the gay... She was pretty. She could get a man if she wanted."

"She doesn't want one. That's the point." Eva was annoyed.

"You had me worried for a moment with all that. Remember when you told me you liked men and women? I'm so glad you went the right way. Look at you now. Married, baby. You are wasting your bachelor and master's degrees, but you have them. There's nothing you can't do, Eva."

Eva remembered the time she attempted to come out to Nana. Sadly, it had not gone well. The old woman had refused to speak to her for almost 6 months.

"Yeah. Look at me now." Eva sighed.

TRUE TO HER WORD, WHEN she returned to work Lauren had left information from her clients about the local running group. They had a Facebook group that she could join, and they post runs daily that anyone can join.

She went on the social network and signed up. She saw several of the members were training for the same race she had signed up for. She wrote down notes on where to meet up for a few runs.

She wrote a thank you note to Lauren and stuck it in her employee locker.

Eva put herself on autopilot.

She put a mental schedule together. Train. Race. Justin's first birthday. Work. Family. Repeat.

And so she began. She started running with the group and making friends with them. Britt would periodically join them too. She found a welcome distraction in the physical exertion of the daily runs and the often self-deprecating humor of her new-found cohort of runners. They welcomed her with open arms as well.

They ran up and down Lakeshore Drive along Lake St. Clair, along the old mansions and large waterfront estates, and sometimes through parts of the city.

They talked about their lives and marital woes as well. She thought to herself she could have saved herself so much money on copays had she found a running group instead of therapy.

It was a whole new level of catharsis.

On a long run day, where the group was venturing 8 miles, with a light drizzle of rain and September chill in the morning air, Eva felt pain shoot down the back of her leg and up her back.

"Ouch... You guys, I need to stop. Something is wrong." She slowed her pace and looked at her group.

"What's going on?" Kit, the most advanced runner of the group stopped next to her. Kit was like the guru of the group. She often directed conversations, pacing, and routes.

Eva described the pain to her. "That sounds like your piriformis. It's a muscle in your back side. Are you stretching?"

"Stretching? No. I know I'm supposed to. But I don't."

"Yeah. It's tight. Get a massage. Have the therapist stretch you. Make sure you start stretching."

Eva attempted to finish the run at a slow pace. She drove to her spa after limping her way back to the parking lot to see if anyone had any openings. Doug had Justin for the day, and she was going to take advantage of it.

Kayleigh, the front desk girl, pulled up the schedule. "Lauren has an opening. She would be best for what you have going on."

"Anyone else? What about Suzie or Elle or Lou?"

"Booked, booked, and called off."

"Okay. When can Lauren see me?"

"In an hour and a half. You can do an 80 minute."

"I'll take it."

She went back to the locker room area and took a shower and changed into a spa robe. She went and sat in the waiting room and thumbed through magazines.

Lauren brought her client to the waiting room and handed her a cup of water. She smiled over at Eva. "Give me a few and I'll come back for ya."

Eva felt flustered. She just nodded.

Throughout the service, she forced herself to think about her son. To think about her Nana. To think about her life and what she built. *Nana is proud of me. Let's keep it that way*, she told herself.

She found after the service she felt better than she had in a long time.

"You were tight! A lot of tension," Lauren commented as she escorted Eva back to the waiting room. "You need to do this more often. It's good for you. And not just when you are interviewing new therapists."

"You are right. I will make myself a regular on your books." Eva challenged herself.

"I'm holding you to it." Lauren opened the door to the locker room and let Eva in.

She now had one more thing to fill her overwhelming calendar.

Chapter 4

Thirty-Three

WAKE UP, RUN, SHOWER, WORK, CLEAN, cook, baby, repeat. Eva's life was tightly scheduled into this unbreakable pattern. She was so busy, that she no longer cared that Doug and her never went back to therapy and that their sex life was one bump above nil. She had mellowed and found that as long as she stayed distracted and busy, nothing mattered. It was a fail proof replacement for being medicated.

Race day came and went. Eva and Britt completed the half marathon course in just over 2 hours. Eva hung her race medal over the mirror of her vanity table.

Justin's first birthday came and went as did the holidays. The diehards of her running group maintained doing outdoor runs. Eva, not a fan of cold weather, joined a gym and took to the treadmill and loud rock music on her iPod for the season. She missed the camaraderie but could not face the cold. The gym had a free childcare center that would be good for Justin and his socialization anyway.

She felt good about life for the time being.

It was mid-January and it was snowing. She had the whole day off. She had just finished a run and fastened Justin into his car seat. She settled herself in behind the wheel when her phone rang. It was Doug.

"Hey! How's your day?" she chirped cheerily into the phone.

"I need to talk to you." His voice was gruff on the other end.

"What's wrong?" She was suddenly concerned. She had backed out of her parking spot and was heading down the road.

"I fucked up. I fucked up big. And if you want to leave me, I will understand," he rushed out. It was the first time since she knew him that he ever showed a lot of emotion in his voice.

"Did you have an affair?" She was hopeful. She could deal with that.

"No."

"Well, what the fuck? What's going on?" She was really concerned.

"I have a drug problem. I've had it for a while. And I never told you, because … because… I don't know why. But I've been taking morphine. And I take it from the hospital. And today, I got caught."

Eva pulled off to the side of the road. She couldn't deal with the snow, road conditions, and this. She looked at Justin in his car seat in the back and pulled his blanket a little higher.

"I don't even understand a word you just said. Where are you?"

"I'm on my way home. I got fired. Or I think I got fired."

"You don't know? Oh. My. God. Never mind. I'm on my way home right now."

She hung up and pulled back onto the road. Her head was spinning.

She called Jack. He was a nurse. He would get it.

"Dad, Doug just called me, and he lost his job. Or maybe lost his job. He was taking morphine from the hospital," she blurted out as soon as he answered.

"I would not have guessed that for him. Where is he?"

"On his way home. So am I. I just don't know how to deal with this."

"He's going to get fired for sure. He might lose his license. He works for the Med Center. They don't mess with that kind of stuff. But he's unionized. He might not."

"Great. Good. What do I do?"

"Calm down. Don't do anything rash."

"Ha."

"If you can't be calm, don't go home. Pull over. Take a breath."

"I can't pull over. I need to get home."

"Still, breathe. You will figure this out."

She hung up with her dad and pulled into her driveway. Doug was already home. He came outside and met her on the walkway, taking the baby in the car seat from her.

"This is a fucking joke, right?" she asked a little too loud.

Doug shook his head no.

"Fucking *morphine*?"

Doug nodded. She shoved him hard on the shoulder nearly knocking him down. She instantly regretted it when she saw him stumble to keep from dropping the car seat holding the baby, but couldn't help it. She moved to strike him again but stopped.

"What the absolute *fuck* is wrong with you?" she yelled. "You *selfish* motherfucker!" Neighbors were peering out their window.

Doug went back up into the house to keep the neighbors from witnessing any more of their spectacle. She followed slamming the door.

Doug sat the car seat down. Eva pulled Justin out of the seat and put him in his highchair spilling baby snacks over the tray. She threw her coat and scarf over the back of a kitchen chair.

"Fucking spill it. All of it. Tell me what the fuck you did," Eva demanded.

Doug sat on the couch and slouched forward with his head in hands. He took a deep breath. "Remember when you just had the baby, and I told you I hurt my back lifting a patient? Well, we were so busy and consumed and all, I didn't have time to go to the doctor so one of my other patients had been discharged, and while I was wasting the pain pump, I thought I could take just a little of the morphine. So I filled some syringes. And I just started doing that. I would come home, and after you went to bed, it became my treat. And when patients were not getting discharged, I would go down to the Pyxis and take it from there. Well, today, I got caught taking it from the Pyxis. I was asked to leave and it's all under review."

"You have a stash?" Eva asked.

Doug nodded.

"Where?"

"On top of the medicine cabinet behind the lights in the bathroom, and behind the hot water heater in the basement."

Eva grabbed a chair and dragged it to the bathroom. She felt around up behind the lights and found four syringes with liquid inside them. She grabbed them and marched down to the basement, threw on the lights and reached behind the hot water tank and found two more.

She came upstairs and held them up.

"When you were slamming morphine into your arms at night while me and your son slept, did you even consider us and what this could do?"

"No. I didn't and I'm so sorry." Doug had tears in his eyes.

Eva backed up into the kitchen until she was up against the counter. The knife block was directly behind her. She felt the irresistible urge to grab a knife and drive it into his sappy remorseful face.

"Get. The. Fuck. Out. Of. This. House. Now. I don't care where you go. But you can't be here. I can't look at you right now."

He stood. "Eva... Please."

"Pack your suitcase. Go."

"Eva..."

"Don't. Go stay with your mom. Or your brother. Or anyone else. But not here. I can't deal with you right now." She shook her head as she spoke, gripping the syringes in her hand.

Doug packed a suitcase and left. While he packed, she stayed still in her spot up against the counter. The window over the sink had a draft. She could hear the wind howl and whip past it. Large snowflakes stuck to the window. The morphine filled syringes felt hot in her hands.

Doug came out with his head down, his suitcase rolling behind him. He picked his head up once more to look at Eva. She refused to look at him.

Justin cooed and babbled in his highchair.

Doug closed the door softly and left without another word.

After his car disappeared down the snowy street, Eva sent a text to Drew asking him to come over. She put Justin down for a nap and let Starling out into the yard.

She poured a coffee and added a liberal amount of Kahlua to the drink. Drew arrived and let himself in.

"What is going on?"

Eva scooped the syringes off the counter and poured them onto Drew's lap. "That's morphine. Morphine stolen from the University Medical Center. Morphine stolen from mother fucking *cancer* patients. Morphine that *my husband* was busy slamming into his veins."

"Shut up," Drew said. "That's not true."

"It is."

"Where is Doug?"

"I sent him away. I was going to stab him. I wanted to kill him. I couldn't look at him. So I sent him out."

"Where to?" Drew asked, picking up the syringes. "And what are you going to do with this?"

"I don't know. Turn it back into the hospital? What am I supposed to do with it?"

Drew shrugged. "Are you going to stay with him?"

"I don't know. This would be a good reason to leave him, wouldn't it?"

"Do you want to leave him?"

"I don't know. I've been doing so good lately. I've resigned myself to this is all there will be. I've come to terms with it."

"That's depressing."

"I don't know. I don't know what's next. I don't even know what I should be doing. What's even more depressing is he did this, while working with Camille."

"It's not about her."

"No. It's not. But still. I need to call her and see what everyone knows. See if she knows what needs to be done."

"Do it. I'm here."

Eva picked up her phone and scrolled her contacts looking for Camille's number, selected it and held her breath. She put it on speaker and set down the phone.

"Hey. I was going to call you," Camille answered.

"So, you know what happened?"

"I was there when he got caught," Camille stated.

"I'm so sorry. You put your neck out for him and this is what happened."

"Eva, it's okay. It happens to a lot of nurses. He isn't the first and won't be the last. But hey, he needs to call Jill Beck, his union rep."

"Can you give me the number? I sent him to go somewhere else for a few. I can't deal with him. I will call her."

Camille recited the numbers and Eva took them down.

"Don't be too hard on him. He's not a bad guy. We never saw this coming on the floor."

Eva rolled her eyes. "How's Kyle and the kids?"

"They are great! I see on Facebook how big Justin is getting. What a cute baby! Who would have thought you and I married with kids?" Camille laughed.

"Yeah." Eva didn't offer the laugh in return. "I gotta go. I got to handle all this bullshit."

"Yeah. I get it. It was nice talking to you. I miss you!" Camille chirped.

"Yeah. Me too." Eva hung up.

Drew looked at her. "Wow. That was tone deaf."

"Yeah. That's Camille."

Drew put his arm around Eva, and she leaned into him and cried. He let her get it out. He stuck around and took care of Justin while she made phone calls to Jill Beck, who informed her the hospital has not decided whether or not to file charges against him, but if they do, it's advisable Doug surrender himself.

Eva called a lawyer while Drew rifled through her refrigerator looking for ingredients to cook.

Eva had hung up with an attorney and sat back on the couch, drained by the day when the phone rang. It was Doug's mom.

"Do I answer it?" Eva asked Drew.

"Yes. Just get it over with."

"Hi, Trish."

"Doug is here. He said you threw him out. He won't tell me why."

Eva told her everything. Trish took a sharp inhale. "This is all true?"

"Yeah. That's all of it."

"What are you going to do?" Trish asked.

"I don't know. I don't know what I'm supposed to do in a situation like this."

"Well, if you decide to leave him, I certainly understand. I would be on your side."

Eva raised her eyebrow at this and made an on-the-spot decision. "No. I'm not leaving him. Not in a time like this. That's ridiculous you would even suggest that. No."

Drew's jaw dropped.

"Trish, I've got to go. I will call Doug later." She hung up and looked at Drew.

"I thought you didn't know what you were going to do?" Drew asked.

"I didn't until just then."

After dinner, Eva put Justin to bed while Drew cleaned up the kitchen. He left after making sure she was okay.

Eva called Doug and informed him of the information from the lawyer, the union rep, and the police department.

"Thank you for doing all of that for me," Doug whispered.

"Look. I'm mad. I'm really mad. I'm disappointed. But I'm not giving up."

"I don't deserve you."

"Probably, right now that is accurate. Jill Beck is going to be looking for your call tomorrow. Call her. She will help you negotiate your out, and hopefully you can get out of this with your license intact and get another job elsewhere."

"When can I come home?"

"I don't know about that yet. Just give me a few days."

She hung up and scrolled through Facebook. She looked at all her friends with their seemingly perfect lives. She felt nauseated and threw the phone down.

It would be 2 more days before she would allow Doug to come home. She called in from work and skipped her gym time. She didn't look at her phone. She didn't call anyone. She just focused on Justin. She snuggled him and loved on him and doted on him.

The night Doug came home, she let him cry on her shoulder. She held him and let him apologize.

The next morning, he went in to meet with HR and Jill Beck. Jill had managed to get him a decent deal for resigning in lieu of termination. He would get a buy-out of his vacation time which totaled just about 3 weeks, and the hospital would allow him to maintain his medical benefits for 12 weeks as long as he enrolled in a rehab program.

Doug had to go to the police department on his way home and give a statement.

Once he was home, he informed Eva that he didn't think they were filing charges, and that he found an outpatient rehab program that worked with health care providers and would allow him to keep his license because it was a first offense.

Rehab started the following Monday.

Eva asked him about his likelihood of getting another job.

Doug shrugged. "I can't look for one until I'm done with the 30 days of outpatient."

She nodded. "We can't afford to live here very long without you working. I don't make enough to float our lives."

"I will get unemployment. We will make do with what we can. I am sure that our parents can help us."

"Maybe my dad. My mom, no way."

Jack was able to cut a check to help them get by for the first month. Doug's mom refused to even see Doug, as she was so disgusted with what he had done. Jack was sympathetic having watched this happen to several of his co-workers along the way. Between Jack's help, Eva working and selling off some of her jewelry, they made ends meet enough to not lose their home.

Doug breezed through the month of outpatient recovery and started putting his resume out to other facilities. Eva also convinced him to go back to couple's counseling.

Doug appeared to be a changed man through this experience. He was more attentive as a father and a husband. He showed gratitude for Eva and all the work she was putting in and sacrifices she had made in choosing to stand by him. He cleaned up around the house and attempted to cook dinner while Eva was working.

Eva continued to run, to work, and put herself back into her grind that allowed her to ignore her overall feelings that she was missing out on something bigger and better.

Doug secured a job right after his rehab stint was over at a dialysis center. A benefit for male nurses is being a rare find and in high demand. A condition to keeping his license he could not pass meds for 3 years and had to continue to go to NA meetings and report back to a counselor.

As Doug began to work again, life truly fell back to where it was before the 'big incident'. It seemed that the first 6 weeks after Doug was caught things may have been better than ever before. But slowly, everything went back to the way it was.

It was soon warm enough outside, that Eva could brave the outdoor runs with her running group again. She resumed her every 2 weeks massages with Lauren as well.

Lauren and her began talking through the services as well.

Eva learned that Lauren's girlfriend was older than Lauren by 10 years. Lauren was only 3 years older than Eva. She also learned that Lauren's girlfriend, Olivia, was very possessive and jealous and struggled with Lauren's chosen profession.

Eva would lament to Lauren about Doug's lack of attention and Lauren would lament about getting too much attention.

Eva was no longer intimidated by her attraction to Lauren but looked forward to every moment they had together in the break room or the treatment room.

After several weeks of their carefree banter and growing friendship, while they were having lunch in the break room, Eva worked up the courage and asked Lauren to hang out after work.

"I can't. Olivia would come apart at the seams." Lauren rolled her eyes. "I miss having friends for sure, though."

"That sucks." Eva pouted.

After a few more weeks, Eva and Doug had fallen completely back out of synch and stopped couple's counseling. She was truly back to where things were before his big drug bust.

She numbed herself by staying busy and preoccupied with everything else she could keep her hands on and posting highlight reels of how 'blessed' and 'happy' and busy she was on social media.

She would lament to Drew, Lauren, and her running group, and Britt, and listen to their lamenting about their lives and work, and partners. In hearing how everyone was always complaining about something with their partners, Eva thought maybe that's just what life is. She felt guilty for feeling dissatisfied and took it as a personal flaw.

She began to truly think, this really is all that there is. It won't be any better with anyone else. This is normal. This is what it means to be an adult. She comforted herself in this.

During this time, her Nana began a severe decline in health. She added in weekly visits with Nana either at her home or at the hospital to relieve Geri of her obligation.

She didn't mind, as she loved Nana beyond all words. She attributed all that people loved about her to her Nana's influence.

But Nana was getting mean. She didn't feel good. She didn't feel like herself, and it was coming out in her outbursts lashing out at whoever was closest to her at the moment.

Eva would stop and pick up a strawberry shake for Nana, and sit in her living room, getting Nana comfortable in her chair with her blanket and her shake. She would bring Starling and Justin with her. She would sit and listen to Nana reminisce about the good old days. She would listen to Nana lecture her about her hair. Tell her she was getting too skinny.

"How's your marriage?" Nana asked one day as Starling and Justin played together at Nana's feet.

It was summer now. Nana did not like the temperature on the air conditioner to be too cold as she was concerned about the price of her electric bill and did not like to be cold. The sun was beating down through the living room window, and Eva thought she was baking in the seventh ring of Hell. Nana had not redecorated her house since the 1990's, and the pastel furniture held heavy the smell of smoke and the brass decorations and accents reflected the glare of the sun.

"It was good right after Doug got busted. Now, it's back to what it was."

"You need to have an affair," Nana coached.

"What? Are you crazy? Did your oxygen shut off?"

"No. You are so high strung. You are always busy. You are always adding things onto your plate. If you were satisfied, you would relax more. I had an affair when things were bad with your grandfather. It helped." She really was in Hell.

Eva rolled her eyes and changed the subject. "Gross. I don't want to know that. How's your shake?"

Nana sipped the straw. "Good. But think about it. Of all the kids I raised, you are most like me. I know what you need."

Crazy old bitch, Eva thought. As she sipped her shake and watched Justin and Starling play on the floor, she thought about her running group and all the members she knew were sneaking around with each other after runs or at travel races when their spouses, burnt out on sitting on the sidelines for hours, stopped coming in support. Could she actually do that? Would she do that? She shook her head of the thought and changed the channel on the television.

SUNDAYS WERE EVA'S FAVORITE DAYS. It was her day. It was the one thing that did stick after Doug's drug rehab. It was his day to be a dad and take over primary house and baby duties.

Sunday mornings, Eva would get up and go do a long run with her running group. They would go anywhere from 5-10 miles, sometimes more if one or more of them were training for a long road race.

After her run, she would go to the spa, shower in the locker room, and see Lauren for an 80-minute massage.

It was August, and the heat and humidity in the Detroit area was oppressive. Eva ran 10 miles with her group. She was restless. It was scorching and the sky was heavy with low, dark clouds. It tried to rain while they ran through the neighborhoods and back in front of the lake. The cool mist was a refreshing reprieve from the heat, but she couldn't shake that restlessness.

Eva and the group got back to the parking lot they all used and stretched and said her goodbyes to her friends, and then headed to the spa for her massage.

Lauren called her back to the treatment room. She laid on the table and stared up the ceiling. She was so on edge. She could not let go; of what, she couldn't say.

Lauren came in and began working on her neck. "You need to relax," Lauren murmured. She manipulated Eva's head to the side so she could dig into the side of her neck muscles. When she was content with muscle release on that side she moved Eva's head to the other side and worked. Eva's foot tapped back and forth under the blanket and her eyes remained open. By now she was normally in a state of relaxation barely conscious.

Eva tried to take a deep breath. But she couldn't let it go.

Lauren moved off to her side so she could work on Eva's shoulder and arm. Eva, possessed with a boldness she had not known in so long, reached out, grabbed Lauren by the arm and pulled her down so they were nose to nose. She looked Lauren deep in the eye, before she moved in to kiss her.

Lauren kissed her back, before pushing back.

"I don't do things like this." She shook her head vehemently.

"I'm so sorry." Eva sat up holding the sheet to her chest. "I don't even know why I would do that. I just … I don't…"

Lauren came back and sat next to Eva on the table and pushed Eva's hair back and looked at her for a minute. She leaned in and kissed Eva again. "I can't deny it. You are something else. But you know this is wrong."

Eva was lit aflame inside. "Yes. It is. I don't care."

Eva pulled Lauren closer letting the sheet fall. Lauren had brought herself all the way on to the table with Eva propping herself up.

"So, we should probably stop doing this, right?" Lauren asked.

"Probably, yes. But I hope no." Eva dragged Lauren down on top of her.

Lauren's hand slipped under Eva's waist, her other hand propping her up. Eva felt drunk with endorphins. Lauren's body was sanguineous on top of her. Eva slid her hands up Lauren's back, and to the back of her head pulling her back in. Lauren's hand slid out from under her waist and over her body. Pulling the sheet further down.

Their lips stayed locked as Lauren's hands traveled down between Eva's legs, gently stroking. Eva gasped and let out a small moan as Lauren began to slowly tease around in the spot.

Her hips rocked against Lauren's hand, and her mouth sought Lauren's. She felt her own urgency and sought that release. Her hand pushed Lauren's hand into her with more pressure. Lauren's fingers went inside her.

Lauren's other hand moved and covered Eva's mouth. "Shhhhhh."

Eva's neck went back and her back arched as waves of heat and ecstasy poured through her body.

She had forgotten how it felt to come alive under someone else's touch.

Her legs were spread over the edges of the massage table and her arms were clutching Lauren as her hand refused to relent, grinding against her and inside of her.

Eva's body finally calmed, and Lauren removed her hands, her lips seeking Eva's.

"So that's a happy ending?" Eva asked laughing.

Lauren laughed quietly. "I've literally never done anything like this before. My table is a sacred space usually."

"I'm so sorry. I don't know what came over me. I respect you. As a friend, as a co-worker, and as a professional. This was so not what I had ever intended."

"If I didn't want to do it, I wouldn't have done it," Lauren said sitting back.

Eva pulled the sheet up over herself.

"Do you regret it?" Lauren asked.

"Yes and no. Yes, because I don't want you to think I don't respect or care about you. No, because … Well... It was amazing. Do you regret it?"

"Yes and no, too. Yes, because technically, you are my boss, and you are a client. I never wanted to cross either of those lines, ever. No, because I have felt like we have had a deeper connection for a long time. I can't deny it. I felt it when you interviewed me. I think it was bound to happen at some point."

"Do you feel guilty about Olivia?"

"When you spend just about every day getting accused of something, it's only a matter of time before you actually do it. No. I honestly don't feel guilty. I thought I would, but I don't. Do you feel guilty?"

"No… I have been begging Doug to pay attention to me. To give me what I need and to work on things. He's just not."

Lauren nodded. She stood up and looked at the clock.

Eva looked over as well. "You have another client. I get it." She grinned.

"How do you want to handle this?" Lauren asked.

"I don't know." Eva stood and grabbed the spa robe and put it on. "How do you?"

"I don't know either. I say we just think about it and come back to this another time."

Eva nodded and exited the massage room.

She got in her car after getting dressed and paying at the front desk. She felt awkward paying for the time and leaving a tip. It somehow made everything feel cheap and dirty. She hoped in her heart that Lauren was not in her room regretting it at this moment.

The clouds that had hung low and sprinkled her during her run had broken and cleared. The hot, overbearing August sun in Michigan, was beating down and the humidity never relented.

She called Drew as soon as she got to the car. "I cheated on Doug," she blurted out as soon as Drew answered the phone.

"Well, hi to you too. I was going to tell you I need to call you back, but not now."

"What could you be doing that's more important than talking to me anyway?"

"I'm working. I am catering a baby shower."

"Sounds awful."

"It is. But tell me what happened, I have like 5 minutes."

"Remember Lauren? The cute massage therapist I hired a while ago?"

"Yes! Her?"

"Yes. Oh my god. But it was bad too. She got me off on her massage table."

"You crossed so many lines. You can get sued for that. That's workplace harassment. Prostitution. All kinds of legal drama."

"Don't suck the joy of it out."

"Did you get off?"

"Yeah… Oh my god, yeah."

"Are you going to do it again?"

"Dunno. But I needed it."

"Yes you did. Hey, I'm happy for you. Congratulations on your orgasms, but I gotta get back to work. Come over later around six and have dinner with Jose and I?"

"Okay. Love you. Bye."

She hung up and drove home.

Doug and Justin were playing together in the sprinkler in the back yard. An old and decrepit Starling laying in the shade nearby. Eva grabbed a vitamin water from the fridge and sat out on a lawn chair in the back yard and watched them. She felt like she should feel guilty, but she just didn't.

"How was your day?" Doug led Justin back over to her and toweled him off. Justin crawled up into her lap.

"It was good. It was a good run. Nice massage." She kissed Justin's wet head. "I'm going to have dinner at Drew's house tonight, if you don't mind?"

"I can come with you," Doug offered.

"No. It's good. Drew wants to talk to me about some personal things." Eva shifted her gaze over to Starling.

"Oh. Okay. I was just thinking it's been a while since we had a night..."

Oh. Now he wants to be a husband! Eva thought guiltily.

"Yeah. It has. Tomorrow night after I come back from Nana Duty." Eva smiled at him.

"Okay."

Eva picked Justin up and carried him into the house. She cleaned him up and dressed him and sat him at the table so they could eat lunch. She smiled at him. She still loved looking at his face. It was still the most beautiful thing she had ever seen. She loved his dimples and large brown eyes framed with long thick lashes. His sandy fine hair was long and shaggy.

She spent the rest of the afternoon reading to Justin and snuggling with him until she left for Drew's.

She hugged Drew and Jose when she got to their house. Sitting at their dining table, Jose looked at her and grinned as Drew poured rosé into their glasses. "I heard you were a bad girl."

"I wouldn't say bad," Eva countered.

Drew sat down. "First, let's toast to being satisfied."

They lifted their glasses.

"So, now that you are back to being a lesbian, are you going to move in together next week?" Jose teased.

"I don't do labels," Eva said as she sipped the wine.

"Are you in love?" Jose asked.

"No. The only person I love outside of my Nana, and my mom and dad, and of course you two, is Justin. I don't think I'm the fall in love type."

Drew served Greek salads with chicken and warm pitas on their plates and asked, "It's been a few hours now. You have been home and all that. What are you thinking is your next step?"

"You are asking if I'm leaving Doug? No. I can't do that to Justin right now. I don't know if I could honestly do that to Doug right now either. He still hasn't spoken to his mom since he got in trouble. Honestly, he really was there for me when I was deep in the depression thing. I don't know."

"Do you think you and Lauren will be like a thing?" Jose asked.

"I don't think so. I think this was a one-time thing. She has her girlfriend." Eva waved her hand to shoo the idea away. "Plus, I don't think I can handle a double life."

"You know you deserve to be happy, right?" Drew asked. "You don't have to be in a double life to be happy. You can admit you made a mistake by marrying Doug. You can admit that you don't belong together."

Eva shrugged. "I don't know. I don't even know it will happen again. There's a lot of moving parts at play and I'm not so sure I'm willing to disrupt any of that right now." She took a deep breath. She knew the right thing to do was to leave Doug and admit it was a mistake. She saw the glimmer of light in talking to Drew and Jose. She was also terrified of being on her own and what that would look like.

THE NEXT MORNING EVA WOKE up and didn't feel bad. She looked out the window while she sat alone in the living room with Starling and her coffee. Justin had not woken up yet and Doug was already at work. The clouds rolled back in overnight and it was thunder storming. She thought about texting Lauren but chose not to. It was Lauren's day off and she didn't want to crowd her. She wanted to play it cool.

She went in and checked on Justin and took a quick shower. She assessed herself in the mirror as she toweled off. She felt confident. The running group had lent her that confidence. She felt powerful and competent. She looked better than a lot of other women at her age, she felt. Her hair was still not graying, and she had very few lines compared to a lot of other women her age, which was due to working in the spa and all the free facials, and a ridiculous amount of non-relenting in her personal skin care regime at home morning and night.

She finished dressing and woke Justin up, fed him breakfast, dressed him and headed to Nana's, stopping to pick up shakes.

At Nana's house, while they sipped shakes and watched sitcom reruns on Nickelodeon together as Justin played on the floor by her feet, Eva's phone alerted her of a text. It was Lauren. 'I can't stop thinking about yesterday.'

Eva's pulse raced. 'Is that good or bad?' she responded.

'I don't know. But I think I want to do it again,' Lauren responded with a winky face emoji.

'Me too,' Eva replied.

'When do you think we can be alone together again?' Lauren asked.

'I don't know. Maybe we can figure it out for after work,' Eva responded.

'Well, let's not take too long,' Lauren replied.

Eva smiled and turned her screen off. It felt good to feel wanted.

Chapter 5

Thirty-Four and Thirty-Five

SUMMER MOVED INTO FALL. EVA and Lauren never found a way to make time for each other outside of work. Eva stopped scheduling massages with Lauren as she did not want to feel awkward paying for the time or put Lauren into the position of feeling cheapened by the service. There were plenty of risqué text messages and innuendos in the break room. The interest was still there for both of them.

Halloween passed. Justin's birthday passed. Nana's health continued to deteriorate. Eva was spending more of her off time with Nana.

Eva would spend her time at Nana's or in the hospital room on her many admissions talking to Nana and scrolling on Facebook. She maintained her messaging with Riley and found comfort in their brief communications. Riley was now taking care of her ailing father at the same time.

Christmas passed.

So came the new year and Eva just fell into her groove of apathy and routine. Wake up, feed Justin and self, run, shower, work, Nana, spend time with Justin, squeeze in sexting with Lauren, sleep, repeat. She had started a separate account at the bank where she would deposit money, referring to it as her 'Freedom Fund'. As the account grew she considered the possibilities of a single life where she could pursue happiness with just her and Justin.

Spring came and went. As did summer. The Freedom Fund slowly grew and so did Eva's edginess. Eva daydreamed about having her own place, with just herself, Starling and Justin. She would lament her discontent to Britt over lunches or glasses of wine at Britt's house. Britt suggested that Eva just be patient and when she could, make her move.

It was fall again. Eva and Lauren had been sexting for a year with no resolution. The text messages were detailed, graphic and Eva enjoyed them, but she wanted more. She wanted the physical. But with everything else she resided herself to that this is all there ever would be.

Nana was in the hospital more than she was home.

Eva and Doug had not been intimate in well over 3 months. Eva would escape to the guest room alone or take an additional shower, reliving her text messages with Lauren as relief. For being a married mother with a busy schedule, Eva never felt so alone.

Geri called Eva one night after she had just put Justin to bed. "I'm coming over. We need to talk," Geri said.

"Where are you?" Eva asked.

"I'm leaving the hospital. I just talked to the doctor."

Eva knew what this would be about. Nana was declining to the point that these stents in the hospital were all that were really keeping her alive. She had a diminished quality of life, and she was miserable while she was awake.

Geri showed up. Doug came and sat in the living room with them.

"I think we need to talk about hospice for Nana," Geri said as she sat down.

Eva sat back on the couch and fought back tears. She knew it was the right thing to do. She nodded.

"When will this start?" Doug asked.

"She can come home tomorrow. The hospice people can come over tomorrow afternoon." Geri was surprisingly calm.

Tears flowed hot down Eva's cheeks.

"I need to know you are okay with this, honey." Geri reached out and touched Eva's knee.

Eva assented. "I'm not. But I know it's right," she choked out.

"We will be there tomorrow for the hospice consult," Doug offered.

"Thank you," Geri said. "I need to get home and sleep. I just didn't want to have this conversation on the phone."

"Thank you, Mom," Eva said standing up to walk her to the door.

Eva went back to the bedroom and Doug sat on the couch playing a video game. Eva curled up in the bed and opened Facebook and updated her status. "To those of you who know me well, you know my Nana is my life. Tomorrow she begins hospice. The end of a force of nature is near. I'm beyond broken over this." She hit 'post' and scrolled through her friends' happy posts.

She saw a notice that she had a comment and looked at it. It was from Riley. 'I'm so sorry. I just lost my dad 2 months ago. I know it hurts. Tell Elizabeth Taylor that I love her.'

Eva smiled. She replied, 'I'm so sorry about your dad. I've been so wrapped up I didn't even see that. Nana remembers you fondly. She remembers you calling her Elizabeth Taylor. That was the best compliment from anyone ever in her eyes. One of the only ways I can still make her laugh is regaling our horseback riding adventure with her.' She hit 'send' on the reply.

Moments later she got a private message from Riley. It had her phone number and said, 'If you need anything, call me. I'm always here for you.'

She needed that, responding, 'Thank you. It means a lot.'

Eva put the phone down and fell into a light and fitful sleep.

The next day Eva called Margaret and let her know the situation and requested the next week off work, pending more time as needed. Margaret was understanding and granted the time.

Eva met Geri and Nana at Nana's house shortly after they got back. Geri was in the kitchen smoking a cigarette. Eva put some cartoons on for Justin and went into Nana's bedroom where she was propped up on pillows. The room was done in various shades of peach and pink with heavy cherry wood furniture. Nana looked like an old princess sitting in all the girly glow of the light colors and rich furniture. Her olive skin looked sallow, her hair flatted from lying down.

Eva sat next to her on the bed. "I'm really sick, aren't I?" Nana asked.

Eva nodded. "It's not good."

"I'm tired," Nana said. "I dreamt of my mom and dad last night. Your papa made an appearance too."

The knot in Eva's throat prevented her from saying anything.

"They told me I'm coming soon," Nana continued.

Eva could not control the tears. They fell willfully down and onto Nana's peach comforter with garish pink flowers.

"It's okay. I'm ready. I did what I'm supposed to do here. I raised my kids. I raised you. Of all of them, you know I'm most proud of you. But I also worry about you most. You need to be free. You deserve happiness. But I know you will find it. Just know that it's not wrong to be happy, even if others think it's selfish."

Eva nodded. She gripped Nana's hand and kissed her fingers. Her hands felt ice cold. Eva rubbed them between hers to warm them.

Nana laid herself back against the pillows. Eva stood up and darkened the blinds.

"Rest up, Nana. I will be here." She left the room and sat in the living room and watched Justin zoom Hot Wheels cars around the floor while Disney Jr. cartoons danced around gleefully in the background.

The thought of life without Nana was crushing her heart.

Doug arrived just before the hospice crew arrived. She zoned out all of what was being said. She knew what it all meant even if she didn't hear a word of it.

She got up and got into her car. She didn't say anything to anyone. She just left. She drove 45 minutes away to her favorite tattoo artist. Jeff greeted her as she walked in. He didn't have any clients at the moment. "Do you have any openings?" Eva asked.

"For you, sweetheart, I have all the time in the world."

Eva smiled. He always flirted with her. He flirted with everyone, she knew. But he had a way of flirting with someone that made you feel like you were the only girl in the world. He was not a conventionally handsome or attractive guy, but he had a lot of confidence and personality that made him far more attractive than he was.

She pulled an old letter from Nana out of her purse. "See this line at the bottom, in her handwriting? It says, 'This too shall pass'." Eva pointed to it. "I want this, here, on my forearm. Where I can see it always. Make it pretty. Add stuff around it, definitely at least one tiger lily. Those were her favorite."

"Got it, beautiful," Jeff said, taking the letter. He made the mock up with Nana's handwriting, some beautiful blackbirds in flight, and a tiger lily with soft feminine vines twisting around underneath the writing.

She didn't ask about the cost. She didn't care. She sat through the service, letting Jeff flirt with her, not really flirting back.

He cleaned her up and she paid the way too much money that she didn't really have and drove back to Nana's. Her arm burned under her long sleeve and coat. But it was a good burn. It kept her present in the moment.

Her phone rang as she was driving. It was Geri. "Where did you go?" she asked.

"To see Jeff. I needed to get out of there," Eva said. "Is Doug still there?"

"No. He and Justin went home. He went and laid down in Nana's bed with her and talked to her quietly. It was kind of beautiful," Geri informed her quietly. "You know he's not a bad man."

"I know, Mom," Eva said quietly.

"One crisis at a time though," Geri said lightly.

"Yeah... I'm almost there. I will see you in a few."

All of Nana's meds were discontinued. She was only given morphine now to keep her at peace. Eva made a conscious note to keep Doug out of Nana's house for the time being. She didn't want to have to worry about him being tempted to steal the drugs or take them for himself.

Geri and Eva began a vigil over Nana's bedside. Geri took over the bedroom that was hers as a child, and Eva took over the guest room. As a child, she used to beg Geri to leave her at Nana's for the weekends and the nights. She had grown up in this room. In her Navy days, this was her room on her days of leave. Even through college, Eva would come and spend nights at a time in this small room. The twin bed and mattress had not changed. The small vanity table was used by Nana to get ready every day. It had her brush and cosmetics on it. Her body powder in a tin with a puff on the corner. The window was small and looked out into the back yard Eva had grown up playing in. It was night and it was dark. Snow covered the grass and sparkled in the moonlight. Eva picked up the powder and smelled it while she looked across the glittering snow. She never foresaw this day; it had been unimaginable to her. She put the powder back on the table and turned out the light.

Doug brought Justin over in the morning on his way to work.

Eva didn't let him past the living room, hardly letting him sit on the sofa. Geri was sitting at the kitchen counter with a cigarette and her coffee.

"Where did you go last night?" Doug asked. She wondered if he was ever going to ask her.

She rolled up her sleeve and showed him the tattoo.

"How much did that cost?" Doug asked.

"About $450 with tip," Eva informed.

"You got mad when I bought a new video game," Doug objected. "That was only $65."

"Don't start shit right now," Eva whispered. "I never spend anything on myself. I shop at thrift stores. I take care of the house, the kid, I work... Just go to work. We will talk later." She stepped toward him, each step pushing him backward out the door. She was not about to admit that she had a secret bank account and that was where the money for the tattoo came from.

Over the next 5 days, Eva and Geri took turns watching Justin and going back and forth to their respective homes to stock up on clothes and toiletries in between sitting at Nana's bedside. Doug would drop Justin off on his way to work and pick him up on his way home. Nana had sunk into an oblivion. She was speaking Arabic, the mother tongue of her parents, to an unknown and unseen visitor intermittently.

Eva was helping her get up slowly assisting her to the small bathroom off her bedroom. Nana had quit speaking English apparently. Only speaking in broken Arabic that Eva didn't understand. She didn't even know if it was directed at her or the unseen being that had hold of Nana's attention.

She helped her back into the bed with Geri's help. Nana was carrying on in that strange language that Eva never bothered to learn or pay attention to as a child.

"Did you hear that?" Geri asked, bringing her arms across her chest and rubbing her arms.

"I can hear it, but I don't know what it means," Eva said quietly.

"She's talking to her daddy. She said daddy in Arabic."

Eva nodded. "She said her parents and Papa came to her in her dreams the other day," she told Geri as they put the blankets back over Nana and adjusted the pillows.

Nana murmured some more Arabic rambling.

"She's definitely talking to her dad," Geri repeated as they walked out of the room and back to the living room.

"I only know how to order food in Arabic," Eva reminded her.

It was a Wednesday afternoon. It was unseasonably dark and cold. Justin who fought naps with every ounce of energy he normally could crawled up onto the love seat, arranged the pillows and pulled the Afghan blanket over himself. "I'm tired, Mommy," he informed Eva.

Eva nodded. "Me, too, baby. Me, too." He closed his eyes. Eva got up and went into Nana's room. She froze at the door. Nana's breathing did not sound right.

She gripped the door frame to hold herself up. Every part of her being knew what was happening.

She turned around and ran to the kitchen where Geri was sitting at the counter texting her friend. "Mom. She's dying."

"I know, Eva."

"No. Like right now. We need to go say goodbye. She's going now."

Geri dropped her phone on the counter, bolted up and ran into her mother's bedroom. She crawled into the bed next to her mother and held her.

Nana whispered softly still in Arabic. The language sounded magical in the moment. Nana's voice was but a whisper. It sounded like she was praying or casting a spell. Eva stood at the foot of the bed. The room felt warm. The bedside lamp making Nana's face glow. "I love you, Mama. I love you so much. It's okay to let go," Geri choked.

Eva had no words. Nana took a labored inhale in, and the breath came slowly out, and there was no more. There was a strange emptiness now in the room.

"She's gone..." Eva whispered. "She's really gone." She fell to her knees with her hands on the footboard of the bed.

Geri stood and adjusted the blankets. She wiped tears from her eyes and announced, "I need to call the funeral home."

Eva stood up and said, "You do that. I will call her sisters and friends."

She went through Nana's phone book, sitting at the phone in the kitchen on Nana's favorite stool where Nana would sit and talk her through every problem and every decision, always reminding her, 'This too shall pass...'.

She called everyone in alphabetical order as they were listed in her phone book. She was methodical, and calm. "Hi... It's Eva. Wanda's granddaughter. Yeah. Um... Wanda, my Nana... She's gone. She passed away today. We will be making arrangements at Palazzolo's Funeral Home on Gratiot." She said it over and over again.

She was concerned about Justin. He was sleeping so hard, the child that never even liked naps. He was peaceful and oblivious in his slumber. She listened to his steady breathing between phone calls.

She called Doug. "You need to come get Justin," she demanded.

"I'm working," Doug informed her.

"Nana died. The funeral home is coming. I don't want Justin to see her brought out in a body bag."

"Oh. Oh. I'm so sorry. I will be there. Just give me a few."

Doug made it to Nana's house just minutes before the funeral director pulled up in the hearse.

She woke Justin up, and packed him up, kissing his beautiful, dimpled cheeks before pushing him and Doug back out the door as the funeral director was coming in with the stretcher and body bag.

Eva went into the guest room and slammed the door shut. She couldn't watch this. She did not want to see her Nana in that bag. She did not want to see her lifeless and wrapped in a canvas waterproof bag carried out inert into the cold.

She packed up her things so she could go home tonight. As she packed, she heard the funeral director and his assistant enter the living room. She heard the clanging metal of the stretcher. She felt bad leaving this to Geri to handle, but she had hit her limit. She heard the stretcher wheel past her little guest room on the hardwood floor and heard them fussing that they couldn't navigate the stretcher into the bedroom where Nana lay.

She sat on the bed and brought her knees to her face and put her hands over her ears to muffle the sound of them lifting Nana into the bag and the sound of the zipper. She could smell Geri in the other room smoking a cigarette. Geri wasn't watching either.

She heard them place Nana's body on the stretcher. She heard them wheel past the room.

She listened for the sound of the stretcher exiting the small home.

She came out and looked at Geri who was standing at the front door watching as they loaded Nana's body into the back of the shiny black hearse. It was beginning to snow.

"Meet me at Palazzolo's in the morning?" she asked.

"Yep. I will bring the picture of Nana so they can do her hair and makeup."

"Let's pick out her outfit to bring," Geri said, walking back toward Nana's bedroom. Neither of them were really ready to leave.

They went through Nana's closet laughing at what Nana would think about various options. They settled on a black skirt and red blouse. They selected jewelry for her and put it all in her overnight bag to be brought to the funeral home.

Eva drove home slowly in the snow. She felt hollow and numb. She called Britt who patiently listened as Eva cried. Britt stayed on the phone with her while she sat in her car in the driveway not ready to go inside. "Just take your time. You just lost Nana. It's okay if you feel hurt and you don't want to go inside yet," Britt coached.

Eva took a deep breath. "Thank you for being there and answering the phone."

"Of course. Love you."

"Love you." Eva hung up.

She dragged herself into the house. Walked past Doug on the couch watching NFL Network. She walked into Justin's bedroom, and he was sitting up in his small toddler bed.

"Hi, Mommy." He smiled at her. He had several books pulled off the shelf around him. She smiled at him.

"Do you want me to read you a story?"

"Yes, Mommy." He grabbed his favorite book, 'Sleepy Baby Owl' and crawled into her lap.

"Nana is an angel in Heaven now," Justin said in his soft voice.

"Yes, she certainly is. She is going to look after us and protect us from Heaven now." She held him close in the rocking chair and kissed the top of his head.

She read him 'Sleepy Baby Owl' and then two more stories before he was sleepy enough to lay back down in his bed.

She dragged herself from his room to hers. She laid down, still in her clothes and fell asleep.

She dreamed of Nana. Nana was wearing the white jumpsuit she had worn to her wedding in Key West. She was standing in the bedroom doorway, and she was smiling. Her olive skin was healthy and glowing and her hair was perfect. Her eyes were sparkling.

Eva woke up and looked at the bedroom doorway to find it empty. She got up and looked at the clock. It was three in the morning.

She tried to go back to sleep and laid in bed with her eyes closed. Doug was sound asleep next to her. She could hear Justin's white noise machine across the hall. She tried to focus on that but couldn't.

After an hour, she got up out of the bed and went into the living room with Starling. The poor old Chihuahua was slowing down for sure. She picked up the little dog and sat on the couch with her under a blanket. She grabbed her phone and scrolled through social media.

She updated her status informing her friends that her Nana had passed. 'Hey loves... Can't sleep. Nana passed away about 12 hours ago, and I am just broken.'

She put Starling on the couch and got up and decided to make coffee.

As she was pouring her cup, her phone vibrated alerting her she had a call. She looked at the caller ID and it was a number she didn't recognize from California. She looked at the clock, it was almost 5 in Detroit, making it almost 2 in California.

"Hello?" she asked quietly.

"Hey, it's Riley."

"Holy shit. It's like 2 in the morning over there. What are you doing up?"

"I couldn't sleep, and I saw your post. I thought I would call you."

"Hold on just a sec." Eva poured cream into her coffee and grabbed the cup and went down to the basement so she could talk without whispering.

"Oh my god. I haven't heard your voice in like 12 years," Eva exclaimed.

"I know. I know we kept talking about getting together or talking and we never did. I figured you're awake and so am I, so I'm going to call."

Eva sat on the old rec room couch in the corner of the basement. "It really means the world to me that you called."

"Of course. I know how you are feeling," Riley lamented.

"Yes... I'm so sorry about your dad. I know it was a hard time. He was sick for a while."

They spent over an hour on the phone trading stories about their lost loved ones and going back into reminiscing about their time in the Navy. She learned Riley was a busy real estate broker in Southern California now, but Eva couldn't bring herself to ask which girl in the pictures was actually her girlfriend. She told Riley about being a mom and running someone else's business.

Eva could hear Doug's alarm go off for work. She knew Justin would be getting up shortly too. "I gotta get going. Everyone is slowly getting up. I need to tend to the fam. I am so happy you called!"

"I'm glad I called, too. Maybe we can talk again soon?"

"Yes! For sure!" Eva hung up.

She made breakfast for Doug and Justin and got ready to meet Geri at the funeral home to finalize arrangements for Nana.

She sat with Geri and picked out a casket, flowers, gave the funeral director a picture of her Nana and the overnight bag of clothes.

She called the people she needed to reach to share the arrangements. She posted on Facebook the information as well.

The wake would be the day after tomorrow. She packed Justin in the car and drove to the mall to find a dress.

She walked around and couldn't find anything. She stopped at the indoor playground and let Justin run out some kid energy. They made another lap around the mall, and she settled on a plain black basic long sleeve form fitting dress. She felt like it was too much money, and after splurging on her tattoo, she thought, *What's another hundred bucks?*

She paid for the dress and found Justin a cute black suit that would fit him. She went back to Nana's and let herself in with the hidden spare key.

She turned on the television with cartoons and placed Justin in front of the brightly colored animation with a Happy Meal and his toys and sat in Nana's kitchen and breathed in the smell of spices and cigarette smoke. She got up and went into Nana's living room and picked up the Afghan blanket that Nana used while she would watch her classic sitcoms. She picked it up and tossed it over her arm. She went into Nana's bedroom and took the sheets and blankets off of the bed and pushed them down the old laundry shoot to the basement.

She opened the closet and pulled out all the boxes of photos and photo albums that Nana kept stored on the shelves. She checked on Justin and started to take trips out to the car, the Afghan, the boxes of pictures, and other small items that held more significance for their memories than their value.

She picked Justin up and put him back in the car when she was done, locked the door and vowed never to set foot in that house again. She couldn't.

The wake was more difficult than she could ever imagine. She was the first person to arrive at the funeral home. The director ushered her to the room where Nana's body was displayed in the pink casket flanked in the corners by carved angels. She was holding Justin and Doug was standing just behind her.

"What do you think? How does she look?" the funeral director asked expecting praise.

Eva was mortified. The body did not resemble her beautiful and spunky Nana. Nothing looked right to her.

"She looks dead," Eva choked out.

Justin reached his hand to the edge of the casket. "Nana is sleeping. Shhhhh," he said innocently.

"Yes, baby. Nana is sleeping." She kissed Justin and looked hard at the funeral director.

He clearly was not sure how to respond to Eva's comment. He closed his eyes, bowed his head and clasped his hands behind his back. "I'm sorry. I know death is hard for many," and with that, he exited the room.

The next day, the snow was coming down thick and heavy. The family and Nana's friends piled into the old Catholic church that Nana had belonged to since Geri was born and baptized there.

Nana was laid out in her pink casket like a sales display in front of the altar with the priest standing in front. After the ceremony, the priest closed the casket ceremoniously, and Justin screamed in the church. "Nana won't be able to breathe and wake up! Open her back up!" he shouted running up the aisle toward the priest.

The priest caught him and picked him up. He smoothed Justin's hair and whispered quietly into Justin's ear as Justin cried. He brought the child back to Eva who was sobbing. She reached for her son and Justin asked in his innocence, "If she's locked in there, how will she be an angel?"

"I will tell you the story of how that works later, my Beautiful Boy," she whispered to him. He laid his head against her shoulder and buried his face into her neck. Britt helped Eva calm Justin down, taking him from Eva's arms and quietly taking him out the large doors to the entrance of the old church.

After the obligatory luncheon, Eva went home. Doug left to work the afternoon shift. Geri was going to go to Nana's house with her brothers and cousins and aunts to parcel off Nana's goods. Geri's real estate agent, off again on again, boyfriend, would be listing the house once all of the items were removed and it was painted with new carpet.

She sat Justin down on her lap on the couch in the living room and pulled the Afghan she brought home from Nana's up around them. It smelled like Nana's house. She could smell Nana's scent mixed with cigarettes.

"You comfy, Beautiful Boy?" she asked. Justin smiled and snuggled into his mother. "Did you know, Nana made this blanket herself?"

Justin shook his head no.

"So, let me tell you about Nana in the casket. I know that looked like our Nana. But her spirit was not in there. See, we all have spirits inside of our bodies. That spirit is who we really are. The body we have, is just a means of getting around in the world. The spirit lives here," Eva tapped over Justin's heart. "When someone dies and goes to Heaven, the spirit leaves the body. Nana was not really in the box today. Just her body was. Her spirit has been in Heaven for many days now. That's how she can be an angel in Heaven. She is going to always look after you and look after me and Gramma Geri."

"How do you know she was not having her spirit in her body anymore?" Justin asked.

"Because you have faith. You trust. Just like we always say our Angel of God prayer, that Nana taught me when I was your age. Her Angel of God, guardian dear, helped her spirit to Heaven so she can be our newest and brightest angel looking after us."

Justin absorbed this information, then wriggled himself free. "Can I play with my toys now?"

Eva smiled at him. "Yes, Beautiful Boy. Go play."

EVA THREW HERSELF INTO TRAINING for a spring race. She busied herself with work. Margaret was opening yet a third location for her spa, and Eva was training the new manager and helping to hire new therapists.

She and Lauren continued their meaningless sporadic sexting, never able to fully connect. They had stepped it up by sending occasional pictures to accompany their messages.

It had now been a full 4 months since she and Doug had been intimate. She had stopped caring.

She found the secret to happiness is to understand there is no real happiness. There's just reality and you need to be content with what you have.

She ran her race, in a state of Zen. Focusing only on one foot in front of the other. Inhale, exhale. The music in her earbuds. Move to the left to pass this person. Move to the right to pass the next. Keep pushing.

She crossed the finish line and took a selfie of herself with her medal and posted her stats on Facebook. Smiling, looking happy and fulfilled. She clicked 'post' and sat on the ground to stretch. Doug, like so many other spouses of avid runners, had stopped coming to cheer her on at the sidelines of every single race.

After stretching she made her way to her car and checked Facebook one more time before starting the car. Riley commented on her selfie, 'I really miss you!'

Eva replied, 'I miss you too! Let's plan this reunion we've always been talking about!' She clicked 'send' and made her way down the street. She was getting ready to turn into Starbucks when her phone rang. It was Riley.

"Hello?" she answered.

"Am I coming to you or you coming to me?" Riley asked.

Eva laughed. "It's probably easier if you come to me."

"Okay. I'm coming. I'm on Expedia now. Can you take time off work like next month?"

"Sure! When?"

"I will come in on Friday, April fourth, and leave on the ninth. How's that?"

"That's amazing! I'm so excited! I have a guest room. You can stay with me! Are you bringing your girlfriend?"

"Oh, god no. Long story. But it's just me."

Eva was so excited when she hung up the phone. She called Drew to share the news. "Riley is coming to visit, and you have to meet her!" Eva blurted out.

"How exciting!" Drew exclaimed.

"Yes! She will be staying for like 5 days. I have to show her a good time. I mean, Detroit is no New Orleans, but we have fun stuff, right? I've been hibernating for so long I don't even remember what we have to do."

"Ohhh! When is she coming?" Drew asked.

"April 4-9."

"There's a big party at The Aut that weekend. It's their anniversary of being open. Take her to that!"

"Yes. And I think I'm going to take her downtown to Greektown and maybe the Henry Ford Museum or something."

"I think you sound like you have it under control," Drew reassured her. "I can't wait to meet her!"

Eva went home, showered and told Doug they were going to have a house guest.

"You planned to have her come that weekend? Can you change it?" Doug asked.

"I think she bought her tickets. I don't think it's refundable. Why?"

"I really wish you would talk to me before you make grand plans. That's my parents' anniversary. It's their 40th. There's a big party up north. We are staying in the family cabin. I don't want to miss it."

"When is it?"

"Saturday April 5th."

"Why don't you take Justin and go up there? Stay home Friday night so Riley can meet you and Justin, though. You guys can leave Saturday morning and stay a few days. That will allow me to have time off mom duty and go party with my friends." Eva smiled.

"Everyone is going to wonder where you are," Doug said.

"Tell them I'm drunk at an Ann Arbor gay bar. Because that's where I'll be!" Eva grinned.

"Okay… I just wish we talked this over first. No use arguing about it since it can't be changed," Doug said sensibly.

Eva texted Riley that everything was cleared, and she was planning some fun itinerary for the trip.

'Can't wait!' Riley responded with a smiley face emoji.

APRIL 4TH FINALLY ARRIVED. EVA WOKE up, went for a run, came home showered and took Justin with her to the airport.

She texted Riley that she was waiting for her in baggage claim.

Eva eagerly looked at all the people waiting for her tall blonde friend to arrive. Justin busied himself watching the carousels of bags and people swarming around.

Finally, Eva saw her. They made eye contact across the crowds. Riley, nearly 6-foot tall, with a blonde spiky faux hawk, still moved like she owned the world as she made her way across the baggage claim. Her black Harley Davidson t-shirt and loose-fitting jeans looked like they were being displayed on a runway the way she walked. Eva grabbed Justin and ran to her friend.

"Oh my god! He's adorable," Riley exclaimed as they embraced.

"I know, right? I can't believe I made him!" Eva exclaimed.

"Hi, Miss Riley," Justin said shyly from Eva's arms.

Riley grabbed her suitcase off the luggage carousel and they made their way to Eva's car. They talked avidly on the way to the car. Eva found it hard to look at Riley. She felt all of the old familiar stirrings within her. She was suddenly very aware that her old crush on Riley was still very present.

As Eva snapped Justin into his car seat, Riley opened her bag. "I forgot; I have a present for the little man!" She pulled out a stuffed boxer dog toy. She handed it to Justin, and he hugged it tight. "I have two dogs at my house that look just like this guy," she told Justin.

"Thank you, Miss Riley!" Justin said. "I love him. His name will be Terry."

"That's a good name," Riley said.

It was an hour drive back to Eva's house from the airport.

Eva pointed out various sights along the road and they talked about losing their loved ones and making the most of life.

Justin fell asleep in the backseat cuddling his plush dog.

"So, where's the girlfriend? What is the story there?" Eva asked.

"Ugh. We are breaking up," Riley told her. "I tried. I gave it my all. But here's the story. You know she's a dancer, right?"

"Dancer ballet or dancer on a pole?" Eva asked. Eva was not sad in hearing that Riley and the girlfriend were breaking up. She was internally, very satisfied with this news.

"Pole."

"Oh my god. You fell in love with a stripper! Like the Wyclef Jean song?"

"No. I didn't meet her at a strip club. I met her at a winery. I didn't know she was a stripper when I met her."

"Okay. Not as bad. Go on."

"So, I thought in the beginning this was going to be good. It would be good sex and she would be all fun… And it was in the first couple of months. But then she moved in and like, stopped having sex and slowly stopped working. Next thing you know, she's depending on me for everything and giving me nothing. We've been together for 4 years now. She's lived with me just over 3 of those years, and the last two she's been fully dependent on me. It's kind of bullshit. I didn't sign up for a housewife. We haven't even had sex in almost 6 months."

"Woah! That's insane! Although, I'm coming from a similar situation," Eva confided.

"What do you mean?"

Eva explained her state of marital affairs.

"So here we are! Our parental figures died within months of each other. We have the same relationship issues. Anything else we have in common?" Riley laughed.

They arrived at Eva's modest home, and she showed Riley to the guest room, and where everything was located.

Doug was playing his video game in the living room. Eva introduced the two.

After dinner and putting Justin to bed, Doug retired to the bedroom himself. Riley had brought several bottles of wine from one of her local wineries with her. They had opened one and retreated to the basement rec room so they could talk.

Sitting on Eva's old beat-up couch from her Navy days, one on each end facing each other as they talked, just like when they were roommates, they finished off the bottle together, lamenting about their partners. Eva told Riley about Lauren. "I didn't even realize you were into girls too," Riley remarked.

"Yeah, that's because you were so up your ex's ass you couldn't see anything else. I had a big crush on you back then, too. I literally broke up with my boyfriend because I thought you were so hot," Eva confessed, her heart suddenly beating hard and loud.

"Um… What?" Riley laughed her green eyes sparkled in the recessed lights of the basement.

"Yeah. When I went with you for New Year's Eve. You were wearing that tux… Oh. My *god.* And you looked at me outside the bar over your shoulder. My fucking heart *stopped.* And this wine is *so* fucking good."

"I brought 3 bottles of it," Riley offered.

"No… I can't. I am such a lightweight. Listen to me. It's like truth serum."

"Yeah… So you had a crush on me when we were young. You like girls and boys apparently. What else am I going to learn?" Riley was grinning and looking directly into Eva's eyes.

"Nothing. I'm shutting up now." Eva was blushing, and felt her whole body was on fire.

"So, what are you going to do with Lauren?" Riley inquired.

"Nothing. I am not doing anything with anyone. It was a one-time shot. I honestly think I was or am chasing something that is not possible. I mean, happiness is not focusing on what you don't have. It's focusing on what you do have. Maybe this is all that there is?" Eva was trying to be rational in the moment, failing miserably.

"Fuck that," Riley said. "I watched my dad suffer and die and he was barely sixty. He spent most of his life working his ass off. Twelve-hour days. One day a week off. He never lived. You don't think you deserve more than to be on a rat wheel for the rest of your life?"

Eva was quiet. She wasn't sure if it was the wine or if Riley really made that much sense. "I mean yeah. I see your point." She thought about her Freedom Fund at the bank and didn't say anymore.

Riley looked at the clock on her phone.

"Oh my god. It's 3 in the morning! You have to be exhausted," Riley said.

"Yeah... I have a lot of plans for you tomorrow. I'm going to take you to Ann Arbor to go look around my college town. Then we are going to have dinner with my best friend Drew and his man, Jose. Then we are going to an 80's party to celebrate our favorite gay bar's (and the scene of so many scandals) anniversary." Eva stood up and Riley followed.

"Come here, you!" Riley said, pulling Eva close to her. She gave Eva a big hug. "I'm so happy to be here spending time with you."

"I'm so happy you are here!" Eva said smiling. She loved the way Riley smelled. It was not helping her mental state or the fact that she was so sensitive to how she was feeling for Riley in this moment. She was raw inside and out. The feeling of Riley's arms around her and her scent had Eva hypervigilant in her senses.

The next morning Eva woke up with less than 5 hours of sleep to help Doug get Justin ready to leave.

Eva balanced a cup of coffee in one hand while she packed Justin's bag with the other. Justin was pushing cars around on the floor behind her.

Doug was packing his own bag in the other room. Eva had not spent more than a few hours at a time away from Justin since he was born. She found it bitter sweet. She put down his packed bag and sat in the rocking chair in the corner of his room. "Come here, Beautiful Boy," she said quietly.

He crawled into her lap.

"Have fun at Grandma and Grandpa's. I'm going to miss you."

"I love you, Mommy," Justin said, putting his arms around Eva's neck.

Doug came in, "Okay. We are ready to go."

Eva patted Justin's bottom. "Go on, Beautiful Boy," she said.

Justin slid off her lap, grabbed his stuffed dog from Riley off his bed, and walked up to his dad. Eva got up and handed Doug Justin's bag. "Okay. We'll be back Wednesday morning. I have to work Wednesday afternoon."

"Okay. Be safe. Call me when you get there so I know you made it safe." Eva followed them to the door.

"OK. Love you." Doug leaned in and kissed Eva on the cheek.

Eva didn't realize Riley had woken up and was standing in the kitchen behind her and Doug filling a coffee cup.

"Bye, Doug! It was nice meeting you!" Riley called.

"Bye!" He waved to her.

"Bye, Miss Riley, I love you!" Justin called.

"Aw, little man, I love you too!" She smiled.

Doug and Justin got into his car and backed out.

Eva turned to Riley, "You are up early. I hope we didn't wake you."

"Nah. I just was restless anyway. It happens sometimes when I travel. But seriously. He's going for 5 days and he just kissed you on the cheek. That's it?"

"Yep."

Riley rolled her eyes.

They had breakfast and got ready to go. Packing a small bag for clothes to change into before going to the bar later that night.

The drive was just about an hour, and they talked about their post-Navy lives and listened to music and laughed. Eva felt happy and light in Riley's presence. She watched as the sun filtered through the windows and lit Riley's features. She caught herself wondering what it would be like to kiss her. She pushed the thoughts aside and continued to look at the road.

Eva parked in downtown Ann Arbor. "This is the coolest city in Metro Detroit," Eva informed Riley.

Riley looked around at the quaint Main Street area and smiled. It was a sunny, perfect spring day in Michigan. Cherry blossoms were blooming, trees were budding around them, and the sky was actually blue and cloud free. "Okay, where first?"

"This way!" Eva grabbed Riley's arm and pulled her down the street.

Eva pulled Riley in and out of the various shops and up and down the streets.

They stopped at her favorite New Age shop. Riley looked around at the various displays of crystals, jewelry, tarot decks and books. Eva picked up a bracelet of amethyst beads and fingered it gently before placing it back. "There's an upstairs, too," she informed Riley who was standing close behind her. She dragged Riley up the stairs. "They make the best chai latte's here. It's my favorite place in Ann Arbor," Eva said as they ascended the dark stairs.

"This is a cute little shop," Riley said as they got to the cafe on the second floor.

They walked up the counter to order. "Hi, ladies. How can I help you? Or are you here for the couples' seminar in the meeting room?" The barista pointed to the meeting room in the back of the space slowly filling up with couples sitting together on yoga mats.

Eva blushed, laughed and looked at Riley. "Um no. We are just here for the Chai lattes. Two please."

"I'm so sorry to presume." The barista smiled. "I just would assume you two were together. You look like you would be cute together."

Eva blushed deeper. "I had a crush on her way back in the day. She's just a great friend from way back."

Eva paid for the lattes, and they went and sat on a couch near the open window that overlooked Main Street. "This is my favorite place to just sit and be." Eva settled in smiling.

Riley sat close to her and looked down out the window smiling.

They sat back and waited for their drinks to be brought out. They were sitting close. Riley put her arm across the top of the couch and Eva was sitting under her wing. She could feel Riley's warmth and her body was very aware and very lit up with every sensation that came from Riley's presence.

They were both quiet, but it was not awkward. They were just enjoying the fresh breeze and the soft couch. DJ Drez's most recent album played softly in the background.

"I love this song," Eva said quietly.

"I've never heard music like this before," Riley said. "It's interesting."

"It's DJ Drez. I was in a yoga class and the instructor played it."

The barista brought the lattes to the couch and set them on the coffee table in front of the two women. She smiled. "Are you sure you aren't together? I mean, look at you!"

Riley laughed and leaned forward to pick up her cup. "No. She's just my beautiful little friend." Riley winked at Eva. Eva's heart skipped and she blushed.

Eva smiled at Riley and cast her eyes away. She was fighting the impulse to lean and kiss Riley.

"Okay, you two… enjoy. If you need anything else, I'm at the counter." She walked away.

"Did you ever tell me you had a crush on me?" Riley asked bluntly.

Eva sipped her chai latte. "Did you try this yet? It's so good, right?"

"Don't change the subject on me." Riley grinned at her.

"No. I was scared. Plus, you had a girlfriend you were obsessed with."

"That's fair," Riley said.

Eva turned herself on the couch and sat cross legged so she could look at Riley. "If I had told you I had a crush on you, would it have made a difference?"

"Probably not back then," Riley said.

"Exactly," Eva said.

After making their way around Ann Arbor, they drove to Drew and Jose's home. Riley brought another bottle of the fantastic wine she brought from her home.

Jose answered the door. "You were not joking. She is a sexy fine woman!"

Riley looked over at Eva and grinned. "Jose, Riley – Riley, Jose!" Eva introduced walking in.

Riley handed the bottle of wine to Jose. "So nice to meet you! I brought this from my favorite winery near my house."

"Oh! She's classy too! I approve!" Jose exclaimed. "Drew is busy finishing the dinner. Let's go sit and I will open this."

Jose ushered them into the living room. He disappeared to the kitchen and Eva sat close to Riley on the couch.

"This is a gorgeous home!" Riley stated as Jose came back in with glasses and the bottle corked.

"Thank you. We just moved here last year. I wanted to be closer to Ann Arbor, and so did Drew. Most of his jobs are in this area. Where do you live in California?"

"I live in North County San Diego. I'm close to the wine country, in Temecula, but also not a bad drive to downtown San Diego, just about 45 minutes. It's nice out there. Not as crowded as living in the cities."

"I'm a flight attendant. My favorite overnights are San Diego! I love Hillcrest!"

"Look me up next time you are there overnight. I will meet you for a drink!" Riley stated as Jose poured the wine.

"I will have to do that!" Jose agreed.

Drew came out with a charcuterie board and sighed as he sat down on an armchair across from the couch. "I'm caught up! The chicken breasts are in, and everything else is warming. Let's try this wine. Hi! I'm Drew!" Everything came out in one exhausted breath.

"Hi!" Riley laughed. "Thank you for making dinner and hosting us!"

Eva rolled her eyes. "He lives for this shit!"

"Well, my bestie called me and told me you were coming, and I had to meet you," Drew said.

Dinner flowed seamlessly. Riley rose and excused herself to the restroom. Drew turned to Eva and grabbed her knee. "You so need to jump on that."

"Drew, stop. It's tempting. Believe me. I could be in love with her. But you are forgetting there is a history of friendship. Separate states…"

"I'm not saying marry her. I'm saying blow the dust off and have fun. You have 5 days with no husband, no kid, and a hot ass lesbian in your house. You do you. Take care of your needs."

Riley came back in, and Eva blushed as she sat next to her.

"I'm going to grab the dessert." Drew got up.

They got ready for the bar after finishing their desserts and headed out.

It was crowded and the 80's music blared. Several of the attendees were dressed in their finest 80's looks.

They paid the cover charge and went up the stairs to the bar. Riley kept herself close to Eva.

Several of the other women were looking Riley up and down trying to assess the new and unfamiliar face.

One woman approached and boldly slid her arm around Riley's shoulder. Eva could not hear what the woman said to her over the music. Riley slid out from the woman's arm and patted her on the back and smiled and said something back to her.

The woman left.

Drew leaned in. "You better stake your claim before someone else does."

Jose bought tequila shots for the group. Everyone participated in good nature.

Eva ordered a cosmopolitan, and Riley ordered a beer. Drew and Jose disappeared to go dance.

Eva was feeling self-conscious and suddenly unsure.

"Let's go out to the balcony." Eva leaned in to Riley, talking loud enough so she could hear.

Riley nodded in agreement.

They made their way outside. It was less crowded and quieter than inside.

They could look down and see the crowded courtyard in front of the bar.

"This reminds me of New Orleans, a bit," Riley said amused.

"Less crowded and far less cool," Eva laughed. They were standing close together. Eva could feel Riley's breath close to her face. Riley placed her hands on Eva's hips and pulled Eva closer to make room for a passing group of people.

Eva looked up at Riley, they were nose to nose, eyes locked.

"We are friends," Riley said softly. Eva felt like she was inhaling Riley's being as Riley exhaled, their lips close, not quite touching.

"We are," Eva agreed. Riley didn't let go and neither woman moved. The world stopped in that moment for Eva. Nothing else existed or mattered as she looked into Riley's eyes.

"If we do anything, anything at all that crosses that line, we are always friends first," Riley stated.

"I never want to jeopardize our friendship," Eva agreed.

Riley pulled her over to an out of the way corner of the balcony and lowered her lips to Eva's. Eva felt every nerve in her body explode as their lips met. In her whole life, she had never felt so much as she was feeling during this kiss.

Riley pulled back and smiled at Eva.

Eva bowed her head into Riley's chest. She sat her drink down on a nearby table. She leaned Riley into the wall behind them and kissed her again, deeper. "I think we should get out of here," Eva said to her.

"I agree," Riley said.

Eva and Riley made their way through the bar and found Drew and Jose on the dance floor. "We are going to head out," Eva informed them.

Drew grinned at her. "Have fun! Be safe. Call me in the morning!" he called out over the music.

Eva led Riley down the stairs and to her car. Riley pushed Eva against the car and kissed her again. Eva felt all the wind in her body leave at once.

She was shaking as she got into the car, and they didn't have much to talk about the entire drive back to Eva's. Eva just prayed that Riley didn't change her mind before they got home. She barely breathed the entire time.

Eva led Riley into her bedroom. She unbuttoned Riley's shirt and looked up at her. Her hands caressed Riley's body as she pushed the shirt from her shoulders to the floor. Her pale skin glowed against the moonlight and was soft and warm.

She unfastened Riley's bra and let her hands explore and touch her. Riley kissed her slowly, leading her closer to the bed.

Eva's heart was thundering in her ears. She sat on the edge of the bed and unfastened Riley's jeans pulling them to the floor. Riley stepped out of them. Eva kissed her belly, and let her hands caress her hips and backside. She stopped as Riley's hands reached down and pulled her top over her head and unfastened her bra, her hands soft caressing Eva's bare flesh.

Riley pushed her back onto the bed and took control. She unfastened Eva's jeans and pulled them off. She knelt next to Eva on the bed as Eva scrambled further back toward the head of the bed.

Riley was on top of her, her mouth on hers. Eva's hands were reaching for Riley. Her hand reached between Riley's legs, and she felt the warmth. Riley took a sharp inhale. Her hand seeking out for Eva. They moved together, and against each other. Riley arched against her, crying out.

Riley pushed Eva back and away and moved her face between Eva's thighs. Her tongue lapped against her. Eva's body was on fire. She arched up and away. Riley grabbed her hips and pulled her back down, keeping her mouth in contact.

Her body, wracked, her flesh hot, Eva finally moved away, shaking and trembling.

Eva had not slept so deep or felt so much peace since she stopped taking her medications. She slept wrapped in Riley's arms peaceful and content.

She woke up well before Riley and went to the kitchen to make coffee and let Starling out.

She made two cups of coffee and brought them back into the bedroom. She sat on the edge of the bed near Riley setting the cups down. She kissed the back of Riley's neck and let her hand roam down the side of Riley's curves. Her hand resting on her hip.

Riley's lip curled into a smile. "Good morning," she managed groggily.

"I made you coffee," Eva said.

Riley rolled onto her back, so she was pinned beneath Eva. Her hands caressed under Eva's t-shirt.

"How do you feel about last night?" Riley asked.

Eva smiled and bit her lip. "I feel amazing. I feel like it was supposed to happen."

"This feels... right? It does, doesn't it?"

"I feel like it shouldn't stop just yet."

Eva moved on top of Riley and buried herself between Riley's thighs. She soaked up every bit of her taste and scent as Riley rocked and moaned against her.

They spent most of the morning in bed, unable to keep their hands off each other. Eva was insatiable and Riley was more than willing and able to meet her demands.

Eva felt content in this moment for the first time in her life. She didn't feel that familiar anxiety, sadness, or gaping hole in her center. She felt full, warm and satisfied with Riley next to her. She wanted to hold this moment forever.

It was close to noon before Riley finally said, "I think you are going to need to feed me real food soon."

Eva obliged and took her to Greek Town for lunch.

Over Saganaki and spinach pies, Riley gave Eva a serious look.

"I need to know how you are really feeling right now."

"I'm fine. I'm content. I feel good." Eva shrugged.

"You have a husband and a kid," Riley reminded her.

"I do."

"Do you feel guilty?"

"No. I honestly don't. I mean I could parlay this out so many ways, in why I have every right to not feel guilty right now."

"Well then, let's hear it," Riley implored.

"Well, first and foremost, if he was a good husband and cared truly for me, I would not be so eager to jump into bed with my Navy roommate. Part two, many people would argue that it's not the same, it's not cheating, because you are a female."

"Nah. That's a shitty argument. It's the same. It's worse, actually because many would argue that the level of connection and emotion is deeper."

Eva shrugged. "I've never been the fall in love kind or type. So I don't know about any of that."

"Never? You've never been in love?" Riley asked.

Eva shook her head. "Not that I'm aware of. I don't know if I believe in it." Although inside, being with Riley, the stirring inside of her soul was awakening to what love might be, no matter how hard she was trying to stomp it back down.

"You never felt love for Doug?"

"No. Honestly not. I settled. I think outside of my parents and Nana, the only person I love is Justin."

Riley sat back against the booth. "That's deep."

"It's sad. It's true," Eva said.

They left the restaurant and strolled through Greek Town hand in hand. Eva drove down to the River Front and Campus Martius so they could walk around there. Clouds were slowly rolling in. Eva found a bench and pointed across the river. "That's Canada," she told Riley.

"I didn't realize it was that close," Riley mused. She put her arm around Eva. "What do you plan on doing now?" she asked. "Are you going to go back to your life as it was or are you going to make changes?"

"I don't know. I am scared of so many factors."

"We are always friends, right?" Riley asked.

"Always," Eva confirmed.

They wandered the area for a while longer and had dinner at the Hard Rock before making their way back to Eva's. The clouds continued to roll in darker and heavier.

They snuggled on the couch and watched a movie, before making their way back to the bedroom. The rain began to come down and low rolls of thunder could be heard in the distance. Eva, satisfied, and warm slept well for a second night in a row.

It was still rainy and storming in the morning. Eva took Riley to her favorite diner for feta and spinach omelets and then to the Henry Ford Museum.

They walked hand in hand and made their way around the exhibits. They had lunch in the museum cafe and while sitting there with soups and hot sandwiches Riley looked at Eva long and hard. "I know this is weird, but I really don't want to leave tomorrow."

"I don't want you to leave. For the first time in my life, I feel content. I feel happy. I feel loved. I feel like I love you. Like I know it seems fast and silly and extreme. But the thought of you leaving pains my heart." Eva was finally honest with her feelings for the first time. It felt good to confront them head on and bare her soul to Riley about how she felt for her.

"I think since we have a history, it doesn't seem fast or crazy. What do you want to do going forward? Do you want us to just step back into being friends and let this be like some great memory of a whirlwind romance?"

Eva shook her head vehemently. "I can't do that. I know friends first and all, but the idea of you with someone else, pisses me off." Her heart felt like lead at the very thought of Riley not being hers. She was so very cognizant of her heart and how it felt in this moment and of this overwhelming fear of not having this very thing she wanted and needed more than the oxygen she was breathing.

"I don't want to do that. But I can if that's what you want or need. You have a husband and a kid. And we live on opposite sides of the country."

"I want the fuck out of this state. I will move if we get to that point. I can't go back to my life with Doug now. Not after this weekend with you. Knowing what it's like to be with you. I can't." Eva's throat felt tight.

"We will figure this out then," Riley said. "But know this, I have zero expectations of you, and I will not be responsible for the choices you have to make. I will not be mad at you if you change your mind."

Eva locked her gaze in Riley's. "I'm not changing my mind. I've waited a long time to feel this way about someone. I can't throw it away." She knew this feeling was worth fighting for. Suddenly all of it made sense to her. Love songs, movies, poems and love stories were real. She got it now.

They left the museum as the rain continued to pour down. They spent their last night taking complete advantage of the peace around them and every last minute they could spend together.

The next morning, Eva ruefully watched Riley pack her bag. "I feel like you need to have something from me. From this weekend together," Eva said sitting on the bed watching Riley.

"I have you," Riley said, smiling.

Eva took off her OM necklace and put it on Riley. "You have this, too. It's my favorite necklace. I wear it all the time."

Riley fingered the necklace and looked at it. "What does it mean?"

"OM," Eva said. "It's the sound of the vibration of creation and it's sound is supposed to bring you back to peace and center."

"Well, we drank the three bottles of wine I brought. Aside from my clothes and my toiletries, I don't have anything to give you right now. Watch your mail box though," Riley grinned.

"I have you, though," Eva copied, and kissed Riley on the nose.

Eva drove Riley to the airport. She parked and walked Riley as far as she could to the TSA line. "This is goodbye then?" Eva choked.

"No. It's see you later. No matter what. It's see you later."

"I do love you," Eva said, convinced for the first time. She finally knew it was real.

"I love you, too," Riley whispered, choking up herself. She kissed Eva. "I will have internet on the flight. I will be able to message you on Facebook."

Eva wiped a tear away. "When do you think we will see each other again?"

"Maybe we can work something out soon. Let's just see what happens next." She kissed Eva one last time. "I have to go. We are boarding soon."

Eva watched Riley go all the way through the line until she couldn't see her any longer.

She drove home. The house was empty except for Starling. "It's like the olden days," she said to the dog. "Just you and me."

She opened her laptop and opened a blank word doc. She had to get her feelings out while they were fresh. And she owed it to Doug for him to know.

'Dear Doug,

I'm trying hard to make sense of how I feel and explain it to you in a way which you will understand.

I feel like we are bad for each other. Not in a violent way or hurtful way. Just not good though. I think we have both grown complacent and taken each other for granted this entire time. I stayed with you because you didn't abandon me when I broke down. I stayed with you through your drug episode because I couldn't do to you what you refused to do when I was broken.

But I've been unhappy for a long time. I've been going through the motions.

Life is short. I want more, and that more is something you don't wish to give.

I think its time we separate. We can discuss what and how to move forward in an amicable way soon. But I can't talk right now. Please respect my feelings.

I'm sorry.

Eva.'

She printed the letter and folded it. She turned on the television and checked Facebook. She had a message from Riley waiting. 'I miss you already. Thank you for all this weekend was.'

'I miss you, too. I'm leaving Doug,' she replied.

After a few minutes she received, 'Make sure this is truly what you want, and you are not acting rash. I remember you've always been impulsive. :)'

She read it over and thought briefly. 'The house is quiet. I'm alone. I know what I want. What I've always wanted. You.' She clicked 'send'.

'I never knew until this weekend that you were going to be my match. You truly showed me what I need and want,' was Riley's reply.

Eva chatted with Riley until she landed and went off to bed. She tucked the letter to Doug into a drawer. She would leave it for him tomorrow.

EVA LEFT THE LETTER TO Doug with his name scrawled on the outside of the folded paper, propped on the counter so he would see it when he arrived home. She was safe at work. She would be asleep when he got home from work. She had chosen to move most of her clothes and items into the guest room before she left for her shift. She would sleep there when he came home.

He didn't text her. He didn't call her.

She picked up Justin from Geri's house. She told Geri what had happened and what she planned to do.

"Eva, this is foolish," Geri said.

"I know you think it is. But, Mom, I'm in love. I know what I feel. And for the first time in my life, I feel content with someone. Like I belong."

"What are you going to do? Live in two states? Just see each other occasionally? That shit doesn't work."

"We haven't figured it out yet. I don't know how that is going to work."

Tony, Geri's boyfriend was sitting at the table as well. Eva had known Tony since she was 16. They were never fond of each other but learned to accept each other over the years. He was the world's laziest realtor and always looking for a hand out. Geri practically supported him between real estate deals. They were always breaking up and getting back together. His daughter had also recently come out of the closet, and she thought she would have an ally with Tony. She looked at him.

"Doug is a good guy, and you are about to wreck his world for a folly," he said. "You aren't even really gay."

"Did you tell your own daughter that?" Eva sniped.

"No. Don't compare my daughter's situation with yours. She didn't break anyone's life in two for her lifestyle choices. Or upend her kid's life."

"Having a kid doesn't mean I need to stay chained to a wet noodle for the rest of my life or that I need to forsake my own happiness," Eva defended hotly.

"You've always been selfish. You will never change," Tony said getting up and leaving the table.

"He's such a dick," Eva said to Geri.

"Yeah. About that. Aren't you going to miss ... you know?" Geri asked in typical fashion. Geri had been young when Eva was born, causing the two of them to have a more sisterly dynamic, hence why Nana was the major influence in her life. And God, how she missed Nana right now.

Eva rolled her eyes, "That's never been important to me."

Eva got up and packed Justin up and took him home. She got him fed for dinner and bathed and snuggled him before bed. She read him his favorite stories and said his prayers with him.

Could she give this up every night? she asked herself. How many nights will she have to give it up? she wondered.

After he was asleep she retired to the guest room and put her things away in the drawers.

She could hear Doug's car pull up. She turned out the lamp and held her breath. She heard his footsteps come to the master bedroom. She had changed the sheets that morning so they wouldn't smell of Riley.

She heard him exit the bedroom and stand in front of her door. She wasn't ready to talk about it. She said what she said. She couldn't unring the bell. And she wasn't going to back down. But she didn't want to talk to him yet.

She texted Riley to tell her what had happened.

'I'm proud of you for standing up for what you want,' Riley replied. 'Sleep tight.'

Eva laid back in the guest bed. She kept the pillowcase Riley slept on and slipped it on a pillow on the guest bed. She slept deep and sound.

The next morning, she woke up and made a pot of coffee. As it was brewing, Doug came out with the letter in his hand.

"Did you and Riley have an affair?" he asked.

"No," she lied. She knew it was a lie. But she wasn't about to rub that in right now. "Just having the time to be free, and to be myself, I felt like it was time. Life is too short. I am unhappy. This is not working for me anymore."

Doug looked down and leaned against the counter. Never one for a confrontation he said, "I understand. I mean, I don't understand why out of the blue like this. But I do understand that you are not happy. I do also understand that I will never be able to change your mind. What should we do about Justin?"

"I want to move to California. I want to take him with me," Eva stated.

"I do think you are the better parent. I can't argue with that. But when would I see him?" Doug asked looking at the floor.

"You can have all of the holidays and all of summer break. He's starting pre-kindergarten school next year. I don't plan to move for several months. It's going to take me time."

"Why California?" Doug asked.

"Because there is more opportunity out there. I can work within my degree field, or even get a teaching credential," she had researched these things on her downtime at work the day before, "and I can get out of this shithole state." Eva added cream to her coffee and sat at the table.

"I know you. I know once you make up your mind that there is no changing it."

"That's true."

"So are you just going to stay in the guest bedroom until you move to California?"

"I don't know. I might ask Drew and Jose if I can stay with them."

"You don't want to stay with your mom?" Doug asked.

Eva wrinkled her nose. "And deal with Tony on the daily? I did that for 2 years in high school before I left for boot camp. No thanks."

"Well, stay here as long as you want. I guess we can just work through this a day at a time." He poured his own coffee and went off to the living room.

Eva texted Lauren and told her about Riley, and that their sexting escapades had to come to a close. Lauren's reply was, 'It was a good run, kid. I had fun. Thank you for making life more interesting.'

Eva got ready for work and called Riley on her way. "Doug was strangely calm about the whole deal." Eva recounted the entire conversation for Riley.

"He didn't even fight for you?" she asked.

"No… Not that I'm some prize worth fighting for. I've been a nag and a bitch most of our relationship."

"Don't talk about my girl that way," Riley said, smiling.

"Oh, am I your girl?" Eva asked.

"I think you are," Riley affirmed.

"I want to start planning to move out there. I am not setting a date or a timeline. But if this is going to work, one of us needs to move. You have a whole business out there and I can't ask you to close shop and move here. So I need to start considering my options out there."

"One step at a time, love," Riley said. "So Doug doesn't know that we are together?"

"No. With his ED and stuff, I don't want to push that in his face. He will know. But not now."

"Got it," Riley said.

When Eva got home from work, she and Doug continued their conversation. "I don't want lawyers," Doug said. "I think we should sort this out for ourselves."

"I agree," Eva said.

They sorted out a visitation schedule for once Eva moved out, and once she ultimately left for California. Doug would get every single holiday, and the entire summer break, and they would split the cost of transportation and plane tickets. Once Eva actually moved out, they would alternate weekends based on Doug's work schedule and it would be 50/50 time.

They sorted out what she would take and what she would leave. It felt very productive.

Once she retreated to the guest room, she texted the update to Riley.

'I'm impressed he's handling this so well,' she replied.

'Me too. It's almost too easy.'

The next day, Eva dropped Justin off at Geri's so she could go to work. She updated Geri on everything briefly. "Mom, it's all working out as it should."

Geri looked skeptical.

Eva left for work, completed her day and picked up Justin. Tony was in the kitchen when Eva arrived.

"I don't think what you are doing to Doug is fair at all. You are lying to him," Tony stated, dripping with judgment, arms folded across his chest.

"You don't live my life. You don't live Doug's life. Stay the fuck out of it," Eva said coolly.

"Doug is my friend," Tony said. "I care about the guy, which you obviously don't."

"Tony, you don't know the first thing about my life, or our lives together."

"The hell I don't. Your mother tells me everything. She feels sorry for him too."

Geri waved her hands in front of her. "I'm out of this."

"Why would you tell him about my private business? You know what, never mind." She picked up Justin's things and went home.

Doug was working. She made dinner. Talked to Riley, put Justin to bed, researched online filing for divorce without an attorney and then looked up job postings and educational opportunities in California.

It was 4 days since Riley had left. Eva checked the mailbox. A package from Riley was there, just as she had promised. Coming inside and grabbing the scissors, she ducked into the guest room and opened the package. A letter was on the top, penned in Riley's neat and measured handwriting, 'My Beautiful Eva, Thank you for making me feel loved and special. These last few days were more than I ever could have wished for. Love, Riley.' Eva smiled and tucked the letter into a small wooden box she saved all of her special mementos in.

Under the letter was a small velvet pouch, she opened it and inside was a bracelet made of amethyst beads and a charm with an angel or bird wing dangling from it. Eva had admired this same bracelet at the new age shop before they went upstairs to the coffee house. She put the bracelet on and took a selfie of her with it and texted a thank you to Riley.

It was 11 days since Riley had left, and 10 days since Eva told Doug she wanted a divorce. Doug came home from work one afternoon, while Eva was sitting in the kitchen looking at job postings in San Diego County after applying for an online teaching credential program.

The late afternoon sun was pouring in, and Eva was feeling optimistic about life and opportunities. She was looking at the requirements to get into the program to obtain a teaching credential, taking notes and making a plan.

"Hey!" she greeted Doug as he came in. They had been getting along better than ever with the expectations of marriage taken out of the picture.

"Tony told me everything," Doug said. "You lied to me." His voice was dark. His eyes were narrowed as he glared at Eva.

Eva froze, her pen mid stroke on the paper.

"He told me how you and Riley had this grand romance the entire time I was gone. Did you plan that?"

"No." She didn't look at Doug and her voice was quiet. She kept her eyes fixed on the laptop in front of her. The flashing cursor on the screen matching her increasing pulse.

"No you didn't have an affair, or no you didn't plan it?"

"I didn't plan it."

"You are not taking Justin with you to California. I will not let you move him for some fling. If you want to go, fine. But he stays here."

"Doug... You are being unreasonable."

"No, Eva. You are unreasonable. You are crazy. You can have the same visitation we agreed to. But it's getting flipped. You are mentally insane if you think I'm going to let my kid go so you can pursue some chick in a midlife crisis fit of fancy."

"This is not a midlife crisis. For fuck's sake."

"End of story," Doug said, and he walked out of the room.

Eva went outside and called Geri. "What the absolute fuck? Tony told Doug about Riley."

"I don't have any excuses, but honestly, Eva, he deserved to know."

"Whose side are you even on?" Eva asked. "You know what? I don't care." Eva hung up.

She called Riley and told her about Doug knowing the truth about their relationship. "I'm looking at plane tickets right now. I'm coming out there for a few days. I don't think you should go through this alone."

"I can't take any more time off of work."

"You don't need to. But this way, I can at least be there for you while all this is going down."

Eva choked back tears.

"I also understand if you choose to not move your life out here."

"I don't know. I mean I would get all of the best times with Justin. And it's almost fifty fifty still. I deserve to be happy, too." Eva felt defiant and bitter.

"I'm booked for the day after tomorrow. If you can't pick me up, I will take a shuttle. I'm going to be staying at the Hyatt. I don't think Doug will be okay with me staying at the house now."

"That's about right," Eva affirmed.

The next day, after work, she took Justin to Drew's. She told him everything that had happened and what was going on.

"Baby Girl, you need a lawyer. No one in their right mind is going to give that man custody."

"Can I move in here? I mean it's a long commute for me for work. You have two extra bedrooms. I can pay rent. Just till I know what I'm doing and when I can leave, and this is all settled? Now that custody and all of that is going to start ramping up, I don't know that I can stay in the guest room."

"Of course. You don't need to pay rent. Just pitch in for the utilities. When do you want to move?"

"Let me get some folks together and I will set a date. Thank you for always being my hero."

"Baby Girl, you got it."

"Also, can you pick Riley up at the airport tomorrow? She's coming in while I'm at work. Margaret is getting bitchy about my time off requests."

"Yep. I got you both." Drew sighed.

The next day, after she got out of work, she made sure Doug had Justin and told him she was not coming home that night. She told him she was not coming home for the next four nights. She also told him two of those nights Justin would be with her. "This is non-negotiable," she said.

She drove like a bat out of Hell when her shift ended, and she was heading to the hotel. The elevator took entirely too long. She hit the button four more times as she fidgeted.

Once it arrived and took her to the fourth floor where Riley's room was waiting at the end of the hall, she darted out of the doors and down the hallway.

Eva knocked on the door and waited. Riley opened the door and she flung herself into Riley's arms. Her lips locked in with Riley's, Eva melted.

"Hi, to you too," Riley murmured.

Being with Riley was like coming home for her. She felt peaceful and happy. On her 2 days off, she brought Justin to stay with them on the pull-out sofa in the room. Justin thought it was an adventure. They took him to the zoo and to the park. Riley was a natural with him and he loved her instantly.

When Riley left again, Eva felt like a part of her left too. She realized her entire life from this moment on if she stayed with Riley would be saying goodbye to a piece of herself constantly. So long as she was in Michigan, it was saying goodbye to Riley. Once she moved, it would be saying goodbye to Justin.

A month later, in the middle of May, she was moved in with Drew, and Riley was planning another visit.

Eva's life began revolving around her visitations with Justin and talking every spare moment with Riley.

Eva's life became a new routine. Commute to work. Spend the entire commute on the phone with Riley. On days with Justin, they would FaceTime at bedtime so she could say good night to Justin too. Eva would FaceTime her back after Justin was asleep. She would fall asleep FaceTiming. Wake up and repeat.

She started taking prerequisite classes online to get herself into the

California teachers' credential program. She would work on her classes on her off time. She was able to get a deferment on taking the admissions tests when she planned to visit Riley.

Drew was busy with his business so they didn't get to hang out as much as she would have liked. Jose was gone on flights most of the time as well. Britt was there for her, supporting her and encouraging her to make it through.

Eva no longer called Geri or hung out much with her because of the fear that Tony would tell Doug everything.

Eva met Britt for lunch before an afternoon shift at work. She told Britt everything that was going on. "You need a lawyer," Britt advised.

"I know. I just don't have the money for one," Eva relented. Her Freedom Fund had been dwindling with paying for utilities at Drew's, signing up for courses online, and impending plane tickets.

"You might be able to get your dad to help. Maybe Riley will help. Sell the house, use the equity."

"We are underwater on the house," Eva informed Britt.

"Sell your ring. That will cover a retainer. You need representation. You need to fight for Justin."

When Riley came in for her next visit, she and Eva went to interview lawyers. They settled on one that would take payments after the retainer was burned through. Her name was Kate, and she came across as smart and even keeled, calm and very conservative, which Eva thought would work to her advantage. Eva sold her ring and used the last of her inheritance money from Nana's estate to cover the retainer.

"If I file for this, this is going to forever fuck my standing with Doug," she said aloud as she sat in the living room with Drew and Riley.

"Do you think he's a capable parent on his own?" Riley asked.

"No... He's floundering. He can't do anything on his own. He's letting the house foreclose and moving in with his mom as we speak."

"Wait. Is your name on the house?" Riley asked.

"No. My credit was too bad when we bought the house, so he went on it by himself."

"When are you thinking this will be finalized?" Drew asked.

"I'm not sure. I know my goal is to be moved by February though."

"It's summer. That's just over 6 months. What if this is not settled by then?"

Eva shrugged.

The paperwork was filed, and Doug was served at his mother's home the following week. Riley had gone back to California. Doug called Eva, "What is this paperwork? Why do you feel the need to do this?"

"Doug, I don't feel like you are capable of making decisions for Justin on your own. You can't even live on your own. You let the house go because you didn't want to be by yourself. You can't deal with making decisions. This is ridiculous. You are trying to punish me for leaving you."

"You are Hell bent on ruining me. Taking my kid. Leaving. This is all on you," Doug said and hung up.

From that moment on, their exchanges were no longer friendly. They were frosty and in the end existed only to exchange Justin.

Justin loved his room at Drew's house and loved the big spacious back yard. He did not seem to mind that he lived in two different houses and saw his parents separately. Eva maintained their precious bedtime routine when she had her nights with him.

Eva and Justin took a trip to California together in August so that Justin could get his first plane ride and Eva could show him it was nothing to be afraid of and she could take her entrance exams for the teaching credential.

It was hot when they landed, with the sun beating straight down on them. Riley was waiting for them in baggage. She had a bouquet of lilies for Eva and a San Diego Padres shirt for Justin.

Eva stood outside in the sun and looked at the palm trees and wondered if she was home. She realized she was dancing a fine line between two very different lives, and nothing seemed permanent or stable.

With Eva scheduled to take the requisite exams for the Credential program, the schedule was packed. She crammed the exams into 3 days, knowing she had to nail them in this one shot, or she would be dropped from the program.

Eva soaked up the time in California with Riley and Justin. Riley had set up a bedroom just for Justin with books and toys. Justin got to meet her two big boxer dogs named Milo and Frank that enjoyed chasing him through the yard.

Aside from taking the exams, Eva enjoyed each and every one of the days being with Riley and Justin, living like they would once she relocated. A family.

On their last night with Riley before having to fly back the three of them were sitting on the patio finishing dinner. "I'm scared," Eva confessed.

"Of what?" Riley asked.

"Of not getting this." Eva gestured to the environment around them. "I'm so happy right now, but if I don't win the case, what will happen? Will I get to have these moments still?"

"Of course. You will get those moments when Justin is here with us. But if you don't feel like you can do it, you are not obligated to move," Riley reassured her.

Eva took a deep breath in and sipped her wine. Justin was eating a hamburger at the end of the table, oblivious to the conversation she and Riley were having about his future.

"I know I belong here. I feel that in my bones," Eva said. "I'm just scared for Justin. It's funny because I didn't even want kids to begin with… And he was the very thing I never knew I wanted. I love him so much, but I also love me. It's unfair that I potentially have to choose me or him."

Riley took her hand and looked deep into her eyes. "You are not choosing yourself or him," Riley said quietly. "Parents need to be happy. Kids deserve to see parents who are strong, and happy and willing to live life. Being a parent doesn't resign you to a life of unhappiness."

"I'm full. Can I go play with the dogs?" Justin asked at the end of the table.

Eva looked down the table to her son. The market lights adorning the patio glowed against the setting sun. "Yes, Beautiful Boy. Go play." She looked back at Riley. "You are right," she resigned.

Chapter 6

Thirty-Six

THEIR FIRST APPEARANCE IN FRONT of a court referee was in October. Doug's lawyer decimated Eva's argument. The referee looked at Eva, "You don't have a job in California. You don't have a home in California. You have nothing out there except a relationship. I don't agree with giving you custody. But we will let a custody investigator determine this. You can schedule the investigation after you leave here."

Eva looked at Kate as they walked out, giving Doug and his attorney as much distance as possible. Her attorney looked at her, "I know you are taking your teaching credential classes online, but you need to show that you have a future in California meanwhile. Get a job lined up. One that can show you can be self-sufficient if you and Riley don't work out. Have that lined up before the investigation."

After her court appearance Eva met Britt at their favorite diner and sat across from her.

"I can't believe they would consider letting Justin stay with Doug. He has a drug abuse history. He's a large child. One that cannot handle life on his own much less with a child."

Britt looked at her. "They won't. They can't do that." Britt seemed so confident in the outcome that it bolstered her own confidence.

In November, Eva took Justin on another plane ride to visit Riley together.

Justin loved being on the plane. He looked out the window and busied himself with watching a movie on the screen in the seat in front of him, before falling asleep on Eva's shoulder.

Riley was waiting for Eva in the baggage area, smiling and bright.

Eva stepped outside of the airport and looked at the large palm trees. She breathed in the warm air. This time, it felt a little bit more like home. "Let's go get some lunch. You must be hungry!"

They went to a Mexican restaurant in Old Town San Diego and sat in an outdoor booth. Justin was enthralled with watching the women making tortillas and all the people wandering outside.

After lunch, they took Justin to see the ocean and play on the beach. "How does it feel to be here?" Riley asked as they watched Justin play in the sand.

"It feels good. It feels right," Eva said.

"What if we don't win?" Riley asked.

"I will eventually. I may not win this time, but Doug will inevitably fuck up. He always does," Eva said.

"Let's get you guys home," Riley said standing up. "Come on, Buddy! You ready to see Milo and Frank?"

Justin picked himself up and grabbed the pile of sea shells he had amassed and handed them to Eva. "Treasure," he informed her.

"It's a beautiful treasure," Eva reassured him.

The next day they took Justin to Disneyland, and the day after that they spent the day around the house watching movies and cooking. Eva took the time to apply for jobs in the area.

She secured a couple of interviews right away. But they were not for jobs that would meet the requirement for self-sufficiency. But a job was better than no job.

She and Justin left with a sense of normalcy in California, and a job as an assistant spa manager for a chain company.

She could start at the spa right after the holidays. She was given the position in hopes that she would be taking over as manager at the newest franchise site opening in the spring. She hoped that she would be able to secure a teaching position and not even have to be there for very long.

Eva went back to Michigan and started closing up her affairs.

Thanksgiving week just days before the holiday she and Doug met with the custody investigator. The investigator was a squat woman who was stuck in her days as a Goth Girl teenager. She dressed in all black, and her hair was dyed jet black, with a Betty Paige style haircut complete with bangs and winged eyeliner and a too red lip. "You had a child with a man from Michigan. Don't you think taking that child to live in California to pursue your relationship is selfish?"

Eva had no response. Several times during the meeting the investigator used air quotes to refer to Riley or her relationship. She looked at Kate for help. Nothing.

Eva was heated when she left.

"For fuck's sake, Kate. Why am I paying you? You didn't help me with anything in this."

"Eva, I'm trying. I've never had a case like this before. I can only do so much within the constraints of the law."

"Try harder," Eva demanded, frustrated, before marching off.

Her departure date for California was December 26. She was due to start work January 2nd. Eva tried to not focus on how hard it would be to say goodbye to everyone and to focus more on how much her life was going to improve.

She scheduled lunch with Britt and Drew. Sitting across from them she tried not to cry. Both of them encouraged her to go make her life with Riley.

When she met up with Geri, it was initially less supportive. "I don't think you are doing the right thing. I have a very bad feeling about all of this. I've had a lot of nightmares lately."

"Mom, I can't stay here. I just can't. I need to be happy too."

"If you want to be gay, can't you be gay here?"

"It's not just about 'being gay'. It's about being with the one person who I know in my heart I'm supposed to be with. Remember when you left Tim for

Tony? It's like that. I don't think I could truly be happy with anyone else. It's about her. It's about Riley…"

Geri burst into tears in the restaurant. Eva sat next to her and put her arm around her. "I'm just going to miss you. I lost my mom and now you, too… And soon Justin. I hate Tony but I can't leave him."

Eva took a deep breath. "I'm sorry, Mom. I can't live for others anymore. You shouldn't either."

RILEY BOOKED A ONE-WAY FLIGHT coming in just a few days early so they could spend Christmas together.

It was Eva's last Christmas in Michigan. They spent Christmas Eve with Geri and Justin. Tony was gone to Florida to spend the holiday with his own lesbian daughter, as Eva refused to go into Geri's home if Tony was present.

They opened presents and had a modest dinner focusing more on cookies and sweets. Doug was going to pick Justin up from Geri's and this was going to be her goodbye with her son for several weeks.

Eva tried hard to not focus on the clock. She soaked up every minute with Justin, picking him up and snuggling him every chance she could get. She had prepared him that they were going to start seeing each other less soon, but that didn't mean she didn't love him. She was scared he didn't understand.

When Doug arrived, Eva did what she could to hold herself together. She put Justin's coat and hat and mittens on him. She held his face so he was looking into her eyes. "Okay, Beautiful Boy, do you remember everything we talked about?"

"That you are going away to California with Riley and that you love me, and I will be flying out to see you soon, but it might be a long time."

"Yes, you are so smart, Beautiful Boy. What else?"

"And that you love me a lot and that you will only be a phone call away. And that I deserve a happy mom who lives a happy life so we can all be happy together."

She hugged him close and kissed his beautiful cheeks.

"I'm so proud of you, every day. The best thing in life I ever did was having you. I love you so, so much. Never forget that. I will call you on your dad's phone tomorrow."

She hugged Justin close to her and he hugged her tight.

"I love you, Mom Mom."

"I love you too, Beautiful Boy."

Doug glared at Riley as Justin and Riley embraced and said goodbyes. Geri stood in the doorway next to Doug and cried.

Riley and Eva spent Christmas Day with Drew and Jose. Dinner was quiet and subdued. Drew's kids were with Mona and Jose had to leave after dinner for a flight. Drew, Riley and Eva drank a bottle of wine and said goodnight with a lot of tears.

Early morning, Riley and Eva got up and made their way cross country, stopping for breakfast with Jack. Jack was melancholy and said he understood, but he feared Eva would have regrets as she was going to ultimately miss out on life with Justin. He knew, because he had regrets on all that he missed out with Eva in her youth.

Riley and Eva drove for 4 days across the country. They made the best of it by blasting music, finding fun pit stops along the way and finding interesting restaurants to try. They posted their journey to social media and chronicled the start of a new life together. Starling rode in the passenger seat with whoever wasn't driving. The poor old Chihuahua would sleep or stand on her old failing legs to look out the window.

They enjoyed the quiet and exhausted nights together in the different motels along the route.

Eva FaceTimed Justin every night of the journey.

Her heart felt an impending sadness.

"Am I selfish for this?" she asked Riley.

Riley held her close, "Do you regret it? We can turn around and go back."

"No. And yes. But mostly no. And I don't want to go back." She looked into Riley's eyes. Riley put her hand on the back of Eva's neck.

"They haven't ruled yet," Riley said hopefully, kissing the top of Eva's forehead.

"I don't feel good about it," Eva said forebodingly.

"Why?"

"You were not in there with that investigator. She looked at me like I was dog shit on her shoe. Like how could I leave this poor man for some woman...?"

"You are going to get a lot of flak for this choice for sure. But you need to know, this is your life, and they are not you. They can judge you all day long. Are you going to live your life for you or other people? Are you ready for that?"

"I don't have a choice. I deserve happiness and to be loved and to love as well, don't I? And by being with you, I am giving Justin a role model, another person to love him, and show him a new side of life he won't get with his dad."

"I think you are going to be okay. I think you know in your heart what is right and wrong. We are all going to be okay. For sure," Riley reassured.

Part 2

For Love and For Drama

Chapter 7

Thirty-Six (Continued)

EVA BEGAN HER JOB, WHICH she hated. But she also began student teaching, which she loved. Her first day in front of the classroom was electric. She showed up nervous and full of self-doubt, but the moment she stood in front of the classroom and began the lesson, she lit up. She enjoyed watching the kids grasp the concepts of rhetoric and participate raising their hands and asking questions and engaging.

She was busy every minute of every day, either working, doing homework, or student teaching. On her down time, she would try to FaceTime with Justin. Being busy kept her from missing her son. On days off, she and Riley would do day trips running up to the mountain towns of Idyllwild or Julian, or over to the coast to sit at the beach.

Just as night-times were her favorite with Justin, they were her favorite with Riley. It was not just the sex though; it was the depth of intimacy. She enjoyed snuggling into the thick white comforter and lying next to Riley and sometimes just looking at the dynamics of her face were enough for Eva. She would admire the shape of Riley's nose, the curl of her lip when she would smile, the dimples in her cheeks. The way Riley would seek her out under the blankets and hold her close, the way her cologne mingled with her skin and the softness of her touch. Eva found that she could lose herself in just being near Riley. She could shed the stress of the day and her sorrow for not having her son with her by losing herself in feeling loved and loving in exchange.

About 2 weeks into January, Eva received the ruling from the investigator, which ruled in Doug's favor.

She ripped it up and cried.

"We have him for the best times," Riley reminded her softly.

"You are right, you are right," Eva said regaining composure.

She and Doug finalized and settled everything negotiating through their lawyers and avoiding a long expensive court decision. She tried to remain friendly with Doug though it was difficult. She would call him to talk about Justin and he would get defensive and combative when Eva asked questions.

In February, Doug finally found a new girlfriend. She found out from Britt, who ran into Doug and the new girl at the MGM Grand in downtown Detroit.

"Tell me about her," Eva inquired. "Is Doug happy?" She did wish him happiness, and that was genuine.

"I don't know. But the girl is haggard. She looks rode hard and put up wet. And that was with makeup on and what I presume is dressed up."

"That's unfortunate," Eva said.

"She wasn't really friendly either," Britt added.

"That's *really* unfortunate." Eva exhaled.

"It is. I don't think it will last," Britt said.

"I hope you are wrong. Truly… I know it sounds awful, but I want him to be happy and move on. If he can be happy, and she's a good woman, it's the best thing for Justin."

She hung up with Britt and called Drew. She filled Drew in on what Britt had told her.

"Oh my god! I saw her on Facebook," Drew exclaimed. "She's rough. Hold on. I will send you screenshots from Facebook."

"You and Britt are so mean. Are you willing to fly with Justin in March for a spring break visit? He's not old enough to fly alone yet."

"Of course," Drew said. "I need a vacation too."

"Are you bringing Jose?"

"Nope. I need a vacation from his ass too."

"Trouble in paradise?"

"No. Just a long-term relationship."

"Aw… Well, we will have fun!" Eva's phone pinged to let her know Drew's screenshots arrived. She put him on speaker so she could look. Eva opened the picture and looked. The woman with Doug was named Lucy according to the tag. She was taller than Eva was given the way they were standing. Lucy was thinner than Eva, but her dyed blonde hair looked like bleached straw, and her roots were in bad need of touching up. She had thick black eyebrows, and a large hawkish nose. Her skin was a darker complexion than Eva's, lending her a more exotic look. Her makeup was sparse, and her features came together in an odd way. She had the potential to be pretty if she worked at it. "She's not that bad," Eva said.

"Definite downgrade," Drew said.

She had to love her friends for their unfettered loyalty to her.

THE NEXT 6 WEEKS WERE A blur. On top of managing school, work, student teaching, Eva and Riley planned to buy a new home to start fresh together. Riley wanted Eva to feel as though she had a stake in what they were building together.

Eva loved going to the different listings and open houses with Riley and putting together their list of must haves. Riley wanted a large home with plenty of space for a home office and Eva wanted a pool and outdoor entertaining space. They would go through home after home and try to picture their lives in each one.

They found a perfect listing not far from where Riley was already living. It was a new build, single story ranch home with almost an acre of land. "This can be the one…" Riley suggested as they walked through the model, reaching for Eva's hand.

Eva looked at the perfect model home and tried to picture it as they walked through. She pictured the dogs in the back yard and Justin running around. She loved the sprawling floor plan and the small casita that would be in the back yard for guests.

They walked through each room slowly.

"Let's talk about this," Eva said sitting on the couch in the model living room.

Riley sat next to her and turned so they were facing each other. "What's on your mind?" She smiled.

"I'm just scared. I'm so scared right now. I'm happy and everything is going so good. I'm just fearful of the other shoe dropping."

"What would be the other shoe? I think you have already been dealt the worst blow in this process."

"That you are going to decide that I'm not the one and you are going to move on."

"Are you serious right now? We are getting ready to buy a house together. I think I'm pretty serious that *this* is it. This is the most serious I have ever been about any other woman."

"I know... I know. Things just never work out like this for me. They never have. I just am so scared."

Riley stood up and pulled Eva up. She kissed the tip of Eva's nose. "Stop it. Let's go make arrangements. We have a house to build. A future to build together. You and me, and Justin too."

They went back to the sales office and initiated the paperwork. They filled out forms and the house would be completed just in time for summer break.

A few days after deciding on their home, Eva and Riley went to the airport to pick up Drew and Justin from the airport.

When Justin saw Eva in the baggage area, he broke free from Drew and ran into Eva's arms. Eva's heart broke. She had missed him, but it hit home holding him in her arms just how much.

It had been easy to numb that pain in her heart by throwing herself into work and nice dinners out and quiet nights at home. Seeing Justin again, and knowing the inevitable goodbye was only days away, reopened the wound in her heart.

The first stop was taking Drew and Justin by the construction site to see the progress on the new home. Justin was fascinated with the process looking at the beams and nails.

Eva stood on the foundation and said to Justin, "Your bedroom will be right here."

"There will be a roof, right?" Justin asked.

"Nope. You will sleep outside" Eva teased him, chasing him back to the car.

They got back to the house and set Drew up with his guest room and sent Justin up to his room to settle in. Eva felt over the moon to have her loved ones with her.

Throughout the visit with Drew and Justin they packed in as much fun as they could. Sea World, beaches, San Diego Zoo, movie nights, barbecuing, playing in the pool.

When she took them back to the airport, she tried hard to remain stoic and strong. Justin was so young, he didn't fully understand why Eva was so quiet.

"Beautiful Boy, I will see you soon, okay? On FaceTime."

"Okay, Mom Mom. Aren't you going to come with us?"

"Not this time, Beautiful Boy. But you will be back in a few short weeks to see me again. And I'm just a phone call away, okay?"

After Drew and Justin disappeared down the walkway and through TSA, Eva made her way to Riley's waiting car and fell apart.

"Are you going to be able to do this? This is going to be a lot of goodbyes." Riley put her hand on Eva's.

"I'm fine." Eva closed her eyes and took a deep inhale and pulled herself together. "I'm so fine. Let's go to Temecula and get lunch and some wine." She wiped her tears and breathed in deep to steady herself, shoving her feelings back inside.

This was life now. She was going to have to be strong and hang in there. It was not a matter of choosing love over her child. She had resolved herself to the knowledge that she was going to spend her life saying goodbye to either Riley or Justin. But it was, in a sense, self-preservation. She believed in her heart that it would only be a matter of time before Justin was living with her.

EVA WAS WRAPPING UP HER student teaching hours. She passed on the promotion to full manager with the spa chain since she knew she would get hired at the high school that she was student teaching in. The principal, Dr. Cynthia Tilman, after observing her teach a complicated lesson plan, adored her, and encouraged her to apply, and she did.

She aced all her remaining courses and became good friends with her master teacher Melanie.

But she lived for her downtime with Riley. They would curl up in the bed and the moment she would look into Riley's green eyes, she knew everything was okay. The stress, the hurt, whatever she was feeling would melt away. Time would stop and nothing else mattered when Riley would reach out for her and touch her, hold her, kiss her.

Starling's health had continued to decline since the cross-country move. Eva, teary eyed finally made the decision to take her to the vet after the old dog refused to eat her breakfast. Riley held her as she cried, and the vet told her "it was time."

Outside of her busy schedule and her escaping in Riley, she would attempt to FaceTime with Justin every chance she could. She was noticing that she was getting less time with him on the phone.

She attempted to talk to Doug about it, but he dodged any questions.

"I had to put Starling down a few days ago," Eva told Doug trying to make small talk and be friendly.

"That's terrible! I loved that old rat dog," Doug said, no real emotion in his voice.

"Tell me about your new woman," Eva finally implored.

"Her name is Lucy. She works at The Big Coney Diner. She's pretty great.

She's great with Justin. She's never been married. No kids. I think I like her a lot. I think it's serious."

"That's great. That's awesome. The Big Coney Diner in Flint?" Eva asked.

"Yeah. Her mom owns it."

"Very cool." Eva hoped it didn't sound as bitchy to Doug as it did to her.

"We are moving in together."

"You are moving out of your mom's house? With Justin?"

"Yeah. We haven't found a place yet. Maybe over the summer. Or in the fall."

"Okay. Great. Maybe we can plan a meet up with the four of us. Just so we can all stay on the same page and Justin can see that. We can try to be a united front."

"Yeah. Let's plan that. When are you coming back to Michigan to visit your family?"

"I don't know. I will let you know." In all honesty, Eva didn't want to go back to Michigan for any reason. She had grown accustomed to her life in California and didn't understand why she should ever leave. Shouldn't people just come to California?

EVA WAS EXCITED ABOUT FINISHING her credential and her upcoming job at the high school. She quit the spa before Justin came to visit. She had one full week before Justin came to visit with no work, no school, no obligations other than moving into the new house.

Eva packed boxes while Riley worked during the days. She would load up what she could into her car and take loads to the new home.

After dropping off a load of boxes she stood in the center of the barren living room. She assessed the gray slate tile floors that replicated the Mediterranean style homes she saw pictures of growing up. Intricate mosaic patterning in different shades, arches in the support beams. She looked over the open floor plan into the kitchen and the marble countertops. She wandered into the room that would be Justin's, and then into the bathroom that would be his, and then back through the center of the house to the other side where her and Riley's master suite was located. She looked at the large fire place and the French doors that led out to the outdoor patio. This was hers and Riley's. Together. She texted Riley a simple, 'I love you. I love our new nest.'

'Nest?' Riley texted back.

'Nest. It is our nest to build and customize,' Eva sent back.

'Love nest,' Riley sent back.

After a full week of packing and taking loads and one big day spent with furniture being moved, sold, and delivered, The Nest, as it was now referred to, was complete, except for the bare walls that drove Eva nuts. She wouldn't even consider furniture store art prints. "What goes on the walls of this house has to tell our story," she said. "I'm not compromising on that."

They set the small casita out back up for their impending guest, Geri, who was bringing Justin out the next day. Geri had offered to fly with Justin since he was unable to fly unaccompanied yet. She needed time away, she said.

Geri spent a week in the casita. Eva would see her in the morning sitting on the small casita patio outside the bedroom, overlooking the pool, smoking her morning joint, soaking in the sun.

"California looks good on you, Mom," Eva said, bringing them each a cup of coffee on her last morning. Justin was eating his cereal inside on the kitchen island.

"I wish I could stay. This little casita would be perfect for me!" Geri exclaimed. "I need to go back though. Tony needs me."

Eva rolled her eyes. She hadn't spoken to Tony since he spilled everything to Doug, and she had no intention to ever speak to him again.

After taking Geri to the airport, the remainder of the summer went fast. Riley and Eva took Justin to Las Vegas, and up to the Central Coast. They spent days at the beach and Eva relished having her Beautiful Boy there with her.

Michigan schools and California schools not being on the same schedule required Eva to start work the last few weeks before Justin went home, but it worked out fine. Several days a week Riley would bring him to the office with her, and they found a nice, retired lady in the subdivision who babysat her grandkids that were about Justin's age.

Jack flew out at the end of the visit to stay for a few days and fly Justin back with him. It was his turn in the casita.

One evening, after Justin had gone to bed and Riley was inside helping one of her junior agents with a client crisis, Eva brought Jack out a peanut butter and jelly sandwich, which was his favorite bedtime snack.

The patio doors were open letting the hot breeze in. Jack hated air conditioning. Eva sat on the small couch in the living room and handed him the plate. "Thank you! What a great daughter you are!" he exclaimed.

Eva smiled back at him.

"You did good, kiddo," Jack said.

"I know! I mastered the PBJ." Eva smiled.

"No. I mean all of this." Jack gestured around. "Making a life out here. You have a great career starting. A beautiful home. You found love. I just wish I didn't have to bring Justin back with me tomorrow. That kid belongs here with you."

Eva looked down. "I know. But there is nothing I can do about that."

"Just don't quit. Stay on Doug. You know he's an idiot. He will screw things up sooner rather than later."

She knew he was right. She looked over at his open suitcase on the floor and stifled her hurt as she said goodnight and walked back across the yard.

Eva's heart broke into pieces watching Justin and Jack walk off and through the TSA line early the next morning.

Riley drove them home from the airport. Eva was sullen and quiet.

"I have a surprise for you," Riley said, side eyeing Eva with a smile.

"What?" Eva asked, forcing herself to smile.

"We are leaving for Cabo next week. You will have to get a sub for a few days, but I felt like we needed a little romantic trip. We need some us time. It's been go time since you moved here."

Eva smiled. "I can't wait! You are right... I need it."

She would not see Justin until Thanksgiving which was about 86 days away. She busied herself with packing and lesson planning and writing sub plans for the next week until they left.

Once they arrived in Cabo, it was easy to feel good about life and her future with Riley. They stayed in bed late almost every morning, ordering room service for breakfast. They went kayaking to El Archo, lounged by the pool at the resort, explored the town and drove to Todos Santos to see the infamous Hotel California, and took walks along the beach. Eva had never been on such a romantic vacation before.

Three nights into the trip, Riley asked Eva to get dressed up, they were going somewhere special for dinner. Eva swept her hair up so that loose ringlets framed her face, the remainder of her curls swept up in a twist, and she selected a loose flowing peach dress with chiffon layers that caught the breeze. Riley in linen pants and a pink button-down shirt grabbed Eva's hand and raised it. She spun her around, "You look like a dream." She pulled Eva in and kissed her lightly.

Riley took Eva to an idyllic sunset dinner at another resort. As cocktails came to the table Riley looked at Eva. They had their fingers interlaced across the table. "Where do you see us in the future?"

Eva smiled devilishly. "How far into the future? Tonight? I see us naked in the bed -"

Riley grinned and cut her off before other tables overheard. "Shhh... No... Like the future. Like years from now."

Eva raised her eyebrow. "I don't know. I have been so busy making it day to day I haven't really given much thought to the long game."

"Do you see us together?"

"I wouldn't want my future without an 'us'. You are all that I ever wanted," Eva answered without hesitation.

Riley let go of Eva's hand and stood up. She made her way over to Eva's chair and dropped to her knee.

Others in the restaurant turned to watch.

"Eva Jayne Brooks, I want to spend the rest of my life with you. I've never been more sure about something in my life. Will you marry me?"

"Yes! A million times yes." Eva was crying openly. The patrons cheered and applauded, and the mariachi band came and serenaded a love song.

Chapter 8

Thirty-Seven and Thirty-Eight

UPON GETTING BACK TO NORTH County they came back with more than just news, picking up several small pieces of art to hang on the bare walls and commemorate this trip (as Eva had demanded, the art in the home should tell a story – the story that represents them), Eva called everyone she knew to share the big news about her engagement to Riley.

Britt was ecstatic. Drew was thrilled.

Jack was not surprised, indicating how Riley asked him for his blessing before he left with Justin.

With wedding planning with Riley and writing teaching plans, her days went fast. Riley wanted a big wedding, and all Eva wanted was Riley. She indulged Riley's wishes and they spent hours each day on Pinterest sending each other ideas on work breaks. They spent afternoons touring venues, and evenings planning the honeymoon.

She broke the news to Doug as they discussed Justin's progress in school. The moment she sprang the news, he unceremoniously hung up.

A few weeks later, shortly before Thanksgiving, Geri told Eva, "Tony told me that Doug proposed to Lucy."

"Well, that's quick," Eva said.

"I think he's doing it because you and Riley are engaged. He's jealous," Geri speculated.

"Maybe. Or maybe he really loves her," Eva hoped.

"He downgraded for sure," Geri said. "I met her when they dropped Justin off to visit this weekend. She's rough."

"I saw pictures, she isn't that bad. I've never met her though," Eva informed Geri. "She won't even talk to me. And when she's watching Justin, I can't seem to talk to him."

Doug informed Eva that he and Lucy signed a lease and they moved in together, it was rent to own, and they were hoping to eventually buy it. During her FaceTimes with Justin, Eva was trying to notice what the house looked like or to see if she could get a glimpse of Lucy in the flesh. Justin only FaceTimed from his bedroom, a converted room in a finished basement. The walls were white and the ceiling was made of drop tiles like the ones in her classroom. Lucy never made an appearance on the camera, just shouting in the background that it was time to hang up.

When Justin arrived for Thanksgiving, he was old enough to fly unaccompanied.

Eva picked him up at the gate and he ran into her arms. Eva covered him in kisses and got him outside to Riley's waiting car.

When they got home, Eva put Justin in the bath and as he was playing, Eva asked him, "How do you like Miss Lucy?"

"She's mean to me," Justin said frankly.

"What do you mean?" Eva asked.

"I dropped my milk glass on her kitchen, and she picked me up and threw me on the couch and hit me on my butt."

After she loved him up and tucked him into bed, she told Riley what Justin had confided.

"I don't know how to handle this," she finished.

"You need to tell Doug. You need to also tell him that it is unacceptable," Riley counseled.

Eva agreed. "But I'm going to wait until Justin is gone. I'm going to talk to him when he is boarded."

"Yes. Let's not drag drama into this visit. It's already a short one."

They enjoyed the holiday, going to the Queen Mary for Thanksgiving Dinner, and the next day decorating the Christmas tree as a family.

On Sunday, Eva walked Justin to his gate and watched him board the plane, telling him the short number of days before she would see him again at Christmas.

After she got out to the car, she called Doug.

"Hey, he's boarded the plane."

"Great. Thanks!" Doug chirped.

"Hey. Um. I heard you are engaged to Lucy. Which is great. Congratulations. But I have a concern. Justin told me she hit him. He dropped a milk glass while she was watching him, and she threw him on the couch and hit him."

"Lucy wouldn't do that. I don't appreciate the accusation."

"Why would Justin make that up?" Eva was genuinely confused.

"He wouldn't. I don't appreciate you trying to start drama."

"Um, okay. This makes no sense."

"It makes no sense for you to accuse my fiancée of something like that. I don't know why you can't just let me be happy."

"I want you to be happy. I want nothing more than that," Eva said. "Make sure she doesn't hit our son ever again."

"She never did that. I will talk to you later." Doug hung up.

Eva hung the phone up and looked at Riley as they made their way down the road. Eva repeated the conversation to her.

"Unacceptable," Riley said angrily.

"He doesn't like to be alone. He's protecting her over our son," Eva said.

"You need to go to court. You need to bring this up and bring Justin back home with us," Riley said.

"I need a new lawyer, first. Kate was awful."

"Bring up how you never get to talk to Justin when he's with this Lucy person either. This is shady."

Eva appreciated how calm and logical Riley was in this situation. She was grateful for the cool head, as she was ready to implode.

EVA AND RILEY FOUND A NEW lawyer, Max, after researching divorce groups in Macomb County on social media. They did their homework on Max and learned that he was part of the 'boys club' of attorneys and judges and well connected. He looked like a stereotypical lawyer in all his pictures online. Tall, and broad shouldered, dark hair and deep-set eyes. He looked intimidating, and spoke with authority.

Max was able to schedule a court date for January. This was the first time any of them would actually appear in front of the judge. Everything had settled outside of court and had only gone to the judge for a rubber stamp.

Judge Sean Gleason sat at the bench. The Honorable Judge Gleason came from Macomb County legal legacy. His brother was a judge as was his father and his father's father. He was elected on name alone and held zero passion for his profession, he would have much rather been doing anything at all than sitting on the bench, and it showed. He was not much older than the parties involved. He had shaggy brown hair with graying sides, and high cheekbones. His expression was what scared Eva. He looked bored as he sat at his bench above the courtroom. She watched the cases come before him waiting for theirs to be called. His eyes showed nothing. His expression was unmoved like stone. His tone of voice was flat as he ruled on case after case. Riley and Eva sat next to each other. Riley's hand wrapped around Eva's. They looked at each other. Eva whispered, "I don't think this is going to go anywhere."

"He has to protect Justin," Riley said back quietly. Hopeful.

Their case was called, and they went up in front of the judge. Doug refused to make eye contact with either Riley or Eva, keeping his head down and playing meek. Riley sat back in the gallery and Eva stood next to Max. The judge didn't seem to care. He made no movement or change of expression as Eva detailed what Justin had told her. Doug denied all allegations, and everything was dismissed.

Defeated, Eva and Riley flew home without Justin.

A week after court Britt called Eva. "I don't think Doug realizes he's still friends with me and Harry on Facebook. But check your text messages. I just forwarded you some screen shots."

Eva pulled her phone away from her ear and looked at the screen. It was a series of pictures of Doug and Lucy in Las Vegas at a wedding chapel. They had eloped. It was only the second time Eva had actually even seen a picture of Lucy. She didn't attend court with Doug. Drew and Britt were right, she was not an attractive girl. She was scrawny, and her nose was too large for her face. Her eyes were deep-set with dark circles. She wore little to no makeup even to get married. She was the antithesis of Eva. She was wearing a white dress that looked out of date. Eva was unsure if she was intentionally trying to have a vintage look.

"Wow!" Eva said sitting down on the couch. "That was quick. I wonder if she's pregnant or something."

"You know better than that," Britt said. "His dick doesn't work. Remember?"

Eva laughed. "Yeah. I'm still trying to forget."

"I just don't know how he could marry her after what Justin said she did. Why would he protect her and not his son?"

"Excellent question." Eva ruminated on the question, trying to figure it out for herself.

AFTER MONTHS OF DOUG PLAYING games with communication times and Eva not being able to talk to Justin for almost a week, she finally broke down and hired a private investigator to look into Lucy as she correlated her times of not being able to talk to Justin were when he was primarily in her care.

He brought the background investigation over and handed her a printout and a thumb drive. Amazing what $180 will get you. As it turned out, Lucy's mother was an immigrant from Macedonia (which is not uncommon in Detroit). Lucy's dad was German Irish (also not uncommon in Detroit), and worked in the auto industry on the line until that wasn't a thing anymore. Her given name was Lucy Ann McFadden. She had a list of aliases and several social security numbers. "That's because she's most likely been involved in some identity theft, but it doesn't look like she's been caught and or that she's taking part in it now," the investigator informed Eva. "Given the last date correlating the usage of the fraudulent socials, the statute of limitations would be up on pressing charges against her for it."

Riley's eyebrows shot up.

"I also looked into some of her known acquaintances, they are not good people. There's a lot of shadiness going on. Looks like some of the folks have been under FBI surveillance and some have gone away to the federal pen. They are a rough crowd."

"This doesn't make me feel better," Eva said after the investigator left.

"What are you going to do?" Riley asked.

"There's nothing I can do. She's never been indicted or under investigation. She is just a bitch with shitty friends."

"What a great choice. Man, your dad was right. It wouldn't take Doug long to fuck things up."

Eva called Max the next day.

"Is there anything we can do with this information?" she asked.

"No. But it's nice to know. As far as the communication goes, I will talk to Doug's attorney and see if we can get a schedule going for you to talk to Justin on a regular schedule."

Doug and his attorney, to avoid going to court, settled on a schedule that allowed contact 4 days a week at a regular time. Eva was satisfied with this as it took the guesswork out of when she would talk to her son.

EVA AND RILEY FINALIZED THEIR wedding plans, picking an outdoor venue and an art deco twenties theme.

Riley found a tailor that made her a custom tuxedo and Eva found a bejeweled gown that fit the designs of the era.

Riley took Justin to get fitted for a tuxedo on his spring break with them. He was excited about the fancy tuxedo and the spectator shoes.

They planned a Mediterranean Cruise for their honeymoon. All of this would be coming up in a year. Their wedding date was coincidentally Mother's Day weekend. The actual wedding being on the Thursday before, as that was the only available May date they could secure at the venue.

Eva had Max send Doug's lawyer a letter requesting Justin for that week so he could be part of the plans. They received confirmation in writing that Justin would be there, and Eva was able to breathe better.

As plans settled and finalized and final checks were written, another summer rolled by and then another holiday season.

It was drama free, and Justin seemed to be okay with the way his life was rolling out. There was no more talk about being hit or Lucy being mean.

Shortly before the May wedding, Britt texted Eva, 'I'm not trying to start anything or tattle, but I think you might need this information or be able to use it. Lucy posted this.' A screenshot was attached. Lucy had tagged Doug. 'You left your kid for a life of sin. Getting married and pulling kid out of school for your sham wedding shows how you only care about yourself. Kid will be missing a week of school to go see you be a sinner.'

Attached was a meme about the biblical definition of marriage, and another one about the rainbow not being a symbol of gay pride but of God's love.

Eva gagged. 'Bitter bitch,' she responded.

This had to be about the nightmare of arranging flights for Jack, Geri and Justin to fly together. Geri did not want to fly alone and asked Jack to fly with her. Jack wanted to fly with Justin. So now, three schedules had to be managed. Geri liked direct flights and Jack liked layovers so he could walk around and break up the monotony. Justin would have to be picked up but who was going to pick him up?

Eva showed Riley, and she just shook her head. "I don't understand what this bitch has against me. She's never even met me."

"She is just an unhappy person," Riley reasoned. "Let's not focus on them though… We have our wedding coming up soon."

Three days before the wedding, she picked up Geri, Jack and Justin at the airport. When they got back to the house, Geri in the guest room, Jack in the casita (they flipped a coin, best of three to decide) Eva walked back into Justin's room with him. He was digging in his backpack and handed Eva a stack of the picture books she had made him over the past couple of years. One for each of their visitations together.

"Why are you giving me these?" she asked. "Those are for you."

"Lucy doesn't want them at our house. She doesn't want things that remind her of a person she hates in her home."

Eva bit her lip. "Beautiful Boy, do you like these books?"

"Yes," he said.

"They are yours. If you want them, you take them back with you and you keep them. Just maybe don't put them where she can see them. Look at them when you are by yourself."

Eva got up and went to the kitchen where Riley was preparing chicken breasts to barbecue.

"Lucy sent Justin back here with all of his picture books," Eva said.

"Why?"

Eva made air quotes with her fingers, "'She doesn't want things that remind her of someone she hates in her house.'"

Riley wiped her hands on a towel and looked at Eva. "She's doing that to mess with us during our wedding week. Don't even think about it further. Don't feed into it. It's what they want."

"You are so right. I'm not even going to address it."

The next day Drew and Jose and Britt and Harry arrived and took over a local hotel. Riley's family and friends began to pour in as well. The rest of the week leading up to the wedding was one big non-stop party. They were surrounded by love and support, and they chose to focus on that instead.

The night before the wedding, Eva and Justin stayed in a hotel room down the hall from Britt and Harry and Drew and Jose's rooms. After the rehearsal dinner, Eva took Justin back to the room instead of going out to party with her friends and family. Throughout the week, she had not had time to focus on him.

After Justin got into his pajamas, she sat him down on the bed and handed him a small velvet box. He opened it slowly. Eva explained as he opened it, "This is your first real big boy gift. It's not a toy and you need to be very careful with it." Inside the box was a sterling silver dog tag set. On one tag it was engraved, 'To the end of the universe and back' and the other tag had the wedding date. "This is to symbolize how on tomorrow's date, we are officially a family, you, me and Riley."

Justin put the tags around his neck and hugged his mom. "Thank you. I will never take them off or lose them."

The morning of the wedding was a blur. Harry and Drew came down and swept Justin away so they could all get ready. Britt and Geri and Eva went to the salon for hair and makeup.

This wedding day was so distinctly different from the last. She was not concerned or feeling the need to drink herself into oblivion. She wished Nana was there, but felt a strange reassurance that she was indeed with her.

They went from the salon to the wedding venue. While she was in the bridal suite getting into her dress, Jack knocked on the door. Geri let him in.

"You are not going to talk to me about turning back are you?" Eva asked as Britt buttoned up the back of her dress.

"Absolutely not," Jack said. "I just wanted to say again, that I'm proud of you. I think you really did find the right one, this time." He smiled and kissed Eva on the cheek. "You look amazing."

The brides had opted for a first look ahead of the ceremony knowing that would allow them time to have makeup touch ups in the event that emotions took over.

After the photographer had contented himself with pictures of Eva getting ready, they set up for the first look. They had ushered Riley out to a grove with a bridge and a man-made waterfall and stream. The plan was for Eva to walk across the bridge and greet Riley at the end by tapping her on the shoulder. Staged, but would be great for photos.

Eva got midway down the bridge. She stopped, thinking about the New Year's Eve in New Orleans all those years ago. She believed in that moment that that New Year's Eve was foreshadowing her destiny. Some part of her must have known all those years ago that Riley was her person. She put her hands over her mouth to stifle a cry. Riley heard her and looked over her shoulder. It was the exact look from that night. Eva reached for the railing of the bridge and Riley came to her with tears glittering in her eyes.

Eva's arms wrapped around Riley's neck.

Eva thought it would have been a perfect moment had it not been for the photographers clicking cameras.

"You look so amazing," Eva whispered into Riley's neck.

"I can't even believe we are here," Riley said.

After the obligatory pictures, the ceremony began. Justin stole the show as ring bearer.

Jack and Geri flanked Eva and walked her down the aisle. Eva could not have planned for a more beautiful day.

After the ceremony, Riley took Justin to talk to him privately. She vowed to love him and protect him always. They agreed later that evening that he would call her Mum instead of by her name.

THE WEEKS AFTER THE WEDDING and honeymoon, Riley was busy hanging more art that they had selected on their honeymoon paying to have it shipped to their home and Eva took time to get her name changed, taking Riley's last name (Mares beat Brooks by a long shot in her opinion). She and Riley also took time to enjoy extended honeymoon days, languishing with late mornings in bed on the weekends.

Work days were tough, as all they wanted to do was continue the honeymoon. Nana would have been happy for her, if she could understand the whole gay thing, Eva thought. Eva was happy. She was in this beautiful relationship that she had always longed for. She had a spouse who matched her desire for wanderlust, lust in general, and constant personal growth. She had someone who understood her and loved her for who she was. The only thing she was missing was her son. Eva fully understood at this point, love is indeed real. She felt loved and she gave love in return.

Summer vacation arrived, and Justin got off the plane running to Eva full throttle. He was exceptionally clingy with her as she got him home.

They were sitting outside on the patio near the pool. Riley was barbecuing in the outdoor kitchen. She and Riley had glasses of sparkling rosé and Riley had made Justin a Shirley Temple.

"Mom Mom, I have a question." Justin looked at Eva, his thick eyelashes squinting against the sun.

"Well, I have an answer," Eva said.

"Why do Lucy and Dad keep saying that you abandoned me and that you are a liar and a bad person? They threw away the dog tags you gave me at the wedding and told me it was lie."

Eva's chest tightened. Riley slammed the tongs she was using to flip the turkey burgers down on the side of the grill.

"Am I bad for asking that?" Justin asked.

"No, Beautiful Boy. No. You did nothing wrong and that is a great question. It's a question I unfortunately can't answer really." She couldn't breathe.

"Buddy," Riley began, "some people don't understand other people's choices. So, since they don't understand, they make guesses and sometimes those guesses are not right. Lucy has never met your mom or me, and she can only make guesses about us and what we are like. As for your dad saying those things, well, he's very mad at your mom and I and that doesn't make what he said right, but I understand that he's mad."

Eva got up and walked inside the house and went into the powder room. She tried to catch her breath. Her anger and her pain were both coursing through her. She took deep breaths in and out and focused on the feeling of the cool tile under her bare feet until she felt herself return to her body and control her emotions. It would be so easy to just give up. Quit. Not deal with it.

Eva went back out and sat in her chair next to Justin. "Beautiful Boy, let me ask you a question."

"Okay, Mom Mom."

"Do you think I love you?"

"To the end of the universe and back and everything in between," he answered.

"Do you know what abandon means?"

"To leave and never ever ever come back."

"Do you think I could ever do that to you?"

He shook his head no and sipped his pink drink.

"Have you ever seen me do something that was mean or hurtful to anyone?"

He continued to shake his head no.

"Do you think I'm a bad person?"

"No. You are a teacher. Teachers are good people. You help kids. And you are always loving to everyone you know."

"Okay. So do you think that those ugly things you heard about me are true?"

"No."

"How did it make you feel to hear those things? Did you think even for a moment those were true words?"

"No. It made my heart sad to hear Lucy say those things about you."

"Okay. Listen, Beautiful Boy... I'm not going to say bad things about Lucy or your dad. It's not my place to tell you negative things about them. They are your family just like Mum and I are your family. You are allowed to love all of us the same and that is not wrong. But some people, like Mum said, may say some ugly things. When you hear those things, you listen to your heart. You can always ask me if you don't understand, and I will help you."

"Okay, Mom Mom." Riley had placed a plate of food in front of each of them and sat down next to Eva.

"Are you okay?" she asked quietly.

Eva shook her head no and refilled her rosé. "We will talk later," she said quietly.

After dinner they played in the pool and walked the dogs and Eva put a very tired Justin to bed after reading him the first chapter of Harry Potter.

Eva crawled into bed next to Riley and laid her head down facing her wife. "I can't fucking believe they would say shit like that to a child."

"You need to confront Doug," Riley said.

"After summer. I can't do it now. I don't want it to interfere with what time I do have."

"I think you need to do it while it's fresh."

"Let me think on it." Eva leaned in and kissed Riley. "On that note, goodnight, my love."

A few days later, while they were coming back from the beach, Justin told Eva that Lucy had hit him again.

That was the straw that broke her back. When she got home, she sent Justin to shower off before dinner. She picked up her phone and called Doug.

"Oh, I thought it was going to be Justin," he replied after hearing Eva's voice.

"No. He's in the shower. We need to talk. I understand you are married to Lucy, but there's a real problem. Our son is showing up saying things like you and her are telling him I'm a bad person and I abandoned him and he's saying that she's hitting him."

"I'm not going to sit here while you insult and accuse my wife of things that are not true. Why can't you just let me be happy?"

"Why can't you protect our son?"

"Have Justin call me later." He hung up.

Eva set her phone down.

She braced herself with the counter and looked up at Riley.

"I don't want to send him back."

"We don't have a choice, babe."

"I can't believe he is letting this happen. Wait... I can believe it. This is the same man that took morphine willingly, knowing the repercussions. He's a fucking idiot. He and that judgy bitch are doing irreparable damage to our son."

"Maybe Justin needs to see a therapist to kind of mitigate this damage? Someone that can help him get some coping skills in dealing with these people?"

"I will see what I can do with my insurance provider," Eva stated.

"I will help you pay for it if we need to go out of network," Riley offered.

BY THE END OF THE summer, Justin had seen a therapist a handful of times in between his vacation to Sedona, swimming lessons, camping, and staying busy. He was sent back to Michigan with a dark tan, and new skills that ranged from jumping into the deep end of the pool, to deep breathing when he was upset.

One week after his return, Doug sent Eva an email. 'I don't know who you think you are. Justin told us all the lies you filled his head with. Don't expect me to bend over backwards for you ever again. No extra days, no extra time on the phone. Nothing.'

Eva, perplexed, responded, 'I think there is a miscommunication. What are you talking about?'

Doug never responded.

Later that same day, after her FaceTime with Justin was coming to a close, she asked him to put his dad on.

Doug came on the screen. Eva had not seen him in almost a year. She was shocked to see that he had shaved his head and grown a beard. His eyes looked sullen. "What?" he asked, irritated.

Riley was sitting off screen near Eva, listening.

"I don't understand your email," Eva offered.

"You told Justin that my wife and I are liars," Doug offered.

"I did not. Not at all. I asked him to think about the things that you and your wife, who by the way has never even met me, said to our son. I asked him to think about how they made him feel, and if he felt they were true."

"The truth is, you left him here. You traded him in for a lifestyle. You traded him in for money. You are a gold-digger. You are a sociopath."

"Doug, where is Justin?" Eva's voice was low.

"He's sitting right here. So he can hear you. He can hear you admit how you left him."

Riley grabbed the phone from Eva.

"Who do you think you are? Eva loves Justin more than you could ever imagine. She lives for that child. She thinks of him morning noon and night. You took him from her. You kept him from her, and you do nothing but use that child as a pawn to hurt her. How dare you say those things about her in front of that boy."

"This has nothing to do with you," Doug said to Riley.

"It does. It has everything to do with me. I love that child and I love his mother. I can't stand to see the damage you are doing to them. You and your bitch wife."

"My wife didn't abandon her son. Your wife did. She can deal with what she did." He hung up.

Eva tried to call Justin back, but no one would answer.

She tried tirelessly to call him for almost a week, but no one would respond.

Eva just did what she always did when she was distraught and in pain. She threw herself into everything that would keep her busy.

She went to the yoga studio.

She and Riley went to the wineries.

She worked over her scheduled days so she could get ahead on her lesson planning.

She read extra chapters in her book every night.

She drew pictures.

She avoided even talking about it.

"You need to talk to me," Riley demanded.

"I can't. I don't want to talk about it. It hurts too much," Eva said.

Eva called Jack. "Have you been able to talk to Justin?" Eva asked.

"No. I tried. No one answers."

It was the same thing with Geri and Drew. No one connected to her was allowed to talk to Justin.

She contacted her lawyer after it had been 10 days.

"I will file a motion," Max informed her.

Max filed a motion claiming parental alienation, including the therapist's notes, and demanded that in the very least, Eva have scheduled phone and FaceTime conversations with Justin, court ordered.

Eva and Riley flew into Michigan for the court appearance.

Doug refused to even look at Eva or Riley again, keeping his head down and looking like a victim. Lucy did not show up either.

The referee overseeing the case, came down hard on Eva and Doug both. She looked at Eva, "Why would you leave the state and leave your child? You understand it's hard to parent from over 2000 miles away."

"Your honor, it's not that simple. I don't have a simple answer for you."

"Well, I'm not the one you will have to answer to. Your son is," she quipped.

She read through the motion and read through the notes. She slammed the paper down and looked at Doug. "You need to stop your smirking, sir. These things I'm reading, they are disturbing. You told that child that she left him. You don't do that. You don't speak ill of that woman to that boy, do you understand? That's his mother."

"She's not his mother. She doesn't do anything for him. She left him. She doesn't deserve to be called his mother," Doug hissed.

By the end of the motion, it was ordered that Doug and Lucy were not allowed to disparage Eva to Justin, and Eva was to have scheduled phone calls with Justin between visits.

Eva and Riley left feeling victorious.

Chapter 9

Thirty-Nine and Forty

THE REST OF THE YEAR went smooth with very little drama. Eva loved her life despite missing Justin constantly. She took on advising the Mock Trial team at the high school. It was the school's only academic competition club. She loved spending time with the kids she affectionately dubbed her 'nerds'. They were smart and creative and highly competitive. She relished their after-school club meetings and how astute and socially aware this group of teenagers tended to be. She threw herself into her morning workouts before work, yoga and running. As long as she was busy, she could not be overwhelmed by her emotions.

Summer vacation arrived and Justin came back, barreling off the plane into Eva's waiting arms.

Justin was so grown up in her eyes. She was amazed with the subtleties he would notice and the questions he would ask. He noticed the little things like new pieces on the walls, wanting to know the story behind them, or other knick-knacks around the home.

As she was tucking him into bed at night, she asked him how everything was going at his dad's.

"I don't like Lucy. I don't like living with her," Justin said.

"Why not?" Eva asked, sitting on the edge of his bed.

"She's mean. She pushes me. She hits me. She's always yelling at me."

"I'm sorry, Beautiful Boy."

"She still says mean things about you. I just don't like her."

"I will see what I can do." Eva sighed.

The next morning, she contacted Max. "Eva, there is not much we can do. I can file a motion, but you know the court's opinion and they are not going to change up custody."

"Maybe. Can't they talk to Justin?"

"No. Even if they did, his opinion on what he wants isn't that weighty."

"Okay. Just see what you can do."

Eva tried to keep the focus light throughout the remainder of the visit. She allowed Justin to talk to her and she would listen. She didn't pry nor did she say anything negative about Doug or Lucy, though she wanted to say, "I'm sorry your dad sucks. If I had known he was such an ignorant, lazy, apathetic douche I would never have married him." She kept her lips sealed and would snuggle Justin and say instead, "I'm so sorry you are dealing with this. Maybe you can tell someone at school?"

Justin would just shake his head no. "My dad says I'm not supposed to talk about what goes on in our private home with people who don't live in it. He doesn't even think I should talk to you."

Eva bit her tongue. She knew with the details and words Justin was using this was not made up or embellished. What it told Eva is that Doug knew what was going on in his home and knew that it was wrong.

AFTER SUMMER, THERE WAS ANOTHER scheduled court appearance in early fall. A show cause, as Max called it. They called Doug in front of Judge Gleason to explain why Justin was still saying that they were speaking ill of Eva. Max also charged him with continued parental alienation.

Judge Gleason sat at his bench, looking bored. His head was propped in his hand like he was ready to fall asleep, and he listened without changing his expression or hardly moving. Eva wondered if he was even paying attention.

After hearing the motion Judge Gleason sat up slowly, moving at a sloth-like pace placing his hands in front of him like he had literally just been awoken from a deep nap, and in his monotone and apathetic voice he ordered a forensic psychologist to read into the situation.

Eva felt like she was walking out with a major win. Someone would see the truth and things would change.

That afternoon she called the office of the forensic psychologist and made her appointment. It would be several weeks, almost Thanksgiving before they could get into the psychologist. Meanwhile, she would just throw herself back into avoiding her deeper feelings.

Things with Riley were still great. She loved Riley, and Riley was always cognizant to show her love in return.

But deep down underneath, there was the emptiness. The accusations of abandoning her son. The missing him. The guilt. The words and accusations had gotten the better of her. They had triggered her in a way she couldn't get over.

She dealt with it every time she had to talk to someone new. They would look at her like she sprouted a second head the moment she said her son did not live with them. She dealt with it every time she FaceTimed with Justin.

She tried to start therapy but didn't feel like she could fully relax enough to tell the story to the therapist. She was so guarded because of what she perceived to be the constant judgment, she never got anywhere with the therapist.

She and Riley flew back to Michigan to meet with the forensic psychologist. She sat in front of the much older, very pale man. He seemed to focus on asking her questions that had little to do with parenting and focused more on her sexuality. He pushed her. He asked her about leaving Doug.

He observed Justin with her and Riley. He questioned Riley. Everyone had to fill out questionnaires for personality inventories.

Thanksgiving break came. Eva asked Justin how things were going. "It's good. Lucy stopped hitting me and she stopped saying mean things about you."

"Well, that's good. But remember, you need to tell the people who ask you about it, what you have been through. It's important."

"I didn't tell the doctor because it stopped. So I don't need to talk about it anymore." Eva felt her heart sink into her gut. Without Justin disclosing his experiences, they were sunk.

Right in time for Christmas the report and recommendation came from the forensic psychologist. He tore into Eva in his evaluation of her, calling her narcissistic. He found that her allegations of mental and physical abuse were unfounded, and no changes were required. She had suspected that this would be the case when Justin mentioned that Lucy had stopped her abusive behaviors, but she never realized she would be labeled in such a way.

She sat down with Riley and handed her the copy of the report. "We lost and I'm a narcissist," she said. She laid her head in her hands and choked back the sob.

Riley started skimming through the report. "There is nothing in here. We paid over three grand, and this is 60 pages of bullshit and nothing."

"I know... I don't even know what to think right now." Eva's eyes were glassy, and she worked hard to control her tears.

Eva called Max on speaker and she and Riley confirmed with him that the best they could do was adopt a few of the recommendations from the forensic psychologist as orders. The biggest being that Lucy is not to discipline Justin, ever.

CHRISTMAS BREAK CAME AND WENT, and Justin was still doing good. He didn't spew out any stories of horrific punishments but did lament how he still wished he could stay with Eva and Riley.

As spring break approached, Eva was talking to Justin on FaceTime and he seemed particularly upset.

"What's going on, Beautiful Boy?" she asked him.

"Lucy is upset with me because I didn't load the dishwasher the way she does it. So she made me write 100 sentences about following directions. My hand hurts and I missed baseball because of it."

"Well, that seems excessive," Eva stated, "but you do need to work on following directions." She had to work hard at keeping her mouth shut. What she wanted to say was, "Tell that bitch that there is a court order stating she is not allowed to punish you."

A few days later, when Eva was FaceTiming with Justin again, he seemed upset. "I had to write 100 sentences again. This time for not folding my laundry fast enough. And then, she said they were too messy and made me start over."

Eva had Max file another show cause the next day.

Justin came for spring break and the day he was supposed to go back to Doug's, he broke down crying. "Please don't make me go back." He sobbed as she packed his backpack.

"I have to send you back, Beautiful Boy. If I don't, I'm breaking the law, and I go to jail."

"Mom Mom, I don't like her. She's so mean to me."

"I know, but you need to talk to your dad about it," Eva informed Justin.

"My dad doesn't care what I have to say about it. He just loves Lucy," Justin whined.

"I think he loves you more," Eva corrected.

Justin shrugged. "I don't want to talk about it anymore."

Shortly after spring break, Eva and Riley flew back to Detroit for the show cause hearing. Britt and her husband and Drew and Jose sat in the gallery and observed for support.

Judge Gleason took the bench. He had his usual look of boredom and apathy on his face. "Why are we here today, Counsellor?" he asked in his monotone voice, putting his head on his hand.

"Your honor, the minor child is disclosing to his mother that the defendant father's wife is still disciplining the child though it was ordered the *last* time we were here that she is not to do so any longer. These punishments to boot are abusive. Also, the defendant father is no longer allowing the minor child to have any communication with the maternal side of the family as punitive measures to punish the mother."

"Does the defendant have anything to respond?"

"Your honor, these are baseless allegations because the plaintiff mother is making yet another play for custody. She feels guilty for abandoning her child. The forensic psychologist even said she's nothing more than a narcissistic and guilt-ridden woman who can't get over what she has done. The child has never told anyone but the mother about these alleged punishments. If the child was so traumatized, wouldn't he tell someone else? A therapist? A teacher? And as for the communication with the maternal side of the family, grandparents do not have rights in this state. The defendant father is merely not comfortable with allowing them unsupervised time with the minor child. The maternal grandparents have histories of drug abuse," Doug's attorney pontificated.

The judge turned his gaze to Eva. "You up and moved to California. It's hard to parent from 2000 miles away, wouldn't you say?"

Eva closed her eyes and took a breath. She was so over that question. "Your honor, it shouldn't be difficult with modern technology. The defendant is what makes it hard. He plays constant games with communication and tit for tat pettiness every time he doesn't get his way. He is allowing his wife to continue to punish Justin and it's affecting how Justin is responding to school, peers, and more."

The judge turned to Max. "Counselor, what would you like to see happen today?"

"Your honor, I would love to see the defendant be held accountable for his refusal to comply with this court's orders. I would like to see him fined or jailed in contempt."

The judge turned his gaze to Doug. "Is your wife still disciplining the child? Are you keeping him from seeing his family members?"

Doug shifted his gaze down. "My wife spends her time taking care of the child while I work. She takes care of him more often and better than my ex-wife has or can. If the child acts out, she contacts me. These are my punishments delivered through her. As for seeing my ex's family, she flies to town three times a year for visits. If she wants her family to see him, they can see him then."

"Your wife is not to even deliver punishments, even if they are yours. I'm not going to sanction you or fine you this time. Your child is going to hate you when he grows up if you continue on this path. That's punishment enough for me. All motions denied. Court is adjourned." The judge delivered in one monotone breath, hit the gavel and sat back in his chair.

Eva turned to Riley. Riley had her mouth hard set and she shook her head. Britt and Drew both had a look of shock on their faces.

They all exited the court room and walked to the diner down the street.

"He's like a Teflon Don," Harry said.

"Seriously," Drew said. "There has to be something that can be done."

"Have you ever even met this Lucy person yet?" Britt asked.

"No," Eva said. "She's never come to court. She's never had a conversation with me. Nothing."

"That's just weird," Britt commented.

"It's immature," Eva finished. "For someone who loves to boast how much she hates me for no reason and takes her hatred of me out on my son, the least she can do is show herself to me. See me face to face."

"What are you going to do?" Jose asked.

"There's nothing we can do," Riley answered. "We keep doing this over and over again dumping money expecting solutions and nothing changes."

Eva looked down. "I'm going to keep fighting. I have to. This is my son."

JUSTIN CAME OUT FOR SUMMER vacation. It was the same pattern as the other vacations. He got off the plane and divulged more trauma courtesy of Lucy. They went on vacation as a family, and Doug sent hate messages accusing Eva of not letting him have enough access to Justin. Eva also spent time teaching Justin about meditation, crystals, and talked to him about being strong. It did not stop him from having a complete come apart when it was time to fly back to his father. "Mom, I just want to stay with you."

"Justin, I love you and I'm only a phone call away."

"I don't have a phone," Justin responded.

"Well, you ask your dad or Lucy and tell them you want to talk to me."

"When I ask for the phone, they tell me I shouldn't want to talk to you because you are a bad person."

Eva pursed her lips. She wanted to say, "Well, they are just assholes." But she refrained. "Well, we will have to work on that," she said instead.

After he left on the plane, she went to the store and purchased him his own phone and had it shipped to him.

Two days later she was FaceTiming with him when she had him open it. She walked him through setting up and charging it.

When she went to call him a few days later on, it went right to voicemail.

She tried again the next day, same thing.

She texted Doug's number to request to talk to Justin.

He called her back from Doug's number. "They took the phone away from me. They said I'm too young," he said.

When Eva got off the phone, she sent a message to Max. Doug had been playing games with the communication times and now he took away Justin's phone.

Yet another show cause was scheduled.

Eva and Riley appeared via phone for this hearing. The judge in his ruling to dismiss all motions stated, "Not my kid not my problem. You two need to figure it out."

After hanging up, Eva went outside and stuck her feet in the hot tub. "I can't keep doing this. The court does not care."

"They don't. Do we move back to Michigan?" Riley asked.

"I can't... Michigan is notoriously bad for teachers. I would be giving up my retirement and all. Regardless, if we move back to Michigan, it doesn't remove Justin from Lucy and Doug."

Riley sat down next to Eva and put her arm around her. "I'm sorry. I feel like this is all my fault."

"How is this your fault? You didn't do anything wrong."

"I started this relationship with you. I moved you out here. If it were not for me, Justin wouldn't be in this position."

"I wanted to leave Doug. It was inevitable. I hated living in Michigan. I was going to leave the state as well. All you did was expedite the process," Eva said.

"It's hard to not feel responsible for this," Riley confided.

"Well, stop. It's not on you. This is my mess." Eva stood up and went into the house. She made her way into Justin's bedroom and picked up his favorite plushie. She held it to her nose and sat down on his bed. She felt the entirety of the weight of her mistakes on her. Her chest felt like it was collapsing. She felt like she did the day she fell apart in her office.

She pulled herself together. She didn't like for Riley to see her in this state. She didn't like Riley feeling responsible for this mess.

Chapter 10

Forty-One

ON THE OUTSIDE LOOKING IN and looking at Eva's social media, one would be jealous of the life she and Riley lived. And Eva recognized she had a lot to be grateful for. They traveled to beautiful places, hiked, and were still very visibly very much in love. Justin being the only missing piece. *Maybe I'm not meant to have it all? Something will always be missing*, Eva rationalized.

Justin came out for Thanksgiving and then Christmas. He came with more stories of being terrorized by Lucy. Doug had sent the phone back with Justin. Eva just internalized all of the stories.

The court didn't care, and she was not going to pour more money into attorney fees for Judge Gleason to just look bored and say, "oh well". She had decided she would just focus on making the best of her times with Justin. She would be supportive and listen and talk to him about being strong and finding his own voice, and like a good English teacher – finding common ground with strong characters in the Harry Potter books. She would draw parallels between their stories and struggles and Justin's.

When Justin came back for summer, he came barreling off the plane. Eva took notice of his appearance as he ran to her. She noticed that he had been gaining some weight, normally a slight kid, small for his age, he looked heartier and thicker.

Eva took him to see a therapist. She knew if she had a hard time dealing with the information he spewed forth every time he got off the plane, he must be struggling, too.

Eva looked at the older gentleman sitting in a comfortable worn leather chair. His office was comfortable and masculine. Large wooden furniture, and dark rich colored paintings. Corner lamps and tissue in boxes on the end tables. Eva sat on a small sofa next to Justin. "What is the goal you have for Justin?" Dr. Arthur asked.

"I really want him to find his voice. To speak up for himself. To talk and confide in people other than me. I can't handle what he's telling me. I don't know what to do with it. With that being said, I'm going to get up and let you and Justin talk."

Forty-five minutes later, Justin came out of the office. His eyes were red. He had been crying.

"Are you okay, Beautiful Boy?"

"No. I told him everything Lucy does to me. How she punishes me if I don't eat enough food fast enough. How I don't like I'm getting fat. How she hits me. Pulls my ears. Calls me names. I let it all out."

She hugged him hard. "I'm so sorry you are dealing with this," she whispered into his ear.

"It's not your fault, Mom Mom." She wanted to tell him it was indeed her fault.

The next morning as she was sitting on the back patio having her coffee, her phone rang with a Michigan number in the identification.

"Hello?" she answered.

"Hi, is this Eva?"

"Yes. Who is this?"

"This is Amanda Jones, Genesee County CPS. I have a report here in front of me. When can Justin come in and speak with me?"

"He doesn't come back to Michigan until the end of August. Is there a way you can do a video call? And what is this about?"

"Tell me what you know about Lucy," Amanda demanded gently.

"I know that she is mentally, verbally, and physically abusive to my son. She terrorizes him."

"Explain to me what that means."

"Justin tells me that if he doesn't eat enough food fast enough, she pulls his ears and grounds him. If he doesn't do things the way she wants him to, she makes him write sentences, and if they are not to her liking, he has to keep writing. She has hit him upside the head and dropped him on his face when she thought he dropped her cat. She calls him stupid; she tells him he's not a good person." Eva choked up as she was recounting the things Justin had told her.

"That has to be hard for you to hear your son talk about as a mom. Do you believe that he's telling you the truth?"

"Why would he lie to me?" Eva asked.

"Kids lie sometimes for attention."

"I don't think my son is lying. He's been telling me these stories since he was five."

"Okay. I'm going to reach out to the CPS office near you. I am going to send one of their officers to take a look at Justin and talk to him."

"Sounds good."

The next morning, while Eva and Justin were having breakfast, two women knocked on the door.

Eva opened the door, still in her pajamas with her hair piled on top of her head. "Can I help you?"

"I'm Krista and this Theresa." They both showed their ID's. "We are here from North County CPS. We were contacted by Genesee County CPS regarding Justin. Can we come in?"

Eva stepped aside and made room for the women to enter the living room. "Amanda told me I would be hearing from you. I'm sorry. We are just having breakfast. Come on in."

"Do you mind if we talk to Justin alone?" Theresa asked.

"No. Go ahead. Would you like to sit outside or inside? Do you want anything to drink? Coffee? Water?"

"We are good. Thank you," Krista stated.

Eva led them into the kitchen. "Justin these ladies would like to talk to you alone. I'm going to go to my room. You can send him in after you are done to get me."

Eva sat down on the bed and texted Riley letting her know what was going on.

'I just hope he's honest with them,' Eva typed into the response.

'He will. You are teaching him to be strong and honest,' Riley replied.

Eva busied herself by scrolling on Twitter and Instagram while she waited.

It was just over an hour later when Justin knocked on her door. "They want to talk to you now," he said peeking his head into her room.

Eva stood up and went out to the kitchen. She looked at Justin, "Beautiful Boy, go take a shower and clean up your room, please."

"Yes, Mom Mom."

Eva sat at the kitchen table with the two women.

"Who is in charge of discipline in your home?" Theresa asked.

"Me."

"How do you discipline Justin?"

"He gets a time out and then I go and talk to him, and we try to rationalize what went wrong and how we can make better choices in the future."

"Are there any other children in this house?"

"No. He's the only one. Unless you count our dogs." Eva smiled.

The two women were less than humored. "What Justin is stating happens at his dad's home is very serious. Do you know what he is alleging?"

"His stepmother hits him, pulls his ears, force feeds him, calls him names. The courts don't seem to care."

"So, this is an active custody case?" Krista asked.

"Yes and no. I mean we seem to go back to court all the time. But whenever we go, no one cares about anything, and we spend a whole lot of money and time for nothing."

"Did you prompt Justin or tell him what to say?" Krista asked.

"No… absolutely not." Eva shook her head vehemently.

"Who lives in this house?" Theresa asked.

"My wife, myself, and occasionally Justin."

"What's your wife's name?" Krista asked.

"Riley. Same last name, Mares."

"And what do both of you do for a living?" Theresa asked.

"I'm an English teacher, and Riley owns a real estate brokerage."

"Do you mind showing us around the house?" Theresa asked.

Eva showed the women around the house. They checked the refrigerator and pantry and looked at all the rooms.

"Thank you for your time," Krista stated.

"No problem." Eva showed the women back to the door.

Justin came down the hall way and looked at Eva with a concerned look.

"Mom, they are going to be so mad at me," Justin blurted out with tears in his eyes.

"Who is going to be mad at you?"

"Dad and Lucy. I'm not supposed to talk about what happens there with anyone. They told me not to talk about it with you, or therapists or doctors."

Eva sat Justin down. "Justin, if something doesn't feel right, you absolutely need to talk about it. If you don't like the way someone makes you feel, you absolutely talk about it. Trust your heart and trust your instincts."

Justin put his head down and walked back to his room and shut the door.

A MONTH LATER, EVA HEARD back from Amanda. "I interviewed Doug and Lucy. If Justin was with them at the time we would have filed this case as a moderate risk and opened services on them. However, since he is with you, he is in a safe place and this case is closed with a safety plan in place."

"Amanda, Justin has to go back there in 3 weeks."

"Well, if it starts back up, he will have to make sure to speak up."

"Are you kidding me?"

"No. I'm sorry. We did all that we could do."

Eva hung up the phone and called Max.

"Can we please file for another change of domicile? I can't send him back."

"You know it probably won't go anywhere. But I will send a request for the CPS reports and do what I can."

"Will I have to send him back meanwhile?"

"Yes. You can't just keep him," Max retorted. Eva could tell he was frustrated with this case. She just hoped he wouldn't quit on her.

JUSTIN WOKE UP ON THE day he was supposed to fly back to Doug's and refused to get out of bed.

Eva stood at the foot of his bed and shook his toes. "Justin, we have to go. We are going to miss your flight."

"I don't care. I don't want to go back," Justin choked out.

Eva's heart cracked. "Honey, I don't want you to go back, but you have to. If you don't, I will go to jail."

"Lucy should be the one to go to jail," Justin cried.

Eva sat on the edge of Justin's bed. "I understand this is so hard, Beautiful Boy. But we have to do what is right. That includes you going back."

"She is going to hurt me again."

"No. No she won't. CPS knows now that she's hurtful. If she continues to hurt you, you need to talk to your teacher, or counselor, or therapist, or doctor."

"I can't talk to them when I'm there. If Dad and Lucy find out I will be in more trouble."

"Justin, I'm doing all I can. I swear. I'm trying. But unfortunately, this is one of those situations where you have to help me help you. You must be strong. You are part me, too. You need to dig deep and find that part of you that is part of me and stand up for yourself."

Justin sat up and leaned into his mother.

Eva was broken inside.

Riley drove, and Eva continued her pep talk to Justin the entire way to the airport.

At the gate, when it was time for Justin to board the plane, he clung to Eva. "I love you, Beautiful Boy. Be strong. Be so strong. Don't let ugly souled people break you down." She slipped her tourmalated quartz beaded bracelet off her wrist and put it in the palm of Justin's hand. "These beads are for protection. Hold them tight when you feel weak or scared."

Justin looked at her with tears in his eyes.

She kissed the top of his head. "I'm fighting hard, but you need to fight, too."

He walked silently onto the plane with the flight attendant. He stopped once and looked back at Eva. She choked up and blew him a kiss. "I got it in my heart," he called out and blew one back.

As she walked back out to the parking lot to find Riley waiting, Britt called her.

"I'm sending you some screenshots. I don't know. I know I've said it before, but I feel like I should tell you when I see these things. Maybe it can help you in court. It shows what a terrible person she is."

"What the fuck..." Eva exhaled as she got into the car.

Her text alert went off and she put the phone on speaker. Riley was looking over at her perplexed.

"It's Britt... Lucy posted some shit on Facebook, Britt thought we should know."

"Did you get it?" Britt asked through the speaker.

"I'm opening it now." Eva opened the file. Lucy's posting stated, 'Stupid bitch. You left your kid. I raise your kid. You tried to take me down, but all I do is win. I got your man, and I got your kid. I'm living the life you wish you were living and now you feel bad and try to go after me. Fuck you. I win all day long.' Eva read it out loud. "Is she serious? Like really? I left that man for a reason. Have fun with my sloppy seconds. But for real? What is her point?"

"I know... I know today is hard for you as it is. But I felt like I should share it," Britt stated.

"I appreciate you. I love you, always," Eva said.

"Thanks for looking out," Riley quipped.

"Always," Britt said.

Eva hung up and looked at Riley as they made their way back home.

"I'm so disgusted with this whole situation."

"We are doing all we can do," Riley offered.

"I know."

"I mean, we can try to move back to Michigan. Maybe only temporarily?"

"No. It's not an option. We've already discussed that. And it won't get Justin away from her. He will still have to deal with her. Maybe less often. But it won't stop her."

A few days later they sat on the speakerphone as the court was called to order. Max pleaded the case, and Judge Gleason, who Eva was glad she didn't need to see slouched on his hand on the bench, in his monotone apathetic voice stated, "I don't see a reason to change custody at this time. Where CPS put a safety plan in place, they did not see a reason to remove the child from the home. Sir, I will ask that you stop allowing your wife to discipline the child though." How many times would they order this? Eva felt the heat rising in her face.

After court was adjourned, Max called Eva. "What the fuck?" Eva asked.

"I'm sorry. You got stuck with a judge that never really wants to make an effort. You have to realize that these courts see kids with broken bones, cigarette burns... Yeah, Justin has a shitty stepmother but in the big scheme of things, it's not as bad as they see often times."

"It's still my son's childhood. Don't they get it? They can change his life for the better with a stroke of a pen and they choose to let him stay there and get beat down."

"Eva, I do feel your pain. I understand. We are all working as hard as we can for Justin."

~ 183 ~

"I know you are. I just don't understand the courts and their lack of competence." Eva hung up the phone and looked at Riley.

"I know, babe…" Riley looked heartbroken at Eva.

"I fucked my kid's life up because I was selfish," Eva lamented. "And I can't fix it."

Riley was quiet and looked downcast waiting a few breaths before saying, "You were not selfish. We talked about this before you even moved. Justin is getting older. The older he gets, the less likely he is to deal with this torment. He will find his voice."

Chapter 11

Forty-Two

LIFE KEPT ROLLING FORWARD AFTER the disappointment of court. Eva threw herself into work and her relationship with Riley and their dogs, and projects around the house. She did everything she could to keep her from feeling caught in her guilt and heartache for missing Justin.

She had everything she could ever ask for or want. Her students adored her at work. Her room was always swarming with students. She had developed a reputation on the campus as "one of the cool teachers," and students felt comfortable to confide in her and seek support and advice. A small faction of young gay girls hung out in her room during lunch seeking relationship advice or to just fill Eva in on the gossip going around school. Eva would offer motherly advice and show requisite sympathy when someone would bring their heartache to her. Many of the girls faced parents who either did not know their daughters were gay, or did not approve, so Eva became their mother hen. On the other side of the classroom hanging out and seeking her attention were her Mock Trial kids.

Being busy and being distracted was always her go to coping mechanism, but she understood she had to get deeper. She felt she needed to heal, or at least start to heal.

She found a new therapist to talk to, Zack.

She was sitting in his office looking at him, knowing that during this time she would have to come face to face with everything she has spent weeks, months and years avoiding.

She looked at the older gentleman. He was short, with thin graying strawberry blond hair, and a thick mustache. He wore wire framed glasses and dressed in khakis and a white button down. He looked kind, she thought.

She sat in his office and didn't say anything for a good 3 minutes.

"So, Eva... Why are you here?"

"I have everything. I literally do. I have a great career that I love. I have a wife who is amazing and loves me and takes excellent care of me. I am loved by my students. I am respected by most of my admin and coworkers. I have everything. Everything but my son."

"Explain to me why you don't have your son."

"I don't have him because I have everything else. I literally had to choose my happiness or my son. But I never thought in choosing my happiness that my son would be forsaken."

"And how is that, exactly?"

Eva did her best to summarize the last several years.

"So you believe that your son's pain and suffering are your fault exclusively?"

"I mean, if I never left, his dad would not be with that Lucy bitch."

"And where would you be?"

"Miserable," Eva answered. "But how do I mitigate what my son is dealing with?"

"I can't answer that for you. I can help you understand your decisions and make decisions, but I don't have the answers."

"I realize that," Eva said.

"What do you do when you are feeling regretful or sad about your situation?"

"I bury myself. I pick up extra duty at work, or Riley and I go on vacation. Or yoga. I love yoga."

"Do you pray or meditate? Do you ever find silence?"

"No. I fill my life with as much noise as I can. When I'm silent, I am forced to feel. I don't want to feel. I want to avoid the feeling."

"We are almost out of time for today. I challenge you in the next 2 weeks to find 3 days where you meditate for just 10 minutes. There's apps and audio books that have guided meditations."

Eva stood up to leave. She thanked Zack for his time and walked down the stairs. She wandered into the Starbucks and got a chai latte and sat out in the courtyard near the fountain. She felt the sun warm her face.

She tried to enjoy the silence and focus on her breathing like they teach in the yoga studio. Her mind went back to the first visit when Justin told her about Lucy hitting him. She pushed that thought aside and she tried to focus on the moment and counting her breaths. She took a sip of her latte. And tried again.

Her phone rang. She looked at the caller ID. It was Riley. "Hey, baby. Where are you?" she asked.

"I just finished my therapy appointment," Eva said. "I got a coffee. I'm on my way home."

"Meet me for dinner. I'm hungry," Riley said.

"Sure."

Eva met Riley at their favorite Mexican restaurant. They were seated outdoors on the patio. The sun was setting, and it was getting chilly. The waitress turned the outdoor heater and the firepit on. Eva pulled her hoodie on.

"We got invited to a party this weekend," Riley offered.

"Really? Whose?" Eva asked.

"Samantha's party. She has a medium coming," Riley informed her. Samantha was a client of Riley's, who like many of her other clients, had become a friend. She was wealthy, having inherited a sizable sum from her late father's estate, and lived off that interest. She was a hippie at heart and took style cues from Stevie Nicks. She was deeply spiritual, and Eva loved spending time with her as they would geek out on crystals and tarot cards together.

Eva rolled her eyes. "I grew up around all of that. So many of those people are charlatans."

"Apparently this lady is the next big deal. She's huge here. Let's just go. It will be fun."

Eva sipped her jalapeno margarita and agreed. "But seriously, we need a safe word if it's hokey and we want to go."

"Deal. If we say 'bison' we are so out of there!" Riley laughed.

Eva felt instantly better being in Riley's presence and her smile warmed away the angst she had been feeling earlier in the day. "Okay. Okay. You know I can't resist you when you smile like that." Eva gave in.

SAMANTHA'S LIVING ROOM WAS PACKED with four couples sitting on the large sectional. The medium was sitting in an overstuffed chair facing the couch. The fireplace was on, and music was playing softly in the background. Samantha had put out a charcuterie tray and other finger foods. Almost everyone had a glass of wine in their hand, including the medium.

Samantha got a large pillow and sat on the floor near Eva and Riley.

The medium, a short, voluptuous blonde woman, dressed in jeans and a button-down blouse cleared her throat. "I'm Kathy. I'm a medium. That means I can communicate with those on the other side. Communication can vary from symbols to actual words or just pointing. Sometimes I can hear, but mostly I see. I will try to be as specific as I can."

Eva took a deep breath in and a swig of her wine. Growing up, Geri and her Nana were always going to the psychics and metaphysical fairs. Eva had always been surrounded by crystals and tarot readers. She had learned to read cards when she was a teenager and still kept several decks. She had seen real deal readers and mediums, but mostly, her experiences were of the variety of people saying vague generalizations that made their audience feel better.

Kathy began talking to a woman on the other side of the sectional. Eva clued in for the typical generalizations, but instead, was surprised by the details Kathy was able to discuss. She described what turned out to be the woman's father. Kathy described him down to the wheel chair he was in before he died, describing how he stood up out of the chair to tell his daughter he's better now.

Eva's heart raced as she watched the woman dab tears from her eyes.

She watched and listened as Kathy picked person after person with messages from their loved ones. Kathy kept looking over at Eva out of the corner of her eye. At one point, she looked over and nodded her head. Eva did not understand the gesture.

After almost everyone had gotten a message from a loved one, Kathy looked at Eva. "I've been waiting all night for you," she said.

Eva sat back. "Me?" She pointed at herself.

"Yes. There's a woman, she has olive skin, dark hair, short, she's very curvy, and loud. She is standing with her hand on her hip, and she said, 'Lady, I'm her Nana, and I have to talk to this one, but it's going to take a while.' She also tried to hurry everyone else along so she could talk to you."

Eva's eyes burst with tears. "Oh. My. God."

"She said that she's sorry. She said you tried to tell her, but she didn't accept it because she didn't want you to have a hard life. She was wrong and she's sorry. She says she is worried about you, and she is with you almost every day. She said to look for signs that she's there. Dreams. Butterflies? She's now standing behind you." Kathy pointed to Riley. "She has her hands on your shoulders. She says she loves you and you are 'our people'. She says she appreciates how you take care of her granddaughter. But she's concerned with how sad you are because of your ..." Kathy paused and squinted. "Your child, I think. She's nodding at me. Your child. She wants you to know that babies choose their moms. Your child chose you. You are its mom. Your child loves you and will be with you. Be patient. She is yelling at me, 'Tell her the truth will come out.'"

Riley looked at Eva wide-eyed. "Holy shit," she whispered.

Eva blew her nose and sobbed. She needed the release, and she needed the verification from something beyond herself that everything would be okay.

She got up and hugged Kathy. "Thank you for that," she whispered.

On the way home, Riley looked at Eva, "Everything is going to be okay. Nana said so."

Eva smiled. "Yes. It will be…"

The peace she gained from that reading lasted her for months. Eva threw herself back into her spirituality. She bought more crystals and began reading more. She made time to meditate and stuck around the yoga studio she had been attending for their meditations and kirtans.

She started keeping a dream journal chronicling several visits from Nana. She also noticed the various random times she would see butterflies. She would smile, feel warmed and thank Nana for being there for her.

During Christmas break, while Eva was looking up one of her dreams and putting it down in her dream journal, Justin sat down next to her and asked her what she was doing. She showed him the dream dictionary and her journal. "Do you remember Nana?" she asked him.

"I do," he said looking at her.

"Sometimes, after our loved ones pass away, they come and visit us, and guide us and check on us. One of the ways they do that is to come in our dreams."

"Is that the same thing as a ghost haunting?" Justin asked.

"No. It's just a way that they let us know they are still there for us looking out and helping us," Eva explained.

She wasn't sure if Justin got it or if it went over his head. He got up and poured himself a bowl of cereal and never mentioned it again.

He probably thinks I'm loopy just like I thought Geri was loopy, she thought and went back to translating her dream.

On Christmas Eve, it had become their tradition to go drive around the various neighborhoods and admire the Christmas lights, while listening to holiday music and sipping hot cocoa they would pick up at Starbucks. Before they would leave, Eva would always 'forget' her phone and rush back into the house. She would grab gift bags that were made out to the three of them and set them next to the fireplace, early presents from Santa, containing matching pajamas for all three of them to wear that night, and a book for each of them and a special ornament for Justin to hang.

After driving around the neighborhood, they came back in and Justin, who normally would rush to the fireplace, meandered over to his room. Eva cocked her head and made her way to the fireplace and called him back out. "Hey… Looks like there's some gifts…"

Riley sat down on the couch and Eva handed her the bag addressed to her.

Justin came back out. "It's okay, Mom Mom… Lucy and Dad told me already. There is no Santa and it's a big lie."

"Is it a lie?" Eva asked sitting down, disappointed.

"I think it's a game parents play with kids," Justin said quietly.

"Is it fun?" Eva asked.

Justin shrugged. "Yeah. I guess so."

"As long as you believe you shall receive," Riley said. "The holidays are a time for magic and love. You can believe, receive your gifts, and enjoy it, or you can be a sour puss and not see the magic in the season."

"I will believe. I will enjoy it," Justin said sitting next to Riley. Eva handed him his bag and they all sat down to open their pajamas and books. They giggled at the silly pajamas selected (this year it was giraffe print pajama pants) and Justin hung his ornament on the tree.

After he went off to bed, she looked at Riley, "I realize he's getting older, and he is probably ready to know there is no Santa, but who kills a kid's joy like that?"

Riley looked at her and shrugged. "We will always keep the holidays a magic time for him. If he wants to act like them and be a sour puss, that's on him. We keep our traditions. They are for all of us."

Eva smiled at her wife, grateful for her continued sense of logic and patience.

Her sense of peace continued through the new year and on to her visit to Michigan in February. Even though she hated going in February, she refused to miss any time with Justin.

That peace was shattered when after returning from visiting Michigan for midwinter break and spending time with her friends and family and Justin, she suddenly stopped being allowed to talk to Justin.

Drew sent her a screenshot of Lucy's social media posts. There were several ramping up from the summer vacation one that Britt had sent her. The posts were calling her a deadbeat mom, calling her a bitch, and a psycho. Post after post detailing how Eva lost and deserved to lose and how vindicated she and Doug were in each win.

"Nine days and counting since I've been able to talk to Justin," Eva said to Riley.

"This is ridiculous," Riley lamented. She grabbed her phone and made a phone call. "I hope you actually listen to this, you spineless puss of man. I know you are bitter and angry. Eva left you for me, it's been years, man. Aren't you tired of the games? Let your kid talk to his mother." She hung up.

Eva looked at Riley scared. "You just opened a whole can of worms."

"I don't give a shit. I'm done giving a shit. How many years is this going to continue? We've been dealing with this since Justin was 5 years old. We have several more years of this to go. I'm tired of seeing you hurt. I'm tired of seeing you sad. I love you. I love you with all that I have. I love Justin. He's my world, too. But I hate seeing you so broken all the time. I blame myself for this. It hurts me, too."

Eva stood up. "It's not about you."

"It is about all of us. Don't you see that? It's not just about you. It's not just about Justin. It's about us as a family."

Eva rolled her eyes. "Stop. I can't deal with it. I just can't." She left the room and went into the bedroom. She grabbed her car key from the top of her dresser and went to walk out. Riley was standing in the doorway. "Move."

"No. You need to stop. You can't just shut down and go dark on me every time you are upset. I have feelings, too. I'm in this with you, I've been in this with you."

"You don't understand."

"Oh, I don't? What I do understand is you shutting me down and shutting me out every single time your friends notify you with a post from Lucy. Every time you get served. Every time Doug withholds Justin from you. Every time Justin comes here and shares some other story about his mistreatment. You literally turn into the ice queen. You get so quiet it's like sitting next to a corpse. You don't look at me, you don't talk to me. You just disappear."

"Maybe I do need to disappear for a few days."

"Yeah. That's the answer. Run away. Fill your time and avoid dealing with whatever's bothering you."

"I don't run away."

"You do. You stopped going to therapy after one session. You left Doug and ran right to me. You left Michigan. You keep yourself busy so you don't have to deal with what is really bothering you."

"Fuck you," Eva said pushing past Riley and storming out to her car.

She got in and took off. She didn't know where she was going. She didn't have anywhere to go.

She drove west toward the coastline.

The silence in the car was deafening. She turned on Lana Del Rey and turned up the volume. Lana's voice crooned through the speakers.

Eva gripped the steering wheel harder. She accelerated faster down the divided road. She saw a large truck barreling in the opposite direction. *How easy it would be to jerk the wheel and go head on. Just be done with all of this*, she thought. *I'm tired of feeling like I'm fucking crazy...* Her eyes glazed with tears, and she held her breath.

She didn't do it. She was not fazed by the thought though.

She made it all the way to Tamarack State Beach in Carlsbad.

She got out and kicked her shoes off and sat down in the sand. Her phone kept alerting her that she was getting text messages.

She didn't care.

It was getting cold, and she didn't have her hoodie or a sweater. She didn't care.

She just sat there, cold and numb.

It was starting to get dark. The lifeguard came and told her it was time to go. She got up and brushed herself off and went back into her car.

She looked at the clock on the dash. She had been there for over 2 hours. She was hungry. But she didn't care.

As she was making her way back down the road, listening to Godsmack now, her phone rang. It was Riley. She answered. "Hello."

"Where are you?" Riley asked.

"The beach."

"You sound like you're driving now."

"I am. They kicked me out of the beach."

"Where are you going now?"

"I don't know."

"Come home."

"I'm not ready."

"I didn't do anything wrong."

"I know you didn't."

"You didn't do anything wrong, either."

"I know."

"Then come home."

"Okay."

Eva drove home. Riley was sitting in the living room watching CNN when she entered the house. She turned the television off and looked at Eva. "Babe, you need to figure out what you want to do."

"As far as?"

"These next several years. Justin will most likely start talking and standing up for himself. Or we can hope anyways. But you can't keep on like this. I can't keep on watching you like this. You beat yourself up over this. You internalize it. It tears me apart to see someone I love deconstructing in front of me every day. I feel like I'm losing you bit by bit."

Eva wanted to stay shut down, but with looking at Riley as she plead with her, she couldn't.

"I hate this so much. I complicated your life. I complicated my son's life and because of my own impetuousness, I fucked my own life up. I can't help but wonder how much better life would be if I were not in it, for all of you."

"Do you need to be 5150'd?" Riley asked cautiously.

"No. No. I just … I'm not in a good place right now. I think I just want to not talk about it. Not with you. Not with anyone."

"Please, baby. Just don't do something like that."

"I'm not. I couldn't."

Riley stood up and put her arms around Eva. "I love you. We will get through this."

Eva wiped her tears and composed herself and let herself fall into Riley's embrace.

DOUG PLAYED GAME AFTER GAME with communication times. Some days only allowing Justin to call while Eva was at work, or making Eva wait anywhere from 7 days to 2 weeks without talking to him.

Justin finally came for his spring break. "I missed you so much, Mom Mom," Justin said as he got off the plane.

"I know. I feel like I hardly got to talk to you after I left in February."

"Dad and Lucy won't let me use the phone. I got grounded from the phone a lot, too."

"Well, you are here now, Beautiful Boy. Let's not focus on them."

Eva took Justin and Riley to Universal Studios toward the end of his visit.

As they were walking around The Wizarding World, Eva stopped to buy them all butter beers. She took Justin to a shaded spot and sat on a bench with him while Riley wandered off to a gift shop.

"Justin, why do we love Harry Potter so much?"

"Because it's a good story and magic is fun."

"Yes, but what is so special about Harry as a character? Or Snape?"

"They stood up for what they believed in. They were good."

"I need you to be like Harry, Justin. I need you to stand up for what you believe in. If you want to talk to me, you need to let your voice be heard."

"Mom, I don't like to even ask anymore because when I do, they just say horrible things about you, and I can't stand it."

"Well, I don't care what they say about me. You shouldn't either, because you know in your heart what is true and what is not."

"I get in trouble; I get yelled at just for wanting to talk to you," Justin informed her, his voice quiet.

"I understand, Beautiful Boy. I do. They are scary. But be like Harry. She is like Umbridge or Voldemort. You are stronger than she is because you have love in your heart."

Justin just looked off into the distance. "I don't want to talk about this while we are here," he said.

Eva gave an exhale. "You are so my child."

"What does that mean?"

"I don't like to talk about difficult things either. I like to avoid them. It is so bad for us though."

"Can we talk about it when we are back at the hotel or home?" Justin asked.

They enjoyed the park and enjoyed each other. Heading back home the next morning, after breakfast, Eva broached the subject again.

"Justin, you need to be strong when you go back, understand?"

"Mom, you don't understand. I am grounded all the time. Lucy finds reasons to ground me for everything. If I don't eat, I'm grounded. If I don't eat enough, I'm grounded. If I say anything I'm grounded. She yells non-stop. She throws shoes at the cat. She's terrifying."

"Justin," Riley began. "Have you ever heard about the buffalo?"

"Like the big animals that roam in the meadows?"

"Yes... those. But there's a whole story," Riley explained. "So, when it rains, or it's getting ready to rain and storm and the buffalo and the cows are all out in the pastures and fields, the cows run away from the storm. Running away, actually makes them stuck in it longer because it follows them. Buffalo will actually go into the storm head first, facing it, that way they push through it faster and they are out of it quicker."

"Do you understand why that story is important to you?" Eva asked him.

"Lucy is the storm," Justin answered. "I can be a cow or a buffalo."

"Exactly," Riley said.

"Be the buffalo," Eva said.

Justin didn't respond. He just looked out the window of the backseat as they drove back south.

Eva worked with Justin on meditation, and focusing energy, and crystals and what they mean, for his last 2 days. Justin had a lot of curiosity in the different stones, picking them up and touching them and asking about their qualities and what their intentions were, picking through the large bowl Eva kept her stones in on her bedside table while sitting in at the table in the yard.

"Do you still have my bracelet?" Eva asked him.

"I keep it in my pocket during the day, under my pillow at night, and when I'm scared it will get found I put it in my sock drawer." He reached in his pocket and pulled it out.

Eva curled his fingers back around it and held his hand. She pulled him in and hugged him close. She saw a butterfly flit past them, and closed her eyes silently thanking her Nana for being there.

He put the bracelet back in his pocket and looked at the display of crystals and stones Eva had shown him. He picked up a piece of onyx and held it in his fist. "Can I have this one, too?"

"Of course you can."

WHEN JUSTIN WENT BACK AFTER spring break, Doug continued with his games with communication. Eva went another 10 days without talking to Justin.

Doug had learned that no matter what, the court didn't care about its orders and he could play whatever games he wanted with no penalty. He had such little control over all else in his life, that controlling his son and making Eva's life as miserable as possible were all he had for joy.

Eva went back to see Zack for therapy again.

She sat in his office and looked at him. "I don't even know what to talk about or say. Nothing has changed. I still feel guilt and anger. I fucking hate my ex. I hate his bitch wife. I feel hopeless and helpless. I feel guilty for even thinking that, because I have everything else. Maybe I'm not supposed to have Justin. I mean, I really didn't want kids to begin with. Maybe it's karma for how I began my relationship with Riley. I don't know."

"Do you feel like you are putting too much pressure on yourself for this perfect life?"

"I mean, maybe. I can be. I don't know. I just feel like this heaviness, all the time."

"What kind of heaviness?"

"Like a weight inside my chest. My heart hurts constantly. Not like chest pains like I'm having a heart attack. It just feels like a weight. I feel sad. I feel like I'm missing a part of me. Which is weird, because like I said, I didn't want kids in the first place. It's like having Justin was the one thing that Doug got me to do, that I didn't even know I needed until I saw him for the first time. It makes zero sense, I know. And to boot, now I've fucked up this little person for life because I had to have this perfect relationship and be happy. I mean, I see all these posts where they say that moms are supposed to live for their kids first. I chose me over my son. That's messed up, right?"

"To be a good mom, you need to be all of yourself. Your authentic self, and you need to be healthy and happy. That is a huge misnomer that moms need to sacrifice their happiness or self-satisfaction for their children," Zack offered. "When you subtract that guilt out of your life, how do you feel?"

"I feel so happy. I'm so in love with my wife. She is amazing in every way. But that happiness is constantly fucked with by my ex or by his wife. When my son tells me what he's dealing with it hurts me. And then the guilt creeps in."

"Can you control what happens to your son when he is not with you, when he is with his father?"

"No." Eva shook her head.

"Even if you lived next door, would you be able to control or mitigate what happens in his father's home?"

Eva shook her head again.

"Our time is up for today. I want you to start keeping a journal. Log what you feel each day and what is creating those feelings."

"Great. Will do." Eva stood up. "Thank you," she said as she walked out.

EVA AND RILEY FLEW TO Michigan for a long weekend for Mother's Day, since Eva was awarded that time with Justin through the court.

They spent the weekend with Justin in a rented cabin near Lake Huron, near Jack's side of the family. Jack was also staying in the cabin with them.

Eva and Jack were sitting on the back porch, overlooking the lake in the late afternoon. Riley was inside preparing dinner, and Justin was down by the water wading in the shallows looking at rocks and wildlife. Eva watched as a brightly colored butterfly flitted around the table. *Happy Mother's Day, Nana,* she thought.

"How are you?" Jack asked.

"I'm good. Mostly."

"What does 'mostly' mean?" Jack inquired.

"I just hate that Justin doesn't get to see you. Or you see him. He's being robbed of that. You both are. I hate that I've made a mess of things."

"I made a mess of things with your mom, too. You turned out okay."

Eva snorted. "Yeah. I'm totally great. And you and mom at least pretended to get along. Or do get along. I'm not sure which."

"Your mom is a different type of person. She marches to the beat of her own drum. I didn't agree with the way she raised you, for sure. She was definitely too permissive, more of a girlfriend or sister than a mom. But she had your Nana. Nana balanced that out a bit. I wish I had more time and influence with your younger years. But you did turn out okay. You're smart and have a good career and a great wife and you are doing the best you can as a mom, which is all any parent can do. Do I wish things were different? Yeah, but like I've always told you... You can shit in one hand and wish in the other. See which one fills up first."

Eva smiled. "Thank you, Dad."

Between her sessions with Zack and this talk with her dad, she knew she should feel better. But, deep down, the band aids of words were doing little to stop the bleeding.

Sunday morning, as they were eating breakfast on the patio of the cabin, Drew shared a screenshot with Eva. It was another post from Lucy. 'Have fun on your pretend Mother's Day, fake ass bitch, sad excuse for a mom. Your "son" knows who his mom really is. You just gave birth to him. I'm the one who is his real mom, and he knows that.'

Eva put the phone down on the table and pushed it across to Riley.

Riley picked it up and read it.

"What's going on?" Jack asked.

"Dad, why don't you take Justin down by the lake. He was showing me some neat things last night. You might want to see them."

Justin and Jack got up and went down by the water.

Riley looked at Eva, "Don't let this ruin today."

"It's hard not to."

"She's threatened by your relationship with Justin. That boy adores you. He hangs on every word you say. He follows you around all day long. He hates her. She's a miserable, ugly person."

"I know. I know," Eva said.

"Let's just pretend we never saw this today and we go on about the rest of today. Your mom is coming up for lunch. Let's have a good time."

Eva grabbed her phone back. She typed to Drew, 'I understand why you sent that to me, but please not today.'

'I'm sorry,' he typed back with a broken heart emoji.

'I'm good,' Eva typed back.

Jack stayed for lunch to see Geri. They had a fun afternoon sitting outside and listening to music and eating. The entire time, Eva felt like she was faking it. Her heart felt heavy, and she did her best to enjoy the time.

Geri and Jack each left, and Eva packed Justin's things.

"Can't I just stay one more night? You can take me to school in the morning."

"I wish I could, but your dad will not allow it."

"Did you even ask?"

"I don't need to. I've asked in the past and your dad said no, he only wants to stick to the court orders without any extras."

Justin plopped on the couch and folded his arms across his chest.

"If you want more, you need to speak up," Eva told him.

"Be the buffalo," Riley reminded him.

His eyes welled with tears. "I can't," he said.

"You can." Eva's throat was tight.

"I just don't feel welcome in that house. I don't feel loved. I feel like I just am, when I'm there. When I'm with you, I feel like I belong," Justin said.

"I know, Beautiful Boy. But everyone has lessons they need to learn in life. This is just one of your lessons. You must learn to stand up for yourself. Tell your dad and Lucy what you want."

"I did tell them," Justin said. "And they told me you were just brainwashing me."

"Well, keep telling them," Riley insisted.

"We need to go," Eva said looking at the clock on her phone.

Justin was quiet the entire drive back to his dad's home. They stopped for dinner, and he hardly ate.

Eva picked at her food, too, watching Justin.

"Hey, it's just a few weeks before you are back in California for the summer!" Eva tried to be cheerful.

"I know," Justin said quietly. "It's just really hard to go back there after spending time with you. I am going to have to hear about what a terrible person you are. I'm not allowed to love you or talk about the fun time we had together, none of it. It's like it's a dirty little secret."

"Like you have to keep our love and our time in a locked closet," Eva said quietly. "I understand it's not an easy way to live. But just know, Beautiful Boy... This too shall pass. One day you will be grown and old enough to do what you want, see who you want, talk to who you want and love who you want."

Justin grabbed Eva's left forearm and turned it over and traced the tattoo with his finger. "That's what Nana always said to you."

"Yes. And it's true. Everything ends in time."

They left the restaurant and Justin remained quiet in the backseat. Riley grabbed Eva's hand in the front seat.

They pulled into Doug's driveway and Eva got out and pulled Justin's bag out of the backseat.

She handed him his backpack and they hugged hard. "I love you so much. I love you to the end of the universe and back and everything in between," Eva whispered to him.

"I love you more," Justin said.

"Don't you let them break you down. Stay strong and be the buffalo," she whispered.

Doug opened the front door and glared down at Eva.

Eva looked up at him and stared him down.

"I need to talk to you," Eva called out to him. "Alone."

"You can talk to my lawyer," Doug called back.

Eva shook her head. "Weak," she called out as Justin clung to her.

"Come on, Buddy," Doug called to Justin.

Justin looked up at Eva. "It's all good. Just know I love you."

Justin reluctantly made his way up the walkway and into the house. Doug slammed the door behind him.

"What a fucking pussy," Eva said as she got in the car.

Riley got out of the car and stormed up the walkway to the door. Eva got back out and stood near the car.

Riley pounded on the door. "Doug and Lucy. Get out here and talk like adults," she pounded.

No one answered.

"Oh, real brave of you, keyboard warrior talking shit about my wife online, but can't face either one of us! Nice!" Riley yelled out. "I know you can hear me!" She pounded a few more times, kicked the door and turned and left.

They headed back to the cabin in silence. Not even the radio was on.

"I'm so fucking sick of them," Riley broke the silence after a half an hour in the silent car.

"You and me both," Eva said quietly.

"I could see the sadness in your eyes all day."

"I tried to hide it."

"I know you did, baby. But it was there."

THE MONTH BETWEEN MOTHER'S DAY and summer vacation, Eva went back to her old ways. Keeping herself so busy she had no time to think about her sadness.

Every morning she woke up extra early to do yoga or run, rush through a shower and make it to work just in time for the first bell, stay late to grade, plan, advise Mock Trial, come home, clean, make dinner, go to bed. Weekends she would wake up, help Riley work in the yard, grocery shop, go out to dinners or they would take off for a weekend trip somewhere.

Doug continued to play games with Justin's ability to contact Eva. She didn't acknowledge it. She only did her daily routine. She stopped going to therapy again. Therapy made her think about things.

Wednesday nights she and Riley would FaceTime with Britt and Harry for "happy hour."

One Wednesday night, a week before Justin was due to come back, Britt came on the screen. "Lucy is posting again. She's saying you are not paying your child support and that you owe them for a new front door."

Eva rolled her eyes. "I'm paying my child support. And their piece of shit door was dented before Riley kicked it."

"How long are they going to keep this up?" Harry asked.

"I don't even know. It's so stupid," Eva commented.

Riley poured two glasses of wine and sat in front of the screen next to Eva. "This has been a long, few years. It's going to be a long few more," she said.

"Can we just not talk about it?" Eva asked.

Britt cocked her head to the side. She had watched Eva go through her avoidance phases for several years. "Are you sure?"

"Yeah. I'm sure. I just wish everyone would stop telling me what that stupid bitch posts."

Britt sat back. "I'm sorry," she said. "I don't tell you because I'm trying to make things worse. I really thought they would help with character in court." Eva felt bad. She knew that of all the people in the world, Britt was not the person who would intentionally make her feel bad. If Britt shared anything with her, it truly came from a place to help.

"I'm not mad at you. I'm mad at the situation. I just have a difficult time keeping myself together as it is, and the extra noise is just too much sometimes." Eva sipped her wine and looked at Riley plaintively. "I appreciate you and all of the information. I thought it would help, too. But honestly, it doesn't. The court doesn't care what kind of person she is. They only care that I left Michigan."

"So, let's talk about summer plans!" Riley changed the subject.

Chapter 12

Forty-Three and Forty-Four

FOR ONE WHOLE YEAR, EVA was lulled into a sense of security. After Mother's Day came summer, which was riddled with Doug sending Eva messages telling her what she should do and how to run her time with Justin. Eva ignored them. She felt that was the best way to deal with Doug, and mostly, it worked.

She just ignored him and ignored it when her friends sent her posts about Lucy. She just worked, found joy in her chaotic schedule in the day time and peace at night in Riley's embrace.

Summer, Thanksgiving, Christmas, Mid-Winter Break, Spring Break, Mother's Day... All sailed by with very little drama. Justin still lamented his hatred for Lucy, and how he didn't like living at his dad's. Justin was given a phone he could use at his father's house, and use was heavily monitored and restricted. Eva and Riley just told him he needed to start talking and speaking up for himself.

Summer vacation rolled around, and Justin came running off the plane into Eva's arms. As they were driving back from the airport to home, he said, "Lucy said she's going to sue you. She said you lied about her in court, and you dented their door last year. She said she looked it up and talked to a lawyer."

"Let her sue me. She has no grounds," Eva said as she navigated the heavy traffic.

"I just don't want to have bad things happen to you," Justin said.

"Don't worry about me, Beautiful Boy. This situation is not your fault, and you shouldn't stress about it."

"I think I am starting to hate her," Justin said. "And I don't like that I'm stuck with her."

"You are only stuck with her until the courts either let you be heard (and they listen), or you graduate high school, or your dad divorces her."

"Dad's never going to divorce her, he said he will never get divorced again. When can I talk to the courts? I would like to do that as soon as possible. I don't want to wait to graduate to be rid of her."

"I will talk to Max and see what we can do," Eva sighed.

"You know she's still hitting me and calling me names?" Justin stated.

"I did not know that."

"She hit me upside the head because I knocked the vacuum cleaner over because she left it in the hallway, and it scratched the wall."

"Is that the only time she hit you?"

"No. She hit me a few other times as well."

"Did you tell anyone at school or anything?"

"No. I'm scared I will get in more trouble because CPS will come back."

"What's the worst they can do to you?"

"Punish me more."

"If CPS is involved, not likely."

"Mom, please... Don't pressure me."

"Done," Eva said.

Five days into summer vacation, Max called Eva. "Doug and his attorney have filed a motion to terminate all of your parental rights including visitation, stating you are not stable. They filed an emergency motion to have Justin sent back."

"What do we do?" Eva asked, her knees weak beneath her, as she sank onto the couch.

"Of course we fight it."

"When is this being heard?"

"The soonest the court could hear this was 2 weeks from today."

"What grounds are they saying I'm unstable?"

"This is just a bullshit motion, they don't have anything other than your history of depression and the forensic psychologist stating you have narcissistic tendencies. This is just to rattle your cage. They had nothing else. You know his lawyer is a shyster who likes his billable hours. This will go nowhere. It's just to fuck with your time. This will be tossed within a matter of minutes."

"What's the likelihood that this isn't tossed, and it goes through?"

"Like 5-10%. Tops. I'm emailing you the motion."

"Okay… Can we file a counter motion? Justin says he wants to talk to the court so he can stay here."

"Of course we can. But be prepared… His opinion counts very little."

"I know. But it's worth a shot."

"Of course. It always is."

Eva hung up and went into Justin's room where he was laying on his bed playing a video game on his phone. Eva stood in the doorway and just looked at him for a moment before speaking. She looked at how tall he had grown. The sunlight was filtering through the blinds of the plantation shutters and his ceiling fan spun lazily. His room was still decorated in the steampunk aesthetic he favored when he was young. Eva had asked him each year if he wanted to redecorate, and he declined.

Eva finally broke her silence and spoke, leaning on the door frame. "Hey… I just want you to know… There was a motion filed in court. They are asking that you come back from summer early and that you don't get to come here anymore. It most likely won't get past anyone. But in the small chance it goes through… I want you to know what the real deal is. I never not want to be around you. I never agreed to that. And I'm sorry that things are this way."

Justin put his phone down. "I will just run away then. I will find a way to be with you. I'm not going to never see you again."

"I wish it were that easy. And I wish this wasn't happening."

"It's Lucy. She tells Dad what to do. She bosses everyone around in the house. Me, Dad, even the cat. She's always unhappy and yelling. We all just do what she wants to keep her quiet. She says every time I come to see you I come back worse than when I left. She says you ruin me, and I shouldn't be around you."

"Well, I'm not going to repeat out loud my thoughts. I just want you to know how much I love you, and that it's a very small chance that you will have to go back earlier than we planned."

"I'm not going to go back early. I don't even want to go back at all."

"I understand. It's also too pretty out. Why don't you text one of your friends so you can go do something outside. Go swim or something. Your skin is Michigan pasty. You need your California tan."

"Okay…" Justin picked his phone back up and scrolled through his contacts.

Eva went and sat in the office and opened her email. She read through the motion that Doug had filed. She focused on the words 'narcissistic personality, depressive states', and how they used the words from her statement to the forensic psychologist and his assessment of her against her.

"Mom, I'm going to Trevor's!" Justin called from his room.

"Okay. Wear your sunscreen. Take a towel," she called back. "Be back around 6 for dinner."

"Love you, Mom Mom." Justin came to the office door.

Eva stood up and went to him and gave him a hug. "I love you. Go have fun."

She watched him walk out and called Riley. "I just forwarded you the motion that Doug and his dick attorney just filed. They want Justin back early and say I'm unstable."

"For fuck's sake," Riley said. "Let me read it and we will talk about it when I get home. Are you okay? Did you talk to Max?"

"Yeah. Max said they are doing it just to fuck with me and not to take it seriously."

"Your pocket book is going to take it seriously paying for the legal bills."

"I know."

"Alright, babe. I gotta go. I will read this, and we will talk later."

"Okay. Love you." Eva hung up and went to the living room. Her and Riley's big, flashy brindle boxer dog Guinness, who replaced the recently deceased Milo and Frank whose old ages finally caught up with them, jumped up on the couch with her. They had gotten him after Milo and Frank both passed within weeks of each other. She rubbed Guinness's large head and he laid his head in her lap. She grabbed the book she had begun reading off the coffee table and opened it trying to read. She couldn't focus on the words though.

She turned the television on and flipped the channels. She couldn't focus on anything being said and turned it back off.

She put on her workout clothes, loaded the work out app on her television and selected a yoga class.

She did her best to make it through the 45 minutes of class. The yoga instructor was one that she typically enjoyed because she incorporated meditations into the class, but today, the constant talk of intentions, and heart opening made her unbearably irritated. Opening her heart to make herself more physically receptive to emotions was the last thing she wanted or needed.

When it was over, she took a shower and sat on the shower bench under the running water.

Narcissist. Depressive Mood. Bad influence. Negative. Selfish. The words kept playing in her head.

Riley came home and saw Eva sitting in the shower.

"You are hyper focused on it right now, aren't you?" she asked.

Eva looked at Riley through the glass. "How can I not be?"

Riley removed her suit jacket and hung it back in the closet and removed the rest of her clothes so she could get in with Eva. She opened the door and grabbed Eva's hand and pulled her to stand. She held Eva under the water. "You can't let them get to you. Letting them get to you is letting them win."

"I know. In all reality, I know these things. But I can't seem to believe them. Everyone tells me I'm not a bad person. They tell me all the right things. But I just don't believe them. It's so much easier to believe the bad things than the good, I guess."

"Hey, I'm a good judge of character. I wouldn't be with you. I wouldn't stay with you if any of that trash was true." Riley kissed Eva on the forehead and on the lips. "I love you. Stop listening to the noise and listen to me. I love you and Justin loves you. That's all that matters."

Eva kissed her back. "I'm sorry. I've complicated your life. It's not fair to you. You don't deserve that."

"You are not the cause of the complications. Your dumb ass ex is the problem. It will all end."

Eva did her best to take solace in the words that Riley spoke, but struggled to remove the echo in her head of the words on print in the reports and in the courts.

On the day of court, Eva and Riley were prepared to be heard via phone. They were dressed and caffeinated and ready at six in the morning Pacific standard time. They waited and waited for the court to call and patch them in. Eva was texting Max the entire time. Doug and his attorney didn't even bother showing up. The case was tossed out.

Max filed a motion to have Justin speak to the courts while he was there. The courts would hear them shortly after Justin would go back.

Eva and Riley made their way to the kitchen and Eva cut oranges in half and pressed them through the juicer to make orange juice. She found the process strangely cathartic imagining each orange half as Doug's smug face. They were both quiet as they made their way around the kitchen. The sun was slowly peeking in and dancing off the pool. Riley opened the patio slider and let the breeze in.

"Even Doug doesn't believe his own bullshit," Riley said as she made her way back to the kitchen island grabbing the juice Eva squeezed to make mimosas for the two of them. Eva moved on to cracking and whisking eggs to make scrambled eggs.

Justin came into the kitchen shuffling and sleepy. "Do I have to go back?" he asked rubbing his eyes.

"No, Beautiful Boy. You get to stay," Eva said as she turned the heat off the stove.

"Forever?" Justin asked.

"No, until the end of August." Eva portioned the eggs onto plates.

"Do I get to talk to the court?"

"I filed the motion. I get to ask them in September."

"Okay." Justin sat on a stool at the kitchen island and poured himself a glass of orange juice. As he poured it, he accidentally dropped the orange juice carafe and his glass tumbled to the floor and broke.

"Woah!" Riley cried out jumping off her stool to mitigate the mess.

Justin blocked his head with hands and ducked down. "I'm sorry! I'm sorry!" he cried out.

"Justin, what is wrong?" Riley asked as she picked up shards of glass with the paper towels Eva handed her.

"Lucy would have hit me."

"Lucy isn't here. She can't hurt you here. It's an accident. Accidents happen," Eva told him.

"I know. Lucy says I have too many accidents. She says I do them on purpose," Justin informed them.

"No, Justin. Accidents happen. You are just clumsy. Some people are. And some people are clumsy around certain ages. That's just where you are right now," Riley offered. She stood up and put the paper towel and glass shards on the counter and hugged Justin.

Eva's heart broke to see her son react as he did over a broken glass. She wondered if she could fly to Michigan and meet Lucy in a darkened alley somewhere.

A WEEK LATER DOUG WAS served with the papers to request Justin speak to the court. Eva became aware because Britt saw another post of Lucy's online. This one hit her the hardest. 'You think you are such a great mom? You are nothing. Your kid doesn't even want to go see you. He begs to stay home. You chose to leave. You left him and his dad because you are a gold-digging fake dyke. You chose to leave for money instead of staying with your child. You are now forcing your child to make a decision to leave his family for your fake life. You should just kill yourself. You are not worthy of anyone's love, much less that child's.'

Below the post, in a comment, one of her friends stated, 'Or I can just kill her for you.'

'Call it a plan. A done deal,' Lucy had replied.

Eva sent the screenshot to Max. "File a restraining order," he instructed.

She called the police department in the town Doug lived with Lucy. They said she needed to file it in California where she lived.

She called her local police. They said it needed to be filed in Michigan, but they made a formal report.

She called Max back and told him.

She and Riley were in their bedroom with the door cracked discussing the post.

"She is crazy, and I'm not comfortable with her posting these things," Riley said.

"I think it's just talk. She knows her posts get back to me. I don't think Lucy is really going to kill me. She posted for me to kill myself. Her friend is just playing her sick game."

Justin pushed the door open. "Lucy is planning to kill you?" He was visibly shaken.

"Justin, how long were you outside the door?"

"I heard you call and talk to someone on the phone, all the way to now. Mom, I don't want her to kill you."

"She's not going to. She's just trying to mess with your mom," Riley consoled him.

"You don't live with her. You don't see how crazy she really is." Justin had tears in his eyes.

Eva hugged Justin close. "She's all talk. I promise."

THE MORNING JUSTIN HAD TO fly back to his dad's was another emotional mess. Justin refused to get out of bed.

"I don't want to go back. Please, don't make me go back to her."

Eva walked out of his room and looked at Riley. "I wish I could record this and submit it to the court."

"I know… But honestly, I don't think that will even help."

Riley walked into Justin's room and Eva stood near the door and listened to her encourage him. "Hey, just remember everything me and your mom have taught you. You are strong. You are smart. There is no need to fear her or anyone. We will always be there for you. We are always here for you. Just be strong. Have courage."

Eva's heart broke for her son. Lucy's post echoed in her brain. She felt responsible for Justin's suffering and pain.

It was an emotional drive to the airport and getting Justin on the plane was not easy for either her or him. Because he was nearly a teenager, he was reluctant to show too much emotion in front of the crowd, but he found every way he could to delay the boarding process and stay with his mom. He stopped to tie his shoe. He stopped to double check the contents of his backpack. He stopped to make sure he had his phone. As he was escorted on the plane, he stopped and looked back once more at Eva. She blew him a kiss. "Got it in my heart," he said putting his hand over his heart.

Eva felt like her work was suffering as she got back into the groove of life without Justin at home with her.

She found herself distracted in the classroom, and constantly checking her text messages and emails looking for correspondence with Max.

As she was assigning argumentative essays for Juniors, she was trying to focus on breaking the essays down for the students.

"You have all week to work on them," she reminded as the period ended. It was lunch time and the several students who enjoyed hanging out in her classroom during their lunch began filing in. Mock Trial kids on one side, LGBTQ on the other side.

She sat back behind her desk and grabbed a protein shake from her mini fridge under her desk.

Jessica, a favorite student of hers moved to a desk closer to Eva. "Are you okay? You seem very stressed."

Eva smiled at her. "You are so sweet. Just grown-up problems. I will be okay. How are things with you and Jake?" She welcomed the teenage melodrama as a distraction.

"He's under so much pressure. He's trying to get into UCLA, because that is where his dad went. He wants pre-law so bad. He's not talking to me much right now. You have him after lunch. You should tell him to be nicer to me!" Jessica laughed.

"I had him last year. He's also the president of my Mock Trial team. I am well acquainted with his intensity He will be in shortly."

"He has to be. His dad is a JAG lawyer, and he doesn't allow for any slippage."

"Yeah. I met his dad at competition," Eva offered as more students filed in and the noise level amped up. Several of her Mock Trial students and past and present students filed in. Many vied for her attention. "Speak of the devil!" Eva said quietly to Jessica as Jake came in and took a seat next to her. Jake was tall, muscular, and brooding. His dark hair was cut in a military fade, and he looked like a panther ready to leap at any moment all the time. His very presence was constant tension. He had mastered the 1000-yard stare, and rarely smiled. He looked older than his classmates, mostly due to his intensity. Eva hated putting him in group projects because he would take charge, boss the other students around and get agitated when things did not go as planned. She couldn't fathom what Jessica saw in him. She was light, fun, and always perky and easy going. She was petite, blonde, and sunshine. She reminded Eva of a girl who would be voted Miss Congeniality in beauty pageants; she was always building people up around her.

Jessica smiled at her boyfriend as he sat down next to her. She pulled an extra lunch she had made for him out of her bag and sat it in front of him.

"Did you get the case packet for Mock Trial from the county?" Jake asked Eva, barely acknowledging the lunch that Jessica had put in front of him.

"Yes. We will go over it in the meeting after school tomorrow. Are you taking pretrial this year? I would prefer it if you did."

"My dad said I should," Jake agreed. He stuffed a bite of food in his mouth and pulled his calculus book out of his bag and started working on an assignment. Jessica spoke to him quietly. "I can't right now. Just back off. I need to get my work done."

Jessica sat back and looked dejected. Eva made eye contact with her in a silent question.

Jessica shrugged and ate her sandwich pulling out her laptop to work on her essay.

Another student had gotten Eva's attention and she began to focus on that instead.

After lunch, Jake took his assigned seat and put his calculus away.

Eva roamed the class as she talked about the hero's journey and its various points. Jake stared ahead at the projector with his deep severity.

When Eva got home, she sat down on the couch with a glass of wine next to Riley and propped her feet up. Guinness was laying between them with his head on Riley's lap.

"I have a kid who scares the shit out of me," Eva said.

"What do you mean?"

"He's just off. He's like dark. His aura just freaks me out. He's on my Mock Trial team as well."

"Have him switched out," Riley offered.

"It's not that simple. I can't contact his counselor and say I don't like his energy. His dad is a dick, too."

"Is this the kid from last year? His dad is a JAG?"

"Yeah. That kid."

"Oh yeah... I remember you talking about him. He got super upset after they lost the last round and didn't make it to semi-finals."

"Yeah. What's weird is he has a girlfriend now. I thought it would mellow him out, but he treats her like trash. It bugs me."

"Can you refer him to a counselor or her?"

"We have a mental health support person on campus, but she's overwhelmed with kids who are like in foster care or abuse situations."

Riley shrugged. "You are going hyper focus on this right now to avoid your own situation, aren't you?"

"Probably, you are right," Eva agreed.

AS IT TURNED OUT, JESSICA and Jake would not become a welcome distraction. The court agreed to have her case re-heard by a court custody investigator. Eva and Riley were hopeful. They went back to Michigan for their October visit with Justin. They pumped him full of courage and built him up as they always did. Of course, pending investigation, Lucy had backed off him.

Max assigned her to put together a binder with the last 8 years of conflict when she got back from her visit. Putting together the binder became Eva's full-time job. Teaching became her side gig as well as coaching Mock Trial.

Eva would grade assignments without giving feedback for better performance. She also was not focusing or paying attention during Mock Trial meets. She let the students lead their meets without really offering much as she was busy printing and organizing the information she wanted to include for the investigator. Her excuse being it was supposed to be student led anyway.

She spent 5 weeks putting together a perfectly organized binder with margin notes, flags, annotations. She had it organized by sections including correspondence, medical records, letters of recommendation, text messages, phone logs.

Eva and Riley flew in for the meeting with the investigator.

Eva and Max were seated on one side of the room, Riley was not allowed in. Per usual, Lucy was not there. Eva and Riley still had never seen Lucy in person. Not once. Doug and his attorney were on the other side of the room. The investigator, a curt older woman sat behind a large desk with her hands folded in front of her. Eva's binder, which she shipped a week in advance was sitting in front of her. Eva felt encouraged by seeing it there.

Doug refused to make eye contact with Eva. Keeping his head down, looking like the meek victim, true to his form and all his past performances.

Doug's lawyer started first. "Ms. Jones, we are only here because the plaintiff mother is trying desperately again to undermine my client, the defendant father. She is pathetic in these attempts, and her complaints have been constantly thrown out by the court."

Max interjected, "My client is only ever here because the defendant father and his wife constantly and flagrantly refuse to follow the orders of this court. My client has been desperately trying to get someone to please enforce these orders that are put in place, most importantly, the one that states the defendant's wife should not be physically punishing the child, Justin."

"Before I hear all of that, I want to know, what is this?" Ms. Jones, the investigator, held up the binder.

"That's the last 8 years of my child's life, ma'am," Eva said.

"All of this? I'm expected to go through all of this?"

Eva could see Doug sneering in her peripheral vision.

"All of that represents what my son has been subjected to, ma'am," Eva commented she couldn't help the bitterness in her voice.

The investigator rolled her eyes and plopped the binder down in front of her, it smacked the desk with a loud thud. Eva's heart sank.

Throughout the entire meeting, the investigator cut her off, mocked her, and ridiculed her.

Doug whined, pleaded, and lied his way through the investigation.

When Eva brought up that she had not been able to talk to Justin for 10 days at a time, consistently, Doug lied and stated that Justin didn't want to talk to her.

When Eva brought up that Lucy was still disciplining Justin, Doug lied and said it was not true. The investigator challenged Eva. "How do you know what's going on in their home?"

"My son tells me," Eva said.

"Are you questioning him? Are you sure he's honest with you?"

"I don't question him. He just spills it as soon as he gets in my car from the airport," Eva said.

"How do you know he's honest with you?"

"Why would he lie?" Eva challenged back.

"Because he likes the attention he gets from you," Ms. Jones answered. "I want to see the child in my office tomorrow at two in the afternoon," she instructed Doug. "We are done here."

EVA AND RILEY FLEW BACK to California early the next morning.

Eva was heavy in heart. She had told Riley verbatim what went on in the office. Riley couldn't do much other than offer words of encouragement which fell on deaf ears.

Eva put her headphones on during the flight and watched two movies. She tried to feel optimistic about what Justin was going to say, but she didn't know how it would be received. At this point, she had not spoken to him in 11 days.

THE NEXT DAY, EVA'S MOOD was heavy as she stood in front of her classes trying to stay focused on the lessons.

She had to take her Mock Trial students to the court house that afternoon to do a practice with another school's team.

She just felt empty and didn't care. When her students were trying to joke with her, she just responded with a wry smile.

She didn't care.

Lucy's posts rang in her head. She had asked her friends to stop sharing those with her, but they still played in her mind.

She sat in the back of the courtroom and let the other teacher act as judge for the practice. She took no notes and offered little to no feedback for her students.

Jake was pushing her, "I think that the other teacher was questioning me unfairly about my motion. My argument was solid and so was my case history."

"Yes, Jake. You were great," Eva said flatly as they walked to the bus.

Jake pushed back at her. "Are you even paying attention? You know that I need to win this season. This is my senior year. I can't go out as a 4-year loser. I need this."

"Jake, it doesn't really matter in the long run if you win or lose on your transcripts or anything. Your scholarships will not be because you won Mock Trial competitions."

"You don't understand. I don't know why you teach or coach," Jake growled and stormed off across the parking lot to the bus. She overheard him muttering about how she was worthless.

She waited 5 minutes before getting on the bus. She was trying to compose herself. She felt worthless in so many ways. Worthless as a teacher, and worthless as a mom. She had barely cooked a meal or initiated any form of intimacy with Riley or pulled out the vacuum cleaner. So she was a worthless wife too.

She sat at the front of the bus and rode quietly back to the school.

When they got back, she grabbed her bags out of her classroom and a stack of essays from her senior class.

It was close to the end of term. The large stack of ungraded essays sat on her desk mocking her in her uselessness. She put her bags back down and texted Riley that she was going to work late to grade, feeling grateful Thanksgiving Break was coming followed by a short 2 weeks before semester finals and then Winter Break. A glorious 3 weeks off work and 2 of those with Justin.

She barely skimmed the essays, and again, left little or no feedback, just scribbling a grade on each and putting the grade into her online gradebook.

She got to Jake's essay. She was expecting more, but it was lackluster. She couldn't come up with adequate words to give him feedback. She scribbled a 75% on it, entered the grade, and felt she was being generous.

Eva entered the grade in the online grade book and finished grading another 5 essays before calling it a night.

AFTER A QUIET THANKSGIVING BREAK, Eva could feel herself wearing down through the end of the semester. The Mock Trial club was nearing competition, she had an accumulation of gifts to wrap, and last but not least, now the recommendations of the custody investigator had arrived.

The envelope was sitting sealed on the counter. Eva and Riley stared at it. "No matter what, we will make peace with whatever it says, right?" Eva asked.

"That's on you, babe," Riley replied.

"Should we call Max and do this together?"

"Just open it."

Eva tore the envelope open. Riley stood behind her reading over her shoulder.

Eva could see the repeated lines referencing the forensic psychologist, "Narcissist." She skipped to the back where the recommendations lie. The investigator recommended that she lose all legal rights to Justin. All rights were to go to Doug and Lucy as Eva was deemed a pariah. No change in custody. No change in visitation. Eva threw the report down on the counter. "Fuck. I can't." She sank to the floor in tears.

"Babe, we talked about this. We knew this is what might happen."

"I know. It doesn't make it any easier though." Eva was crying hard.

"We are going to just make the best of the times we have Justin. We maximize every moment. We teach him to be strong. We teach him to enjoy life and all there is to offer. He knows we love him. He knows we are here. He knows we fought hard for him," Riley offered sinking down next to Eva.

Eva looked at Riley through her tears. "What if he grows up, hates what his life has become and blames me for everything? It's not wrong. I left. No one can deny that."

"But you were always there. You never really left him. He may go through a phase in life where he does blame you. But as he grows up, he will see and understand," Riley reassured.

Eva went on autopilot doing the bare minimum. She put absolutely no effort in going above and beyond for any task. She was numb. She was confused. She was guilty.

Jake came in during lunch the next day. "I need to talk to you." He glared at her. Jessica looked from him to Eva worried.

"Why did you only give me a 75% on my essay? I asked you if we could meet and discuss it and you never got back to me. All of the grades I have gotten in this class have been low. I think you have a problem with me." He threw the essay and a stack of other lowly graded assignments on Eva's desk.

"Maybe you need to calm down before we have this talk? Or maybe we need to have this talk in the admin office with someone there?" Eva offered dryly.

"The scores in this class tanked my grade and my GPA. College applications are getting ready to go right now. This is going to blow everything for me!" Jake shouted.

"If you don't like the grade, maybe I didn't like the work," Eva said hotly.

Jessica's eyebrows shot up. "What did you just say?" Jake asked. The whole room got very quiet.

Jessica slid out of the room unnoticed by Jake.

"I said, if you don't like the grade, maybe I didn't like the work. This essay was not to standard, and frankly, a 75% was being generous, and the rest of this is pure laziness," Eva said quietly, with a level iciness in her voice standing behind her desk, her finger pointing at the stack he dropped on her desk.

"There is nothing wrong with my work. You just have it out for me. You are just a man hating dyke!" Jake shouted.

"Dude… This is uncalled for," one of the lunch time students intervened. Eva didn't remember his name. She knew she had him last year, but he was always quiet and never really engaged with her or in class. Even at lunch, he came in and never really said anything to her. Just ate his lunch, talked to a friend or two, and played games on his phone. "Mrs. M. is one of the good guys. She's a good teacher. You don't want to go there with her."

"Oh yeah. She's such a good teacher. Look at this!" He held up his paper.

"Dude… It's a better grade than I got. She's a tough grader on our essays so we learn. It's all good, bro. She has high expectations of us. Everyone knows that. But don't hate on her, okay? Chill." The student tried to de-escalate.

"Stay the fuck out of my business. This is between me and this bitch," Jake said between gritted teeth. His eyes narrowed on Eva. She stood her ground with her fists on her desk staring back.

Jessica re-entered the room with two campus supervisors behind her.

Jake turned and saw. "Oh, it's like that?" he said to Jessica.

She looked down.

"Come on… Let's go," the larger of the two supervisors encouraged.

Jake turned back to Eva. "We are not done," he said.

"Is that a threat?" Eva asked, cocking her head to the side.

"It's a fucking promise. We will end this," Jake said as he turned and walked out.

Eva waited until Jake was out of the room before she collapsed into her chair shaking.

"Mrs. M, are you okay?" Jessica asked.

"The better question is are you okay?" She volleyed the question back to Jessica trying to smile. "I'm from Detroit. You can't rattle me that easily."

Jessica smiled. "I'm okay. Jake will be okay, too. He just needs time to chill. He's under too much pressure right now."

Eva nodded. She took a deep breath to control her nerves, slowly exhaling. "Jess, you need to be careful. Does he ever get that mad with you?"

Jess refused to look Eva in the eyes. "I mean, everyone gets angry."

Eva looked at the group of students being purposefully quiet trying to hear what Eva and Jessica were saying. "You guys, I'm so sorry... I love all of you." She looked directly at the student whose name she couldn't remember. "And thank you for what you tried to do. Can all of you go, please. I need a moment with Jessica."

They packed up their things (albeit slowly) and quietly said goodbyes to Eva. Jessica sat down across from Eva. "Mrs. M., I'm fine. This is not necessary."

"Jessica, does Jake talk to you like that a lot?"

"I mean, like I said, everyone gets angry. He's said some things in anger, but he always apologizes."

"Jessica, I want you to think about some things. You are young. You do not need to tie yourself to one person right now. No one should say hateful, hurtful things just because they are stressed out or angry. Has he ever hurt you physically?"

"I mean once... Once he grabbed me and threw me against the wall. But he didn't mean it."

"I think you need to evaluate this relationship and how you deserve to feel and be treated by your significant other."

"You are not going to tell anyone are you?"

"I'm a mandated reporter," Eva informed her.

"Mrs. M., it was months ago. He hasn't done anything like that since. He just yells and says things," Jessica pleaded, her big blue eyes glassing over with tears.

Before Eva could say anything else, the classroom phone rang.

"Mares," Eva answered.

"Mrs. Mares, it's Cynthia." It was the principal. "I am sending a sub down to cover your next period. I need you to come down here."

Eva hung up the phone. "I have to go see Dr. Tilman. Think about what I said," Eva said to Jessica.

Eva grabbed her phone and locked her laptop in the cabinet. She grabbed her sweater and put it on. Jessica was quiet as she gathered her things. Her eyes were wet from tears. Eva scribbled some directions onto the white board for her next class.

Eva let Jessica out of the room and locked the door.

She knew she was going to have to write a report on what happened. She also knew she may have to face Jake in the office.

She steeled her nerves and thought ironically, how at least this was keeping her mind off the disaster she created for her son.

She made her way to the admin offices. She greeted the students she saw in the corridors on the way. Smiling, high fiving and all the normal interactions she would have with students in between classes.

She made her way into the quiet of the admin building and knocked on Dr. Tilman's door. She didn't see Jake, and for that she was relieved.

"Eva, sit down." Dr. Cynthia Tilman was a stout woman, a few years younger than Eva, but with years of experience as an educator. Eva had deep respect for her and always felt that Dr. Tilman was fair and precise in her actions and direction. Her copper hair was in a flat ironed bob, and she wore very little makeup. She always wore polo shirts tucked into dress slacks and sensible shoes. Dr. Tilman folded her hands on her desk.

"I had to suspend Jake in lieu of an investigation, potentially expelling him. After what happened, and what he said not just to you, but to us, we feel he is a credible threat. He threatened your life."

Eva sat back and took a deep breath. "Um. Okay. I don't know how to feel right now." Her hands gripped the armrests of her chair.

"That's understandable. I just want you to give me your statement directly. You will also need to write it up in the system. But I need to know what happened. Are you okay with talking about this? I also need Officer Murphy to be in here and witness your statement."

Eva nodded. Her heart was racing. Dr. Tilman got up and flagged the School Resource Officer, Officer Murphy in. For those who were unfamiliar with him, he looked imposing, but he and Eva became fast friends. He would often come into Eva's room during class debates and give his two cents as the students debated sides.

"Hey, E.M.," he said smiling. "You okay? I always thought you would get someone mad someday with those heated discussions you host. I just never thought it would go down like this." His deep voice resonated through the room and his smile helped Eva feel a small bit of peace.

"Yeah. Right," Eva said trying to smile. "Let's do this." Eva summarized Jake's interactions with her over the last month. Dr. Tilman sat and listened attentively. Officer Murphy took notes.

"Do you feel like it was a credible threat?" Murphy asked.

"I mean... Given what Jessica said, I think it can be."

"What did Jessica say?" Murphy asked.

Eva summarized Jessica's statement to her.

Murphy put his pen away and looked at Eva. "Call me before you walk to your car for the next few days. When you get here in the morning and when you leave at night. Me or one of the campus sups will walk you to and from."

"Do you really think he would do anything?" Eva asked, narrowing her eyes at Murphy and Dr. Tilman.

"No one can really say. But none of us want to take that chance either," Dr. Tilman said.

"He did say he was going to go get his dad's gun and come back for you," Murphy informed her.

Eva's eyebrows raised. "So, where is he now?"

"We had him taken down to the police station. Not sure he will be charged with anything ultimately. But it will scare him a bit in the very least."

"Or piss him off further," Eva said. "This kid thinks I ruined his chances at getting into college. If he thinks he's going to have charges pressed, or expelled... He's really going to go."

"Eva, he has a low B in your class now, he's barely passing Econ. He's so stressed out that he's slipping in all of his classes right now. He's most likely not getting into his dream college anyway," Dr. Tilman informed. "You are just his scapegoat. He used to be a straight A kid, but not this year. Something else is going on with him."

"We did find a packet of Adderall in his backpack when he was searched," Murphy explained.

"That explains a lot," Eva said. "I am going to go back to my room now, if that's okay? I will write my incident report when I get back. I will let the sub stay for the whole period."

"We appreciate you," Dr. Tilman said.

Eva smiled wryly. "The joys of teaching, right?"

"You are a great teacher. The kids love you. They love your class, which says a lot about you since who loves English?" Dr. Tilman stood smiling.

"That's just because you used to teach science," Eva teased as she left.

"I will walk you back to your class," Murphy offered.

"He's at the station. He's not going to teleport back here," Eva said. "I'm good."

She left Dr. Tilman's office and took the long way through the admin building stopping at the bathroom. She didn't know how to feel about the events of the day. She knew she should be more worried than she was.

She stood at the sink and listened to the dripping faucet and counted her breath.

She thought about Justin. She thought about Riley. She tried to let the thoughts of the two people she loved and who loved her, warm her.

She pulled her hair up into a messy bun and took a deep breath, stood up tall and made her way back to her classroom.

When she came back in, the class got very quiet. "Don't let me stop you," she sang out forcing a smile. "Carry on. You were working with partners or solo, creating an outline for the in-class essay for your final." She made her way to the front of the room to talk to the sub. "Can you stay until the end of the period? I need to fill out some paperwork."

The sub nodded her head.

Eva sank behind her desk into her chair and unlocked her cabinet to retrieve her laptop. She opened it and opened the screen to fill out the incident report. She stared at the empty boxes and her throat tightened, followed by her chest.

Everything just felt like it was too much for her.

She just wanted to curl up with Riley. She could hear some of the students whispering. Word had already gone around about the incident, and they were talking about it. She couldn't blame them; it's what teenagers do. She didn't have the energy to tell them to stop or to clear up any rumors.

She looked over the top of her laptop at the cluster of students whispering. They looked back at her, knowing she heard them.

She raised an eyebrow at them. They leaned back and made themselves look like they were working on their assignment.

The bell rang and she thanked the sub as she left.

She started to slowly fill in the boxes for the incident report. Her fingers felt like lead and her vision blurred as she fought off the tears.

There were still two more periods to go. The pressure was overwhelming, and it seemed she just couldn't get a full breath. Dr. Tilman appeared at her door. "I should have offered this in my office, but I honestly forgot. You want to go home? Get some distance? Or do you want to talk to anyone?"

"I think I just want to go home," Eva said, her voice hoarse.

Dr. Tilman was leaning in the door frame with her hands in her pockets. "I got you. I will cover. What do I need to know for the next two periods?"

Eva forced a smile. "It's on the board. They know what to do." She stood up and packed what she needed into her bag. "Thank you, Cynthia. I appreciate it."

Eva ran the short distance to her car. She loved that her classroom was so close to the staff parking lot since she always pushed it with her timing in the morning, often getting into her room with little to no time to spare before the morning bell.

She sank into the driver's seat of her SUV and started the engine. The engine hummed and She sat and listened to it before turning on the radio. She selected Morrissey from her playlist and turned the volume up and drowned herself in his crooning as she backed out of the parking lot and made her way home.

Her tears flowed hot as she drove the route home. With her vision blurred and her hands were shaking, and her chest felt like it was filled with concrete she navigated the roads on autopilot.

As she opened her garage door and pulled in, she saw Riley's car parked safe next to hers.

She turned off the ignition and grabbed her bag. Riley was there at the garage door before she could open it. "Are you okay? Why are you home?" her brow was furrowed with concern.

Eva fell into her sobbing.

"You are not okay. What is going on?" Riley supported Eva's weight as she backed up through the doorway and into the house.

Eva slid to the floor, pulling her knees up and curling into a ball. "I just can't right now. I can't."

"You can't what, baby?" Riley asked, coming down to the floor with her.

"Everything. I can't."

"Okay… It's going to be okay. All of it." Riley wrapped herself around Eva.

Eva composed herself, drawing strength from her wife. Once she found her composure, she told Riley everything that had happened today.

"I think you need a leave of absence," Riley reasoned.

"No… I think I will be okay. It just got to be too much. We have finals week next week. Then we are off for 3 weeks for Winter Break. Everything will be okay."

"Maybe you should take tomorrow off in the least?"

"I don't know. I will think about it."

"Take the rest of the week and we can head up to Pismo for a long weekend? We can stay at the hotel you like with the ocean view and bring Guinness. A 4-day weekend if you take the rest of the week. It will be a much-needed break from all this trauma. You just got bad news from the court last night. You had a shit day today. You deserve it." Riley placed her hand under Eva's chin to force her to make eye contact. She grinned at Eva. "If we leave now, we are there in time for dinner. Clam chowder…" Riley tried to entice her.

Eva put her hand on Riley's wrist. "It's tempting."

"You don't even need to bring many clothes…" Riley winked.

Eva forced a smile. "Okay."

She put in for a sub and emailed Cynthia and finished her incident report. She put together a small carry on with some essentials.

As promised, Riley had them in Pismo in time for dinner. Eva went and sat on the balcony while Riley ran out to pick up clam chowder from their favorite restaurant near the pier.

The sun was setting, and Guinness was seated close by her. She watched the seagulls flying back in to roost for the night.

She looked at her phone it was just before 8 pm Michigan time. She texted Justin's phone. "Hey, Beautiful Boy. I miss you, call me if you can."

A few minutes later, her phone rang with a FaceTime call from her son.

"Hey you!" She smiled, her heart warming.

"Hey! Where are you?" he asked.

Eva flipped the camera around so he could see the view. "Wow! That's beautiful. Where are you?" he asked again.

"Pismo," she answered. "How are you? Are you ready to get here for Christmas break?"

"Yes! I can't wait! Are we going to go camping with the Jacobs?"

"Yes, we are for New Years, like last year!" Eva said.

"Yay! Is Grampa or Gramma coming?"

"Not this year. But we will still have fun," Eva said. "How are you?"

"Lucy is having a baby. She's extra crabby," Justin informed her.

"What? Really? I don't think you ever told me that?"

"That's what she tells me. I think she's just getting fat."

"That's not nice. Even if she's not nice to you," Eva corrected. Although inside she was laughing.

"Sorry," Justin offered.

"It's all good. I miss you. I just needed to see your face."

"Dad said the court made a recommendation," Justin blurted. "Mom, they didn't listen to me. They don't care, do they?"

Eva pursed her lips and cocked her head. She didn't want to talk about this right now. "Beautiful Boy, we will talk about this while you are here for break."

Justin's eyes welled with tears. "I just don't want to be here," he whispered.

"I know you don't. I'm so sorry. We are just going to have to work on you being strong though," Eva coached. Her throat got tight. The sun sank lower. Guinness laid down at her feet.

Justin looked at her through the screen. "I'm trying, Mom."

"Keep trying until it works," she said mustering strength in her voice.

He changed the subject to a video game he played with his classmate. She lost herself in his chatter. Riley came in and brought the Styrofoam container of hot chowder to Eva. She peeked down into the screen and called out to Justin.

Eva ended the call with Justin and Riley joined her on the balcony. They ate in silence and watched the sky darken.

They spent the next 4 days lazing late into the day in bed making love like they did when the relationship was young and new, walking on the beach in the afternoons and pretending the rest of the world did not exist.

Sunday afternoon they drove back to their home, content, rested and ready to resume life.

MONDAY MORNING, THE BEGINNING OF finals week for her students, one week before Winter Break, Eva went into her classroom and started setting up for the day. She was laying out packets for the finals on the desk when Murphy popped in. "Hey, you. You didn't call to get an escort in."

"Murphy, it's been almost a week. I'm sure it's fine and blown over."

"You are a hard-headed girl." He smiled, tapped the door frame and left.

Finals weeks are always exhilarating. The promise of weeks off looming. Only having students for the first part of each day and spending the afternoon grading and submitting final grades and cleaning off her desk and organizing and prepping for the next semester always brought a sense of ease to Eva. She enjoyed finals week and the structure of it.

As Monday drew to a close, one day closer to break and time with her son and gift wrapping and sleeping in, she packed her bag and grabbed her travel mug and locked the door behind her. The campus was empty, with only a few other teachers lingering and finishing their days as well. The students had long since cleared out after their second final of the day completed.

It was nearly four in the evening and the sun was low and the sky was bright blue and cloudless. The crows that hung out near her building were cawing and picking through the trash. She used her key and let herself through the gate to the staff parking lot.

Eva made her way to her SUV parked in the middle of the lot. As she approached, she heard, "Hey... Mrs. M."

As she turned, she heard a loud boom and felt heat burning through her chest.

She heard nothing but the beating of her heart in her ears. Her vision blurred and went dark.

Part 3

Deus Ex Machina

Chapter 13

Post Mortem

SHE WAS SUDDENLY STANDING NEXT to her body, looking at her shattered mug on the ground next to her, she could see her co-workers rushing around as a lockdown was called, and she saw Jake standing over her frozen. "I told you it was a promise." He was crying and shaking. Snot was bubbling under his straight nose.

Nana was next to her. She looked at Nana, looked at her body, and looked around. "I'm dead?"

Nana nodded her head.

"What about Justin and Riley?"

"What about you and your mom? I've been here by your side all along. You can be there for them, but differently. I had been by your side so many days helping you and guiding you and sending you signs. Remember what the medium said?"

Sirens were approaching.

Jake had fallen to a sitting position. He was crying and rocking, his knees up against his chest. The gun was by his side and his hands were in his dark hair.

"I'm not even mad at him," Eva said, not acknowledging what Nana had said to her.

Murphy had gotten to the gate and was rushing through as police cars and an ambulance pulled into the lot.

Eva was watching her own blood spill out around on the pavement.

"I wanted to die so many times over the past 20 years. I thought about taking my own life, but I never could do it. I was never ready. I don't think I'm ready now."

"It's like having a baby. You are never ready. Even when you think you are," Nana coached.

Eva was hardly paying attention to what Nana had said as she watched the cops swarm Jake. One used his boot to push him forward, face down on the pavement with a knee in his back. Another cop cuffed him.

A flashing light like a strobe. Someone was taking pictures. A helicopter was buzzing overhead.

Two paramedics came to Eva's body. They assessed that there was no life left in the body. They were talking, but she wasn't listening. She couldn't watch them work over her lifeless body. Her skin had a pale waxy look against the black pavement. The pool of blood around her looked black and shiny and slick against the porous pavement.

As Jake was taken into the cop car, her co-workers began to exit buildings and look.

Cynthia came out and Murphy put his arm around her as she cried out. Eva could hear the sound of Cynthia's voice echoing against the buildings.

Eva sat back and just watched. Disbelieving.

"Am I stuck here?" she asked Nana.

"No. I will help you. You can be anywhere now. Until they decide whether or not you get to come back and do it all again. But time, distance, it's all irrelevant now. Sometimes I am nowhere really, and sometimes I am with you and sometimes I am with your mom. It depends on if someone needs you or you want to be with them…" Nana's voice trailed off as she only half paid attention.

She watched as a paramedic put a sheet over her body. Red bloomed through the white.

News trucks were approaching.

More cop cars were approaching.

Eva had no idea how much time had elapsed. Nana was right, time was irrelevant now. She saw Riley's truck pull up to the melee. She must have gotten wind of the commotion at the school and suspected the worst.

Murphy and Cynthia made their way around the crime scene to her. Eva followed. Riley got out of the truck and looked at Cynthia shaking her head no.

Murphy and Cynthia caught her on each side and held her. The cry that escaped Riley's lips ripped through Eva.

"She loved you so much," Nana whispered. Eva reached out for Riley. She knew Riley could feel it because she looked up knowing.

The crime scene photographer was taking pictures, and evidence was being compiled. Her co-workers were calling their loved ones to tell them what happened and that they were safe. She felt envious of them. Riley could see the car with Jake in the back. "That's the motherfucker who did this!" She pointed and pulled herself up.

"Don't... No..." Murphy and Cynthia were holding on to her.

"Does he know what he took? What he did?" she cried.

Cynthia and Murphy guided Riley back behind the crime scene and on to campus. They were at the gate, feet away from Eva's classroom door.

After the crime scene photographer took pictures, the paramedics loaded her body onto the stretcher.

"What am I going to tell Justin? Her parents?" Riley asked.

Cynthia had no answers and neither did Murphy.

"Tell them I loved them. I will be with them always," Eva said, though Riley couldn't hear her.

"She will do fine. She will be fine," Nana consoled.

It was several hours before her co-workers were allowed to get to their cars and leave. Some left their cars there opting to have family members or Ubers pick them up from the corner.

Some stayed sitting vigil with Riley. Reporters attempted to ask questions of Riley and she just quietly told them she couldn't bear it right now. Cameras flashed in her face, microphones were shoved under her chin. She was pale and stricken. Eva was clueless to how much time had elapsed. She noticed it was dark outside. Lights beamed over the parking lot, the sky was black and starless.

Eva watched as a young female reporter with choice position stood outside the staff lot. The cameras having a view behind the reporter of the pool of Eva's blood shining slick in the floodlights of the now dark parking lot on the ground and the broken mug, just feet from her car.

"Hi, yes, Robert – I'm here live from North County High School where a well-loved and well-respected English teacher was gunned down by a disgruntled student just this afternoon. It appears this teacher and student had had a confrontation just last week over the student's grades. The student has been identified as 18-year-old Jacob Porter. The teacher, identified as Eva Mares had been his English teacher for the last 2 years and coached him in academic competitions."

I'm a statistic now, Eva thought as the reporter caught sight of a group of students who had come to witness the carnage. "Did you know Jacob Porter or Mrs. Mares?"

Eva took herself back down to where her body had lain and bled out. She listened as the coroner was talking. "From preliminarily viewing the body and the entrance wound, the bullet struck right through her aorta. She bled out quickly. The kid was a helluva shot. She probably didn't even feel it. Small favors…"

He's right. I didn't feel it. Not really.

The detective made his way over to Riley, Cynthia, and Murphy.

"You are the wife of the victim?" he asked Riley.

"Her name is Eva," Riley said quietly.

"I'm sorry. I'm sorry for your loss. They are taking her to the coroner's office. Will you be able to come down there for a formal identification of the body and to retrieve her personal effects?"

"I can be there with you, I can drive you," Murphy offered.

Riley nodded. "I would appreciate that, Murphy." She looked back at the detective. "When do you need me to be there?"

"In about an hour or two, that would be great. Meanwhile, do you mind answering a few questions?"

Eva took herself back to where her mug lay shattered. She pondered the insignificance of it lying in the parking lot. She looked at the pool of her blood. She looked back at Riley and the detective. The police car with Jake in the back had left. The ambulance with her body had left.

The handful of co-workers that stayed in support of Riley were texting their loved ones. Students had gathered in front of the school and spilled over to where they were wrapping up the crime scene. Several were crying and visibly shaken.

Cynthia was handling business on her cell phone and the superintendent had arrived.

Eva found that if she centered her attention hard enough on an area or a person, she would be able to hear them or be next to them.

She looked at Nana who had followed her incessantly since she had become incorporeal. "I think you need to go be with Mom. Riley is going to be calling her soon."

Nana looked at her, "Are you going to be okay? I will find you as soon as I know your mom is okay."

Eva watched as Nana disappeared. She wondered how she was even able to see her to begin with, or how she made sense of seeing herself still dressed in today's clothing.

She saw Murphy get into Riley's truck and adjust the seat. Riley got into the passenger seat. Eva got in with them. As they were driving away, Riley took a deep breath and dialed Jack. "Jack, it's Riley." Her voice cracked.

Jack, cheerful on the other end, "Hey, Riley! How are you?"

"Eva was killed today. A student shot her in the parking lot," Riley blurted without warning. As Riley spoke, Eva felt herself pulled to Jack's side.

She could see her dad let the phone slip from his hands and into his lap. Riley's voice crying on the other end. She saw his jaw tremble and tears spill forth from his eyes. He took a deep trembling breath. He was trying to be strong for Riley.

Jack picked up the phone with a shaking hand. "What are we going to do?" His voice was hoarse as he tried to maintain stoic strength.

She could hear Riley on the other end as if she were in Jack's ear. "I'm going to do the formal identification now. I will call you when it's all done, and we will discuss everything. I just thought I needed to call you."

"I can't believe this is real," Jack said. He couldn't control the flow from his eyes.

Eva watched Jack weep silently in his chair after hanging up with Riley. His big old cat Mouser was in his lap purring softly.

Eva wrapped herself around Jack's shoulders. Hoping he could feel her comfort. She thought of all the wisdom he had imparted on her through the years. Nothing could have prepared either one of them for this.

She was pulled back to Riley before she could even think twice. Riley was in the coroner's office standing in front of a window with white curtains on the other side. Nana was next to her as well.

Someone moved the curtain back and Eva saw a metal table with a crisp and clean white sheet pulled over it. Someone moved the sheet back to expose the face. Eva saw herself, bloodless and white. Her wild, curly hair pulled free from her typical messy bun and spread out behind and underneath. Her eyes were closed.

Tears poured like a fountain from Riley's eyes. The detective was kind and held her up as her knees buckled beneath her. He escorted her to the front where Eva's bag, cell phone, and jewelry were placed in a box. Riley opened the bag with the jewelry and pulled Eva's wedding ring out and placed it in her palm holding it to her lips.

She signed the forms and Murphy helped her back to her truck.

"Eva really adored you," Riley told him.

"She was like a sister to me. We started in the district together. We met at orientation, and we have been buddies since," Murphy said smiling.

Riley looked at him. "I need to talk to her son."

She called the phone number for Justin's phone. It rang and rang and rang. When it went to voicemail, she dialed again. Finally, Doug answered after the third round of calling. "It's well past his bedtime. What do you even want?" he answered, his voice bellowed over the car speakers on Bluetooth.

"Eva was killed. He needs to know," Riley said.

"What's he supposed to do about it right now?" Doug retorted. "I will tell him tomorrow." Doug hung up.

"That man needs his ass kicked," Murphy said.

Riley forced a smile. "We've been saying that for years."

"You want me to drop you off at your house, and I can get someone to pick me up from there?" Murphy asked.

"Please," Riley said.

Eva stood by and watched as Murphy and Riley went into the house. They didn't speak much. Eva was grateful for Murphy being there. Guinness seemed to know she was there, looking at her with a cocked head and moving around the space she occupied.

Riley opened a bottle of wine and offered some to Murphy. He declined. "My ride will be here soon."

Riley poured a glass. "Thank you for being here for me. For her."

"I got you. Even when all of this is said and done… I got you. For her."

Riley wiped a tear from her eye.

Murphy's phone pinged. He looked down. "That's my ride. You need anything, call me."

Riley nodded and hugged him.

Eva stood watch all night over Riley. She watched her force herself through her nightly routine. When it came time to get into bed, Riley grabbed Eva's pillows and pulled them to herself. She breathed in Eva's scent and exhaled. She put the pillow back, grabbed her own pillows and blankets and went to the living room. The Christmas tree was lit and now looked garish and ridiculous in the face of her grief.

She pulled the plug on the tree and turned on the television. She found one of Eva's favorite shows and streamed it.

She saw the book Eva had been reading on the coffee table and picked it up. She thumbed through it and put it back exactly as she had found it.

She watched as Riley drifted restlessly in and out all night. She sat herself near Riley's head wishing she could soothe her.

"I know you are here with me," Riley said softly. "I can feel you. This is so unfair. I miss you already. I know I will be okay without you, eventually. But I never wanted to be without you."

"You never have to be," Eva replied.

Riley couldn't hear her. "I'm not just losing you. I'm losing Justin, too. Everything we built has come apart."

"Justin will seek you out when he can and when he's ready," Eva offered. She didn't know how she knew this, but she felt with all that she had, that it was the truth. This was something she had a difficult time believing when she had been alive, but with death came the certainty that had eluded her in life.

Riley rolled onto her side on the couch. Guinness shifted at her feet. She drifted back off.

In the early hours of dawn, Riley tried calling Justin back. Doug again answered the phone. "He's at school. I will talk to him after school."

"What is wrong with you? This child needs to grieve. He needs to know what happened to his mother."

"You are not his parent. You don't get to say what is right and wrong for my child," Doug retorted and hung up.

Riley called Jack and informed him of Doug's refusal to talk to Justin or let Riley talk to him.

"I will go to Justin's school and talk to them," he offered after Riley explained to him what was going on.

Eva felt herself be pulled to Jack. She was sitting at the table with him as he put the last of his coffee down. Cold sun poured in through the kitchen window. The newspaper sat folded on the table next to his mug. He stood up and grabbed his car keys and went out to his car. Eva sat herself in the car with him.

He entered the address to Justin's school into his GPS and drove slowly. He still hadn't even begun to process what had actually happened.

Eva watched him as he navigated the side streets and then the highway.

She looked at his hands and remembered riding next to him as a child going back and forth between his home and Geri's on weekends listening to Cat Stevens and telling made up ghost stories. She would watch his hands on the steering wheel as a child as she listened to him create scary stories for her entertainment. His hands looked older now as she observed them. His veins showing thick through the thinning skin of age. How she so loved his ghost stories. Now she was a ghost story.

He pulled into the parking lot of Justin's school. He took a deep breath and slowly exited his car and walked up to the doors to the office. Ringing the buzzer, he explained that he needed to talk to the principal and counselor about a student, that it was an emergency.

The secretary hit the buzzer and Jack walked in. He went to the office and looked at the secretary. Tears welled up in his eyes. "My daughter is… was? Justin Franz's mother. She was murdered yesterday. Justin doesn't know." His voice cracked in a hoarse whisper.

"Oh. Oh my god." The secretary stood and brought the box of tissues over to Jack. She placed her hand on Jack's. "I'm so sorry. Let me call Ms. Cartwright. She's the principal. Ms. Elmhurst is the school social worker. I will call her too. Come this way. You can sit in here."

The secretary opened the counter and let Jack back, ushering him into a conference room next to the principal's office. It was a small room, cramped, with a round table and a filing cabinet and a large whiteboard. The whiteboard was probably the only thing that had been updated in this room since it was built in the 1950's.

Within minutes, Ms. Cartwright, the principal, was sitting in the room with Jack. Eva had met her once in the fall. The two women had extended professional courtesy to each other but did not particularly like one another. Ms. Cartwright, with her short gray bob, and beady brown eyes had written Eva off as had everyone else in the State of Michigan in regards to her involvement with Justin. Eva did not expect much from her in this moment. Jack introduced himself. "I think you have met my daughter a few times," he said.

"Yes. She was a teacher in California," Ms. Cartwright stated.

"Yes, that's right." Jack took a deep a breath before continuing. "She was murdered by a student yesterday afternoon after school. Justin doesn't know yet. His father would not let her wife talk to him and tell him."

Ms. Cartwright nodded. "I'm so sorry for your loss," she said quietly as Ms. Elmhurst entered the room.

Jack went through the entire situation with them both in the room. Ms. Cartwright stood and asked the secretary to have Justin sent to the office.

Justin came in and saw his grandpa and grinned and ran to him. "Grampa!!" he yelled running into Jack's arms.

Eva felt pain for the first time since her death as she watched her dad come completely unglued, tears falling from his eyes and wetting Justin's hair. "Grampa, what's wrong?" Justin asked.

Jack sat down and Justin took the chair next to Jack's. "It's about your mom, Justin," he said. "One of her students was not very happy about something that happened at school. He felt your mom was to blame. He... he..." Jack couldn't finish the sentence.

Justin shook his head vehemently. "My mom is okay," he said assuredly.

"No," Jack said. "I'm sorry, Justin. She's not. She's dead. She's in Heaven."

"No. I'm not. I'm right here!" Eva felt herself yelling it. A light flickered, but no one heard her.

Justin burst into tears. Jack moved over to him and held him as he cried. Eva could do nothing but observe. She enveloped Justin in her energy. He felt the warmth. "I'm with you always whenever you need me," she promised him. He couldn't hear her. He was deaf to the words she spoke. But in his heart, she knew he felt her promise.

Ms. Elmhurst spoke first. "Justin, if you need to talk about anything, I'm here for you, okay? I know this is a lot for you to take in."

"Does Justin's father know?" Ms. Cartwright asked.

Jack looked at her hard. "Yes. Eva's wife called him last night."

"Wait. My dad knew? My dad knew and didn't tell me?" Justin yelled. "Why didn't he tell me?"

Jack shook his head. "I don't know. That's why I came out here. Riley and I thought you needed to know."

"Am I still going to California for Christmas? I can spend it with Mum. She will need me there. Mom Mom was all she really had. We were a family. I'm still her family."

"I don't think your dad is going to want that. I don't know that Riley is going to have Christmas this year," Jack explained. Eva knew Justin loved Riley, but to see the depth of his concern for her really touched her.

"I would offer to let you take Justin home, but you are not on the emergency list," Ms. Cartwright explained. "But please, take as long as you need in the room." She excused herself.

Ms. Elmhurst looked at Jack and Justin. "Do you want to talk about anything now?"

Justin shook his head no. "I want to talk to my grampa," he said quietly.

Ms. Elmhurst left the room. "Grampa, my dad doesn't let me see you or talk to you. I only get to see you or talk to you when I'm with Mom. How is this going to work?"

"I don't know, Bud. I don't have any answers. Just know no matter what, I love you. If I can't see you or talk to you, it's not by my doing or my choice." Jack felt rage and bitterness creep in and take over.

"You are right to be angry, Dad," Eva said. "Get angry. Fight for Justin since I can't anymore." No one heard her, but the lights flickered again.

Jack stayed with Justin in the conference room until school let out. They talked mostly about their favorite memories of Eva. When the final bell rang, Justin hugged him hard. "I have to take the bus. I have to go."

"I can drive you home," Jack offered.

"No. If my dad sees you, he will be mad."

Jack set his jaw. "Justin…"

"I know. As Mom would say, 'You know that's fucked up, right?' Yes. I know it's fucked up."

Jack didn't bother to correct Justin for cussing. "I love you, Justin. I will always be here for you."

"I love you, too, Grampa. I know." Justin's voice was tight as he hugged his grampa one last time.

Eva followed Justin home. She sat with him on the bus and watched as a pretty young girl sat beside him. It seemed this was a familiar pairing of seats the way the girl passed several empty spots and sought this spot. "Hey, Justin!" she chirped as she sat down, pushing a piece of chestnut brown hair out of her face.

"Hi, Nessa…" Justin whispered.

She saw the look on his face and didn't speak further. Justin looked at her and shook his head, indicating he didn't want to speak. His sadness bled out from him, and the girl could feel it. She talked to another girl across the aisle instead.

Eva sat with him in his basement room as he looked through his drawer and found the picture books she had made him. Lucy had tried to make him take them to his mom's house, and when that backfired, she tried to throw them away. Justin had taken to keeping them stashed at the bottom of a drawer.

He traced the outline of Eva's image with his finger. It was a picture of them on a cruise ship to Alaska. Riley had taken the picture, they were getting ready to go to the dining room for dinner, and they were dressed nicely. Eva and Justin were looking over the balcony of the suite, standing identically, with their arms folded on the balcony rail, looking out to the distance. "Mom Mom," he said to himself.

Justin sat on his bed with the picture books spread out around him. He waited for Doug to get home. His anger was rising as he looked at the memories of him and his mom.

Eva sat and watched him unable to do anything. Nana was next to her. "You can't do much, but you can do your best to reassure and to guide them. It's not wise to interfere though." She said to Eva. "You can send signs to them to make them stop and think, or to let them know they are on the right path. But you really don't get to change their course." Nana as she had in life was doing her best to guide her in death.

"When you are not with them, where do you go?" Eva asked.

"It's just a kind of nothingness. A peace, like sleeping. When you are ready to find that peace, you just get to go there."

"And if I'm not ready to leave them? To stop guiding them? Stop being there for them?" Eva's mind was already in gear.

"You are stuck here then," Nana said shrugging.

When Doug's car pulled in, Justin picked up the books and hid them safely under his clothes in the drawer.

He reached in his pocket and pulled out Eva's bracelet. He kissed it and put it back in his pocket. "I think I found my voice, Mom," he whispered.

Justin ascended the stairs. Lucy was laying on the couch with her feet propped up rubbing her growing belly and watching Judge Judy. Lucy was, as everyone described her, Eva finally saw her in the flesh. Her bleached out hair, with dark roots, her large nose, and oily skin, her flat soulless, dark eyes narrowing in on Justin. Eva felt the years of hatred and turmoil build inside of all that she was.

"My mom is dead, and you didn't tell me," Justin accused, his voice firm and loud, bordering on yelling.

Doug just stopped in his tracks. "How did you find out?"

"Were you ever going to tell me?" Justin asked.

"Your father asks the questions. Not you," Lucy hissed.

Doug set his lunch bag down on the table. "I was going to tell you after school. I didn't want to send you to school on that note. Riley didn't call me until after you went to bed last night. Now tell me, how did you find out?"

"Grampa came to my school and told me." Justin's arms were folded across his chest, his voice and posture defiant.

"Of course. He's still fighting your mom's battles for her," Lucy said, her voice bitter acid.

"Don't you ever speak of my mom again!" Justin yelled at her. It was the first time he had ever truly spoken up for himself or his mom against Lucy. He felt emboldened and felt that he had no choice any longer. His mom couldn't fight for herself or for him any longer. He had to become the son she had raised him to be.

She sat up and whacked Justin upside the head. "You don't raise your voice to me, child."

Eva was raging. She had questioned whether or not Justin was fully truthful in what he experienced with her after the investigator and forensic psychologist sowed seeds of doubt. There was no questioning it further. Justin had been telling the truth all along.

Justin stood back and looked at Lucy.

Eva felt the rage inside her build so hot that the light bulb in the lamp popped loudly.

"What did you just do?" Lucy glared at Justin.

"You saw he was over here. Don't get excessive," Doug said. "A fuse probably blew, or the light bulb just died."

Lucy picked her phone up off the couch and stormed off to her room.

She looked at Nana. "I made that happen?" She asked.

Nana nodded her head.

EVA WENT BACK TO WATCH over Riley as she made arrangements for the funeral. Riley arranged for cremation locally and to transport the ashes to Michigan for a memorial service.

Cynthia canceled finals for the students and arranged a memorial in the theater of the school. She had reached out to the students to request they share photos they may have had with Eva and invited Riley to be present and speak if she felt up to it.

The morning of the public memorial at the school, Riley donned her best black suit. She slicked her hair back and went and stood at the front of the theater with Cynthia. It was the day that would have been check out day for the staff, before heading to Winter Break.

Riley and Cynthia watched as the theater filled with students, past and present, parents, and staff members. Projected on the screen was a slide show of pictures of Eva interacting with her students throughout the years. Selfies of her smiling and laughing with her kids, graduations, lessons, Mock Trial competitions. Eva was there watching. Looming in the background. There but not. Nana was by her side. "This is the hard part. The goodbyes," Nana said. "Most of them don't really get it, that we are still here with them."

Riley was quietly watching the slide show. In the background a playlist of Eva's favorite songs played softly. Set to speak were Riley, Cynthia, Melanie – Eva's classroom neighbor, mentor, master teacher, and the closest person she had as a friend locally, and then they would open it up to anyone who felt the need to speak.

At noon sharp, Riley took the podium.

The theater was filled to capacity, with several people standing in the wings and in the back.

"Thank you all for coming here today. Eva was my wife. The love of my life. I know she didn't just impact my life. She impacted so many others. She lived her life to serve the community. She wanted to make the world a better place. A smarter place. A more creative place. She loved her career, and she loved her students. She didn't leave her job at 3 in the afternoon, when she came home. She would talk about how proud or how concerned she was every day. She was always looking for what she could introduce or read with her students. She called her students her kids. Even if they graduated. They were hers. She loved her kids. I had to share her with her kids. I didn't mind. I didn't mind because her kids brought her joy, brought her pride, and anything that made her happy, made me happy. I don't want to monopolize the time, as this is your opportunity to say your peace and say your goodbyes to her. So, just know, she loved every one of you that sat in her room." Riley cleared her throat and wiped her eyes.

Cynthia spoke warmly of first meeting Eva as a student teacher and how she observed Eva through the years and their many interactions together and her passion for teaching and education, and how the building Eva's classroom was in would be renamed for her as the Mares Building.

Melanie came on and talked about how she first met Eva and how she would miss their collaboration and their pre-semester and post semester get-togethers. How her son and Justin would spend time together through the summers.

One by one students from the last several years took the podium to say what an impact Eva had made. She felt a warmth throughout her as she watched. Riley sat in the front row and listened as each one detailed the mark Eva made on their lives. Eva put her hand on Riley's hand as it rested on the armrest. Riley couldn't feel it, Eva knew. But it made her feel better. Nana stood behind them. "I'm proud of you, kid. You did good. Look at all of this. You made a mark. You made a difference. I always knew you would."

"Thanks..."

THE NEXT MORNING, 5 DAYS AFTER her death, Riley went to pick up Eva's ashes. As she was waiting at the crematorium, Britt sent her a text, 'These people are sick,' it said with a screenshot of another post from Lucy. 'Dumb bitch got what she deserved. Karma stupid ho. Rot in Hell.' It was dated for the day after Eva died.

Riley shook her head. She had listened to Eva talk about the numbness she would feel when her depression took hold, but she finally felt it for herself. She texted back to Britt, 'Unbelievable. See you in a few days at the memorial.'

The attendant came out with a sleek silver jar, and a bag with a handle and tissues filled with something Eva couldn't identify, and handed it to Riley. Eva looked at the beautiful jar that contained what was left of her mortal self. *Ashes to ashes...* she thought.

Riley signed the requisite forms and went home, the jar occupying the passenger seat.

When Riley arrived home, she sat the jar on the coffee table and pulled out her laptop, Eva's phone, and went to the closet in the guest room, where Eva stored her things that she wanted to keep but used little.

Riley pulled out the bin that had all of Justin's baby items that Eva had kept. She selected the blanket that Eva had shown her as her favorite to snuggle Justin with. She folded it and set it in a separate bin. She pulled out and went through each of the photo albums and photo books Eva created, Justin's baby book, clothing items, plushies, and mementos of Eva's life.

Riley spent 10 hours compiling three blue tubs. She put one together for Jack and one for Geri and one for Justin. She had gone through all of Eva's digital photos on her phone and laptop and posted to social media and created a jump drive, and put one in each bin as well. She then drove to the 24-hour Walgreens and printed all the copies to add to each bin.

When she got home, she carefully put the stacks of photos on the top of each bin and put everything away that she was keeping. She looked at the three open bins, and the jar on the coffee table. She took a deep breath, and with a lump in her throat, she opened the bag with the tissue that she took home from the crematorium, and pulled out six velvet jewelry boxes. She lined them up in front of the jar and opened the first one. A silver pendulum shaped charm gleamed in the light.

Riley pulled the charm out of the box and unscrewed it. She picked up the urn next and unscrewed the lid, exposing a plastic bag tied with a wire.

Eva knew if she were still corporeal, she would feel sick. She felt her energy run cold as she looked at the dark gray ashes in the bag.

Riley shivered with goosebumps appearing on her arms. Inhaling deeply, she untied the wire. She slowly pulled the plastic bag. "Oh my god…" she cried softly as she slowly dipped the pendulum charm into the ashes filling it. She sealed it tightly to its top. Eva looked closer, the pendulum was engraved with her initials in a feminine and swirly font. It hung from a sturdy silver chain.

Riley made sure it was sealed tightly, and systematically filled each one, placing each one in a purple gift bag with black tissue, and placing that one on the top of each bin.

She tied the plastic bag back in place and replaced the lid of the urn.

Riley slowly stood up and placed the lid on each bin and labeled them and taped them shut. Two gift bags filled with the pendulums on the coffee table, one unwrapped for herself next to those. She placed it around it her neck, pressing the pendulum against her palm next to her heart.

She stacked the blue bins on a dolly and placed them next to the garage door.

She returned to the living room, retrieved Eva's ashes and went to the bedroom. She placed Eva's urn on the mantle over the fireplace, lit a fire and laid in bed quietly. The house was quiet. No television. No music. No sounds. Even Guinness remained quiet laying in front of the fire.

Eva watched Riley lay still and breathe. Her hand reached out to Eva's side of the bed. "If you are here... Can you tell me? Show me something?"

"I'm here. You just can't see me or hear me," Eva whispered. "I'm here."

Nana appeared by her side. "You can go to her. In her dreams. Or, if you try really hard, you can make things happen. You can make smells; you can make things move. You can direct animals to cross their paths. You have to focus on everything though. It's hard. But you can do it if you will it hard enough."

"How do I do it? How do I show up in dreams?"

"When she's asleep, you can tap into her mind. Just focus on her, with all that you have..."

Eva waited for Riley to fall into a fitful sleep. She waited for the measured deep breaths. She willed her energy into focusing on Riley's thoughts. She saw a beach in Washington state. She saw other symbols that made no sense to her. She focused on making herself visible to Riley.

"I see you. You are whole," Riley said to her.

Eva smiled and reached out to Riley. "I'm okay. I'm here. I'm with you."

Riley's eyes popped open, and the dream was gone. Eva was back in the bedroom in the dark.

She willed herself to Justin's bedroom. She tried to pop into his dream as well. She made herself visible in a living room chair in his dream. She said, "Can you see me?"

"I can see you, Mom Mom."

"Good. Beautiful Boy, you know I'm always looking over you. I'm always here. I will do what I can to protect you from here on out."

"I know, Mom."

"I love you."

"I love you more." And she was gone, sitting in the darkness of his room. His gray and white cat looked at her in the blackness.

"You can see me," she said to the cat.

It just stared at her in response.

She moved and the cat's eyes followed her.

She remained in Justin's room all night watching him sleep. When he woke up, he looked at his calendar on the wall. He saw his mom's writing on the date. Today he was supposed to fly to California to see her. His heart sunk. He traced her writing with his finger.

He went up the stairs to the kitchen and sat at the table. Lucy was cooking eggs; his dad was watching a video on his phone laughing.

"Good morning," Lucy said.

"Morning." Justin put his head down on his arms on the table.

"Good thing you don't have to fly to California today. You would have had to get up way earlier," Lucy said.

Eva focused on the grease in the pan Lucy was using. She focused as hard as she could and caused a large pop. Grease splashed up and burned Lucy's hand.

"Motherfucker!" she shouted.

Doug jumped up. "Are you okay?"

"Grease just splashed and hit me." Doug steered her to the sink and ran cold water for her. He took over the cooking.

Eva was proud of herself.

"Dad, what day is the funeral?" Justin asked.

"Yeah, bud... I don't think you are going. It's not a good idea."

Eva was not surprised.

"Why?" Justin implored.

"It's all going to be people who are not good people. People who will fill your head with lies," Lucy said.

Justin felt sick in his stomach. "I want to be there."

"No. Final answer," Doug said.

Eva saw the cat had come upstairs. She startled it, causing it to jump on the counter and knock the egg pan off the stove and crash to the floor.

Justin got up and went back down the stairs.

"Get back up here!" Lucy cried out. "You need to clean that up. Your cat made that mess."

Justin turned on the stairs and stormed back up. He begrudgingly cleaned the mess. Eva felt bad that he was forced to clean up after her antics.

She found her way to Riley who was at the airport. She had checked the large totes and had with her a carry-on suitcase and a backpack. She was wearing the pendulum necklace; fingering it gently, she then opened her backpack to see the urn was still safe. She zipped it back up and hugged it to her chest.

She called Max. "Doug sent me an email. He's not letting Justin come to the funeral," she stated. "I have some of Eva's things to give him."

"I will call an emergency hearing. You may not get him at the wake, but you will be able to meet with him," Max assured.

"The only thing Doug wanted was access to Justin's portion of the life insurance."

"Eva had that expressed in her will. It's in a trust, one part at eighteen, for tuition and books only and the rest not until he's thirty. Doug can't lay his hands on it. You are the power of attorney over that money. Justin will get a portion of her social security survivor benefits until he's eighteen. That's it."

"Thank you, Max." Riley hung up and boarded the plane.

RILEY KNEW THAT EVA WOULD not have wanted a traditional wake or memorial at a funeral home. She had called the new age bookstore Eva had taken her to in Ann Arbor all those years ago when they reunited, and asked if she could rent the coffee house for the day. The bookstore owner was touched by the sentiment and allowed it for a fee. Eva and Nana hung back and took it all in.

Screens that normally played peaceful and psychedelic images now rotated with pictures of Eva throughout her life. A playlist, similar to the one that played at the school, featuring Eva's favorite songs played softly in the background. Riley had the bins for Jack and Geri in the corner of the room. Eva's urn stood on a pedestal cloaked in black velvet in front of the window she loved to sit and look out of, overlooking Ann Arbor's Main Street.

A barista was behind the coffee bar to serve coffees, teas, and finger foods.

Britt and Harry and Drew and Jose were the first to arrive. Britt and Drew stood next to Riley.

"I can't believe Justin can't be here," Drew said.

"They are truly awful. I knew they were evil, but this is a new low, for even them," Britt sighed.

Riley nodded. "I will get a meeting with him at the courthouse this week, according to Max."

"What are you going to say to him?" Drew asked.

"That he's got a large investment I will be holding onto for him, his mom loved him more than anything, here's a necklace with some of her ashes and some things of hers I think you might want," Riley said, frankly.

"Can you make sure he has my phone number. I want him to reach out to me when he can," Drew offered.

"Me too," Britt added. "I would like to tell him the truth about his mom, the stuff they won't tell him."

"Of course," Riley said. She excused herself and came back with two of the purple bags. She handed one to Britt and one to Drew.

"You were her chosen family," Riley said. "She would want you to have these."

Britt and Drew each pushed the tissue aside and pulled out the velvet boxes and opened them.

Britt's large blue eyes spilled over with tears.

Drew clutched the pendulum in his fist and embraced Riley.

"Thank you," he said.

Jack and Geri showed up shortly after. Riley took them to the small conference room that was used for group readings, occasional yoga classes, and seminars with psychics, mediums, and other new age gurus, and on the day that Eva first brought her here, was used for a "couple's seminar." She sat them down and came back in with the two bins. She gave Jack his and Geri hers.

"I went through some of Eva's things and pulled out stuff I thought you would want. If there's something you know she had that you would have wanted, and it's not there, tell me and I will make sure you get it."

Geri shook her head. "This is unreal. Just unreal." She dabbed her eyes with a tissue.

Jack opened his bin and looked at the gift bag. He picked it up and opened it.

Geri followed suit.

Riley sat quietly with her elbows on her knees and her head in her hands.

Both Jack and Geri pulled their pendulums out and looked at them. "Forty-four years and this is all that is left," Jack said.

Geri put on her pendulum and kissed it. "We have Justin. We have Riley. We have memories. No one can take those away."

"Doug is keeping Justin away," Jack corrected.

"He will come back to us. He is his mother's son. He knows in his heart," Geri said sternly.

"I hope you are right," Jack said.

Geri and Jack stayed in the room for a while going through their bins and showing each other the contents. They laughed together and talked about their favorite memories associated with the various items and pictures.

Riley excused herself and went back to the growing crowd of friends and family. She had met most of them at one point or another over the last several years, but many she did not know.

She shook hands and hugged people as they came in and expressed their grief and shock.

"What do you think is going to happen to that psycho?" one large lady with thick blonde curly hair and bright lipstick asked Riley. She didn't remember ever meeting the woman, but she acted as though they had known each other for years.

"I don't know. I hope life," Riley said.

"In the very least," the lady said moving on to the coffee bar for a drink and something to eat.

Riley couldn't wait for the day to be over but she knew it was her due diligence to allow for everyone to be able to mourn and have closure.

Riley turned down the music and stood next to the urn in front of the window.

Everyone got quiet and turned to look at Riley.

"Hi… It seems like not very long ago I was addressing many of you at the wedding, and now…" She paused. "So, it's fitting that this is where we say goodbye to Eva. This was her favorite shop, her favorite coffee house, her favorite place to spend an afternoon. She brought me here when we first realized we were falling in love with each other. We sat here by this window and contemplated life together as us. She showed me from that day on, what love was. She made me feel loved and appreciated me like no one else could. She was taken from me. From us. Unexpectedly. She used to tell me that people come into your life for a reason, a season, or a lifetime. I thought she was my lifetime…" Riley's voice trailed off. "I don't know what else to say. I thought I could do this. Turns out, I can't." Tears spilled down her cheeks. Drew jumped up and wrapped his arms around her.

He and Britt spoke after Riley and Geri and Jack each said a few words.

People poured in and out for the next several hours. Riley settled the bill with the barista, and when the last of the mourners left, it was just her, Drew, Britt, Jack and Geri.

"I don't want this to be goodbye," Jack said to Riley. "Please stay in touch with me," he requested.

"I will," Riley promised hugging him tight.

"Same with me," Geri requested hugging Riley. "I'm only a phone call away."

Riley smiled. "Eva used to say that to Justin."

"Where do you think she learned it?" Geri asked smiling, wiping a tear.

"Let me help you with that," Drew said, taking Geri's tote. "I will be right back," he said to Riley and Britt. He went down the stairs with Geri leading him. Jack followed behind with his own tote.

Eva watched sorrowfully. "I didn't think it would be this hard," she said to Nana.

Nana smiled dolefully at her. "Trust me, time is nothing on this side. Before you know it, they will be here too."

"I'm at peace with not being alive. Kind of. It's seeing how sad they all are," Eva said.

"They will learn to get on, just like you did after I left," Nana said.

"I know," Eva said. "But to see them."

"You didn't have to be here."

"I wouldn't miss my own party," Eva said sarcastically.

Drew had returned. Riley, Britt and Drew sat on the couch by the window. Riley was holding Eva's ashes, all three of them wearing their pendulums. Drew laid his head on Riley's shoulder. Britt sat with her hands on her knees. "What now? What would she want?"

"She would go to The Aut Bar and have a drink," Drew informed her.

"She would," Riley agreed.

They took the urn and made their way to The Aut. The urn sat placed in the middle of a high-top table near the bar, they ordered appetizers and drinks. The first round was free after the bartender realized the silver jar was what was left of Riley's wife.

From The Aut they made their way to Eva's favorite Indian restaurant.

After dinner, Drew dropped Riley off at The Residence Inn. Riley entered her room and put Eva's ashes on the bedside table.

She turned the television on and then back off. She just wanted quiet.

A FEW DAYS LATER, CHRISTMAS Eve, Riley was sitting in a conference room in the courthouse with Max. They were waiting for Doug and Justin to arrive.

The blue tote was in the center of the table. Eva's urn was next to the tote.

Doug and his attorney stood outside of the room and Justin came in. He rushed to Riley and hugged her, his eyes welling up with tears.

"Mum..." he said.

"Hey... I'm so sorry that this has happened," Riley whispered.

Justin broke from the hug and looked at the silver urn. He picked it up, having seen enough movies, knowing it was his mother's ashes.

"I had a dream about her a few days ago," Justin said, hugging the urn to his chest.

"Me too. Wanna tell me about it? I will tell you about mine."

Justin recounted his dream, telling Riley what Eva said and what she looked like and what she wore. Riley explained hers was shorter because she woke up.

"So, I have some stuff for you and some stuff I need to tell you, and I forgot your Christmas presents, so I will have to ship those to you when I get back."

Justin smiled softly. "I don't need presents."

"Well, we bought them, and they are waiting for you. So I will make sure they get to you anyway," Riley said sitting down next to Justin at the table. "First, do you know who this is?" Riley motioned to Max.

"No," Justin said.

"This is Max. He was your mom's lawyer. He is going to talk to you first."

"Nice to meet you," Justin said to Max extending his hand.

"Nice to meet you, too. I've been hearing about you for several years now," Max said.

Max explained to Justin that his dad would get survivor benefits from Eva's social security until he turned eighteen. He then explained to Justin about Eva's life insurance. "She had a large policy. You are getting $300,000. But not all at once. She has it set that you will get $150,000 for tuition and books at eighteen, and the rest at thirty. It will be controlled by your mum here. She's in charge of it for you. Do you understand?"

"Yes."

"Tuition and books means exactly that, your mom wrote. Max showed Justin Eva's margin notes on the document. So, how that will work is when the bill comes, you give the receipt to your mum and she will pay it for you. Anything that is left over after tuition and books will roll over and be added to what you receive on your thirtieth birthday."

Justin nodded that he understood.

"This money will not and cannot be dispersed earlier than that, no matter what you may be told. If you have questions, here is my card. You can call me. Or if you need anything else."

Justin picked up Max's card and put it in his pocket.

"It was nice meeting you." Max stood.

Justin stood and shook his hand again. "Nice to meet you, too."

Max left the room and shook hands with Doug's attorney, and they moved off down the hall to talk.

Riley stood up and pushed the tote closer to Justin. "This is some of your stuff and your mom's stuff. Things I thought you might like to have. If you don't want it now, I will take it back with me and keep it until you are ready."

Justin stood up and opened the lid. He picked up the purple bag and looked at Riley questioningly.

Riley laughed softly. "You do the same eyebrow thing your mom used to do." Her heart cracked. "Open that, though. That's important for you to have."

Justin pulled the tissue paper out and lifted the velvet box out. He set it on the table and opened it and looked at the pendulum.

"That has some of your mom's ashes in it. That way you have a piece of her always." Riley's voice was quiet.

Justin pulled the pendulum out its case and put it on, flattening the pendulum to his heart, in the same manner Riley herself had done when she first put on the pendulum.

He then went through the tote, piece by piece taking his time. He looked at every piece.

When he took inventory of all of it, he put it all back in and put the lid on it. "I want all of it. But I'm scared they will throw it away. Will you hold it for me?" he asked Riley.

"Absolutely," Riley said. "When you are ready for it, I have it. Remember when you used to go to the office with me? You used to mock me leaving my phone number for people. You knew my number by heart. Do you still know it?"

Justin grinned at her and recited it back to her in the same sing song way she would leave it for clients.

"Good. If you ever need me, call me. I will always be here for you. No matter what. Not just to hold your mother's things or manage your trust. I am here for you because I love you and we will always be family."

Justin fell into her arms and cried hard. "I know. If I don't call you it's because they don't let me."

"I know," Riley said. She kissed the top of his head and Doug peeked his head in the room.

"It's time to go," Doug said.

Eva focused her hate and anger hard on him. A gust of cold air blew through the room and the door slammed against Doug.

Justin whispered to Riley, "You know that was Mom, right?"

"Probably. It's something she would do," Riley whispered back.

Riley grabbed the tote off the table and Justin followed Doug out of the room. Eva followed behind Doug and Justin.

Neither Doug nor Justin spoke until they got to the car. "Well, at least your mom set you up for college," Doug said bitterly.

"Yeah. She was smart," Justin said buckling his seat belt. He rested his head against the glass.

"What does that mean?" Doug asked Justin.

"It means that she protected my money so I would make smart decisions with it when I'm older."

"Well, she obviously forgot how expensive it is to take care of a kid," Doug said backing out of the parking spot. He looked at Justin and saw the silver chain peeking out of his shirt collar. "What's that?" he asked. "Around your neck?"

"Mom," Justin answered.

"That's morbid," Doug commented.

Justin didn't speak the rest of the way home. He just pressed his palm against the pendulum into his heart.

When they got to the house, Justin went straight to his bedroom in the basement and laid on his bed still holding the pendulum against his heart. In his other hand was the bracelet Eva had given him years ago. He was still counting the measures of his breath and staring at the mildewed water stains on his drop ceiling tiles. His fluorescent lights hummed dimly in the background of his thoughts.

"Mom Mom, I hope you can hear me," he whispered.

"I can," Eva answered. Justin didn't hear her.

"Help me be strong these next few years until I'm eighteen and can leave."

"I'm here with you. I will do what I can to help you," Eva replied, hoping he could at least feel that she was there with him.

A few minutes later, a very pregnant and round Lucy burst into Justin's room. "Hand it over," she said.

Justin sat up. "What?" he asked, confused.

"That disgusting necklace. That's evil. You will not be wearing some piece of a corpse around your neck in my home," she spat.

"I'm not giving you this," Justin said.

"The hell you are not." Lucy stormed to Justin's bedside.

"Get away from me!" Justin's bed was against the wall. He moved as far as he could from her and attempted to crawl to the foot of the bed. Lucy's hand gripped the silver chain. She cranked it around so that Justin could feel his air supply cut tight.

Doug came in. "What is going on here?"

"It's evil. It's voodoo to wear someone's corpse. This is a Catholic home. I will have none of that witch shit in my home." Lucy let go of the necklace.

"It's morbid. Yes. But there's no need to be excessive about it," Doug said doing absolutely nothing to stop his wife. Justin looked to his dad to intervene, but Doug stood idle.

"Give me the necklace," Lucy demanded.

Doug remained silent.

Justin relented and handed her the necklace, fully disappointed in his father's lack of intervention. "That's okay. Because my mother's love is always in my heart. I don't need the necklace," he said defiantly.

Lucy stormed back up the stairs with the necklace in her hand. Justin could hear her slam it into the trash bin. "Any part of that bitch belongs in the trash," he heard Lucy exclaim.

Justin held his tears back until he knew she wasn't coming back. He didn't want her to see him cry. "I'm sorry, Mom Mom," he whispered as his tears flowed unrestrained.

"It's not your fault, Beautiful Boy," Eva said, trying to direct her warmth and strength into Justin. She wished he could hear her.

She sat in Justin's room until he went to sleep. She waited for Lucy and Doug to go to sleep as well.

Eva targeted all her energy on the trash bin. She pulled the necklace out and brought it back to Justin. She slipped it into his sleeping hand.

He woke up when he felt the cool metal pressed into his palm. "Thank you, Mom Mom," he said sleepily, curling his hand around the smooth metal.

He made a drowsy commitment to keep the bracelet and necklace hidden together so as not to be found ever again.

Chapter 14

Mama's Boy

A FEW DAYS AFTER CHRISTMAS, right before New Year's, a package for Justin from Riley arrived with all the Christmas presents from his mom and Mum.

Lucy called Justin to come upstairs and get the large box that was sitting on the porch in the snow addressed to him. Justin ran up the stairs and plucked the box from the porch and took it promptly back down to his room.

Eva watched with a heaviness in her being as he sat down on the floor with the box in front of him. He opened the flap, and he could smell the lavender vanilla scent of his mom's house. He sat there and relished the scent for just a moment before reaching in. He opened the bag that would have been his 'early present' first. He looked at the pajamas. It was a sports theme this year. New Orleans Saints pajama bottoms and a Drew Brees 9 t-shirt. Justin rooted for both the Lions out of respect for his dad and The Saints for his mom and Mum who chose that team due to their coming of age hanging out in New Orleans together. The book was Neil Gaiman's The Graveyard Book. Justin read the back of it and smiled. It would be a fun book to read. The ornament was a buffalo. "Be the buffalo," he whispered.

The remaining gifts, some were wrapped, some not. Given the date his mom was shot, he figured she hadn't gotten around to wrapping them and Mum probably couldn't bring herself to. He opened a box that was from

Riley. It was a t-shirt with a buffalo printed on it. He smiled. He understood the message. He also got AirPods and some things for taking care of his guitar. He suddenly missed his guitar that he kept at his mom's house. His dad made it clear that was an "at your mom's thing". There was also a stuffed buffalo not yet wrapped, and some video games for his Switch, and some Legos.

Justin grabbed his phone and texted Riley, 'I got my Christmas package. Thank you.'

She texted back, 'I know it was not a very Merry Christmas, but you should try to enjoy it.'

Justin took a picture of himself wearing the t-shirt and holding the plush Buffalo and sent it to her. 'I will be the Buffalo for u & mom.'

He deleted the thread so that his dad and Lucy would not see it, and put away his gifts so they would not be taken from him.

Eva struggled in this moment, wanting so desperately for Riley and Justin to know she was there, and to feel them in her embrace. She was bitter and sad. Death was not any easier than life.

LUCY GAVE BIRTH TO A baby girl that she named Desiree shortly after the New Year. For a few weeks, Justin was able to escape her wrath and just focus on school and healing his broken heart. He began to re-read the Harry Potter books, after finishing the Neil Gaiman book he was sent for Christmas as an escape, also keeping those hidden just in case.

He learned that he could text Jack, Geri and Riley and delete them so as not to be found when his dad or Lucy went through his phone.

He couldn't spend too much time messaging them, but he would send little notes periodically. Erasing their responses as soon as they arrived. This exercise in defiance gave him a sense of connection to his mother.

Eva spent her time mostly following Justin around in his life. She enjoyed watching him learn and navigate life. She was proud of him as she saw so many of her own traits reflected in him. She also enjoyed going back to see Riley. She mostly saved those visits for when Riley slept. Occasionally making herself visible in Riley's dreams. Nana spent most of her time in that mysterious other place that Eva had yet to see or experience, coming to sit with Eva and watch over Justin and guide Eva occasionally.

Once spring had arrived, Lucy's annoyance with Justin returned.

Justin was sitting at the table working on his math homework. The yellow paint on the kitchen walls made the space seem cheerier than it was, almost mocking the constant dark cloud that seemed to hang in this home. The old, round oak kitchen table was scuffed and marred from years of use without placemats. The white appliances were scuffed from wear and tear from less than gentle hands. Lime green Formica countertops lined the kitchen work space and framed the sink. The window was open, and the breeze gently rustled the white cotton curtain into the room. The space was provincial and dated, and Eva felt at one time, maybe even a happy place. If Riley were there, she would be suggesting various updates to modernize the space.

"I asked you to load the dishwasher," Lucy spat at him as she was feeding the baby.

"You didn't," Justin said as he got up from the table, closing his books and putting them into his backpack.

"I did, but you didn't listen, or maybe you are just stupid," Lucy said.

Eva could feel her anger rising.

"No, Lucy. You never asked me to." Justin put his homework back in his bag. "I would have heard you."

"You are still a liar, just like your mom was," Lucy spat.

Eva focused her anger on the light bulb above Lucy's head. It flashed on radiantly making the kitchen ever brighter, before popping loudly and fizzling out.

Lucy jumped startled, and the baby started to cry and she feebly tried to console the baby. Justin moved to the sink and began rinsing the dishes and placing them on the rack in the dishwasher to avoid further ire.

Lucy moved with the crying baby to right behind Justin. "You are such a fucking idiot. You are doing it all wrong. I taught you how to do it. But you are too stupid to pay attention and learn. Such a waste that your mom left you money for college. You won't get in anywhere anyway. Too stupid to even load a dishwasher. Never going to make it to college. The glasses go on the side, bowls in the middle, moron." She hit Justin upside the back of the head as Desiree continued to cry.

There were two glasses on the side of the counter near where Lucy was standing. Eva concentrated her source of current on them, and they flew off the counter smashing against the wall.

"What did you just do?" Lucy asked Justin moving back away from him.

"Are you too blind to see? I'm standing here, those glasses were over by you. Maybe you did it and you are too crazy to remember," Justin retorted, his own hatred boiling over. He was no longer going to feign love or respect for her.

Lucy left the room with the crying Desiree, shooting Justin a look of pure hatred. "Clean that up," she spat at him.

Eva felt satisfied in finding an outlet for that residual pain and sadness that seemed to keep her anchored to this life.

Justin finished the dishwasher, swept up the glass, and went down to his bedroom. He pulled out his phone, and texted Riley. 'Hey, Mum. I would be on my way there next weekend. I miss you.' After it sent, he deleted it.

Riley replied, 'I wish you were coming here as well. It's really quiet here.'

He read it and deleted it.

He pulled the necklace and the bracelet out of his pocket and placed them on the bed.

Eva took herself back upstairs. Lucy had put Desiree down for a nap. She was in the bathroom washing her hands. Eva concentrated herself on being seen just enough in the mirror. Lucy looked up and saw the vague impression of Eva's eyes behind her. She shrieked and spun around and saw nothing.

Eva was having entirely too much fun. She turned the water in the bathtub on. Lucy could see the faucet spinning slowly as it opened, and water came pouring out.

Lucy cautiously moved over to the tub and turned the water off looking around.

She bolted out of the bathroom.

Feeling satisfied with herself, Eva took herself to Riley.

Riley had made the mantle over the fireplace Eva's permanent spot for the urn. She was sitting outside on the patio with Guinness. She had gotten a second dog to fill the void now, as well. She was a flashy fawn boxer Riley named Stella.

Stella was quietly chewing on a plush dog toy at Riley's feet. Guinness was lying peacefully in the sun. Humming birds were darting around the feeders and the smell of jasmine hung heavy and sweet in the air. Bright pink bougainvillea climbed the lattice work of the pergola over the outdoor table. This was always Eva's favorite time of the year to be outdoors. She loved the bright flowers and fragrant blooms.

In the dappled shade of the lattice work of the pergola, Riley was working on her laptop. Eva peeked in on what Riley was doing.

She was creating a listing for the house.

Eva's heart sank. She loved their home. When they bought the place, it was an empty slate. They had done so many projects to create the peaceful haven the house had become; now Riley was going to sell The Nest. For their fifth anniversary, which according to all of the old school gift traditions was wood, Riley had a wooden sign made that was staked into the back yard garden that read, 'The Nest – Eva and Riley and Justin, too' it had the 'established' date for their wedding day.

Her breath held at the top of a sharp inhale, Riley hit the 'submit' button and the listing went live. She got up from the table and walked to the edge of the pool. She kicked off her flip-flops and rolled her pants up sitting on the edge with her feet dangling in.

Eva could see she was upset. Her brow was furrowed and her green eyes glittered with tears. Riley looked up to the cloudless blue sky and took another sharp, ragged inhale. This was not how she had planned their life. Every corner of the house reminded Riley of Eva and Justin and now their home was hollow and haunted by memories and a future that would never be.

Eva wished there was something more she could do. But she understood Riley's dilemma. They built their home, 'The Nest', together. She knew if the tables were turned, she would be doing the same thing. Knowing that she would have been doing the same thing didn't, however, make her feel any better.

LUCY HAD BACKED OFF JUSTIN for an entire week after the dishwasher and bathroom incident.

For the most part, she left him alone. He would come home from school and do his homework, complete his chores and retreat to his basement room until dinner, and then go back to his room after completing dinner.

Eva feeling protective, stuck around close to Justin, lying in wait.

Almost a week to the day since the bathroom incident, while they were eating dinner, Justin found himself to not be particularly hungry, he wasn't feeling good, and the smell of the food wasn't helping matters.

He sat at the table and pushed his food around the plate. "Is something wrong with your food?" Lucy asked.

"No. I'm just not hungry. My stomach hurts," Justin replied.

"Well, you need to eat," Lucy said. She was bouncing Desiree on her lap as she ate.

Doug finished his last bite. "It was delicious, honey. Thank you," he said.

"I don't feel great," Justin said. "Can I just be excused?"

"No. We don't waste food in this house. You will eat what you are given," Lucy said.

"My stomach hurts," Justin said.

"Too bad. Eat," Lucy said. She looked at the clock on the microwave. "It's 6:04. You will finish that plate by 6:30," she said, adding food to Justin's plate. "You will eat all of it, or else."

Doug stood up and took his plate to the sink, ignoring the situation unfolding under his nose.

Eva was as disgusted as she had ever been by him.

"Or else what?" Justin asked exasperated.

"I will take everything out of your room, and you will be grounded for the rest of the week." Lucy was sneering as she spoke.

Justin picked at his food and tried to take a bite. His stomach turned.

"Eat. Goddammit," Lucy growled at him. She stood up and handed Desiree to Doug, who took her and left the room, not bothering to speak another word or even look at his son.

Justin felt resentment for his father's lack of ability to defend him.

Lucy slammed her hand on the table. "Eat. Goddammit," she repeated, picking up her dishes and emptying them into the sink.

Justin took another bite and felt his stomach lurch. He got up.

"Where do you think you're going?" Lucy asked spinning to face him.

"I need to throw up," Justin said rushing to the bathroom.

He barely made it to the toilet as he vomited.

The temperature in the bathroom dropped as Eva's anger rose to fever pitch as Lucy followed followed Justin.

Lucy stood in the doorway while Justin emptied the contents of his stomach into the toilet. "You still have to finish your plate," she taunted. She could feel the temperature shift in the bathroom as she rubbed her arms in the door frame, unable to bring herself to enter the small room.

Eva zeroed in her anger on the lamps in the living room outside of the bathroom door, blowing both bulbs at once.

Lucy turned to look at them. The room was now dark, save for the light filtering out of the bathroom. Eva antagonized the cat, causing her to squeal, hiss and run across the room. "What is going on?" Lucy asked out loud.

Justin stood and flushed the toilet. He rinsed his mouth out. "I'm going to go lay down now," he said. Eva wished she could hold him close and snuggle him until he felt better.

"No. You will go back to the table and finish your food," Lucy said.

Why are you such a bitch? Eva thought as she blew the light bulbs in the bathroom one at a time, allowing them to flicker before popping.

Lucy looked at Justin silhouetted in the darkness. "Go. To. The. Kitchen. Now," she said between clenched teeth.

Justin went to the kitchen and pushed his plate away and laid his head on the table. He closed his eyes to keep the room from spinning, his face clammy against his folded arms.

Lucy stood in the kitchen staring at him. "I told you to eat. You had until 6:30. It's 6:23. You better get to eating."

"I don't feel good," Justin repeated, holding his ground.

In a contemptible standoff, Lucy stood there for the next 7 minutes watching him refuse to move, with his head on the table.

When the clock shifted to 6:30, Lucy went down to the basement. Justin could hear all of his possessions being pushed or thrown out of the bedroom.

Satisfied with herself, Lucy came back up the stairs and pointed for Justin to go.

As Justin got up to go downstairs, Doug came back in the room with Desiree in his arms. "Why is it so dark in the living room?" he asked.

"All of the lamps blew in the living room and the lights in the bathroom. I think we blew a fuse or something," Lucy said.

"What's going on in here?" he asked looking at Justin.

"I don't feel good. I threw up. I'm going to bed," Justin replied as he stood.

"He made himself throw up. He's faking it. I grounded him," Lucy informed Doug.

Justin did not stick around to hear his father not stand up for him again. He went down the stairs and saw all his possessions in a pile outside the door. His books, his tablet, his paper, all of it. The only things left in his room were his bed and dresser and lamp.

He closed his bedroom door and pulled his pendulum and the bracelet out of his pocket and stowed them under his pillow.

He put on his pajamas and went to make his way to the basement bathroom to brush his teeth and wash his face.

When he opened the door, Doug was there. "Hey, buddy," Doug said. "Can you just try to get along? It's a lot of stress on Lucy right now with being a new mom and all. She worked really hard to make dinner for all of us."

"Yeah, Dad. Sure. I just don't feel good, and I want to go to bed now," Justin said, holding back his anger. He wanted to ask why his father could stand up for Lucy but never him.

"Okay… Well, goodnight. Feel better. You have school in the morning."

Justin rolled his eyes once his dad turned around to go back upstairs. He brushed his teeth and went back to his bedroom.

As he put his head on his pillow, his other hand slid underneath holding his pendulum and the bracelet.

From the darkened corner of his room, Eva sat with him and watched him all night.

OVER THE WEEKEND, DOUG WAS changing out the blown light bulbs, Justin helping him. "So weird all of these bulbs blew at once," Doug commented.

"Dad, can I have my things back, now?" Justin asked as he handed his father another bulb. There was a strong indication in Justin's mind of who or what was responsible for the blown lightbulbs.

"I don't see why not," Doug replied.

"I don't think he's earned it," Lucy replied, coming into the room.

"How do you expect him to earn it?" Doug questioned as he balanced on the step stool and removed a blown bulb.

"I think he needs to get outside and do some lawn clean up, and then load the dishwasher properly. Let's see how he finishes his plate tonight, as well," Lucy replied.

Doug nodded in agreement with his wife.

Justin took a deep breath and handed his father the last light bulb for the bathroom.

Eva considered knocking the stepstool over and causing Doug to fall, but did not act on her impulse.

With his phone set to a playlist he made with his mom, consisting of songs she had introduced him to, volume in his AirPods cranked loud, Justin worked on cleaning up the yard of winter debris and leftover leaves most of the afternoon. Eva idly watched over him.

HE WENT INSIDE, AIRPODS STILL playing music and began to load the dishwasher.

He didn't hear Lucy enter the kitchen. "You took too long with the yard. You are not getting your stuff back," she said.

Justin did not hear her, so there was no reply.

"Idiot. Did you hear me?" Lucy asked.

Eva's anger was rising within her. She sat back ready to lash out on Lucy.

Justin was still oblivious to Lucy's presence or her statements. He held the sponge in his hand, wiping the food remnants from the brown ceramic plate as he quietly sang along to the song in his ears.

Lucy whacked him upside the head. Startled he dropped the plate, causing it to crash to the floor and shatter in pieces on the floor around his feet.

Lucy hit him twice more over the head and pushed him back against the sink. "You clueless, careless fool!" she shouted.

Eva manipulated the broken plate shards and zoomed them toward Lucy's bare feet before blowing every light in the kitchen.

Lucy stumbled back in pain, yelling out. Each step backward leaving a bloody footprint as the broken shards stuck out from the sides of her feet.

Justin looked around and down at the pattern of broken pieces on the floor. He knew that was not how the plate had broken when it fell. He bent down in the dim afternoon light from the window to inspect it. His music still playing in his ears. Seeking to let Justin know she was there, Eva manipulated the songs and jumped to 'Would?' from Alice in Chains, a song

Eva would sing to Justin often as a baby. Every time the song would come on while they were together, Eva always felt the need to tell Justin that she used to sing that song to him. It used to annoy him that she would always tell him, "I sang this chorus to you as a baby. I never bothered to learn lullabies. This worked just as well." Justin knew at that moment Eva was there with him trying to protect him. He looked up and around, hoping he could catch a glimpse of her.

Lucy was still yelling and screaming in his background, but he had tuned her out completely. He turned the volume up to further drown Lucy out.

Doug came rushing into the room.

Justin could see that Doug and Lucy were exchanging words. He was sitting on the floor next to the broken plate with Lucy's blood spattered on the floor. He was lost in the lyrics of the song in the chorus.

After pulling some of the larger shards of glass from her foot, Doug had handed Lucy a towel to stave the bleeding and left the room again.

Justin got up from the floor lost in his music. He moistened a dish towel and wiped up Lucy's blood from the cream-colored vinyl tile. He grabbed the broom and began to sweep.

As Justin finished sweeping and moved to dump the remnants of the plate in the trash, Doug came back in and bandaged Lucy's foot.

The kitchen was getting darker. Doug paused in his bandaging to try to turn the lights on. Justin spoke loudly over his music playing in his ears, "The light bulbs are out."

Doug shook his head perplexed.

Without waiting for permission, Justin took himself downstairs. He didn't wait for his dad or Lucy's approval, he started moving his items back into his room.

When he had finished moving his possessions back and organizing them, he sat on his bed and took his AirPods out.

"Mom Mom, I know that was you," he said.

"I know you know. You are smart," Eva said. Justin couldn't hear her.

"Was that you?" he asked.

She flickered the light for him. He caught on.

"Is that you making all the lights go out?" he asked.

She flickered the light again for him.

"Thank you, Mom Mom. I miss you every day," he said, pulling out one of his Harry Potter books so he could resume reading.

She flickered the lights one more time for him.

He pulled the pendulum out of his pocket and kissed it, placing it back safely.

Satisfied with her moment of vengeance, Eva took herself to Riley to check in on her. The house had a for sale sign in the front, another sign advertising 'Open House', and the large French front doors held open by Eva's favorite Fleur-de-lis door stoppers they had purchased on a trip to New Orleans.

Guinness and Stella were penned in the dog run out back and Riley was standing in the kitchen in her suit, her book to 'capture' information on the couples walking through open in front of her.

One couple was walking through the master bedroom, the wife turned to the husband and whispered, "This is the house of the teacher that was murdered."

"You know that for sure?"

"Yep. That's her wife. I recognize her from the news."

"Well, that's creepy." The husband pretended to shiver, and they exited the room. "Well, thank you. We will let you know," he called as he ushered his wife out of the house.

Riley had pretended that she didn't hear the couple's conversation from where she was standing. But to hear that couple speak of her tragedy like it was a sideshow attraction made her bristle inside. Years of professionalism helped to keep her quiet. A realtor she had done several deals with in the past had entered with a young family.

He encouraged the family to go look around and approached Riley. "Hey, Riley, Rick Laird. We worked together on a few deals in the past." He shook her hand.

"Hi. I remember you," she smiled.

"I'm so sorry about your loss. I saw it on the news," he said. "This is your own house, huh?" He looked around.

"Yeah. I can't stay here. There's too many memories," Riley said softly.

"I'm pretty sure this fam here will want to make an offer. It's exactly what they are looking for. Over three thousand square feet, large lot, pool... Are you going to stay local?" He was looking around as he talked to her.

Riley shook her head no. "I'm burnt out on California now. I am looking at building a home up in the outskirts of Seattle. Eva and I had planned on retiring up there. I need to get away from here."

"That's understandable," Rick said. He didn't know what else to say. He busied himself with checking his phone. The family he brought was chatting excitedly as they went from room to room. The two young sons were bickering over which bedroom would be whose, one laying claim to Justin's bedroom, the other staking out the room she used as a home office. The young mother complimented the colors on the walls and the art. Riley's heart hurt. Eva loved to take their guests through the home and explain the different art choices and where they found them and the stories they had made in finding them. Some pieces from art auctions on the cruise ships, some pieces from galleries in local towns or artisan markets from the many places they had visited. Always an adventure and always a piece to mark that adventure, always a story to tell. Riley did not understand when Eva first put her foot down on what would go up on the walls, but as the years went on, and the stories and memories spilled themselves over the walls, Riley had pictured them in retirement with Eva silver haired and lined showing their grandchildren the pieces and telling their story. How she had loved to watch Eva tell stories – getting excited and getting lost in explaining the details making the story come to life for her audience. Riley shook her head to break from reverie.

The young kids walked out of the sliding glass doors to the back yard, "Mom! There's a pool! With a waterfall! Dad! Look at the grill! And the dogs! Do the dogs come with the house?" the young boy asked excitedly of Rick.

The rest of the family joined the young boy outside, "No, the dogs stay with me!" Riley called out to him smiling through her pain.

She could hear the boy ask his parents if they could get dogs too when they bought this house.

Eva remembered back to the time when she and Riley had watched this house as it was being built, and when Justin arrived for the first time and saw the yard. She felt bitter and robbed for the first time in a long time. The mother who was so complimentary of the art on the walls commented on the landscaping. "This is going to be our home..." the mom decided looking at her husband smiling.

"Let's talk about that offer." The husband turned to Rick.

Eva's pain erupted out of her. Riley got chills and felt cold.

Eva could not stay here for the rest of it. She took herself back to Justin, who had fallen asleep with his book open on his chest.

Nana was waiting for her in Justin's bedroom. "He's a good kid," Nana said.

"I know," Eva said coolly.

"You are angry."

"I was robbed. Everything was taken from me. I realize I took much of it for granted. But I was robbed. Riley is selling our house. My son is unhappy and isolated. This is not fair."

"You don't get to pick and choose for the living. Riley cannot hold on to that house and stay stuck. She still has a life to live. Justin has lessons he needs to learn. You can help him, but you can't shield him from his life or what he needs to do or learn."

"So what was my lesson? What was my purpose?" Eva's entire being was a ball of pain. "Isn't this supposed to be clear to me now?"

"You haven't given yourself time or permission to accept your fate yet. You are still busy living."

"What about you?" Eva asked. "You are with me, following me, talking to me, helping me."

"But I had time first. I reflected on my life, accepted what I could have done versus what I did do. I forgave myself. I'm healed. Your soul will heal when it's ready. You still have work," Nana said. "Don't rush. When you are ready. When you understand, you will know."

EVA ENJOYED WATCHING DESIREE PLAY in her Pack N Play; however she felt bad that the baby was stuck with Lucy as a mom. She was a pretty baby with chubby cheeks and soft black peach fuzz on her head and large round hazel eyes. She was a happy baby and very observant. Lucy never read to her, and just seemed to yell and be frustrated all the time. Whenever Desiree cried, Lucy seemed to take it as a personal failing on her behalf, not seeming to understand babies cry to communicate.

Justin would occasionally hold Desiree and read to her, remembering how he always enjoyed being read to.

It had been almost a month since the plate incident. Justin was playing with Desiree on a blanket spread out in the living room.

Eva had found that Desiree could see her just as the cat could. Eva was playing peek-a-boo with the baby behind Justin. Desiree was laughing and cooing. Justin assumed she was laughing at him.

Lucy was sitting on the couch near where Justin and Desiree were playing scrolling on her phone, with the television tuned to some inane show in the background. Justin caught on that Desiree was not looking and laughing at him but looking over his shoulder and pointing.

He looked over his shoulder and couldn't see anything.

"What?" Lucy asked as Justin kept checking over his shoulder.

"I don't know. I thought I saw something," Justin said.

"Are you crazy like your mom was?" Lucy asked, a smile twisted on her face.

"My mom wasn't crazy," Justin said matter of factly.

"Don't talk back to me. You will teach your sister bad habits."

"Don't talk about my mom," Justin retorted.

"Oh. You think because she's dead she was a saint? When will you understand she was terrible? She was trash. She abandoned you. She left your dad so she could be 'gay'," Lucy used air quotes around the word 'gay'. "She didn't love you or anyone else. She only loved herself. How any mother could leave her kid... She should have just sucked it up for you. She would have, if she was a good mom."

"I'm not going to listen to you talk about my mom like that." Justin stood.

"Stay right there, kid," Lucy ordered.

Justin stopped in his tracks and turned to face Lucy.

"You need to understand the truth."

"I do know the truth. You never even met my mom in person. You never talked to her. You didn't know her."

"Don't you dare defend that piece of shit in front of me. She was a selfish bitch. Selfish like you. Your dad told me all about her. She didn't care about you. She didn't care about him. She was crazy, too. She was in a mental hospital. Your dad told me all about it. She thought she was better than everyone. Just like you."

"Liar," Justin said.

Lucy stood. "Call me a liar again." She stepped around Desiree and closed the gap between her and Justin.

"Liar," Justin said defiantly.

Lucy took another step toward Justin raising her hand to strike him. Eva sent the cat across the room by startling her. She tripped Lucy, who came toppling over twisting her ankle. "God damn cat. I'm getting rid of that stupid thing."

"No. She's my cat," Justin said. He turned and picked the cat up and went down to his room.

Lucy slowly got up and limped back to the couch.

When Doug got home from work, he ended up taking Lucy to the Urgent Care to have her swollen ankle X Rayed. Justin stayed home with Desiree.

He fed her, changed her, and sat in the sliding rocker in the ostentatious pink bedroom that Lucy went crazy decorating when she found out she was pregnant with a girl. Everything from the walls, to the area rug, to curtains and bedding were various shades of pink. Justin rocked her and read her a Dr. Seuss story from a book that had been his, and put her to bed in her crib. He made himself a can of Chef Boyardee ravioli and grabbed the baby monitor and watched a movie on the couch.

He texted Jack. 'If I could, I would go live with you or Mum,' he said.

Jack responded, 'I would let you in a heartbeat. Miss you, buddy.'

Justin deleted the thread.

He texted Riley. 'I hope you are doing okay. I miss California.'

She responded, 'California sure misses you. It's going to miss me soon as well.'

'Where are you going?' Justin asked.

'I'm moving to Washington.'

'How will I find you?' Justin asked.

'My number will stay the same,' Riley replied.

'Okay. I can't lose you, too,' Justin replied.

'You never will,' Riley replied.

Justin sent heart emojis and she sent them back.

He deleted the thread.

He texted his dad, 'How is it going?'

'On our way home soon. Lucy sprained her ankle.'

Justin got up, rinsed his bowl and put it in the dishwasher. He took the cat and the baby monitor down the stairs. As he made his way down to the dimly lit fluorescent lights and dankness of the basement, he missed the cool tiles and soft lighting of the long hallway that led to his bedroom at The Nest. He didn't want to be upstairs when Lucy got home. The egress windows and the hastily installed drywall with seams showing, and mildew from water leakage on the ceiling tiles of the basement had become his haven to escape her.

He went into his room and put on his pajamas. He heard them come in. "Doug, the cat needs to go. What if it trips Desiree when she's learning to walk?"

"That's Justin's cat. I'm not doing that to him."

"Suit yourself, but if one thing happens to my daughter because of that stupid animal, it's gone. Got it?"

"Got it," Doug said coming down the stairs.

Justin was sitting on his bed with his book when Doug came in. "Do you have the baby monitor?" Doug asked.

Justin handed it to him.

"Thanks, bud. Goodnight." Doug took it and left.

Justin sat back on his bed. "Mom Mom, I miss our goodnights. Reading together. Talking. You always asked me, 'anything on your heart or mind you would like to talk about…' I want away from here."

Eva flickered his lights so he would know she was there. He couldn't see her or hear her.

Justin understood the flickers were from her and took comfort in the signal. "I have something on my heart and mind… I miss you. I miss Mum. I wish I was in California with you. I wish Mum could come and get me, or that I could still have visits with her, at least. I wish Dad understood me. Or at least took my side once in a while."

Eva flickered the lights. She couldn't offer him any wisdom. She couldn't hug him. She couldn't wipe his tears. But she could let him know she heard him.

The next morning Justin woke up with a sense of purpose and inner strength. This strength in large part due to Eva speaking to him in his dream. She had looked at him and pushed his hair back out of his eyes. She looked in his eyes, nose to nose. "Beautiful Boy, be strong and stand up for what you want. Your voice matters. Be heard. Speak your truth." He marched up the stairs where his dad was cooking breakfast and Lucy was sitting with her splinted leg on a chair. Desiree was in a Pack N Play in the corner.

Justin sat at the table and said, "Dad, I want to go to California and visit Mum."

"She's not your mum anymore," Lucy chastised him.

"She's always my mum," Justin said, biting back.

"I'm sorry, buddy. But that's not going to happen. I'm not going to send you out there for a visit. She's not your family. She has no rights to you. She did a lot of bad things to this family."

"What bad things did Mum do?" Justin asked. He honestly wanted to know. He couldn't think of a time in his life where Riley was not there and in all that time, he had never seen her so much as even step on a bug much less purposely hurt anyone.

"She brainwashed your mom to leave you. She broke your family up," Doug said.

"Your dad said no. That's the end of the conversation," Lucy sniped.

"Well, then I would like to visit Gramma Geri or Grampa Jack," Justin said.

"That's a hard no, as well. You need to understand. I'm your dad and it's my job to protect you. I'm protecting you from bad people."

"How are Gramma and Grampa bad people?" Justin challenged.

"I don't need to justify my decisions to you. You're a child," Doug retorted.

"Gramma and Grampa are my family. I miss them. I lost my mom and now you are taking away everyone else from me," Justin said.

"It really was for the best that you lost her and that you are not exposed to the rest of them," Lucy said. "This conversation is over."

Justin got up from the table and went back downstairs without saying another word. He was frustrated that he was not being heard.

He sat at the shabby second-hand pine desk that sat in the corner of his bedroom. He looked at the calendar. It was close to Mother's Day. Mom and Mum would have been getting ready to come to Michigan and spend the weekend with him. He pulled out some blank paper and drew a picture of three hearts and labeled them, Mom Mom, Mum, Justin. On the back side he wrote, 'Dear Mum, Even though Mom is gone, you are still special to me. Happy Mother's Day. Love Justin.'

He folded it up and slipped it into his backpack.

The next morning, when he got off the bus at school, he walked to the administrative office. "I need to talk to Ms. Elmhurst," he announced to the secretary.

"Let me see if she's available," the secretary stated. She pushed up from her desk and walked down the hall of offices.

Justin sat in the plastic chairs lining the wall, hugging his backpack to him as he waited. A few minutes later the secretary returned with Ms. Elmhurst. "Justin! Hi! How are you?"

"I'm not okay. I need to talk," Justin said. His voice was trembling.

"Of course. I didn't want to bother you. But I figured you might need to talk eventually." She led him down the hallway into her small, cozy office.

In lieu of the bright overhead fluorescent lighting, she had two lamps set up, and the window was open allowing for fresh air to come in. Several potted plants adorned the file cabinets and desk and small end table near the window, and prints of Monet paintings hung on the wall. Justin recognized them from his visits to the Detroit Institute of Arts with his mom when she would come to visit in Michigan.

"How have you been, Justin?" Ms. Elmhurst asked as Justin sat down across from her.

"Not really good. I miss my mom. I miss her family, too. I'm not allowed to talk to or see anyone."

"Have you been talking about this with anyone? Have you seen a therapist or counselor?"

"No."

"What have you been doing to grieve for your loss?"

"Nothing. I can't even talk about my mom in the house. Can you do me a favor?"

"Depends. What is it?" Ms. Elmhurst asked, a gentle smile on her face and her head cocked to the side.

Justin reached into his backpack. "Can you send something in the mail for me? It's to my mom's wife. My mum. I can't talk to her, but I know she is sad, too. We both loved my mom."

"Yes. Of course," Ms. Elmhurst said warmly. "Do you know the address?"

Justin reached into his backpack and pulled out a piece of paper and his pencil and wrote it down handing it to her.

"Do you want to talk about your mom?"

Justin nodded.

"What do you miss the most?"

"Just knowing she was there. Knowing that I could rely on her. I know she always fought for me. Now, I must fight for myself. No one else can or will fight for me like she did."

"What does that mean?" Ms. Elmhurst asked as she set the letter to Riley aside.

"Dad doesn't really stand up for me. I can't have contact with my grampa, gramma, or Mum. People who used to fight for me, too. So, it's just me."

"Who do you have to fight with?"

"My dad's wife. She's like the wicked witch of Michigan." Justin stopped. He didn't want to say too much more. He was afraid if it got back to his dad and Lucy he would be in trouble. "We just don't get along," he finished abruptly.

"Why won't they let you see your mom's family?"

"They don't like them. Ever since the divorce it's been that way. I could only see or talk to them when I was with my mom."

"How about at the funeral?"

"I wasn't allowed to go to that."

Ms. Elmhurst was quiet, her lips pursed and brow furrowed.

Justin reached into his pocket and pulled out his pendulum and the bracelet. "I got one meeting with my mum after the funeral. She gave me this." He held up the pendulum. "It's got some of my mom's ashes in it. I have to keep it in my pocket and keep it hidden. Lucy doesn't like me to have it. She said it's evil to keep such things."

Ms. Elmhurst was in a difficult position with what to say next. She had her opinions about how the poor kid needed to have contact with his family and be able to mourn his mother. She raised her eyebrows.

Justin was always astute with reading body language. "I know, it's messed up, right?"

"It's not my job to say if it's messed up. It's my job to help you deal with and cope with it." Ms. Elmhurst exhaled.

Justin said, "You don't have to say it is. I know it is. Mostly, I was just hoping you could send that to my mum for me. I should get to my class. I have an assignment due." Justin stood up.

"Feel free to stop by and see me. Would you mind if I called you in from time to time to check on you?"

"That would be nice," Justin said.

Five days later, as Riley took a break from packing boxes, she stood and looked at the now barren walls, 311 playing in the background, wiped the sweat from her brow and decided to take a walk to the mailbox. As she was checking the mail, she saw an envelope from Justin's school.

Since the open house, Eva had not spent much time with Riley. She was drawn to Riley as she inspected the envelope. She tore the envelope open. She looked at the drawing and put her hand over her heart. She flipped it over and read the inscription on the back.

Her heart ached for the child that she had accepted as her own. She would have done anything to hop on a plane and spend time with him. Even 5 minutes.

The walk back to the house from the mailbox was slow. She still had to pack Justin's room and Eva's two closets, her daily closet for clothes and the one in the guest room she had used to store her bins of mementos and pictures. Riley hadn't entered either since before the memorial service in Michigan.

She walked through the front door and to the bedroom. "You should see the letter Justin sent me," she said aloud to Eva's urn. "It was for Mother's Day. It looks like he sent it from school. We would have been there in Michigan this weekend with him." She looked at the clock on her phone. "Actually, we would have been picking him up from school right now. He texts me from time to time and checks in with me. I think he misses you. I miss you both. I didn't just lose you. I lost him, too."

Eva felt warm. She felt Riley's love for her and Justin and wished she could soothe Riley's hurt.

Riley sat in the leather armchair in the corner of the room facing the fireplace. Eva used to sit in that chair when she was reading before bed. She sat there for a long time, as song after song filtered in from the speakers in the living room, and the sky grew darker, feeling nothing but the emptiness from within before getting up and grabbing a box. She slowly put it together and taped the bottom.

There were two doors off of the master bedroom that lead into the master bathroom. One for Riley's closet and one for Eva's. Riley opened the door to Eva's closet. This space had been forbidden to her since Eva's death. She knew she couldn't handle it and had honored that breaking point. It smelled like her in there. She looked at the clothes on the racks and the dresser against the wall. On the top of the dresser were two wooden boxes. One with mementos and letters and photos she had kept over the years. The other one had been Nana's, and had important jewelry in it. Between the boxes was a stack of books Eva planned to read, but never would now.

Eva was there in the closet with Riley looking at all her earthly possessions. All of the things she held dear were somewhere in this space. It meant nothing now. She had no use for any of it.

Riley did not know what to do with everything and stood there helplessly looking. She didn't know if she should just pack it all and take it all with her, or if she should donate it and only keep a few items – but if she did that, what should she keep and what should she let go of? She stood motionless for a moment and just breathed in Eva's scent. She remembered that fragrance when they were sitting together at the coffee house the weekend they had reunited, and later that night when they had first kissed. She closed her eyes and felt the tears slip down her cheeks. Wiping them away Riley resolved herself to her task at hand, setting the box down in the center of the closet.

She opened the drawer of the dresser and pulled out a t-shirt. It was one of Eva's favorites – a dark gray shirt with an oversized neckline so that it slid off the shoulder. Riley loved when Eva wore that shirt, and the tips of her tattoos would peek out over the seam of the neckline and where it slid down over her right shoulder. It was adorned with a large raven and said 'Nevermore' in large swirly script.

Riley re-folded the shirt and put it in the box. She grabbed Nana's jewelry box and put it next to the t-shirt, then grabbed the memory box and set it in.

She decided she wasn't ready to get rid of any of it. Nevermore. Her wife was Nevermore.

Melanie, Eva's work friend had packed up Eva's classroom items and brought them to her. That box was already stacked in the garage. Riley thought to let Melanie keep all of it but couldn't. When she had peeked in the box, she saw the lesson plans and notes with Eva's hand writing, and her Edgar Alan Poe bobblehead on the top. She was not parting with it. She couldn't. Not yet. And she couldn't part with any of this either.

On the shelf above the rack in the closet that held Eva's dresses was a neat line of stuffed animals they had bought on each of their trips. Eva took the seal they purchased from the hotel in San Francisco, emblazoned with a nautical wheel and the name 'Argonaut' the hotel's logo and knocked it to the floor. She wanted to give Riley a sign that she was there.

Riley picked it up and looked around. "I know you are here." Riley sat on the floor next to the box with the plush seal in her hands. She couldn't do anymore than she had today.

MOTHER'S DAY JUSTIN WOKE UP and kissed the pendulum and said, "Happy Mother's Day," to the pendulum. Eva flickered a light on and off so he knew she got the message. He smiled and put the pendulum in the pocket of his pajama pants and went upstairs.

Lucy was sitting on the couch with Desiree and Doug was cooking breakfast.

"Good morning," Justin said to Doug.

"Aren't you going to say anything to me?" Lucy asked.

"Good morning," Justin said.

"Isn't there anything else?" she challenged him.

"Is it your birthday?" he asked playing dumb.

"It's Mother's Day," Doug informed Justin.

"Oh," Justin said.

"Eh hem," Lucy said.

Justin ignored her.

"Ungrateful little shit," Lucy muttered.

Eva turned the television on. Lucy looked at the remote which was nowhere near anyone. Lucy reached for the remote and turned the television off.

"Justin, are you going to say, 'Happy Mother's Day' to Lucy or not?" Doug asked quietly in the kitchen.

"No," Justin said. "She's not my mother. My mother got murdered. I no longer have a mother."

Lucy heard the exchange. "Excuse me? I take care of you. I've taken care of you more years than your mother did before she got taken out."

Eva turned the television back on.

Lucy reached over and turned the remote so the television went back off.

"Justin, you need to realize your mom is no longer here. She's never going to come back. Lucy is the next best thing you have. You should be a little kinder to her," Doug said. Doug plated Lucy's breakfast and brought it to her.

Justin poured a bowl of cereal for himself and sat at the table alone.

The house had an open floor plan, so it was not like he was too far away or fully absent, but he chose the chair with his back to Lucy and Doug.

"Are you too good to join us? You think you are better than us?" Lucy asked.

Justin ignored her.

"I'm talking to you, Justin," she said.

"I'm good here," Justin called.

"That's not a request. It's an order. Come in here," Lucy said.

Eva turned the television on. This time she started flipping the channels fast.

"What is going on with this television?" Lucy cried. She grabbed the remote and turned it off.

Justin picked up his bowl and came into the living room. He sat on the floor with his bowl of cereal. Desiree crawled over to him and playfully grabbed at his bowl, causing milk and cereal to spill onto the carpet.

"Damn you, clumsy boy!" Lucy yelled. "Why are you just sitting there? Go get a towel and clean it up!"

Eva flipped the television back on and turned the volume all the way up.

Lucy turned it off.

Eva turned it back on.

Lucy turned it off.

Eva turned it back on.

"Doug, what is wrong with this television?" she asked.

Doug got up and unplugged it.

Justin came back in and cleaned up the cereal and milk Desiree had spilled. "If you don't mind, I'm going to eat in the kitchen now."

Justin refreshed his bowl and sat back at the table. His heart felt happy. He knew his mom was there and had his back.

He finished his breakfast and went back downstairs where he spent the day in relative peace. He could hear the goings on upstairs. In the background he could hear that they plugged the television back in and were watching a concert on television. It was a country artist, Lucy's favorite. Justin didn't care much for country music and was glad he was downstairs. He put his AirPods in to drown the rest of it out, listening instead to the 90's grunge music his mom had introduced him to.

After some time, Justin took his AirPods out and was charging his phone. He could hear the muffled conversation above him. Lucy wanted to go to a restaurant at the mall for dinner. Doug relented. Justin really didn't want to go. He could hear the dialogue from where he was sitting at his desk putting together a Lego set.

Doug came downstairs and knocked on Justin's door before coming in.

"Hey, buddy. Get changed. We are going to the mall for dinner."

"I'm not feeling good," Justin said.

"You look fine to me," Doug said.

"Dad, I think I need to see someone to talk about Mom," Justin said.

"Your mom is dead. There is nothing to talk about," Doug said bluntly.

Justin could hear Lucy making her way down the stairs. "What's taking so long? Are we ready to go?"

"Justin is not going," Doug said. "He doesn't feel good."

"Bullshit," Lucy said. "Get changed. Today is my day. You will acknowledge it. Let's go."

"Dad told you. I'm not going. I don't feel good."

"Doug, he is not staying home alone. This is my day. You don't get to dictate my day," she said.

Desiree began to cry upstairs. Doug looked at Lucy. "If he doesn't feel good, I don't think he should have to go. He'll just dampen everyone's mood."

Lucy looked at Doug and back at Justin. "My day. My rules. He's going." She stormed up the stairs.

As she came up the stairs, Eva turned the television back on.

"For crying out loud," Lucy whispered. She grabbed the remote and turned the television off as she picked up Desiree.

"Come on, you two!" Lucy yelled from the top of the stairs.

"I'm not going," Justin yelled back.

"Ungrateful son of a bitch – and wow – that word was invented for you!" Lucy yelled.

Eva turned the television back on and turned the volume up again.

Lucy walked over and pulled the cord from the back.

Eva blew the light bulb over Lucy's head. She began to stomp to the top of the stairs. Eva blew every light on her path.

"Fine. He's not going. Let's just go. And you need to call an electrician. Something is wrong with our wiring. This television keeps turning on and the lights blew again," she yelled.

"I will call one tomorrow on my lunch break," Doug said as he ascended the stairs.

Justin waited for Doug and Lucy and Desiree to pull out of the driveway.

He grabbed his phone and pulled it off the charger and texted Geri and wished her a happy Mother's Day. He texted Riley next. 'Happy Mother's Day, Mum.'

'Hey, that means the world to me. And I got your letter. Thank you,' she responded with heart emojis.

'Where do you think we would be right now if Mom was here?' he asked.

'Knowing your mom, probably Greektown!' Riley responded.

'Pizza Papalis?' Justin asked.

'Followed by Astoria Bakery! Chocolate mouse!' Riley responded.

'Yum!' Justin said, envisioning his mom's favorite dessert from the bakery. A small graham cracker cookie base, a ball of whipped chocolate mousse, a dollop of whip cream on top, covered by a thin candy shell, all coming together to look like a small mouse- the bakers even decorate them so they have small faces like tiny mice. The little mice were always lined up in the baker's case all looking up and out as the patrons enter the shop. It was Eva's favorite dessert, and it was a must have each trip back to her home town. Justin had grown to love them as well.

He deleted the thread and put his phone in his pocket. He put on his shoes and his hoodie and went out the front door.

He began to walk down the street. It had been overcast and dark all day, threatening rain though nothing came. The air was heavy and cool. It matched his mood.

He walked to the park nearby and sat on the swing.

"I wish I could run away," Justin said softly out loud. "I would run away and go live with Grampa Jack or Mum."

Eva pushed warm air to Justin. It swept around him and blew his hair back.

He lifted his head; he could smell his mom's perfume in the air.

He stayed there at the park on the swing for a few more minutes and rushed back home to make sure he was home before Lucy.

He let himself back into the house and back down to the basement.

DOUG CALLED AN ELECTRICIAN THE next day, and he was able to meet Lucy at the house that afternoon.

Justin had just gotten home from school, and he sat by in the living room to listen and watch.

Eva was highly entertained as well.

Lucy explained, "The lights blew all in one day, here in the bathroom, here in the living room. They've blown in the kitchen. The television has started turning itself on and off."

The electrician was a tall, very thin, older gentleman from Eastern Europe. He had olive skin and graying hair, and sharp angular features. He listened intently to what Lucy said.

Lucy and Justin watched as he went up into the attic space and then came back down. He pulled the plates off plugs and opened switch plates. He was poking around for over an hour before putting everything back. He looked at Lucy and said, with his accent thick, "There's no problems. Your electricity is fine."

"But why are we blowing lights? The television? Justin, you saw it. Tell the man."

Justin shrugged. "He's the professional. I'm just a kid. What can I say?"

"Sounds like you have a ghost," the electrician said smiling. "Or witchcraft. Someone curse you?" he said with his broken English.

Lucy rolled her eyes. "Just leave," she said. "And we are not paying you. You didn't do anything."

"Maybe attitude like that is why you have curse," the electrician said as he left.

Lucy slammed the door behind him.

When Doug came home, she told him what the electrician said. "We need a second opinion," she demanded.

"I will call someone else later this week," Doug relented.

Eva took this as an invitation to have a little fun. She was inspired by the electrician's diagnosis of a curse or witchcraft.

For the next 4 days, Eva blew lights, and messed with the television, now not only in the living room, but in the bedroom.

In the middle of the night, while Lucy was deep in slumber, Eva turned the television on and blasted the volume loud, also waking Desiree and Doug.

The moment Lucy turned it off, she turned it back on.

This struggle went on for 2 straight hours. Lucy was in tears and crying before Eva stopped. Justin tucked into his basement room, didn't hear a thing. He couldn't understand why everyone was so tired.

Doug had replaced all the lights Eva blew on Mother's Day. Eva went back and blew them all again.

She took these 4 days to go out of her way to make their lives miserable until the third day when they stopped plugging the televisions in altogether, resorting to staring at their phones instead.

Nana had shown up on this third day.

"Are you having fun?" she asked.

"They are such bad people," Eva said. "They deserve it. You would think they could at least read books though."

"What do you think you are accomplishing with this?" Nana asked.

"I don't know. Maybe nothing. But this bitch makes my kid's life miserable. I'm just repaying in kind."

"Do you think it helps Justin?"

"I don't know. He knows it's me. He knows I didn't leave him. I couldn't protect him in life. He probably wouldn't have been in this situation had I not fallen in love. So, I am making the best of my bad situation."

"How long do you intend to do this?"

"I don't know."

Nana left. Eva went down to the basement where Justin was reading the final Harry Potter book. She was proud of him. He could have just as easily been staring at his phone or a tablet, but instead, he was reading quietly.

The next day, the second electrician arrived. He was a local, and not an immigrant, which gave Lucy an air of added confidence, she was convinced he wouldn't blow off her concerns for superstitions. He did everything the first electrician did. Justin and Lucy watched again.

Justin knew the cause of the issues. He couldn't believe Lucy didn't see a correlation of her behavior with the incidents. He knew the second electrician would find nothing wrong with the wiring either.

He came back into the room scratching his head. "Ma'am, there is nothing wrong with your electrical wires, circuitry. Nothing."

She plugged the television back in. "Then why does it keep turning on and off? Why do my lights keep blowing?" She was gesticulating wildly as she spoke with frustration.

"Ma'am, I don't know. But it's not your wiring, or your fuses, or anything I can help you with."

"Thanks for nothing," she spat.

Chapter 15

Puppy Love

EVA LAID OFF TERRORIZING LUCY unless she did something to deserve it. It was a quiet month. No lights blowing, or televisions turning on randomly. She mostly just followed Justin around and stayed close to him in case Lucy acted out.

As summer approached, Justin grew increasingly moody. This was the first time he was stuck in Michigan for summer break. He was longing for the Pacific Ocean, and a big vacation.

On his last day of school Justin signed the yearbooks of his friends and sat forlornly on the bus. Nessa, a girl he occasionally talked to, sat next to him. They had bonded over being the center of brutal custody battles. He thought she was cute with her chestnut-colored hair, fair skin and large very blue eyes, but they had never really talked about anything else. Since his mother's death, she had not really talked to him much at all. "Are you sad?" she asked sitting next to him for the first time in months.

"Yeah. I normally go to my mom's for summer. I don't even know what to do with myself."

She grabbed his arm and wrote her phone number on his arm. She smiled at him, with her cheeks turning pink at her own boldness.

"Call me. We will be having a pool party this weekend. It might cheer you up. My mom and stepdad will be there, if your dad needs to know."

Justin smiled at her. "Thank you!"

"No problem. It will be fun. I promise. Just call me and I will give you my address and the time."

Justin smiled big enough that his dimples showed for the first time in months. "I will call you tonight after I talk to my dad."

"You have a nice smile, Justin. I hope to see it more!" Nessa turned a darker pink.

He blushed and kept smiling. He pushed his hair back out of his face.

"What kind of things did you do at your mom's?" she asked.

"We used to go on big vacations. For like 2 and 3 weeks. We would go to Canada, but not like Windsor – like over on the West Coast, Whistler, Vancouver. We would go on cruises, Alaska, and up the East Coast, to Mexico, Costa Rica, camping all over California… We would go to the beach. We would sometimes stay home and just binge movies all day, hang out in the pool, barbecue… Summers were the best time. I would wake up and do yoga with my mom. I know that sounds lame, but it was nice."

"Your mom sounds like she was cool," Nessa said.

"I was a cool mom," Eva said though no one could hear her.

"She was the best," Justin said. It was nice to talk about his mom with someone. Talking about his mom made him feel better.

Nessa smiled at him. She had a nice smile he noticed, even despite the braces. "I will go to my dad's for like 2 weeks in July. It will be boring. We will go up north and spend some time at his cabin. But it's so lame there." She rolled her eyes.

"It might be peaceful," Justin offered.

The bus stopped and it was her stop. "Probably just boring," she said as she stood up. "Call me! I hope you can come to my party!" she sang out.

When Justin got home he was alone. Lucy and Desiree were gone somewhere, and his dad was still at work. He preferred being home alone and could relax without worrying about what Lucy was going to say or do.

He went down to the basement and got his phone out and texted Riley. 'I miss getting ready to come see you,' he said.

She sent back pictures of a very green, lush back yard. There were large trees, and the sky was cloudy. 'This is where you will be coming to visit if you ever get to come see me,' she responded.

'Are you already in Washington?' Justin asked.

'Yes, sir.'

'I want to see the house,' Justin said.

Riley sent him several pictures of a nice craftsman style home with a stone exterior and a big porch.

She sent a picture of Stella and Guinness laying in the sun in the grass.

'It looks really nice. Mom would have liked it.'

'It's so quiet and country out here. Your mom would probably hate it.'

'How far to the grocery store?'

'Less than 30 minutes.'

'Then she would be fine. Remember, that was her rule. Thirty minutes to the nearest grocery.'

'That's right.'

Eva had spent very little time with Riley as the house in Washington was being built. It was hard to watch The Nest be vacated and a new life being built without her. She kept her visits to Riley short, and only when Riley was sleeping. She had begrudgingly given Riley her blessing in a dream. Looking at the pictures on Justin's phone were hard for Eva. She was seeing their plan for retirement playing out and she was not a part of it. Their dream house that she and Riley had talked about ad nauseum. She would have loved it and she knew it.

Justin deleted the conversation and added Nessa's information into his contacts. He waited for his dad to come home to ask about going to Nessa's party. Doug seemed relieved that Justin was going to hang out with a friend.

Justin called Nessa and told her he would be there.

She was very excited and gave him her address and the time to be there.

On Sunday afternoon, the day of the party, Doug dropped Justin off in front of Nessa's house. She lived on the nicer side of the town, which was not actually that far. Only 2 miles from Justin's own house, on the other side of the park. Her neighborhood had the houses that Justin was more accustomed to in California. Large, spacious homes with built in pools and high ceilings, the main difference being the homes here had large yards whereas most of the homes in California were stacked on top of each other with smaller yards.

"Alright, call me when you are ready to be picked up," Doug said.

Justin thanked his dad and got out of the car. He walked up the long driveway and knocked on the door. Nessa's mom answered, she looked like Nessa would inevitably look in about 25 years, with the same complexion and hair color, only she had light blue eyes and blonde highlights throughout her short haircut. "Hi! You must be Justin! You are the last one to arrive! Come on back! I'm Nessa's mom, but you can call me Christina."

Justin walked into the neat living room, full of light-colored furniture and orderly decorations – just enough to look lived in, but not enough to look cluttered. It reminded him of his mom's home. He longed for California and her. "You have a beautiful home Ms. Christina," Justin said. "It looks a lot like my mom's house did in California."

"That's right, Nessa told us about your mom. I'm so sorry." Christina seemed genuine in her condolences. Justin liked her right away.

He smiled at her. "Thank you," he said.

She put her hand on Justin's shoulder and squeezed. "I bet you are looking forward to having some fun. Come on. Everyone is out here."

Justin followed her out to the beautifully manicured yard. The pool was a large built in, not as elaborate as the ones he was used to in California with grottos and waterfalls, but it had a slide and was clean. Nessa was floating on a large unicorn in the middle of the pool. Four of his classmates were also there. Two of the girls he recognized from his and Nessa's English class, Savannah and Nicole, were lounging on chaises on the edge of the pool. Two other boys, Braydon and Hunter, twins that Justin recognized but didn't know well, were chasing each other up the slide. Nessa's stepdad was grilling hot dogs and hamburgers, he had dark skin, and curly black hair with eyes so dark they almost looked black, he was thin and in very good shape. "Justin, this is my husband, Nessa's stepdad, Krishna."

"Nice to meet you, sir," Justin said.

"Nice manners, young man! Burgers will be ready soon," Krishna said, with a slight, barely perceptible accent .

"Hey!" Nessa cried out and jumped off the unicorn and swam to the edge of the pool.

Justin smiled and set his towel down and removed his shirt and walked to the edge of the pool.

Nessa was at the edge of the pool. "Come on in! It's warm!" she sang out.

Justin greeted Savannah and Nicole as the twins came crashing down the slide one after the other in rapid succession. "Hey, Justin!" they called out coming up for air. They had splashed the two girls who squealed out.

Christina turned on the radio to a streaming pop music station.

Justin got into the water and let all his sadness slip away. Nessa's friends welcomed him right away making him feel as if he were a missing part of their group. Justin had a hard time distinguishing which twin was Hunter, and which was Braydon, which they thought was hilarious. The girls giggled a lot, which Justin did not fully understand. One of the twins suggested that they play chicken – the girls each climbing onto the shoulders of one of the boys and wrestling to knock each other off. Justin, being the shortest of the boys, and Nessa on his shoulders, were quickly eliminated.

They took a break from the games and ate and laughed with each other and Christina and Krishna kept the food and sodas (pop to Michiganders) coming. They got back into the pool and played Marco Polo, and then all lazed on floaties talking about classmates and teachers and recapping their sixth-grade year.

Justin had not had this much fun since before his mom had died. He found himself laughing and joking and enjoying himself. He felt, for the first time in months, that everything was going to be okay.

The twins left first, followed by the girls as the sun started to set.

"Do you want us to give you a ride?" Christina asked.

"It's actually not far. I think I'm going to walk," Justin said. He wanted to hold on to the joy and peace he felt throughout the day for as long as he could before going home to Lucy.

"I can walk you halfway," Nessa offered. "Can I?" she asked her mom.

Her mom agreed. "Just to the park and right back though, okay?" Christina affirmed.

"Thank you for having this party." Justin thanked her mom. He shook Krishna's hand.

Justin folded up his towel and put his shirt back on. He was glad he had brought a hoodie as well, as it was getting chilly as the sun sank.

Nessa ran inside and threw on her own hoodie and a pair of shorts.

They both put their flip-flops on at the front door and made their way down the street.

"Thank you for inviting me," Justin said.

"I'm glad you came," Nessa said.

They were quiet for a few yards. Nessa inched in closer to Justin and her arm bumped into his. She looked at him as they walked side by side. He didn't get the hint.

She reached out and held his hand. Her hand was warm and soft in his. He suddenly hoped his wasn't clammy or wet. His heart skipped a beat.

They didn't say anything else. They just walked quietly hand in hand. They got to the park which was halfway. Nessa stopped.

Justin didn't want to let go of her hand.

She leaned in and kissed his cheek, giggled and then she ran off embarrassed.

Justin stood there watching her run into the darkness as the streetlights popped on.

He cut through the park and made his way home.

He was in the best mood he had been in since before his mom died. Eva was grateful to have silently been along for this day. She didn't even mind that, though she considered Justin too young, Nessa had kissed his cheek.

Justin smiled, and put his AirPods in as he walked the rest of the way home.

He let himself into the house and went to make his way to the basement. "Where were you?" Lucy demanded.

"I was at Nessa's," Justin answered pulling his AirPods out.

"You were supposed to call for a ride," Doug responded. "We were worried about you."

"I'm sorry. I realized it was really close and I could just walk, and I didn't want to bother you."

"Bullshit,' Lucy said. "You just didn't think about anyone but you and what you wanted to do."

"No! That's not it! Not at all!" Justin was trying to hold on to the chill and calm he felt all through the day.

Lucy stood up. "You are a liar. It's what happens. They said that personality traits are inherited. You got your mother's sense of being a liar."

"Don't talk about my mom. You have no right to even speak her name," Justin said through gritted teeth, all sense of chill completely gone.

Lucy got in his face, nose to nose. "You. Are. A. Liar. Just. Like. Your. Mom," she repeated.

Eva popped every light bulb in the room with such force they shattered, thin shards of glass raining down.

"This goddamn house," Lucy muttered, the wind in her sails gone.

Justin just turned and walked down the stairs.

"Get back up here. Sweep this up," Lucy demanded.

Justin rolled his eyes and turned and went up the steps and grabbed the vacuum cleaner. He put his AirPods in and began to vacuum the tiny shards of broken light bulbs.

After Justin was done vacuuming the glass, Doug got on a ladder to replace the light bulbs with Lucy holding a flashlight for him to see.

Justin went downstairs and texted Nessa, 'I had fun today,' not really sure what else to say.

She texted back right away. 'Wasn't sure u would come over.'

'Y?'

'Cos i no u have a lot going on.'

'I do but not 2 much 2 hang w u.'

She sent a gif of a heart.

He sent one of a teddy bear with a heart.

He put his phone away. He wished he could talk to Riley or his mom. He would tell them about today. He felt alone and dark again.

Eva could feel Justin's loneliness as she sat and watched him as he lay on his bed. She flickered the lights for him so he would know she was there. He smiled.

"Were you there today?" he asked.

She flickered the lights.

"I had a lot of fun. It was nice. I like Nessa and her parents. I like Nessa a lot."

Eva flickered the lights.

Justin didn't hear from Nessa again for several days. He wanted to reach out to her, but he didn't want to seem like a creep. She finally texted him randomly in the middle of the week, as it was raining and thundering outside. The low oppressive clouds were dark, making the house dark and onerous as well. 'My mom is taking me to the mall. Wanna come with?'

Justin ran up the stairs. "Lucy, can I go to the mall with Nessa and her mom?"

Lucy narrowed her eyes at him. She was wanting to say something nasty, but she thought better of it. She didn't want to be trapped in the house with him moping around. "Sure."

Justin texted Nessa back. 'I can come.'

'Pick you up soon. Text address.'

Justin texted his address to Nessa. He ran downstairs and changed his clothes and made sure his hair looked good, opting for a ball cap instead.

Christina picked Justin up in her white Mercedes. "Thank you for picking me up," Justin said.

"No problem!" Christina said. "Better than sitting at home all day and it's not like we can hang out by the pool!"

Christina reminded him so much of his own mom. He was very

comfortable with her and thought she was very frank and funny. He sat back in the back seat as she turned up the radio. He noticed she wore Alex and Ani charm bracelets like his mom used to.

"I like your bracelets. Alex and Ani. My mum and I used to buy those for my mom for Mother's Day," he commented.

"Oh yeah?" Christina answered. "That's very thoughtful! What ones did you buy her?" Nessa turned around to watch Justin reply, she was smiling at him.

"My mom loved Harry Potter stuff. She was an English teacher. So most of them were Harry Potter."

"I read the Harry Potter books!" Nessa explained.

They had spent so much time talking about their custody situations they had never talked about anything else, so Justin found this new information interesting and fun.

They spent the rest of the drive talking about their Hogwarts Houses and who their favorite characters were. When they got to the mall, Christina hung back behind them so they could walk around and talk, keeping a careful eye on them.

The three of them ordered Orange Juliuses and sat by the fountain after making several passes around the shops.

Christina then took them for lunch at the Coney in the mall. The more time he spent with Nessa and her mom the more he liked being around them.

While they were eating lunch, Justin got up from the table and excused himself briefly. He had brought his allowance money with him. Nessa had commented on a small plushie of Hedwig in a store they had ambled into, so Justin ran back and bought it for her. He had remembered Riley running back into a shop while they were having lunch in Salem on their East Coast cruise. His mom had noticed a hand painted witch doll in a shop that was unique and pointed it out to Riley saying how cute it would look in her classroom, especially when she taught *The Crucible* each year. Riley disappeared from the table at lunch, had run to the shop and brought the doll back to the restaurant to surprise Eva. Justin had taken his cue from that afternoon.

Christina smiled as Justin handed the bag to Nessa. "That was thoughtful of you, Justin."

"Well, it was thoughtful for you to invite me along." He smiled bashfully.

They left the mall and Nessa rode in the backseat with Justin. She had her new plushie on her lap. They talked about starting 7th grade in the fall and what teachers they hoped they would have and some random game on their phones.

It was raining when Christina pulled up in front of Justin's home. "Thank you again for inviting me. I had a very nice time," Justin said.

Nessa smiled. "Thank you for my new friend!" She was beaming.

Justin's heart was warm.

"We will see you soon, Justin!" Christina called out.

Justin ran through the rain and into the house. He kicked off his sneakers at the door.

Lucy was sitting on the couch watching DVR'd episodes of reality television. Justin felt like his dad could not have found someone more different than his mom. His mom hated reality television.

"You have chores to do," Lucy reminded him as she scrolled on her phone, her inane reality show blaring out of the television screen.

"I'm going to do them right now," Justin said.

He went into the kitchen and started the faucet so he could rinse the dishes.

He noticed that the kitchen window was left open, so he went to close it quickly. Lucy yelled, "Why are you walking away from the sink leaving it running? Moron! You are wasting water!" she yelled.

"Someone left the kitchen window open. Rain is getting in!" Justin replied.

Lucy got up off the couch and stomped into the kitchen. She slammed the faucet off. Justin grabbed the kitchen towel and went to sop up the rain water.

"You need to get the mop, idiot. That's too much water," Lucy sniped.

"I'm not an idiot," Justin mumbled as he stood up with the sopping dish towel.

"Don't you dare talk back to me," Lucy said as she slapped Justin upside the head, hitting his ear so hard it rang.

Justin grabbed his head. Eva set her target on Lucy's feet – which were standing in the puddle of water. Eva pushed with all that she had against Lucy's legs, making them go out from underneath. Lucy crashed to the floor with a loud bang.

"Lazy son of a bitch. If you had just used the mop, I wouldn't have slipped." Lucy was crying.

"Don't call me a son of a bitch," Justin said as he grabbed the mop. "My mom wasn't a bitch. *You* are!" he said angrily.

"Excuse me?" Lucy rolled to all fours trying to get up. This time she felt an undeniable force as she was knocked back on her ass for a second time. Stunned, she sat in the puddle as Justin mopped around her.

"My mom," Justin repeated, "is not the bitch. Stop calling her that. *You* are."

Lucy attempted a second time to get up, furious, and Eva knocked her back again. She had had enough of Lucy and her petty power trips lording over Justin. She had been dead for 6 months, and this petty, small minded, insecure wretch of a being still couldn't keep herself from talking shit about her.

"My mom," Justin said as he wrung the mop out, "is with me. She protects me. You wonder why the light bulbs blow? Why bad things happen to you when you are mean to me? It's my mom. Just like the foreign electrician said. It's a ghost. It's my mom. And she is very angry. So I would watch what you do or say to me."

Lucy didn't question or argue. She moved to get up one last time, and Eva pulled her arm out from under her, causing her to hit her face on the tile floor.

"Unnecessary," Nana scolded.

Eva was smug.

Lucy sat up crying, blood pouring from her mouth.

Justin went back to loading the dishwasher. He didn't offer Lucy a towel or a hand. He just left her there bleeding in her puddle.

Desiree started to cry in the other room. Justin turned the water off and went to attend to his little sister. It was 10 minutes later before Lucy came into the living room. She still looked stunned. She had grabbed a towel and sopped up her bleeding. She walked into the bathroom and looked at her face in the mirror. She had chipped her two front teeth; her lip was split and swelling. She pulled up her shirt and could see where she was bruised on her tailbone.

She came out of the bathroom and picked Desiree up. "I'm going to call your dad and ask him to come home and take me to the dentist. Just get out of my sight. I don't want to see you or talk to you for the rest of today." She kept her hand with the towel in front of her face as she spoke.

Justin went down to the basement gladly.

He sat on his bed and took his phone out of his pocket. Nessa had texted him a picture of her with the plushie smiling.

He looked at the calendar. It was the last week of June. Nessa was going to leave for 2 weeks in a few days. He texted her, 'Will u have phone @ dads?'

'Yes,' she texted.

He felt better.

"Mom Mom?" he asked quietly. "Are you there?"

Eva flickered his lights.

"You shouldn't have hurt Lucy."

The lights flickered. Justin was not sure if that was an apology or if his mom had something deeper to say. Eva was not sorry one bit.

"I know she's not a nice person to me. But I don't want anyone to get hurt."

Eva flicked the lights again. She heard him.

Chapter 16

God and Intentions

AS SUMMER WORE ON, JUSTIN was bored. Nessa was gone to her dad's, they texted short and cute messages back and forth most days. But he missed the grand vacations and the daily adventures with his mom and Mum.

They had planned to go on a British Isles cruise this year. After the cruise they were going to spend an additional 5 days in London so Eva and Justin could go to the Wizarding World exhibit there. They would have been departing for England in the next couple of days.

He had one friend that lived nearby, Colin, but as they were getting older, their interests were drifting apart. Justin had become more cerebral, and due to the amount of tragedy he'd lived, more mature. His friend was stuck in the mode of gross humor and preadolescent games.

Out of boredom, Justin had tried to hang out with Colin. Colin's dimness drove him mad. He made an excuse and left early.

Justin was counting down the days until Nessa came back. He missed her quietness and her presence. He also wanted to hang out at her pool and with her parents, since that all reminded him so much of being at his mom's.

Lucy was avoiding him, and her harsh punishments had ceased for now. Justin enjoyed the peace, but had a sense that it was fleeting.

Doug had brought home a kiddy pool and Justin had filled it up and was playing with Desiree in the shallow water, splashing with her in the sun. It was a rare cloudless day. It was hot, but not overly humid. The breeze was soft. It almost reminded Justin of a California day. The pool was bright blue and had brightly colored fishes painted all over the bottom. Desiree was in swimmie diapers, and a pink bikini fitted over them, a large floppy sun hat shielding her face from the sun. Justin was sitting in the water next to her in his swim trunks. He was teaching her to splash and move around in the shallow water.

Doug came out and sat in a chair next to the kiddie pool. "I have been meaning to talk to you for a bit," Doug said as he opened a twist top beer.

"About what?" Justin asked, splashing gently at Desiree while she giggled and cooed.

"Lucy told me a while back, and I just didn't know, still don't know, if I should even talk to you about it. I almost feel like just leaving it alone is better."

"What, Dad?" Justin stood up and sat on his towel on the ground next to the tiny blue pool.

"She said you think your mom is coming to this house as a ghost. I know your mom and her whole family were into crazy dark occult things like ghosts and spirits and fortune tellers. Your mom's grampa that you never met was supposedly a gypsy or something and Gramma Geri's best friend is someone who supposedly talks to the dead. I don't know how much of this shit you were exposed to out there in the land of fruit and nuts – California – but that stuff is not real. It's just not. There are a lot of coincidences I'm sure, and it's easy to write that stuff off as ghosts or spirits, but it's not real. It's not true. Just like Santa Claus and the Easter Bunny... I didn't even want your mom introducing you to lies like that. That's all that shit is. Lies. Make believe. Fantasy. I don't think I even want you reading Harry Potter anymore. I think those books need to go away. They are feeding your head with fantasy and influencing you the wrong way."

Justin gritted his teeth and closed his eyes. "You don't need to believe. I know in my heart what is true," he said.

"Suit yourself. We are going to start going to church together as a family on Sundays. You need a little Jesus." Doug stood up and went back into the house.

Eva couldn't believe what she was hearing. She knew this was all Lucy. Lucy was just too afraid to dole out her punishments at the moment. She had been watching as Justin would push her buttons just to see her hold back from reacting and punishing him. She would watch as Lucy would inhale and hold her breath and fight her basic instinct. She could see Justin with his eyes glinting, gloating internally, feeling victorious. Lucy had sent Doug to do her bidding.

Justin didn't mind going to church. He knew his mom was raised Catholic to an extent. She had told him as much. She had also told him that God was found everywhere, not just in church and God was not man or woman, though some people like to say God is a father or mother figure. God is the universe, she had taught him. She taught him that magic was everywhere, and all religions had magic and beauty and ritual and to respect them all.

On Sunday morning, sitting in the small Catholic church between his dad and Desiree, Lucy on the other side of Desiree, Justin watched as the priest came walking through swinging his incense burner and remembered his mother smudging the house with sage. Justin breathed in the heady scent of frankincense and longed for the smell of sage burning.

The priest lit candles and Justin thought about his mother lighting white candles and meditating, teaching him to feel the floor beneath him and to count his breath. He closed his eyes and inhaled counting to five, and exhaled counting back down, just as he did with his mom.

Justin watched the parishioners go up for communion and he thought about his mother feeding the crows in the backyard and explaining to him offerings to beings of nature.

He smiled inside. Lucy thought this would be a punishment. He knew this directive came from her. She was the one also raised Catholic. His dad was raised Methodist and had not been to church on Sunday since he was a teenager. She thought this would be punishment, but he drew comfort in it.

He saw where his mother drew inspiration from these practices and adapted them as her own way of paying homage to 'God' or 'The Universe'. He put his hand in his pocket and felt his pendulum and squeezed it.

He listened to the sermon, and most of it went over his head until the deacon came up and explained it in layman's terms. It was a sermon on forgiveness and not holding grudges. He wondered if Lucy was listening. He looked over at her, and she was discreetly looking at her phone hidden in the hymnal.

He felt peaceful and light after the service ended. It also helped that Nessa was supposed to be home from her dad's later that night.

Lucy continued to avoid Justin, and midway through the week, he was at Nessa's house swimming and barbecuing with her family. He felt that they were all so easy to be around. Her mom was smart, she was a public defender who was passionate about social justice, like his mom was. Nessa's stepdad was a pediatrician who specialized in childhood cancers. His family had come here from India when he was in middle school. Justin awkwardly shared with Krishna how his mom loved Indian food and did yoga.

Nessa did not have any brothers or sisters and her mom doted on her endlessly. Watching Nessa interact with her mom reminded him of him and his mom. It did not make him sad, it comforted him.

He enjoyed the high spirits and peace that was extended to him while he was there. When it was time for him to leave and go home, he felt a cloud move over him. Even though Lucy had let up on him, he could feel that the peace was going to end and the punishments would resume and that it was coming any day now. He hated that cloud.

Nessa walked him halfway home again. Again, she was a quiet steadfastness next to him, holding his hand lightly, peacefully.

Feeling the warmth in his heart and lightness in his soul when she held his hand, he understood the paradox in which he lived. He understood the darkness and stagnation that was in his father's home. He understood why his mother fled – especially if this was the feeling she got in being with Riley.

When they got to the park, Nessa leaned in and kissed Justin's cheek again. And again, she ran off back to her home.

He spent the rest of his summer soaking up as much time as he could get away with at Nessa's house, or going with her and her mother to the mall. Anything to be around her family and her and avoiding the darkness of his own home life.

Close to the end of summer, after Justin asked if he could walk over to Nessa's to go swimming, Doug called him out. "Why are you going over there so much? Don't you have other friends you can hang out with? Colin?"

"I don't have much in common with Colin anymore," Justin said shrugging. "Nessa is nice, and she has a pool. And her mom and stepdad are cool. I like them. There is more to do over there than here."

"I don't really know much about them."

"Call them and talk to them then. Can I go? They are waiting for me," Justin quipped.

Doug took a deep breath. Justin was reminding him more and more of Eva with her stubbornness and smart mouth. He was also grateful that Lucy was not present for this exchange as it would have set her off. "Yeah. Go," Doug said exasperated.

After returning home from Nessa's, Lucy, sitting in her favorite spot on the couch, told Justin she had enrolled him in a summer Catechism class so he could learn to be a better Catholic and take the steps to become confirmed. "Because you were raised a heathen by your mother, you are behind. Most kids your age have already received communion and confirmation. You will have to do more classes this summer to get caught up."

Justin shrugged. "Okay. Whatever you say."

"I'm trying to make sure you save your soul. You should say thank you." She held out a pamphlet with the course information on it for him.

"Fine. Thank you," Justin said rolling his eyes.

"You need to be ready to be at the church by four in the afternoon, tomorrow," Lucy called out as Justin made his way back to his basement cave.

This, he was sure, was a ploy to keep him from spending so much time at Nessa's house. Justin looked over the pamphlet and saw it was 5 days a week for 3 hours a day over the next few weeks. A crammer course for new Catholics.

The next day, as Justin sat in the church classroom, he was the youngest person there. Every other student was an adult. The majority of them were there because they were marrying a Catholic and converting for the wedding.

For the next 3 hours Justin listened intently to what the deacon who was teaching the class had to say. Eva hung back and observed. She was never much one for the hubris of the Catholics referring to themselves as 'the one true church'. She watched as Justin opened the work book they were given and thumbed through it. He was a curious kid and was always wanting to learn something new.

Justin watched his fellow classmates ask questions and take notes.

Lucy picked him up from the church and grilled him right away. "What did you learn?"

Justin repeated verbatim, "The Catholic Church is the one true church. Communion is a re-creation of the Last Supper."

"That's it? That's all you learned?"

Justin shrugged. "That's all they talked about."

She turned up the radio on the country station and drove home.

The remainder of summer break, Justin was limited to the amount of time he could spend with Nessa being forced to attend catechism.

Justin didn't hate the class. He didn't love it either. If anything, he walked out each day with more questions than answers. He wished he could talk to his mom to ask her these burning questions and listen to her tangents and soap boxing about religion and spirituality.

He focused on the trends he noticed in the Catholic teaching that he learned about other faiths from his mom. Do no harm. Forgive. Live with love. As I will it, so may it be (is that not the same as asking in prayer?).

The irony of Lucy putting him to religious education to force her faith on him when she lived in the least Christ-like way was not lost on Justin.

He showed up day after day. He looked at it as an opportunity to be out of the house and learn something new. He did not speak to any of his classmates since they were adults. On the breaks he would text Nessa, one of the twins, Jack, or Riley.

He would go home and eat dinner and retreat to his room. He made a commitment to not complain about going to catechism, nor would he let Lucy break him down or think less of the beliefs he learned from his mom. He smiled when he sat down in the class, answered when called upon and completed the course by making his First Communion in a quiet ceremony that his dad and Lucy didn't even bother to attend. Eva was there, though, and Justin could feel it. The lights in the church flickered as Justin made his way up the aisle of the church and the host was placed on his tongue. It was his mom's way of communicating with him and letting him know she was there, and she was proud of him. He smiled as he made his way back to his seat.

Chapter 17

7th Grade

WHEN SCHOOL STARTED BACK UP, he and Nessa made sure to sit next to each other on the bus, and they held hands quaintly in the halls. They sat next to each other in the cafeteria, and he was able to get to know her small friend group. They all sat together at lunch every day. Braydon and Hunter treated him like a long-lost brother and he loved their playfulness. He even eventually learned to tell them apart, Hunter was slightly taller, and Braydon's ears stuck out. They were both tall and reed thin, and incredibly smart. They pushed Justin to do better academically as they were intensely competitive. Nicole and Savannah had been best friends since birth since their moms were best friends since childhood. They had adopted Nessa as one of them since the fourth grade. The five of them had been inseparable as a group since fifth grade and Justin was their missing sixth.

It had now been several months since Lucy had lashed out at him and he had been lulled into a false sense of security and thought maybe it was all done. Eva hung around, knowing human nature, she knew Lucy would start again.

It was a month into the new school year and now 3 months since Lucy broke her teeth on the floor. Justin's life routine was church on Sundays, school, homework, chores throughout the week, and Saturdays at Nessa's. He never invited Nessa to his home. He didn't want to expose her to the darkness he lived with. When he was at home, he sat at the kitchen table to do his homework, did his chores, and went down to his room. He would emerge to eat dinner, and then retreat to his room.

Eva hung around and kept a watchful eye. She knew better than to think Lucy would just change her ways. And she was right.

It was a Wednesday afternoon. Justin had finished his homework and taken the trash out. He didn't realize there was a small leak in the bag, and liquid had dripped onto the floor and left a path from the kitchen garbage can out the side door.

When he came back in, oblivious in his seventh grade haze, he went to head to the basement. Lucy yelled as he was halfway down the stairs, "What do you think you are doing, lazy ass?"

Justin, genuinely confused, turned on the stairs. "I'm sorry?" he asked.

"Don't act stupid. I mean, you are stupid, but don't act stupid," she said. "Get up here and clean up this mess."

"What mess?" asked Justin at this point, totally nonplussed.

"This mess!" Lucy was wildly waving her hands.

Justin came back up the stairs and saw the dribble across the floor. He looked at Lucy, and before he could even control it, he rolled his eyes.

Lucy reflexively hit him upside the head, and then pushed him to the floor. He fell against the chair.

Eva let her anger out with ferocity. She busted the kitchen window, glass shattering onto the table. Her force crashing into Lucy and blowing her back against the wall. She was screaming, "You just don't learn do, you?" but no one could hear her. Or so she thought. Justin was looking in her direction, head cocked. In some manner, she knew he could hear her in her rage.

"You just don't learn, do you?" Justin asked for her.

Lucy stood shaking and Justin slowly got to his feet. "I told you my mom doesn't like it when you hurt me," he said. He got up and went downstairs without cleaning up a thing.

Lucy, shaking, looked around the kitchen. Eva pushed the salt and pepper shakers off the counter onto the floor one at a time. She then pushed the jar holding the cooking utensils to the floor, which crashed and shattered loudly. She was tempted to take everything she could shatter in the kitchen and make it happen, but she stopped herself there.

Justin in his room, paced back and forth. He was upset knowing that Lucy was never going to stop. No matter how long between blows they were always bound to come.

He was angry. He was sad. He hated being there.

Eva tried to flicker the lights to let him know she was there.

He ignored it.

She focused on surrounding him in the warmth of her energy. He stopped pacing. He was attuned because he was always looking for her signs. He could smell her perfume and feel her warmth.

"I just wish she would go. Just leave," he whispered to her.

"I will do what I can to make that happen," Eva promised him. She set out to make that promise come true.

ON SUNDAY, AFTER MASS, LUCY dragged the entire family to the office of the parish priest. He was an older man, stout and bald. He had an undistinguishable accent, and bright blue eyes.

"Hi, Father!" Lucy called out. Justin was already embarrassed. Doug stood next to him holding Desiree, both of them behind Lucy.

"Hello, child," he responded standing back up and making his way to the door of the office. "Come in. Come in. How can I help you? Another round of catechism? Baptism?" he asked.

"Definitely a baptism for the baby, but that is down the road. We need our home blessed. There's been some random activity ever since his mom," she pointed to Justin, "died almost a year ago. Lights flickering, things breaking. You know. That kind of thing."

The priest nodded knowingly. "That sounds very disruptive. Was his mom a Catholic? Did she get the Last Rites?"

"She was a heathen. She practiced witchcraft, which is why I'm sure she's become such a bad spirit," Lucy retorted.

Justin cut in, "She was raised Catholic, but she was spiritual. She wasn't a witch. She was murdered."

"Not all souls who practice spiritualism are bad." The priest smiled with kind eyes at Justin.

Lucy frowned. "Can you please just bless our house?" she asked.

"I can." The priest scheduled to come over on Thursday afternoon.

On Thursday, Justin rushed home from the bus stop and just moments after he let himself in, the priest was knocking at the door. Justin was curious about him. He was accompanied by one of the Deacons. The Deacon helped the father put on his sash and handed him the bottle of holy water as they read from The Bible.

Lucy chattered incessantly as the priest was saying his prayers and splashing the holy water. Justin was nervous that this would work and Lucy would banish his mother's spirit from protecting him.

Eva meanwhile followed the priest around and watched. She quietly devised her own plan. She was no longer just going to wait for Lucy to lash out. She was going to up her game. She had a promise to Justin to uphold. She was going to get rid of Lucy.

When the priest finished, Lucy shook his hand. As he was leaving, Justin followed him out. "Do you really believe that not all spiritualists are bad?" Justin asked the priest.

"There are many ways of believing in this world. Just because you call it a different name, doesn't mean, in your heart, it's not the same," the priest offered. "You are a curious boy, aren't you?"

"I guess," Justin said.

"Are you worried about your mother's soul?" the priest asked standing in the driveway.

Justin came down off the porch and stood next to him. "Is it true, whatever I say to you is a secret?"

"For the most part," the priest reassured him.

"Lucy is the bad spirit. My mom's spirit protects me. She only does things when Lucy hurts me."

The priest nodded. "How does Lucy hurt you? How does your mom protect you?" he asked.

"I just hope that what you did didn't make my mom go away," Justin said, purposefully ignoring the priest's questions.

The priest caught on to Justin's willful skirting of his questions and didn't pry. "It sounds like your mom was a good spirit. What I did was drive away anything evil and bad," the priest reassured.

"Thank you," Justin said, and he turned and went back into the house and down to his bedroom.

He sat on his bed. "Mom Mom?"

The lights flickered.

"Good. You are still here."

Eva waited patiently before acting out again. She waited and soothed Lucy into a false sense of security for a whole week. While Justin was at school, Doug was working and Desiree napping, Lucy got into a hot shower.

Eva stood by and waited for the mirror to steam. She wrote 'Boo!' in the steam on the mirror with a happy face next to it.

Lucy opened the shower curtain and saw the writing on the mirror. "Doug? Are you home?" she queried. There was no response. She knew Justin knew better and would not have come in while she was in there. "Hello? Doug? You are not funny!" she called out as she wrapped her towel around herself. She was met with silence.

She felt the hair on the back of her neck stand up. She grabbed the hand towel and wiped the mirror down. She then flitted to her bedroom and shut the door while she was getting ready.

On Saturday, while Justin was passing his day with Nessa's family going to a pumpkin patch and cider mill, Doug had picked up an extra shift at work, Lucy was sitting on the living room floor scrolling through social media while Desiree played with a toy near her.

Eva turned the television on.

Lucy grabbed the remote and turned it off.

Eva turned it back on.

"Not this again," Lucy whispered as she got up. She turned the television off and unplugged it.

Lucy didn't bother saying anything to Doug about the last few days. She didn't want him to think she was crazy.

On Monday while she was home alone, Eva again wrote, 'I see you', on the mirror in the bathroom while she was in the shower. She then turned the hot water completely off. Lucy startled and shut off the water completely, opening the shower curtain to see the writing on the mirror. Eva turned the water back on, this time only the hot. Lucy shrieked, waking Desiree up. Desiree began to cry.

Lucy grabbed her towel, hair still foaming with shampoo to retrieve her baby.

Each day Eva did a little something to let Lucy know she was there. She varied her annoyances. Turning on appliances. Opening cupboards. Pushing items around. Flushing the toilet. Scaring the cat. She would only do these things when Lucy was alone in the house. Lucy didn't want Doug to think she was crazy, so she never mentioned these things to him. Not that she even cared what he thought. She was beginning to understand why Eva had left. He was just a sort of wet noodle that had nothing to offer more than a steady paycheck. Eva would listen as Lucy would lament on the phone to her girlfriends all of the things she herself used to complain about in regard to Doug. As she complained to her friends, she left out Eva's ceaseless tormenting. She didn't want her friends to think she was crazy either.

On Halloween, Eva planned her biggest day. She felt Halloween itself was cliché, but she knew Lucy in her ignorance would see it as significant. She started at three in the morning, not waiting for Doug to leave for work. Eva turned on Lucy's phone next to the bed, making the music play. She played 'Living Dead Girl' by Rob Zombie for shits and giggles. Lucy being a die-hard country music fan would never have saved that song to her phone.

Eva skipped the song over and over as Lucy fumbled with her phone, finally powering it down. The commotion again woke Desiree up. Doug, frustrated and having to work in the morning, got up and went out to the couch to sleep.

It was nearly five in the morning before Lucy went back to sleep. Eva turned the bedroom television on. Lucy moaned and reached for the remote and turned the television off. Eva turned it back on and tuned it into a station airing *Nightmare on Elm Street*. Lucy had tears of frustration in her eyes. She turned the television off. Eva turned it back on. Lucy unplugged it. Eva turned it on anyway.

Lucy got up and left the room. When she got to the kitchen, Eva blew every cabinet open one at a time. Lucy went and closed them one at a time.

After Doug left for work and Justin left for school, Lucy laid exhausted on the couch. Eva woke Desiree up and began to play with her making her laugh hysterically. Lucy came in and saw that the baby was interacting with *something* by the way her eyes tracked movement she herself couldn't see. She was visibly playing peek-a-boo with that something and laughing and moving her head around. Going from one end of the crib to the other, looking to the right and then over to the left and pointing.

Lucy snatched Desiree out of her crib. She went into the kitchen and all of the cupboards were wide open again.

Nana popped in on Eva as she was watching Lucy close the cupboards with shaking hands. "Are you having fun?"

"I have a plan. I know what I'm doing and if I play this right, I know the end game," Eva said petulantly. "Trust me, if this works the way I think it will, I will never have to do this again."

Nana left again.

Every time Lucy, exhausted, would go to sit down, Eva would create more chaos. Her coup de gras being throwing pots out of the cupboard, followed by writing, 'Peek a Boo! I see You!' in the shower mirror. Lucy quickly wiped the words from the mirror. Eva let herself be seen in the mirror by Lucy behind her head, in full form. She stood there still, grinning behind Lucy, whose eyes were the size of saucers. Lucy turned slowly, and by the time she made her way around, Eva was gone.

When Doug came home from work, Lucy announced, "I'm getting a job. I think I need to get out of the house. Desiree is old enough to go to daycare. I can't sit around here rotting all day. I need adult interaction."

Doug shrugged. "If you want to."

SOON IT WAS THANKSGIVING, FOLLOWED by the one-year anniversary of Eva's murder.

Riley attended the sentencing of Jake. She flew from Seattle to San Diego. She was wearing her pendulum with Eva's ashes. She had added Eva's wedding band to the chain shortly after the funeral. She fidgeted with it the entire flight, writing, and scratching out what she planned to say.

Jake had plead guilty to first degree murder. His dad reviewed the case repeatedly and acted as a consultant to his defense attorneys. Given Jake's outburst, and statements, there was no getting around it. He had planned it, told people he planned it. He had to go to his father's gun safe, unlock it, choose the gun, load the gun, go to the school, and had waited in the parking lot for Eva for over two hours, gun cocked and ready. Pleading would get him a softer sentence.

Speaking at the sentencing would be Riley, Jack, Geri, Britt, Cynthia and Murphy. They sat together and watched as Jake was marched in, wearing a bright orange jumpsuit. His wrists and ankles were shackled. His hair neat. He didn't look like a killer. He looked like a nice young man playing dress up.

Eva saw him for the first time since he murdered her. She wasn't mad at him. She felt bad for him. He threw his life away and for what?

She looked at the row of loved ones sitting there waiting to speak for her. Murphy went first. He talked about how Eva made an impact as a teacher and a friend. How Jake responded in the office. The wake of devastation Murphy saw on campus.

Cynthia talked about Eva as a dedicated teacher and how so many students were devastated by her loss and the terror his act caused on the campus.

Britt talked about how she had known Eva more years in her life than not, and how lost she was to know that her best friend was gone, the hole it left.

Geri talked about losing her daughter and her best friend.

Jack talked about losing his daughter, and how Justin was now motherless.

Riley was last to talk. She wore a black button-down shirt, and a slate gray suit. The white polished metal of pendulum and wedding ring set against the stark colors, sitting on top of the shirt gleamed in the lights of the courtroom.

Riley came to the podium and turned so that she was not facing the judge as everyone else had, but facing Jake. She looked him in the eyes and stood silent for 30 seconds. While the others spoke, Jake sat motionless with his head down, as he was coached to do by his father.

Riley stood there, waiting for him to look at her. "Look at me," she ordered him. "I need you to look at me," she said again, when he had not looked up after her first request. She smacked her hand down on the podium. Jake looked up, finally making eye contact with Riley. Looking directly into his eyes, he couldn't look away. He couldn't look down. "You took not just one life, you took many," she began. "You took my wife, which caused me to lose my son." She maintained his gaze throughout her words. "Eva wasn't perfect. She made mistakes. But when she loved you, it was all encompassing. She loved with her whole heart. When you took her out of this life, she was in the depths of a heartbreak over her own child and what he was dealing with. Her work was suffering, but it was no reason for her to be slaughtered in a parking lot. She was her son's only protector and advocate. You took that from him. You took my ability to be a part of his life away. You have no idea how selfish you were in your rage. You stole a mother. You stole a wife. You ruined three lives with one bullet. You destroyed a family. You left a hole in so many lives. No matter what your punishment is, it won't bring her back. It won't make me whole. It won't make our son whole. I'm only here – not to ask for a punishment, or leniency. I'm just here so that you know what you did. So that you understand what you took away from this world. This…" Riley lifted her pendulum, "is all I have left of the love of my life. Our son has one too. That's his consolation prize for not having his mom and advocate. I hope you are happy with yourself." Riley shook her head and walked away.

The court room was quiet. The judge sat in quiet contemplation for a moment. He addressed Jake. "I don't understand your motive or what you thought you would gain by killing your teacher. I hope you heard the sadness and grief you caused by your action. You didn't just impact the life you took, you impacted an entire community and a family. I am going to hand down the sentence of 25 years to life. You will be eligible for parole in 25 years." The judge smacked his gavel down.

Britt looked at Riley. "That's it? That's all he gets?"

Riley shrugged her shoulders. "Eva was opposed to the death penalty and would not have wanted that. Even if he got the death penalty I wouldn't feel better. She's gone. She will never come back. It's all just pomp and circumstance at this point."

IT WAS SOON CHRISTMAS SEASON, and Justin was focused on it being another holiday without his mom so he went and spoke to Ms. Elmhurst.

"Justin, did your dad ever take you to anyone to talk about this? Or has he ever loosened up about you talking about it?"

Justin shook his head.

"And you still can't talk to your mom's family?"

Justin shook his head again.

"Is there anyone you can talk to?"

"I talk to Nessa and her mom."

"What have you been doing to cope?" she asked him.

"I talk to her like she's still here. I think her spirit is with me. I think she protects me," Justin said quietly.

"I think that's a beautiful way to think about it. Like she's your angel," Ms. Elmhurst offered. "Have you thought about writing a journal? You could even address the bad guy who killed her. You can compile letters to the people you don't get to talk to, as well."

Justin pondered that. "I could try that."

The final bell for the day rang and Justin rode home on the bus next to Nessa. He didn't mind going home as much since Lucy started working. She worked afternoons back at the diner as a waitress.

Eva still popped in when Lucy was home alone and tormented her.

Most recently, appearing in Lucy's dream. Eva was seated, lounging gin a chair facing Lucy, legs crossed, hands placed nonchalantly on the arms of the chair. "I'm not ever going to leave you alone," Eva informed her. "So long as you are in the same home as my child and hold such disdain in your heart for who he is, I'm not ever going to stop." She grinned at Lucy menacingly.

Lucy woke up with a start. It was three in the morning. When her eyes popped open, Eva was nose to nose with her. The temperature around Lucy was frigid. Eva was staring deep into her eyes, and Lucy couldn't move, paralyzed with fear. Eva grinned at her, and then was gone. Lucy got up and out of bed quietly. She made herself coffee. And she made her plan.

She looked up airfare to Macedonia. Her grandmother, who she hadn't seen in years, still lived there.

She looked up getting her passport and one for Desiree. She couldn't get a passport without Doug's signature. When he awoke, she looked at him and suggested they take a family trip to Niagara Falls. "We would all need passports." Lucy stated.

Doug shrugged. "Okay. Justin already has one from traveling with Eva and Riley. We all need to get ours." He stated referring to himself, Desiree, and Lucy.

Lucy smiled.

CHRISTMAS EVE ARRIVED. JUSTIN WAS invited to Nessa's family for dinner and presents. He had ridden the bus that morning to the mall and spent the entirety of his saved allowance. He bought himself a decent sweater to wear, and a present for Nessa, a bracelet commemorating her Hogwarts House. He bought her mother a mug in the shape of an owl as she collected figurines of owls, and Nessa's stepfather a Detroit Tigers t-shirt. He rode the bus home and did his best to wrap the presents.

Eva was proud of his generosity. She was proud of the effort he put into getting dressed up and doing his hair in the fashion he used to when he would spend time with Eva and Riley. He hadn't lost what they had taught him.

Justin came up the stairs and asked if Doug could drive him to Nessa's.

"Why are you so dressed up?" Lucy mocked. "You are like some little prince!" she snorted.

Eva blew the lamp she was sitting next to.

Lucy didn't say another word as Doug got up and walked to the door.

Justin arrived at Nessa's and Doug informed him what time he would be back to pick Justin up.

Justin walked up to the door. Krishna loved decorating for Christmas. The house was decked out in colorful lights, and a festive sleigh and reindeer adorned the lawn.

Nessa answered the door wearing reindeer antlers on a headband. Justin had a lump in his throat. On the last Christmas he spent with his mom she had worn a similar headband as they FaceTimed Britt and Harry and Grampa Jack just before going to look at lights.

He smiled at her. "Merry Christmas," he said to her.

She let him in, and he could see the dining room table set festively. The home smelled of roasted turkey and sweet potatoes.

The tree was large and decorated with white glimmering lights and beautiful ornaments. Nutcrackers and snowmen adorned all the surfaces throughout the home.

"Merry Christmas, Justin!" Christina called out. "Look at you! You didn't need to bring gifts. Here," she ushered him to the tree. "You can put them here by the tree."

Justin put his wrapped packages down.

Nessa made her way to the table and sat down and tapped the chair next to hers. Justin made his way and sat next to her.

Christina brought the turkey to the table where the sides were displayed.

Christmas music was playing softly in the background.

Justin made easy conversation with Nessa and her family. He felt at ease as always. After dinner they sat in front of the tree and exchanged gifts. Nessa gifted Justin a replica of Snape's wand, since he had told her that Snape was his mom's favorite Harry Potter character.

She had written a note and slipped it inside the box. 'Magic is real', she wrote, in commemoration of the conversation he had with her and her mom about some of his favorite memories of his mom.

Nessa opened her bracelet and beamed. She put it on proudly and showed her mom.

Christina gifted Justin with a new backpack, inside there was a leather bound journal and nice ink pen. "You had mentioned that Ms. Elmhurst suggested you keep a journal..." she offered. The leather was emblazoned with his initials and a quote from Edgar Alan Poe, who they knew was a common link with Justin and his mother: 'Even in the Grave all is not Lost-Edgar Alan Poe'.

Eva was so grateful for this connection in Justin's life. She hoped this would be a bond that he could maintain forever, even if the youthful 'romance' ended.

Christina was not a fan of how Justin was treated at his father's house, especially after she heard Justin recount how he is not allowed to talk to his mother's family or even about his mother. She always made a point to ask questions or listen. For those conversations, Eva was always present and listening, and ever grateful.

After the presents, Christina served hot cocoa, and she made sure to use the mug Justin had gifted her.

They sat in the living room, lit by the fireplace and the tree and watched *A Christmas Story*. Christina sat between Nessa and Justin, of course. Eva approved.

When the movie was over, Justin was reluctant to leave. He wished Nessa's family would just let him move in. He was also sad that he couldn't have his walk through the neighborhood with Nessa at his side.

When his dad pulled up, Nessa and Christina hugged him goodbye, and Krishna shook his hand.

Justin walked slowly out to the car. Even though it was cold, he felt warm. He knew Eva was with him. He looked up at the clear sky and saw the stars and the moon. He took a deep breath and kept moving.

He got into the passenger seat. "What's that?" his dad asked.

"Christina got me a new backpack for Christmas," Justin informed him.

"Cool," Doug said. They drove home.

Christmas morning was quiet. They didn't do the big production that Justin was used to at his mom's. Lucy was against Santa Claus just like his dad.

They had breakfast and Justin went downstairs with his haul of presents. A new video game and some new clothes.

He put away his presents and sat on his bed and pulled out the journal. He began to fill it with his thoughts on Christmas.

He started by writing his favorite memories of Christmas with his mom and Mum. He filled three pages. He finished by writing that if he ever had kids of his own, he would make sure they got to experience magic too.

Chapter 18

Hasta La Vista

JUSTIN'S LIFE HAD MOVED INTO a tempo, especially since Nessa and her family had come into his life. They were his outlet and his sense of normalcy. He looked forward to Saturdays with them.

Lucy had for the most part completely laid off him. His mother had made sure of that. He knew that his mother had been giving Lucy daily reminders. He would see the remnants of broken glass, or hear certain noises in the middle of the night that let him know she was reminding Lucy to stay in her lane.

Lucy, Desiree and Doug all went and got their passports for the Niagara Falls trip that Lucy was planning.

Once they arrived, in March- Eva sat and watched as Lucy's heart raced. Lucy looked at the documents as she put them away in a drawer and bit her lip. She knew if she went forward with her decision, there was no turning back.

Eva could sense Lucy's reluctance and was going to have none of it.

As Lucy was carrying Desiree through the living room contemplating her choices and doubting her decisions, the temperature dropped.

Lucy exhaled and her breath was visible in front of her. Desiree was shivering in her arms, but Lucy felt frozen in her space. She watched as a cloud of black particles swarmed over the couch slowly taking a form.

The temperature continued to drop around her and Desiree.

The black cloud took the shape of a woman's silhouette. "Bitch from Hell, be gone!" Lucy's voice was trembling and her words were barely a whisper.

The silhouette took the appearance of herself. Eva hated that she was appearing in such a fashion, but knew it had to be done. She was expending all that she had to ensure that Lucy would not back out.

Lucy looked at the figure of herself on the couch. Legs crossed and arms draped over the back staring back at her. The eyes were darker, black in appearance. The figure's head moved in a disjointed fashion back and forth and the mouth was attempting to make words but nothing was coming out.

Eva was struggling as making a visible form was difficult enough.

Sound finally came from the lips of the figure, and Desiree was confused, reaching for the other version of her mom, still shivering. The sound came roaring and jumbled at first. It was hoarse and cackling, echoing and reverberating from the walls.

Hot tears fell down Lucy's cheeks as she stood mortified.

"Idiot." Came the words from figure as its neck lolled around loosely. "Moron. Stupid. Daughter of a bitch, ha ha ha ha! And were those words ever created for you!" It was laughing at her. "So stupid. What are you a little princess?" The torments she had spat at Justin over the years were slowly coming out of the thing's mouth with that awful hoarse and cackling voice. It's black eyes gleaming at her, mocking her with her own appearance.

"I'm sorry," Lucy whispered. "I'm sorry." Her voice got louder.

The thing kept going repeating the insults and laughing. Its voice was so loud and it was now echoing in Lucy's head as Desiree covered her ears and now hid her face in her mother's chest.

"I'm fucking sorry, okay? I'm going to leave. I'm going to leave him alone. Please, just stop! Just stop!" She was screaming.

Eva made the figure laugh hard and loud as it disappeared. She had expended all that she had for this display.

Nana stood by in the back shaking her head, disapproving.

With a self-satisfied grin, Eva watched back in her invisible state of barely existing as Lucy went outside to the porch with Desiree. "Nana, I know you don't like what I've been doing, but understand I am protecting Justin the only way I can."

Nana sighed and looked at Eva.

"I can feel your disappointment from over here," Eva replied.

"I just don't like seeing you become something you are not. Vengeful, hateful, and dark. Those emotions can change you. I don't want to see you stuck like that."

"If I did this right, it won't be anything you have to worry about."

ONE AFTERNOON, IN MID-APRIL, Justin came home from school and no one was home. He checked the calendar. It was Thursday, Lucy's day off. Her car was gone. *She must have taken Desiree shopping or something*, he thought.

His dad came home from work at seven that night. Lucy and Desiree still were not home.

Doug came down the stairs. "Hey, buddy... Where is Lucy and Desiree?"

Justin shrugged and paused his video game. "You mean you don't know?"

Doug shook his head.

"I'm sure they will be home shortly," Justin said nonchalantly.

Eva knew where they were. She had watched as the plans unfolded. She beamed within herself. She had been concerned that Lucy would not go through with it after all.

But she knew... Lucy was not happy with Doug either. It was hard to be with someone who remained so emotionally detached and unpassionate. His chronic ED was an issue for her just as it was for Eva. He didn't like to take his meds regularly because he didn't like the side effect of congestion. She felt neglected physically and emotionally, just as Eva had felt. Eva sometimes *almost* felt sorry for Lucy, though Lucy never made it easy in how she took her contempt out on Justin.

With the constant harassment of Eva's spirit and her lack of support within her husband, Lucy had finally broken. She couldn't 'parent' Justin. She had few friends and none that she could talk to about what her home life had become since her home was now possessed with her husband's dead ex-wife.

"Did you eat dinner?" Doug asked Justin.

"No." Justin resumed his video game.

"Pizza?" Doug asked.

"Sure," Justin responded.

Doug went upstairs and ordered a pizza delivery on his app. He then texted Lucy, 'Where are you?' He watched the screen waiting for the bubble to reflect it was delivered.

Nothing. It just hung in limbo.

He tried calling her. It went to voicemail.

He called Lucy's mother, but she didn't answer. He left a voicemail. Lucy's mother and Lucy didn't have a great relationship, so he figured that was a long shot. He didn't know any of her girlfriends' numbers to call them.

The pizza arrived and Doug brought the box downstairs and sat on the floor in Justin's bedroom. He watched Justin play the game and gave him pointers while they ate the pizza from the box.

By nine thirty, Justin put himself to bed, and Doug went upstairs. Concern rising within him, he tried to text Lucy again. The first text had never been delivered. He tried again though anyway, 'When are you coming home?' the delivered status never showing on his end.

He tried calling again, and it went directly to voicemail. "Hey. It's me. Where are you? Are you okay?"

Eva knew, based on the time, where Lucy was. She felt a cold sense of satisfaction as panic gripped Doug.

He went to the Find My Phone app and put in Lucy's information. Nothing showed up. It was not locatable.

He knew he couldn't call the police until it had been 24 hours. He would have to wait until the morning. He went on Facebook and her profile no longer existed when he searched it. Her Instagram was also gone.

He made a pot of coffee and sat at the table. He played a game on his phone. He checked Facebook. He tried to text Lucy again. He repeated this pattern of actions over and over all night in the same order. Eva beamed watching him.

When Justin had gotten up for school in the morning, he found his father haggard at the kitchen table in the same clothes as yesterday.

"Hey, Dad. Did you not sleep last night?"

"Lucy and Desiree never came home," he said gruffly.

"Oh," Justin said. He was mildly concerned because he loved his sister, Desiree. She couldn't help who her mother was.

"Was she here when you left for school yesterday?" Doug asked.

"Yes," Justin said.

"Did she say anything to you about having plans?" Doug asked.

"No. She didn't say anything to me. She was acting like Lucy. Complaining about something. I just ignored her and left."

"We do need to talk about how you treat her," Doug said. "You could stand to be nicer to her. Show her a little more respect."

Justin didn't respond. He poured a bowl of cereal and sat at the table to eat. "What are you going to do?" Justin asked.

"I guess I'm going to call the police. It's been 24 hours since anyone has seen her," Doug said.

Justin ate the rest of his cereal. He felt bad for his dad, but he had asked his mother enough questions and absorbed enough of her frankness that he understood why a woman might leave his dad. He had witnessed for himself his dad's spinelessness, and refusal to stand for anything.

Justin went downstairs and took a shower and got ready for school. He packed his bag and went upstairs to find his dad on the phone with a dispatcher.

Justin had mixed emotions, only because he was concerned for Desiree.

He walked to the bus stop, got on and found his seat next to Nessa. "My stepmom disappeared," he told her.

"She did?" Nessa asked her brow furrowing.

"Yeah. And my baby sister. They just left yesterday and never came back. My dad is calling the police."

"Where do you think they went?" Nessa asked.

Justin shrugged.

"Do you think they are in danger?" Nessa asked.

Justin shrugged again. "I don't think so."

"You should have stayed home with your dad," Nessa said.

"No. Honestly, if she left us, that's the best thing for us," he said.

"But still!" Nessa said.

Justin shrugged again.

Eva went and hung out back with Doug, watching him with amusement as he called the police. His voice trembling as he spoke to the dispatcher.

Two detectives, one tall and clean cut, clean shaven, looking like an old school Fed wannabe, and the other, shorter and less clean looking with a five o'clock shadow though it was only eight in the morning, arrived. They introduced themselves as Detective Posey (cleancut Fed Wannabe) and Jenkins (Five O'Clock Shadow) and started with questioning Doug, who struggled with answering their questions. They looked around and Doug followed them, head lowered.

"Do you mind if we look around the house?" Posey asked.

"No..." Doug answered.

Jenkins headed to the bathroom while Posey went off down the hall to the bedrooms.

"Sir, is this your wife's wedding ring?" Jenkins asked, his eyebrow raised as he lifted the delicate ring out of the dish on the sink between two fingers and held it up to show Doug.

"Yes," Doug said with his voice constricted.

"Is it common for her to leave it behind when she goes out?" The detective asked.

Doug shook his head no.

"Did you notice it was left behind?" He asked.

"No... I didn't think to look around." Doug said.

"Your wife and daughter are missing and you didn't think to check the house first?" Jenkins was annoyed.

Doug shook his head. With his hands in his pockets he made his way down the hall to where Posey was opening the closet in the bedroom. "Do you notice anything missing?" Posey asked, stepping aside.

Doug could see the gaping the hole on the floor of the closet between the shoe rack and the wall where two suitcases formerly sat.

"The suitcases are missing," Doug said softly.

"Is it possible your wife just went to go stay somewhere else for a bit?" Posey asked.

Doug shrugged. "She doesn't have any friends really and she doesn't get along with her family... Or really anyone. I don't know where she would go."

"You didn't bother to check the house. Maybe she left a note somewhere?" Posey asked annoyed.

The detectives continued to look around as Doug followed them around attempting to answer questions. No note was found, and neither was anything else that would concern the detectives. Aside from missing clothes, suitcases and an abandoned wedding ring, there was nothing to note.

The only concern that kept the police involved was that Desiree was missing. Since it was a parental kidnapping or an amber alert situation, the police took it very seriously. Posey and Jenkins questioned Doug about Desiree. He didn't know what Desiree was wearing when she was last seen.

Eva knew that they most likely will not find Lucy unless she reaches out. She had watched as Lucy would come home from her shifts, with half of her tips stashed in a pocket Doug would never see. She would count the money as Doug sat in the living room alone playing his video games. Eva watched as Lucy amassed the tips into enough for airfare, not unlike the Freedom Fund she herself had set up all those years ago.

Doug, being so well versed at being a victim would do great on television, Eva thought as the news vans began to arrive at the house, and pictures of Lucy and Desiree were flashed on people's screens by evening news. Doug, looking ever pathetic and haggard, pleaded for his wife and daughter to return.

Eva knew that no one saw people that resembled those photos. Lucy had taken much care to prevent that. She had been making these plans since Christmas. Eva sat back and watched that morning as Lucy dyed her hair back to its normal color, and then took the trash out to hide the evidence. Eva watched as Lucy dressed Desiree in boy's clothing before they left.

The next morning, the police were alerted that Lucy's car was at the airport. They ran Lucy's information and passport information against the flight manifest and found that she had boarded a plane with Desiree to Macedonia.

Since Macedonia was a non-Hague convention country, there was nothing more that could be done. The government could not intervene to force Lucy to come home with Desiree. No one could.

A few days later, Doug received an international phone call. "Hi." It was Lucy.

"Where are you?"

"Not in the U.S.," she said.

"I get that. When are you coming back?" Doug's voice cracked.

"I'm not," she said. "I'm staying here and raising my daughter here."

"She's our daughter," Doug said.

"Not anymore," Lucy said.

Before Doug could say anything else, Lucy hung up.

Justin saw his dad stoop over the table. He felt bad and he knew he would miss Desiree. But he felt lighter. He felt like some sort of strange justice had just been doled out. He also knew what was the driving force behind Lucy leaving.

Doug held himself up with the table and looked at Justin. "She says she is never coming back. She took your sister, and she is just gone."

"Dad, I don't know what to tell you. But I'm just going to say what's on my heart and mind…" Justin's voice trailed off at having used his mom's line. "She made my life miserable. She was not a good person to me, or to my mom. I miss Desiree. If I never see her again, I will be sad. But I'm glad Lucy is gone."

Doug's jaw dropped. He had never noticed how articulate his son was. He was definitely his mother's son.

When Doug did not acknowledge what Justin said, Justin excused himself to his basement room.

He pulled out his phone and texted Riley. 'Lucy left my dad and took the baby. They are in Europe somewhere.'

Riley saw the text and smiled. 'I'm sorry about your sister. Are you okay?'

Justin smiled. 'I'm going to be fine now.'

'I love you, kiddo,' Riley sent.

'I love u 2 Mum,' Justin sent.

Part 4

Closure and Karma

·

LUCY, THOUGH SHE REFUSED TO come back to the United States, did ultimately allow for sporadic FaceTime calls between Desiree and Justin and Doug. The FaceTime calls started 4 months after she left. They were never scheduled, and Doug never knew when to expect them. If he missed one, there was no telling how long it would be before the next attempt.

Eva, watching this strange justice doled out felt vindicated. "It doesn't feel good, does it?" she asked rhetorically.

Doug never relented on letting Justin contact Eva's family. He held firm, digging in deeper since Justin was all that he had left, growing ever more bitter in his loneliness.

Doug held out hope that Lucy and Desiree would return. He lost hope after a year had past, and on the one-year anniversary of their abandonment of him, Doug rented a pick-up truck and took all of what Lucy left and the items of Desiree's that were left, and dumped them at the Salvation Army.

Justin moved from the basement up to Desiree's old room. He repainted it and decorated it doing his best to mimic the steampunk aesthetic he enjoyed at his mom's house. The house turned into a bachelor pad, anything resembling a woman's touch was gone. Sports memorabilia went up on the walls where family pictures once hung, and it was never really cleaned sufficiently being left to Doug and Justin.

The television in the living room was replaced by a gigantic one that took up almost the entire wall, dwarfing the room.

The basement became a home gym where Doug spent hours trying to get back in shape in case he ever met someone new. Justin would occasionally join him down there and work out beside him.

Doug, never verbose, never really had much to say to his son. They were like two roommates.

Justin's eighth grade year was a solid year for him. He and Nessa did not have any classes together, but they still rode the bus together, ate lunch together and spent almost every Saturday together.

Once Lucy was gone, he and his father stopped going to church. But also, since Lucy was gone, Justin no longer hid the pendulum or the bracelet. The bracelet hung around Justin's bed post, and the pendulum was worn around his neck, to Doug's dismay. Doug, having watched Lucy throw the pendulum away, did not bother to ask Justin how he ever regained it. Doug would just glare at it with disgust when it peeked out over Justin's shirts.

Eva stayed close by watching over Justin, but was quiet. She would still flicker lights when Justin talked to her, just so he knew she was still with him. She could begin her own process of healing in her silence.

One night, as Justin slept and Eva sat watching over him, Nana popped in.

"I told you I knew what I was doing," Eva murmured.

"It's time for you to start letting go," Nana reminded her.

"I know... It's hard though. He's still so young."

"Letting go doesn't mean not being here from time to time or when you really miss them."

"Are you healed?" Eva asked her.

"I've forgiven myself. I feel good about things now. It's why you see me less and less. I've found my peace, and you will too."

"This too shall pass..." Eva said quietly, but Nana was already gone.

Occasionally, Justin would ask if he could call his grampa or gramma or Mum. Doug said no and would not discuss it. It did not stop Justin from sneaking his text messages or dropping letters off with Ms. Elmhurst to mail.

Eva did not intervene, finding that she knew he would find his way to his loved ones.

JUSTIN STARTED HIGH SCHOOL AND was starting to come into his own slowly. His dad was ever less of a parent and even more of a roommate to him. They did not speak much, they divided the household chores, any guidance Justin sought came from Nessa's family. She, and her family were a constant in his life. They were his stability, and they were there for him.

Doug was dating sporadically, but nothing ever stuck or held past three or 4 months. Most of the women saw quickly what Eva had ignored and what Lucy had taken as a weakness she could manipulate – his laissez faire attitude and lack of spine.

JUSTIN'S SOPHOMORE YEAR OF HIGH school, he took his struggle to maintain contact with his mother's family to Nessa's parents. Christina, not one to shy away from any battles, took herself over to Doug's home one afternoon on her way home from work.

It was Wednesday, and Doug would be off that day. Justin and Nessa would be at a speech and debate club meeting, so she could speak to Doug alone. She knocked on the door, and Doug answered.

Christina introduced herself and asked to come inside.

Doug let her in and she looked around at the bachelor pad and hid her disgust well.

"Doug, you have been through a lot, haven't you?" she asked.

Doug looked at her suspiciously. "Yes…"

"You know Justin has been through everything you have been through and then some," she began.

"Are you here to criticize me?" Doug asked, immediately defensive.

"No. I'm here to advocate for Justin."

"Advocate for him? He has everything he needs," Doug said.

"Not necessarily. He's missing out on some vital connections. He has not been allowed to have contact with his mother's family. That's important for him. He had bonds with these people. He needs that connection. Whatever fight you have with them, is with them, Justin is not a part of that. He's longing for that. Especially since his mother has been taken away from him."

"You came here to tell me how to parent my kid?" Doug was angry.

"No. I came here to ask you to consider letting go. I've gotten to know Justin well over the last few years. He and my daughter are close. You know that. You know the time he spends with us. I know his whole life story. I care a lot about him. His mom left you when he was very young. He's almost 16. She's been dead for years now. You need to learn to let go. Holding on to these grudges is not serving you well, nor is it serving your son."

Doug looked down.

"I'm not saying you have to say yes now or ever. I just want you to think about it. Let go. Forgive. That doesn't mean you have to be friends with these people. Let Justin have a relationship with them. If they are as bad as you say that they are, he will see it and let them go on his own. It should be his choice though. And he is a smart kid. An intuitive kid. If they are bad, he will know."

"Great. Thanks," Doug said as he stood up. "Is that all?"

"Nessa wants to throw him a surprise party for his birthday. We plan to invite the people he cares about. I wanted to give you a heads up. We are inviting his grandparents and his mother's widow. You are invited and you can choose to be there or not."

"What if I say my son can't go if you are going to expose him to people he shouldn't be around?"

"You choose, sir. But I can guarantee you that if you go that route, it's you your son will not have a relationship with when he graduates and moves on. Mark my words."

Doug stayed silent, refusing to look at Christina.

After a few minutes of silence, Christina stood up and led herself to the door.

Doug stayed in his spot.

She let herself out without saying another word.

On the day of the party, the Saturday after Justin turned 16, Nessa treated Justin to a movie that they had wanted to see. Krishna picked them up and drove them to the house, where her mom had spent the afternoon decorating and setting up a cake and getting the guests inside.

Nessa and Justin's core group of friends were there, and so were Riley, Jack and Geri. Doug had chosen to not come, but did not prevent Justin from being there. *Small victories*, Eva thought.

Christina got the signal text that they were pulling onto the street. Everyone hid and the lights went out.

Nessa opened the door and turned the lights on as Justin walked in. "Surprise!" the entourage shouted.

Justin smiled and looked around, his eyes falling last on those he missed most.

He ran to Riley first. "Mum." He was trying to not be emotional. The twins were there and would never let him live it down. He let go of Riley and wrapped his arms around Jack and Geri, holding onto them for a long time.

He let go and looked around for his dad. A brief wave of disappointment washed over him when he didn't see him. "I will be right back," he said to them.

He made his way to Christina. "You did this?" he asked.

She smiled at him. "It's a big milestone. They should be here. Your mom would have wanted it, I'm sure."

He hugged her. "Thank you so much. This is the best gift ever."

Justin spent the time mostly with Jack, Geri and Riley. "How long are you here for?" Justin asked Riley.

"Just a couple more days. I'm having dinner with Drew and Jose and Britt and Harry tomorrow. We are going to go to your mom's favorite restaurant in Greek Town."

"Pizza Papalis…" Justin smiled.

"I know it might be difficult for you to come, but everyone would love to see you."

"I will be there," Justin said. "Pick me up at the park, near my dad's house. You know the one."

Riley smiled at him.

Justin opened presents and blew out the candles on his cake.

Geri made her way over to Christina. "Thank you for doing this. Thank you for stepping in. Knowing he has people like you in his life is truly a blessing. It's been hard on all of us. We didn't just lose his mom, we lost him." She pointed to Justin.

"I never thought that was fair. When Nessa said she wanted to throw him a surprise party, I figured this was the best gift we could give. He's always talked about his mom, and his family that he missed."

"His dad is a stubborn one," Jack jumped in. "Bitter. He never forgave Eva for leaving him, and he never got past the anger."

"I saw that," Christina replied.

"Justin is stubborn and has a big heart. He is his mother's son," Jack commented.

Justin's friends began to leave, and soon he was saying goodbye to Jack and Geri as well.

"I'm getting a job, now that I'm 16," Justin told them. "And I already have money saved, and I just need a little more and I am buying a car. Once I have a car, I will see you more," Justin promised.

"I will make you a deal," Jack offered. "You tell me how much you have saved, and I will match you."

Justin beamed at him. "Are you serious?"

"I am. If it means I get to spend more time with you, anything."

"I already have almost $1100. I have been putting my birthday money aside and saving my allowance. Mum talked to me about all of that when I was 10."

"Good for you," Riley piped in grinning.

~ 341 ~

"When you are ready, you text me and I will meet you at the bank," Jack offered.

Justin hugged him and Geri and held them each close.

When Riley was ready to leave, they walked to the door. "I'm proud of you," she told him.

"I'm done being kept away. It's not right," Justin said. "I'm also tired of hiding."

"Good for you. You are finding your voice. You are becoming the buffalo."

Justin grinned at her. "You are really going to pick me up tomorrow at the park?"

"If that's what you want. I will be there at five," Riley said.

He hugged her tight. "I will see you tomorrow," he told her.

When he got home, his dad did not ask him how his party was or anything about the evening. They made small talk about a few things regarding school and the video game they had been playing.

Justin informed him that he had plans tomorrow afternoon and would not be home.

His dad didn't ask him what they were.

Justin went to his room and shut the door.

The next afternoon, at promptly five, Justin stood at the edge of the park and Riley pulled up in her silver rental car.

Justin jumped in. Riley stayed in park for a few minutes. She looked at Justin closely. "You have your mother's eyes," she commented. "You always did. Her long eyelashes. Big and wide-eyed."

Justin smiled. "Thank you."

Riley put the car in drive and made her way to downtown and parked near Greek Town Casino. They walked up the street in the brisk cold air.

Britt and Harry were already there, and so was Drew and Jose. Everyone stood and shouted with excitement at the sight of Justin.

Riley had not told them he would be there in case he backed out or was prohibited by Doug.

Justin was met with hugs and affection. When the excitement died down, he took a seat next to his mum.

He was fielding questions about what grade he was in and what he wanted to do about college and do you know how proud of you your mom would be.

Justin explained to them that his grades were all A's with occasional B's. He was not an athlete to his dad's dismay and did not make the baseball team, but he was part of the academic competition teams though, on Mock Trial and Speech and Debate.

"Nerd, like your mom!" Riley called out.

"His mom was not a nerd in high school! She was so bad!" Britt offered. "She got me suspended twice!"

"It's true!" Drew offered. "She was wild until she found you, Riley!"

"I have that effect. What can I say?" Riley laughed.

Justin was quiet for a moment and listened as everyone shared a little story about Eva and her more wild past.

When there was a lull in the conversation, he asked Riley how she liked living in the Pacific Northwest.

"It's good. It's quiet. Business is good though. Steady."

"I think I will focus on my college search for out that way. I'm tired of Michigan."

"You really are like your mom," Drew said. "She hated living here."

"I mean, it's okay. It's home. But I don't want to be here forever," Justin said.

Riley threw her arm across his shoulder and brought him to her. "You know you are welcome to come out that way. I would love that."

He felt like he found a long-lost missing piece being surrounded by the people who so loved and cared for his mom.

After dinner they all walked to Astoria Bakery nearby. In honor of Eva, they all ordered a chocolate mouse. Standing in the small space near the banister of the stairs that go to a basement no one has ever been in, they stood and ate their treat.

After they finished their dessert, they made their way to their respective cars after long hugs.

Justin sat in the passenger seat and watched the city go by as Riley drove.

"I meant what I said. I want to go to college in Washington."

"I meant what I said, too. I would love that."

JUSTIN POURED HIMSELF INTO RESEARCHING all things Washington State. He decorated his room with posters of Seattle, and literature on University of Washington. He applied for and got his first job as a barista at a coffeehouse that had locations in Seattle.

Justin maintained his good grades, his job, and his home chores and academic competition.

He also stopped hiding his communication with Geri and Jack and Riley.

When his bank account hit two thousand, he looked and found a car for just under four thousand. Jack was true to his word and met him at the bank after receiving the promised text. They went from the bank to the seller's house. Jack took the time to inspect the car with Justin. He helped Justin make a reasonable offer and finalize the deal.

It was not the coolest or newest car, but it was his. He promised Jack he would make an effort to spend time with him and he would learn how to take care of the car.

Nessa was not happy about Justin wanting to go to Washington for college. She was committed to going to University of Michigan – as both Christina and Krishna did.

They avoided talking about what would happen after graduation if Justin did get into the University of Washington. She encouraged him to also try U of M at least as a Plan B.

To Doug's dismay, Justin also decided he would be a Seahawks fan, adding paraphernalia in support of that team to his growing collection of Seattle swag adorning his room.

For his 17th birthday, Riley offered to fly him out to see the town. Though Doug objected, Justin went anyway.

Doug could slowly see Christina's prophecy coming true, though he did his best to ignore it, and refused to acknowledge his part in the growing distance between him and his son.

When he got to Riley's home in Sequim, just over 2 hours outside of Seattle, Justin found that she had kept a room with many of his items in it and his old steampunk aesthetic.

"I couldn't bear the thought of getting rid of your things," she said standing in the doorway.

"What about Carrie?" Justin asked, referring to her new girlfriend.

"She understands. You are my son. Your mom always told me that. I took my vows to the both of you seriously."

Justin sat on his bed and asked if he could see the bin with his mother's things.

Riley brought it to him. "Do you mind if I do this alone?" he asked her.

"Of course not."

Riley left the room and Justin opened the bin. He held his baby blanket and looked through the pictures.

As he grew and matured and got busier, he spoke less to Eva. She understood. For the first time in a long time he whispered aloud, "Mom Mom…"

She flickered the light on the bedside lamp in response.

He smiled.

He continued to look at the baby book. He opened it to a page that said, 'What advice do you have for your baby?' In her flourished writing she had written, 'And this too shall pass…'

He pulled out a picture of her holding his hand and looked at the tattoo on her arm. He touched it with his fingers.

He took a picture of the picture and the page in the book and sent it to Nessa.

She sent back a heart emoji.

He put all of the pictures and book away.

Riley had asked him if he wanted to meet Carrie. He understood that Mum still had a lot of life left and couldn't expect her to be single forever, so he agreed to meet her.

They went to a local diner for dinner to meet her.

Justin found her charming. She was taller than his mother was, but not as tall as Mum. She had graying blonde hair, and her hair was wavy. She dressed like everyone else up in the Pacific Northwest. Practical. Warm.

Carrie was smart, a college professor in the Psychology department at University of Washington, much to Justin's delight.

He liked her. He thought she was a good fit for Mum. Eva did too. She wanted Riley to be happy. She deserved happiness.

Carrie offered to make sure that Justin got a tour of the campus while he was visiting.

Justin was excited. He informed her that he would be filling out his applications next fall.

After dinner, Riley walked Carrie to her car and kissed her goodnight. "I will call you later tonight," she promised.

When Carrie was safe in her car, Riley and Justin made their way back to her home.

"I like her," Justin offered.

"You do?" Riley smiled.

"She's a lot like Mom," he offered.

"I can see that," Riley said after pondering it a bit.

"Thank you for having me out here," Justin said after a few moments of silence.

"Of course. I would have had you out here a lot more if things were different," Riley said.

"I know."

The next few days were a flurry of activity. Riley had booked an Air B n B in Seattle for them. Carrie joined them. Riley had surprised Justin with tickets to the Seahawks game after he told her that he had begun following the team. The day after the game was his tour of the campus for the University of Washington. After the tour the three of them roamed the streets of Seattle.

Justin thought Carrie was perfect for Mum. She was quiet and more introverted than Mum, but they balanced each other. Carrie was born and raised in Seattle but had traveled extensively and was passionate about politics like his mother was.

He told Carrie how excited he was to move to Washington and that he was happy that his Mum had found her.

While they were sitting at a seafood restaurant on the water, he asked them how they met.

"I was sitting at a bar having a beer one afternoon, by myself," Riley began. "And then I saw Carrie on the other side. She was also by herself. She was on her tablet, with a beer. I thought she was pretty, but she looked busy. But then this flicker of light flashed by her head. I thought it was weird but went back to minding my own business. Then the light flickered again. I looked around and no one else saw it. I took it as a sign to walk over and strike up a conversation. Here we are 4 months later."

"I wasn't doing anything pressing. I was grading essays from my intro class. They were so bad. She saved me!" Carrie laughed.

Justin knew the flash of the light Riley saw was his mom. Eva had hand-picked Carrie for Riley, Justin guessed.

Justin had to fly back to Michigan the next morning. He was sad to leave, but excited for his future. He didn't leave the bin full. He brought back with him several of his favorite pictures, his favorite plushie from when he was a child, a beanie bear with a leather vest and green mohawk from The Hard Rock Cafe in Detroit.

Nessa picked him up from the airport. She was happy that he was happy, but sad, because she knew she was going to lose him to the West Coast. She picked him up at the baggage claim area and he filled her in on all the wonderful things he did and saw. He pulled the plushie out of his backpack and showed Nessa. She smiled at him with a heavy heart.

IN THE FALL OF HIS Senior year Justin submitted his packet to the University of Washington, and to be safe, as he promised Nessa, he submitted one to the U of M as well.

On the morning of his eighteenth birthday, he skipped school and drove to Ann Arbor and sought out the tattoo artist he researched to be his mom's.

He showed Jeff the picture of his mom where you could see the tattoo, and the picture of her writing from the baby book. Thirty minutes later, Justin was in the chair and the needle was going.

He did not opt for the feminine flairs that adorned his mother's tattoo but opted for the two black bird silhouettes to frame the writing. One to represent his mom and one to represent him.

As the artist worked the ink into his arm, he said, "You look a lot like your mom. She was one of my favorites."

"I have been hearing that a lot," Justin said.

"How is she?" Jeff asked.

"She was murdered. It's been a while now."

"No shit?" The needle stopped, and Jeff sprayed a paper towel with a cleanser and wiped Justin's arm.

"Yeah. She was a teacher in California and a student killed her."

"Dude… I'm sorry."

"It's okay. I'm okay," Justin said looking at the finished work on his arm. "This is awesome. Thank you." He paid Jeff and left.

He had kept his promise to stay in better contact with Jack and Geri visiting each of them on random days off.

By the time spring rolled around, he received his acceptance letters to both the U of M and the U of W.

Nessa was teary-eyed as he told her. She understood but it still hurt. They would try to be long-distance, but she knew those relationships never worked in the end.

Doug was disappointed as well. He had expected Justin to just stay. He didn't understand Justin's drive to go somewhere else.

He tried to reason with Justin to stick around and go to the U of M instead.

Justin just told him it was non-negotiable.

After graduation, Justin was able to secure a transfer to a coffee house location near the campus. He persuaded Nessa to come to Washington to see it for a few days. Riley welcomed them both to stay (Nessa in the guest room of course!).

Carrie had moved in with Riley at this point.

Nessa had never really spent any time at Doug's house other than to pick Justin up, and Doug had made little effort to get to know her. All of their time had always been spent with her mom and stepdad.

Nessa liked Riley and Carrie and found it peaceful in Washington. Justin and she walked to the small private beach in the neighborhood of Riley's home in the morning with their coffee.

"I can see why you like it out here," Nessa offered.

"Maybe I can change your mind and you will come out here for college?" Justin implored, hopeful.

"Maybe. Probably not though. Maybe law school though?"

Justin smiled. "Wait until you see Seattle though. I think you will like it!"

The four of them ventured into Seattle and Nessa was charmed by the beauty of the water front, and despite nearly being hit in the head with a fresh fish at the market, loved the feeling of the city.

When they flew back to Michigan, she felt a small temptation to follow Justin out west, but she knew she couldn't give up her own dreams for a boy.

Eva, having seen Justin through coming into his own, and Riley moving on and finding love again, had found that she could relax herself into the peace of the ether, neither here nor there. She popped in as she saw fit or when needed, but she could now heal herself and let go of the pain, regret, and sorrow that carried over into her afterlife. Those she loved who were left behind in the living world were going to be okay, and soon, she would be with them again. She finally let go.

The last 2 weeks before he was due to leave, Justin spent visiting Jack and Geri and saying his goodbyes to everyone.

He thanked Christina and Krishna for all that they helped him with over the years. He promised to stay in touch with everyone.

The morning he set out to drive to Washington, he stood on the porch with his dad, hugging him awkwardly. "I love you, Dad. I do. This is not personal. It's what I need to do."

"I get that. Will you be back for Thanksgiving or Christmas or anything?"

"I will try," Justin said noncommittally. The truth was, he was burnt out on the bitterness and he no longer wanted it in his life. He forgave his dad, but he didn't understand the refusal to move forward.

Justin looked at the house and looked at his dad as he stood in front of his car. "I will check in, okay?"

Doug stuck his hands in his pockets and looked down. "Okay." He knew when the car backed out of his driveway, he was going to lose his son forever. Justin would never really be back.

Karma. Eva thought it loud enough that Doug faintly heard her voice in his ears as Justin backed out of the driveway and waved.

Doug looked around for the sound, not seeing anything or anyone, and then went back into the house. Alone.

Afterword

THROUGHOUT WRITING THIS BOOK, I found so much inspiration in music. Songs that brought me back to specific emotions, thoughts, or timeframes. Music is a huge part of my life. In saying that, I'm including the playlist that helped this book come to life. I would like to give a special thanks to the catalyst in the creative process that these artists have provided.

Santigold – "Disparate Youth"
Santana (feat. Dave Matthews) – "Love of My Life"
Rob Zombie – "Living Dead Girl"
Alice in Chains – "Would?"
Godsmack – "Serenity"
Imagine Dragons – "Believer"
Moby – "Why Does My Heart Feel So Bad?"
Hole – "Celebrity Skin"
Tori Amos – "Crucify"
Dorothy – "Wicked Ones"
Karen O – "Bullet With Butterfly Wings"
Ciara – "Paint It, Black"
Lana Del Rey – "Ride"
Morrissey – "Sing Your Life"

Cat Stevens – "Wild World"

Nine Inch Nails – "Down In It"

DJ Drez – "Wind Talker"

INXS – "Never Tear Us Apart"

Madonna – "Human Nature"

The Pretty Reckless – "Only Love Can Save Me Now"

Marian Hill – "Whisky"